THE DISTANT OCEAN

THE DISTANT OCEAN

BY

PHILIP K ALLAN

ISBN-13: 978-1-946409-78-2(Paperback)
ISBN :13: 978-1-946409-79-9(e-book)
BISAC Subject Headings:

FIC014000FICTION / Historical
FIC032000FICTION / War & Military
FIC047000FICTION / Sea Stories

Editing: Chris Wozney
Cover Illustration by Christine Horner

Address all correspondence to:
Penmore Press LLC
920 N Javelina Pl
Tucson, AZ 85748

DEDICATION

To Lilian, a remarkable lady

Acknowledgements

In writing the Alexander Clay series I have enjoyed the support of many who have helped to bring my vision to the page. These books start with a passion for the Age of Sail. Mine was first awakened when I discovered the works of C. S. Forester as a child. Later I graduated to the novels of Patrick O'Brian, and the research of Nick Rodger. That interest was given some academic rigor when I studied the 18th century navy under Pat Crimmin as part of my history degree at London University.

Many years later I decided to leave my career in the motor industry to see if I could survive as a novelist. I received the unconditional support, acceptance of the belt-tightening required, and cheerful encouragement of my darling wife and two wonderful daughters. I strive to find a balance in my writing that will satisfy those with knowledge of the period, while still being an enjoyable read for those with none. I first test my work to see if I have hit the mark with my family, and especially my wife Jan, whose input is invaluable. I have also been helped again by my dear friend Peter Northen.

Writers are, on the whole, a welcoming church to late converts like me. One of the most unexpected pleasures of my new career is to have experienced their generous support and encouragement. When I needed help, advice and support, I received it from David Donachie, Bernard Cornwell, Marc Liebman, Jeffrey K Walker, Helen Hollick, Ian Drury and in particular Alaric Bond, creator of the Fighting Sail series of books.

Finally my thanks go to the team at Penmore Press, Michael, Chris, Terri and Christine, who work so hard to turn the world I have created into the book you hold in your hand.

CONTENTS

PROLOGUE

'Stand clear there!' roared Captain Barrington, as the main mast of the *General Cornwallis* groaned ominously. A series of sharp cracks sounded overhead, like a volley of muskets, as the shrouds holding the mast snapped under the strain. Ropes whipped and hissed through the air and the main deck grew dark as the tropical sun was masked by spars and canvas. The hundred-and-fifty-foot structure leant heavily to one side, held for a moment, then fell in a torrent, thundering down across the ship and into the sea along side. The East Indiaman dragged to a halt and lay rocking on the swell like an exhausted stag, waiting for the approach of the hunter who would finish her.

Barrington looked around at the devastated ship and knew in his heart that the battle was over. The quarterdeck canon nearest to him lay on its side. The last of its gun crew was being pulled away by another sailor, his wounded leg leaving a brush stroke of crimson on the planking. From down on the main deck the clank of the pumps had resumed as they struggled to keep pace with the flooding in the hold. So many of his crew were dead and wounded, he barely had enough men to serve the guns that were still operable, certainly not enough to repel any attempt to board.

'I fear we must strike our colours, Mr Harris,' he said. 'The men have done all that can be expected of them.'

'Aye aye, sir,' said his first lieutenant, wiping the sweat from his face on the torn sleeve of his jacket. 'They fought well. Who would have imagined that a crew of Lascars and Malays could have held out so long against the French?'

'Aye, and the *General* hit them hard in our turn,' said his captain. He pointed towards the French frigate as she slid through the blue water towards them. Her towering pyramids of sail were pockmarked with shot holes, her sides blackened with powder smoke. Gathered along her rail was her crew, ready to board their helpless victim. The hot sun twinkled and flashed back from the steel of their weapons.

'Oh damn and blast it!' cursed Barrington, thumping the rail with his fist. 'Madagascar pirates I can deal with, but a national ship of France? How does such a vessel come to be in the Indian Ocean?'

'I suppose they must have come from one of the islands they possess, sir,' said Harris. 'Ille de France lies only a few hundred miles to the north, and Reunion is but a little farther off.'

'And where, pray, was our glorious navy to protect us, eh?' exclaimed the captain. 'A whole cargo of best Canton silk and the first of this year's indigo crop, all of it lost to those blackguards.'

'They are nearly upon us, sir,' said the lieutenant. 'Shall I haul down the colours?'

'Yes, carry on, George,' said Barrington. Harris gave the order, and the red and white striped flag of the East India Company drifted down to sag onto the deck beside them. A muffled cheer came from across the water.

'I've half a mind to slip down to the magazine with a loaded pistol,' muttered the captain. 'See if the blighters want to huzzah when I blow them and the *General* straight to hell.' But he remained at his post while the frigate swept alongside. Grappling hooks flew through the air to catch in what was left of the *General Cornwallis*'s rigging, and a cheering mob of French sailors swarmed over the bulwark and jumped down onto the deck. The officer that led the rush made his way up towards the quarterdeck, backed by a number of cutlass-wielding seamen. He saw the two

Englishmen and came across to them. When he drew close they noticed how young he seemed, at best a few years out of his teens. He had a lean, handsome face with tanned skin and a tiny line of moustache visible over his smile.

'Rupert Barrington of the Honourable East India Company, at your service,' growled the captain. 'I am in command of this ship.' He glared at his young victor for a moment, then bowed his head to him. 'Please permit me to name Mr Harris, my first lieutenant. Regrettably, my other officers are all below deck under the care of the surgeon.'

'No matter, monsieur,' said the young man, making an elaborate bow. 'I am Enseigne de Vaisseau Claude Chavency of the frigate *Prudence*. Please, may I prevail on you to give me your swords, gentlemen?' The two officers unbuckled their belts and handed their weapons across. Chavency accepted them with a smile and passed them back to one of his men.

'We were taken aback to find a ship of your size so far from France, monsieur,' said Barrington. 'Are you newly arrived in these waters?'

'Indeed so, captain,' said the Frenchman. 'You are the first ship we have engaged. May I say how delighted I am to hear of your surprise? For once it would seem our navy has managed to keep a deployment from your many spies. There are three of our frigates in these waters now. Soon none of your ships will dare attempt to cross this ocean.

CHAPTER 1 HOME

'God, I hate this journey,' muttered Earl Spencer, First Lord of the Admiralty, glaring out of the carriage window at the green hills of south Dorset. The road was lined by lush hedgerows, over the top of which could be seen a flock of sheep as they grazed in the warm sunshine. The carriage rolled down a slope and rattled across a stone bridge that spanned a stream lined with alder and willow. By the edge of the water stood a shepherd boy in a wide hat, leaning on his crook as he watched his animals drink. 'I dare say we will be made to sup on mutton this evening,' continued Spencer. 'It's all that is to be had in this arse-end of the world.'

'For my part it will still make a welcome change from pork twelve months in the cask, my lord,' said Captain Alexander Clay. 'But why is it that his Majesty favours Weymouth so much?'

'That is all the fault of his damned sawbones,' exclaimed the First Lord. 'According to the court physician, fresh air and a daily immersion in the sea will control his malady. I ask you! If salt water were a cure for lunacy there would be no mad sailors, and we both know that ain't the case, what?'

'Has his treatment proved efficacious, my lord?'

Spencer turned an eye on the young naval captain.

'You mean, is he sane?' he said. 'I believe that he is currently lucid, although I would certainly have run mad if I was required to spend the whole summer this far from Piccadilly. Never mind how his poor ministers are inconvenienced, having to trail down from London to conduct the business of the nation.'

The Earl sat back in disgust and watched his travelling companion from the opposite corner of the carriage. He is a handsome devil, no doubt about that, he thought to himself, taking in the tall frame, tanned face and head of curly brown hair. A pair of calm grey eyes looked back at him. Spencer's gaze shifted to the naval captain's uniform and rested briefly on the single gold epaulet that he wore. Less than three years seniority, no connections of any note to prefer him, and yet this is the man that young Nelson chose to honour with carrying home his victory despatch, he mused. There is more to you than meets the eye, Alexander Clay.

'The news of Lord Nelson's victory came at just the right time, you know,' he said. 'What with rebellion in Ireland, and all these damned Jacobins at home stirring up the mob. We had heard so little from the Mediterranean that the Cabinet were quite resolved the French had given him the slip and would be shortly sailing up the Channel to invade us. They say that Pitt fell down insensible when he was told of the battle. Mind, the Prime Minister finding himself out cold upon the carpet is passing common, once he starts on the port. They don't call him Three Bottle Bill for nothing, what?'

'I am pleased to have been the bearer of such glad tidings, my lord.'

'The chief thing now is for us to make the most of the situation,' remarked Spencer. 'There is nothing like a victory to calm the mob, and God knows we have had precious few of those. Yes, much can be achieved on this tide of popularity. Pitt can proceed with that new tax of his, for instance.'

'What tax would that be, my lord?' asked Clay. His companion looked cunning.

'He believes he has found a way to tax incomes,' he said. 'Extraordinary, ain't it? I didn't think it would be possible to pry into a man's affairs to such a degree, but he says he can make it answer.'

Clay sat back in his seat and looked out of the window on his side of the coach. He thought back to the desperate sea battle he had been through in the heat of an Egyptian night. He could see in his mind the brilliant flash of broadsides as they had roared to and fro between the rival fleets. He felt again the dreadful furnace heat of the fire and explosion that had destroyed the French flagship. He pictured once more the death and destruction his crew and ship had suffered, and he remembered how he had stood, utterly exhausted, looking out on the calm grey water at dawn to find it dotted with hundreds of bodies drifting amongst the shattered wreckage. Had all that been done to help politicians like Spencer and Pitt pacify the mob?

'Ah, I believe we may be near, at last,' said Spencer. 'About bloody time, what?'

Clay returned to the stuffy interior of the carriage and realised that the horses had been slowing for some time as they drew close to the top of the final rise. Now, in place of sheep and hills, he could see below him the long spit of Portland Bill stretching out into the waters of the Channel. In the bay was a scattering of little fishing boats with brown ketch sails. Farther out at sea was a convoy of merchant ships, heading westwards towards the Atlantic, under the watchful eye of an escorting warship. The coach rattled forwards and gathered pace down the hill towards the little town of Weymouth.

*****

'Pray place your hat under your arm, sir, and remember that under no circumstances should you permit the King to have sight of your back,' said the Lord Chamberlain to the young captain.

'Yes, yes, Thomas,' growled Spencer. 'Don't fuss, man! Captain Clay understands perfectly well how to behave. We're not the damned Army, you know.' The chamberlain cast a last look over the two men and then led them towards the double doors. Footmen in powdered wigs pushed them open and the group walked into a large, sparsely furnished room with windows on two sides that looked out into a sunlit garden.

Ahead of them sat a portly man in a gilt-framed chair, with a half circle of courtiers stood at his back. On his head was a grey horsehair periwig, beneath which a pair of bulging, pale blue eyes looked towards them. He wore a scarlet military-style coat over a white waistcoat and britches, with the blue ribbon of the garter stretched diagonally across him. My, thought Clay, but he looks exactly like Gillray's cartoons in the broadsheets.

'His Lordship the Earl Spencer and Captain Clay,' yelled the chamberlain at the seated figure, as if he were somewhere deep in the garden, rather than eight yards away. Then he bowed and withdrew to one side.

'Lord Spencer, so good of you to oblige me with a visit to Weymouth,' said the king.

'Always a pleasure, your Majesty,' said the First Lord of the Admiralty. He bowed low, and when he came up he beckoned his companion forward. 'May I present Captain Alexander Clay? Captain Clay was the officer who brought the welcome news of the triumph of your Majesty's fleet at the Battle of the Nile.' Clay bowed low in his turn, and when he stood upright again he found that the pale eyes were upon him.

'Were you present at the actual battle, captain?' asked the monarch.

'I was indeed, your Majesty. I command your frigate

Titan. It was our honour to lead the fleet into the bay through some troublesome shoals, although the credit for that feat properly belongs to my sailing master, Mr Jacob Armstrong.'

'Handsomely said, captain. And did your ship suffer much?'

'Not as badly as some, your Majesty. We had seventy killed and wounded from a complement of two-hundred and forty-nine. The *Titan* is currently at Portsmouth undergoing a refit.'

The king meditated on this for a moment, before a fresh question occurred to him. 'And how was... was... eh, what's his name, when you left him?' he asked.

'Your Majesty?'

'Oh, you must know whom I mean!' exclaimed the monarch. 'The cove who sounds like a farmer. He can never cease from chattering away.' Clay looked for inspiration from the men grouped behind the throne. Several of them placed hands over one eye, and some made an arm disappear behind their backs.

'Might your Majesty be referring to Sir Horatio Nelson, Lord Nelson as he is now?'

'The very same! How is he?'

'He was wounded in the action, your Majesty.'

'What, again? Upon my word, there will be nothing left of the fellow soon!'

'He was not too grievously injured on this occasion, your Majesty,' said Clay. 'When I left Naples he was convalescing in the house of Sir William Hamilton. Lady Hamilton was being most attentive to his needs.' A choked snort from behind the throne petered out as the King glanced behind him.

'Now, Lord Spencer, how do you believe I should reward this brave officer for his service to me?'

'You have commanded that all of Lord Nelson's captains should receive a gold medal, your Majesty,' said Spencer. 'The design has been completed, and the Corporation of London is to match your largess with medals for every man present at the battle.'

'Pish! That will hardly answer. What sort of distinction can it be if everyone is to get them?' said the King. 'How is it normal for us to mark such an occasion?'

'It is customary to promote the bearer of such tidings, Your Majesty, but as you can see, Captain Clay is already a post captain. By the long custom of the service, his next step to admiral can only come through seniority.'

'By which time he will doubtless be in his dotage,' said the King. 'Ah, I have it! Have you been knighted, captain?'

'I have not had that honour, your Majesty,' said Clay, a little dazed.

'Does he deserve such a reward, Spencer?'

'Captain Clay is undoubtedly a fine young officer, your Majesty, but a knighthood is normally reserved for an exceptional display of gallantry,' said the First Sea Lord. 'It might be thought to devalue the honour if it were to be given for merely carrying a letter.'

'Lord Cecil, what is your view?' said the monarch, looking round at one of the figures stood behind him.

'I believe Lord Spencer's council to be wise, your Majesty,' said the courtier, stepping forward. 'I am sure the singular honour of having been presented to you will be reward enough.'

'Be assured that your Board of Admiralty have not missed the mark of particular favour Admiral Nelson has indicated in his choice of Captain Clay to bring home news of the victory, your Majesty,' said Spencer.

'That is all very well, but we must do something more,' grumbled the King. He tapped one white satin knee with his plump fingers, and his eyes strayed to the hilt of Clay's sword. In a room full of glittering uniforms, its dull brass hilt stood out. 'Ah, I have it! I will give you a new sword. You are not about to depart from these shores, are you?'

'I... eh... am not entirely certain,' stumbled Clay, looking towards Spencer.

'Captain Clay will not be ordered to sea for a few months yet, your Majesty,' said the First Sea Lord. 'His ship is in need of extensive repairs. The Board of the Admiralty are minded to send him as part of the squadron that will depart in the autumn to regain our control over the Indian Ocean, under the command of Sir George Montague.'

'Capital notion,' agreed the king. 'Hardly a day passes without John Company sending me another petition over all these dashed ships that have been seized. Captain Clay looks to be the sort of resourceful officer to put an end to that nonsense, what?'

'Indeed, that was very much my way of thinking, your Majesty.'

'Splendid!' said the King. 'Then that is resolved. Lord Cecil, I want the finest sword the Worshipful Company of Cutlers can produce as my gift to him. Young man, I give you joy of your new weapon. I shall expect you to carry it with you into your next battle.'

*****

In the orchard of Rosehill Cottage a table had been set up under the apple trees. It was late September now, and the canopy above was heavy with plump, red fruit. Sunlight filtered through the leaves to spot the table surface with discs of gold. Despite the lateness in the year, it was still warm enough for the two young ladies who sat writing there to do so with no more than a calico shawl apiece, draped around their shoulders. They made a contrasting pair. The older of the two had thick, dark hair crammed beneath her bonnet. Her dress was white with small blue flowers dotted across it, the colour a perfect match for the eyes that dominated her heart-shaped face. By contrast, her companion was several years younger, with fair hair. Her dress was of pale green, with a broad yellow ribbon that drew the fabric into a high waist. Her calm, grey eyes were the only feature she shared with her older brother.

A single brown leaf spiralled down through the air to land on one of the sheets of paper. The older lady picked it up by the stalk and rolled it between her fingers. Autumn is close, thought Mrs Lydia Clay, and soon my darling Alex will have to leave me again. She looked up to find that her companion was smiling at her.

'You have a very melancholy aspect,' said Miss Elizabeth Clay, laying her pen down by the inkstand. 'What can you have been thinking of?'

'I was reflecting on what a very indifferent writer I am, Betsey,' said Lydia. 'Here I am, struggling to compose a single letter to my aunt, while my companion dashes down line after line of prose for the draft of her third novel.' She indicated the pile of paper next to her friend's elbow, every sheet of which was covered with rows of flowing script.

'Lady Ashton is perhaps not the easiest person to correspond with,' said Betsey. 'But you, too, are a very fine writer. I admire your poems greatly. Might you not think to have them exposed to a wider readership?'

'Goodness, can you imagine what my family would say to that?' Lydia laughed. 'They already consider my marriage to Alex to have been most unwise.'

'Do they still look down on his origins, now that he has been presented to the King?' said Betsey. 'The sword that arrived from the palace last week is truly magnificent.'

'It was a singular honour, I make no doubt, and I could not be more proud of his growing reputation. However, my aunt is the daughter of an Earl, and is well used to such distinctions. Perhaps I should draw her attention to how close my husband came to being knighted. According to Alex the King was minded to do it, but his courtiers persuaded him not to. Perhaps I should sign my letter as Nearly Lady Lydia Clay!'

The two friends laughed at this, then Betsey became serious once more.

'You could still see your poetry in print, without exciting the opposition of your family,' she said.

'How might that be achieved?'

'Why, you publish anonymously, as I have done with my novels,' said Betsey.

'I suppose I could,' said Lydia.

'If you like, I shall write to Mr Turner on your behalf. He has already agreed to publish a short biography composed by Alex's coxswain.'

'Goodness,' exclaimed Lydia. 'Sedgwick's account is to be published? How extraordinary!'

'It is quite the tale,' enthused Betsey. 'Fisherman in Africa, seized by slavers and transported across the ocean, then his time as a slave in Barbados, escape, and finally a Royal Navy seaman. Mr Turner holds that it will do much to forward the cause of Abolition. The only pity is that poor Sedgwick will be far away with Alex when it is placed before the public.'

Lydia felt sadness tug at her again at the thought of her husband's departure. And this time he would be travelling out of Europe to a distant ocean. It would be many months, perhaps even years before he would be returned to her. She looked around the sunlit orchard, and felt it darken as a cloud past overhead. Then her eyes fixed on a particular spot.

'I believe it was just over there,' she said, half to herself. 'Under that tree, with the scar shaped like an ear on the trunk.'

'Is that the place where my brother confirmed his love for you?' asked Betsey, and then she sighed. 'I wonder if anyone will ever make such a declaration to me.'

'Of course they will,' said Lydia firmly. 'A lady with your accomplishments, fine countenance and noble character? Why, the only surprise to me is that it has not happened already.'

'I can write easily enough of romance, but it is so much harder in practice,' said Betsey.

'You underplay your abilities, Miss Clay,' said Lydia, with mock gravity. 'I have seen the way you regard our current house guest.' Her friend flushed pink with embarrassment.

'Is it so obvious?' she said.

'Only to those that know you well,' smiled Lydia, reaching across the table to squeeze her friend's hand. 'And is no more obvious than his attention towards you. Captain Sutton is a very agreeable young man, is certainly unattached at present, and is your brother's closest friend. All of which makes him very eligible.'

'He does cut a handsome figure, does he not?' said Betsey, picking up her pen and brushing the feathered end against her cheek as she pondered. 'But wait. Is Captain Sutton's ship not due to be part of the same expedition that will take my brother away?'

'Yes, it is,' said Lydia. 'But that is not for at least a month. Time enough for your acquaintance to blossom. They will return from their shooting soon.'

'So be it. I shall do my best to make myself irresistible for when he appears,' said Betsey. She adjusted her bonnet. 'How do I look?'

'Very desirable,' said her friend. 'Although perhaps I

should council caution before you lose your heart to a sailor. The long absences are very trying. You might be happier with a nice fat squire.'

'A squire!' laughed Betsey. 'Now I see how low your opinion of me is. Fear not, for I well understand the path you choose when you marry a sailor. Since the age of eleven Alex has been away from mother and me far more than he has ever been at home.'

'Yes, but then a day will come when, like me, you shall have some hope for the future, and will known that you will face that change alone,' said Lydia. Her friend's eyes opened wide with delight.

'Can it be true?' she exclaimed. 'Oh goodness! Am I truly to become an aunt?'

'I have not had it confirmed by a physician, but yes, I am as certain as one can be so early in such a grave matter. But you must not tell Alex – not until I am sure. So much can yet go wrong.'

'Not tell Alex! But Lydia, why did you tell me at all, then? You know I cannot dissemble. I shall turn as red as one of those apples the moment I see my brother!'

'You had better try and regain your composure, for if I am not mistaken I can hear the gentlemen in the garden now.'

'Good afternoon, ladies,' said Clay, as he approached the table with John Sutton. 'What a hive of industry we have here!' Both men were out of uniform for once, with their shirts open at the neck, their long coats unbuttoned and mud spattered up their boots. Sutton carried a fowling piece casually over his shoulder, while Clay had left his propped against the orchard wall.

'Did you shoot well, my dear?' asked Lydia, smiling up at her husband from beneath the rim of her bonnet.

'No, I shot very ill indeed, I am afraid,' he replied. 'Our French opponents will have little to fear from either myself or John on the evidence of today. But it was still very agreeable to be out in the countryside. I must confess to being quite parched.'

'Then let us go in for some refreshment,' said Lydia, pushing herself up from the table. 'I feel a little chill, now that the sun has gone in. Captain Sutton, would you escort Miss Clay?'

Betsey watched the married couple walk out of the orchard, arm in arm, with their heads inclined towards each other. The chatter of their talk faded with the distance, leaving an obvious silence behind them. She turned her attention back to Sutton, who had placed his gun down on the grass, and taken Lydia's place at the table. He really is a fine looking man, she thought. His hat was angled back on his head, which allowed a ring of tousled, dark brown hair to fringe his face. His features were nicely proportioned, with a strong nose between a pair of brown eyes that seemed almost black in the shade of the apple trees.

'How does your latest work precede, Miss Clay?' he asked. 'I presume well, to judge from the quantities of paper that are by your side.'

'It goes tolerably, thank you,' said Betsey. 'I have been a little stuck of late on the look and appearance of one of the characters. It is that of the hero who will be of principal interest to my heroine. But I believe I may now have had some inspiration.' She held her companions gaze for a moment, and then dropped her eyes.

'That is splendid, Miss Clay,' smiled Sutton. 'It is awaited with impatience by some of your admirers in the service.'

'Ah yes,' laughed Betsey. 'My brother has told me of the bold warriors aboard his ship, who none the less indulge themselves with my romantic novels!'

'Since when have King's officer been barred from having such feelings?' he protested.

'Do you place yourself in the category of a romantic, Captain Sutton?' she asked. He rose to his feet, bowed and extended out his arm.

'Would you care to take a turn around the garden with me, Miss Clay, and judge for yourself?'

She rose, made a mock curtsy and took his arm. Sutton was aware of the warm pressure of her hand on his arm as they walked, and the matching warm glow he felt inside at the contact. Behind them in the orchard it was growing dark beneath the trees. A cold wind had begun to blow and it ruffled at the pages of her unfinished novel.

*****

A month later in Portsmouth Able Sedgwick, the captain's coxswain of the frigate *Titan*, tilted the brim of his tarpaulin hat to deflect the worst of the October rain from out of his eyes. The soon-to-be published writer was one of two men trudging along a narrow street. He was a tall, heavily built man with a handsome face and solid jaw framed between his short sideburns. Unusually for a sailor, his black hair was cut short. This contrasted with the thick pigtail of his companion, which would normally have stretched in a blond rope down his back, but was so sodden with rain that today it showed dun brown. His was a much slighter figure, lean and wiry, and he strode with the arrogant self assurance of a trained top man. Startling blue eyes looked out from under his hat, and a gold ring glinted in his ear.

'I reckons this here lane be Mast Street,' said Adam Trevan, in his strong Cornish accent. 'Can you see that there grog shop?' The two sailors peered down the dark, narrow way, searching in vain for the tavern. Sedgwick stepped across the road and looked at the name painted on the house wall that stood at the corner.

'So why is it set down Liberty Street here?' asked the coxswain, pointing to the white letters.

'Ah, must be the next one, then,' said Trevan. He set off down the road again. 'It's been a right long while since I was last in Pompey. Mind, it do help some to have a scholar along as can read them signs, like. Come on, Able, this ain't the weather to linger any.'

With a sigh, Sedgwick hunched his shoulders against the rain and pushed his hands a little deeper into his pockets as he followed his friend over the gleaming cobbles.

The next street proved to be the right one, and half way up one side was the Elm Tree tavern, with a crudely carved tree that hung from a pole above the door. It was a dingy little place, with low beams and a beaten earth floor. The air was thick with pipe smoke and the loud talk of the twenty or so members of the *Titan*'s crew who sat around the few wooden tables inside.

'Ahoy, lads!' came a shout in a broad Irish accent from one of them. 'Over here!' The companions looked around and saw two figures waving at them. The one who had shouted had a long, dark pigtail every bit the equal of Trevan's; the other had shorter brown hair, and at six-foot-six was comfortably the biggest man in the room. They both rose to embrace the new arrivals.

'Sean O'Malley, as I live and breathe,' said Trevan. 'And Sam Evans, too! How have you been, my lovelies?'

'Fecking awful,' moaned the Irishman, who was the owner of the pigtail. He sloshed beer from an earthenware jug into two spare mugs for the new arrivals. 'Since the dockyard chucked us off the barky, I been stuck in a garret here.'

'An' I still can't show me face in London,' said the huge Evans. 'Five bleeding years since I made a cock of losing that prize fight, and the bookmaker's traps is still a-looking for me.'

'So have you two been holed up in Pompey the whole time, then?' asked Sedgwick.

'We have,' said Evans. 'Burning through our prize money on whores and grog.'

'Aye,' smiled O'Malley. 'So it's not been all bad.'

'Have you lads got your Nile medals?' said Trevan. He reached into the neck of his shirt and pulled out a two-inch bronze disk. O'Malley fished deep into his jacket pocket and produced his, along with a clasp knife, to which the medal's blue and white ribbon had become caught.

'I got my fecker too,' he said holding it up. 'But you can barely get a tanner for them at pawn. Not like the grunters, who got silver ones, like.'

'Or the captains with bleeding gold,' added Evans. 'But I likes mine. The wenches are always wanting to know how I came by it, and I makes them work for that knowledge.'

'Drink up, then, lads' said the Irishman. He raised his mug high. 'To the four of us — each one a hero of the Nile!'

'And to those we left behind, like Rosie,' added Sedgwick. The others all paused with their mugs near their lips.

'Aye, you're on the mark there, Able,' said Trevan. 'Let's drink to Rosie.'

'Have you had word of this frigate squadron we're to join, at all?' said O'Malley, once the toast had been downed. The three sailors all looked at Sedgwick.

'Pipe don't share everything with me,' cautioned the coxswain. 'But he did say as we would be part of a squadron led by some bloke by the name of Sir George Montague.'

'Christ, no,' groaned Evans. 'Not Dismal George! I shared a beer with some of the lads from the *Black Prince*. All they did was moan about what an arse he is. They say how he's a proper spit and polish tartar. He has them cleaning brass and scrubbing decks every hour the bleeding Almighty gives.

This fellow was saying as how they only has three rules on his ship. If it moves, you salute it. If it don't move, you shifts it. If you can't shift it, you paints it.'

'Aye, that's right,' agreed Trevan. 'My mate Tom says they never does no live firing on the *Prince* 'cause he won't tolerate smuts of powder smoke on his precious paint work.'

'Handy that, in a scrap,' said O'Malley. 'We've never actually fired our fecking guns before, Monsieur Frog, but you should mark the speed we can polish brass!'

'So there be us in the *Titan* and Dismal's *Black Prince* in this here squadron,' said Trevan. 'Any more ships?'

'Two sloops of war, one of which will be our old barky *Rush*, with Pretty Boy in charge,' said Sedgwick. His friends brightened at this.

'Proper good grunter is Captain Sutton,' said Trevan. 'Pipe's best mate, too. What's the other sloop to be?'

'She's named the *Echo*, eighteen guns. I ain't heard who her skipper will be.'

'What was that name again?' said O'Malley. He cupped a hand to one ear.

'*Echo*,' repeated Sedgwick. The Irishman shook his head as if to clear it.

'Still not fecking getting it. What did you say again?'

'I SAID *ECHO*......oh, you lousy bastard,' laughed Sedgwick, as he finally spotted the grins on all the faces round the table.

'He had you good and proper,' chuckled Evans. 'Which marks a change. It's usually me as gets made game of.'

'Where's this squadron headed for then, Able?' asked Trevan. 'Is it back to the Med for us?'

'I don't know for certain, but I think it might be a deal farther off.'

'Caribbean?' suggested Evans.

'Doubt it, Sam, the Frogs is proper beat over there,' said

O'Malley. 'Fightin' be all but done. Could it be the South Seas, maybe? Now that would be fecking grand! You must have heard tell of the wenches in them parts? Babylon ain't in it!'

'Autumn be hard upon us now,' said Trevan. 'We be sure to be bound for the Baltic.'

'I helped stow Pipe's kit, and there were precious few warm togs,' said Sedgwick. 'No gloves, nor mufflers, no woollen smalls. Instead it were all light stuff. From what his missus has laid in for him, I should say we're bound somewhere devilish hot.'

'Devilish hot, eh?' said Evans. 'We had best get a drink in, while we still can. Hoy! Landlord! Bring another jug of your ale here!'

The landlord of the Elm Tree was a big, cheerful man, and he swayed his large frame through the packed tavern with some skill to arrive at the sailors' table. He banged a foaming jug down with a friendly smile and paused to wipe his hands on his apron. Then he saw Sedgwick and the smile vanished from his face.

'What's he doing in my tavern?' he barked. 'We don't have his sort in here. This is a respectable establishment.' The sound of the sailors' chatter died away across the room.

'What did you fecking say?' snarled O'Malley in the resulting quiet.

'You heard me. I'll have no Blackamoors in the Elm Tree. You others are welcome to stay, but he'll have to clear out.'

'This be Captain Clay's coxswain!' exclaimed Trevan. 'He ain't no ordinary tar.' The Cornishman rose to his feet. Others followed his lead across the room.

'I don't care if he's the Lord High Admiral himself, he can't drink in here,' said the landlord, folding his arms.

'He fought at the Battle of the fecking Nile for the likes of yous,' said O'Malley, brandishing his medal under the landlord's nose. The other sailors at the table lined up behind the Irishman, the huge Evans having to crouch under the beams as he pushed his way forward. The landlord retreated back towards the serving hatch.

'Mary, fetch my cudgel,' he called, keeping an anxious eye upon the Londoner.

'Lads, it's fine,' said Sedgwick, stepping forwards to place himself between the innkeeper and the sailors. 'I was done with grog for today, any road.'

'Listen to your shipmate now,' urged the landlord. 'There ain't no cause for trouble.'

'No fecking cause for trouble!' roared O'Malley. 'Haven't you just insulted my friend?' There was a growl of approval from his fellow *Titans*.

'Let's fire this miserable place,' suggested a voice on the far side of the tavern. Earthenware slid over oak and smashed onto the floor as a table was up-ended.

'Mary, send the pot boy for the parish constables,' yelled the landlord over his shoulder. 'You leave that table alone now! And those broken crocks will need to be paid for.' A jug flew across the room and smashed into the wall next to his head. The innkeeper ducked round in fury, and then his face cleared.

'Calm yourselves, there is no occasion for any riot,' he said, stepping into the middle of the sailors and pointing to the open door. 'See, all is well. He has gone and scarpered. At least the monkey seems to know his place.' He turned back towards Sedgwick's companions, just in time to receive the full force of Evans's right fist as it crashed into his jaw.

The coxswain was not present to witness the blow, or indeed the subsequent destruction of the tavern's interior by his enraged shipmates. He had slipped away and was walking through the rain towards the sea. After a few hundred yards he reached the quayside and looked out over

Portsmouth harbour. It was crowded with rowing boats and skiffs all busy on the water. Moored opposite him, in a line along the edge of the freeway, a row of warships rocked in the current. All around them where gathered Victualling Board lighters, full of barrels and sacks being hauled up onboard. A struggling cargo net swayed through the air towards the deck of a ship of the line, and he heard a bullock's indignant bellow drift through the dank air like a fog horn. That ship would leave on the next tide, he concluded, now they are getting the livestock on board. Just behind the big two-decker he could see the *Titan*, with light coming from her long row of open gun ports, while beyond her was another similar sized frigate. He could just make out that the figurehead was of a horseman in black armour. So, Dismal George is here too, he thought. They would soon sail from this confusing bloody country, sometimes so full of hope, but always ready to disappointment once more.

He pulled out his Nile medal from his pocket and looked at it. The disc of bronze rested heavy in the palm of his hand. On it was the figure of a robed lady who stood barefoot on a rock by the sea with an anchor behind her. Tucked under one of her arms was a shield with Nelson's bust on it, while with the other arm she held out a leafy branch. The Goddess of Peace, said Sedgwick to himself. That is who Miss Betsey had said she was. What an odd choice to commemorate such a destructive battle, he thought. His friend Rosso had been dashed away in an instant by a shot that had flown in through an open gun port. The skeletal form of the Goddess of Death would have been more appropriate.

He stood with the rain pattering down on the top of his tarpaulin hat and the bronze disc in his hand. The green water of the harbour at his feet was speckled with tiny splashes. They were joined by a single, larger splash as he tossed the medal away.

THE DISTANT OCEAN

CHAPTER 2 DEPARTURE

The captain's steward of the *Black Prince* stood back from the damask-covered table in the frigate's great cabin, all the better to admire his work. The warm light from the candelabras winked back off the ranks of polished silverware and sparkled in the glittering crystal. At one end of the table, straight as a line of guardsmen, a row of broad-bottomed decanters were arrayed, each precisely filled to the same level with dark wine.

'Just the squadron's captains for dinner, Sir George?' the steward asked.

'Yes, that is correct, Thomas,' said Commodore Sir George Montague. 'It shall be a last chance to meet with them all before we depart. I have asked the captain of the *Echo* to come over before the others, so pray have the sherry ready to serve. He is the nephew of an old shipmate of mine.' He walked over to the table and moved one of the spoons a fraction straighter. Then he ducked down and pointed towards a glass. 'Half a finger mark on that, Thomas. For God's sake, man, use your damned eyes!'

'Aye aye, Sir George,' replied the steward. He pulled a soft cloth from out of his pocket and polished the offending crystal.

Montague watched him work with an angry frown. He was a short, haughty-looking man in his mid-forties. His dark hair, cut a little shorter than was the fashion, was flecked with grey above his temples. Two intense dark eyes looked out from either side of a large, patrician nose. He pulled out a silk handkerchief from his pocket and flicked a little dust from the sleeve of his beautifully tailored coat. From the look of the broadcloth, it was new. The front was heavy with a commodore's gold braid. Then he paused as the sound of boatswain's pipes squealed from the direction of the entry port on the far side of the bulkhead. A little later there was a knock at the cabin door.

'I trust I am not late, Sir George?' said Commander Nicholas Windham as he stepped through into the cabin. 'It took a little longer for my cutter to reach you with the tide now in flood.'

'No matter, my boy,' smiled Montague, gripping the young man's hand. 'Upon my word, how you have grown!' He stepped back to look at him properly. Windham was a little taller than his host, slightly built, with dark brown hair that had begun to recede over his temples. His eyes seemed sunken in this pale face. My, how he has aged, thought Montague. He can surely be no more than mid-twenties, yet he looks so much older.

'You were no more than a milksop midshipman when I last saw you, on your uncle Percy's ship,' he enthused. 'That would have been back in the year ninety-one or two? But now look at you! Newly promoted to Master and Commander, with your own sloop of war to boot. If he were still with us, your uncle would have been bursting with pride.'

'I wanted to express my deepest gratitude for my step, Sir George,' said Windham. 'I know I would still be a lieutenant were it not for your preferment.'

'Oh, nonsense, boy,' said the commodore. 'A word offered in the right ear, no more than that. What is the use of the Montagues' commanding four seats in Parliament if I can't help out the nephew of an old friend, what? How else do you think I got the plum command of this squadron? Do have a glass of sherry, Nicholas.' Thomas came over with the tray as the two officers took their seats.

'Now tell me how you find the *Echo*?' asked the commodore.

'She is a fine little vessel, sir,' said Windham. 'But I had never realised how much effort it would be to commission a new ship. All manner of stores to be loaded, rigging to be set up, hands to be found, and with the assistance of just one commissioned officer.'

'It can be difficult in a sloop. I trust that your lieutenant is at least competent?'

'At first I had thought so, Sir George. He is a good friend of mine who pressed me for the position. Well bred, from a sound family, but now I wonder if a more experienced officer might have answered better. I might then not be obliged to take on so much myself.'

'Perhaps so,' said Montague. 'I will help of course, if I am able, but I do have my own preparations to complete. The fact is we shall be away very promptly. Have you thought to seek the assistance of Captain Clay or Commander Sutton? They will be joining us presently. Did you not all serve together as lieutenants, under your Uncle Percy?'

'We did, Sir George, but we have become somewhat estranged since then,' said Windham.

'Really?' said Montague, his eyebrows lifting in surprise. 'But they both seem such amiable coves.'

'At first acquaintance they can be tolerable enough,' said Windham. 'But perhaps when you come to know them better, you will see matters as I do, sir.'

'That may be so, but I don't like the sound of this at all. You must affect a reconciliation, Nicholas. I cannot tolerate any dissention within my squadron. We have a long and challenging mission ahead of us. Only the most harmonious relations between my commanding officers will answer. What on earth can have occasioned such a breach?'

'It dates from the time of my uncle's death, Sir George,' said Windham. He rose from his chair and began to pace the room. 'In truth, I was never satisfied with the explanation that those gentlemen were able to supply as to how my uncle came to die.'

'He fell in battle with a French frigate, did he not?' said his host. 'The papers at the time were most fulsome with their praise of him.'

'Yes, that is what Clay and Sutton would have you believe,' scoffed Windham. 'What is less generally known is that Uncle Percy had quite fallen out with Clay, and he planned to have him broken when we reached Barbados. But of course he never arrived. In the height of battle he fell from the ship, and as he was no swimmer, he was never heard of again.'

'And you hold that it was Captain Clay who did this?' asked Montague. 'That he raised his hand to strike down his captain? If true, it is quite the most shocking thing I have ever heard.'

'In fairness it cannot have been him, Sir George. He was on the gun deck with me at the time of my uncle's disappearance. It was Sutton who had the opportunity to do it. He has always been one of Clay's creatures.'

'Can you prove any of this? Were there any that witnessed it happen?' Windham stopped his pacing and shook his head.

'No, I have no conclusive proof of that kind,' he said. 'God knows, I have tried to obtain it. But I know in my heart what I say is true.'

'Nicholas, come and resume your seat before you wear out my carpet, I pray,' said Montague. 'Consider for a moment what you are saying. The accusations you make are of a very grave character, and yet you tell me you have no proof? Surely you see what folly it would be to pursue this?'

'No, Sir George, I do not,' he said, gripping the arms of his chair. 'All I seek is justice for my uncle. How can that be folly?'

'Listen to me now,' said Montague placing a friendly hand on top of the younger man's. 'I can see from your general appearance how injurious all this is proving to your health. You look like a man that hasn't slept for a month.'

'God knows, I have tried to let matters rest,' he said. 'And while I was serving on a distant station, that was possible. But since I have been assigned to my new sloop, and learnt who commands the other ships in the squadron, it has brought the horror of it all back to me. They killed Captain Follett. I know they did.'

Montague looked at his guest, and his face hardened.

'Your uncle was a good friend of mine, you know, Nicholas,' he said. 'If I find a shred of evidence that what you say is true, I give you my word that I shall act. But consider what you are telling me! A warship cleared for action has no hiding place in which such a base act could have occurred. A captain on his quarterdeck is surrounded by other persons. Marines, gunners serving their pieces, quartermasters at the wheel, sailors of the afterguard, other officers; yet you tell me that none of these individuals saw anything amiss?'

'The mizzen mast had just fallen,' said Windham. 'All was confusion!' His host held up a hand to silence him.

'Even with a falling mast, if what you say were the case, someone would have seen it done,' he continued. 'I speak to you now as an old friend of your family as well as your commanding officer, when I say to you that you must let this matter drop. I cannot have bad blood amongst my squadron. Is that clear?'

'Aye aye, Sir George,' said Windham, after a pause. His

grip on the arms of the chair relaxed a little, but his eyes remained cold as flint.

*****

'This is a capital beef steak pie, Sir George,' enthused John Sutton later that evening. He held his plate towards Thomas, who cut him another generous slice. 'It has a most unusual savour.'

'That will be the taste of truffles, Mr Sutton,' said his host. 'Are you familiar with them at all?'

'I cannot say that I am, sir. What, pray, are truffles?'

'Some manner of fungus that grows like a gall upon the roots of diverse trees,' replied Montague. 'My cook is a very talented Frenchman. He was serving the captain of a French West Indiaman I captured back in ninety-two. He tells me that in his country they use truffles extensively in the better sort of kitchen. It requires but a little to flavour a dish, which is deuced fortunate, for they ain't the cheapest of cabin stores. Are you familiar with truffles, Captain Clay?'

'I have had them only the once, on the occasion of my wedding, Sir George.'

'Only once, sir?' queried Windham. 'I have them quite frequently when at home, but then, of course, Fenton Park does have a better sort of kitchen. No more of the pie for me, but I will have some more wine, Thomas.'

'I collect you wedding was quite a grand affair, then?' said Montague.

'Moderately so, Sir George,' said Clay. 'I married the ward of Lady Ashton last year. John here was present to assist me.'

'Yes, I had heard that you did very well in the matter of your marriage,' said the commodore. 'You are to be congratulated for having wed into a family so decidedly above your station.' Clay looked sharply at Montague, but his host smiled at him in a friendly fashion. He settled back into his seat and let the comment pass. Any talk of his marriage could not fail to remind him of Lydia, and the wonderful news she had whispered into his ear that morning.

'Lord Spencer told me that you were presented at court last month,' continued Montague, filling the gap in his guests' conversation. 'Was that your first levee?'

'It was, Sir George,' replied Clay. 'Although it was not at St James's. I was obliged to travel down to Weymouth. Have you met with the King?'

'Oh, frequently,' said the commodore. 'The last occasion was when I was knighted. Spencer said the king thought to dub you, too, for a while, till it was pointed out to him that if he made everyone who successfully delivered a letter a knight, the postal service might become rather too grand, what?' He and Windham laughed uproariously at this, and his other two guests exchanged glances.

'There was some talk of it, but in the end I was presented with a rather fine sword instead,' replied Clay. 'Perhaps now that I, too, am part of a family with some influence in parliament, my next visit may prove to be as rewarding as yours.'

'I have been to court on diverse occasions,' said Windham. 'What about you, Mr Sutton?'

'Not yet, Nicholas,' he replied.

'No? Nor your father either? Pity that, though I suppose he never did rise very high in the service. He is but a lieutenant still, I collect?'

'That is correct,' said Sutton.

'While you and Captain Clay have both advanced yourselves to such a prodigious degree,' continued Windham, his words a little slurred. 'Why, you both command your own ships now, one a post captain, the other a commander. All this in the few brief years since my uncle was killed.'

'Now then, Nicholas,' cautioned Montague. 'Pray let Captain Sutton enjoy his pie.'

'I fear it has defeated me, Sir George,' said the commander of the *Rush*, laying down his knife and fork. 'My appetite for your excellent beef seems to have fled.'

'No matter,' said their host. 'Truffles can sometimes make a remove over rich. You have performed with distinction, for your first skirmish with that noble fungus. Will you take a glass of wine with me to mark the occasion?' As the wine was drunk he glanced at his steward who came forward to clear the table.

'Now, I have some rather fine cheese to follow,' he continued. 'I live in hope that the prospect will restore Captain Sutton's appetite once more. By the way, does anyone have any knowledge of a riot that occurred at one of the taverns behind Gun Wharf, Monday last? Apparently the owner was soundly thrashed by a party of sailors and his establishment turned over. The Port Admiral is most anxious to find those responsible.'

'I had heard of the incident, Sir George' said Clay, his face neutral. 'Some of my people were ashore, but my inquiries have been unable to confirm if any of them were involved.'

'No *Rushes* were ashore at the time,' added Sutton.

'Or *Echoes,* for that matter, said Windham.

'Hmm, how very mysterious,' said Montague. He looked over the rim of his wine glass at his subordinates. 'Perhaps it is for the best that no further shore leave can be granted, as we are about to depart.'

'Really, Sir George?' said Sutton. 'Have our sailing orders arrived then?'

Their host waited for Thomas to complete serving all his guests before answering.

'They have indeed, gentlemen,' he said. He paused to

twist his plate of cheese round till the family crest on the rim was at twelve o'clock. 'Part of my object in inviting you tonight was to share with you their contents. I know you are all aware that we are bound for the Indian Ocean, but I think only Captain Clay knows what our object is to be when we arrive. There is a force of French ships that have been operating in those waters and attacking our trade. Our orders are to hunt down and eliminate them.'

'Do we know what force the French have, Sir George?' asked Clay.

'They have deployed three of their larger frigates,' said there host. 'Two of forty guns and one of thirty-six.' Sutton whistled out loud.

'Three frigates,' he exclaimed. 'They will be raising Old Harry with the East India trade.'

'Where shall we base ourselves, Sir George?' asked Clay.

'At Cape Town. As you would expect, the Dutch had excellent naval facilities there, most of which were captured intact back in ninety-five when we seized the place.'

'And when shall we depart for the Cape, Sir George?' asked Sutton.

'We must all be away from Portsmouth within two days,' replied the squadron's commander, looking round the table. His gaze alighted on the captain of the *Rush*. 'You seem to find this intelligence distressing, Captain Sutton?'

'Your pardon, Sir George. I did have an engagement I was anxious to fulfill before we left.'

'I am sorry to hear that,' said Montague. 'Was it a matter of some gravity?'

'Not really, Sir George. I had promised to call upon Miss Clay before I departed, but I shall not now be at leisure to make such a journey.'

'How unfortunate,' said Windham, staring across at his fellow captain without any trace of sympathy.

'You shall have to blame your absence on the demands of the service, I am afraid,' said the commodore.

'I am sure Betsey will understand, John,' said Clay. 'Hasty departures have led to my failing to honour no end of such engagements over the years.' Sutton nodded in reply, but said nothing. Clay turned back to their host. 'Will we voyage directly to the Cape, Sir George?'

'Not directly, nor together as a squadron. As is normal these days, no warship can be sent out from home waters without the opportunity being taken for them to offer their protection to some of the trade. One frigate will be required to go via the Gold Coast of Africa with a number of our Guineamen, while the rest of us will help to protect a large convoy bound for the Levant as far as Gibraltar.' He turned towards Clay. 'I had thought the *Titan* might nursemaid the ships for West Africa? They are ready for immediate departure. Could you leave with the tide tomorrow?'

'As you wish, Sir George,' he said evenly, while in his heart he felt the dread of leaving Lydia so soon. 'I will need to work my people through the night on the last of my ship's preparations, but that should be in order. I take it we will rendezvous again at the Cape once we have both completed our convoy duties?'

'Quite so,' said the commodore. 'My ship will leave the following day, together with the *Rush* and the *Echo*.'

'Then perhaps I might trouble you for a paper and pen, so that I may send a note to my wife. I, too, had an engagement I must needs break. She will be expecting me ashore tonight.'

'Of course. Thomas, kindly pass the word for my clerk. Have him bring Captain Clay's orders, too.'

While they waited for the clerk to arrive, Montague looked around his dinner table. God help me, he thought, what an indifferent collection of officers I have under my command. Young Windham looks as if he wants to call out

Sutton at any moment. Sutton seems lively enough, but is now fretting about this Miss Clay. The only steady looking cove I have is her brother. His gaze met the calm, wolf-grey eyes of the *Titan*'s captain, and he raised his glass.

'Gentlemen, I fear our evening draws to a close,' he said. 'We must all shortly return to our various preparations for departure. We have an excellent squadron commanded by three of the most able young officers the service can boast. I give you a successful voyage, and damnation to the French!' The toast was drunk with approval, and then there was a pause while all looked at Windham.

'W...what now?' he muttered, peering around him.

'You're the youngest!' hissed Sutton.

'Oh, yes.... Gentlemen, the King!'

*****

The straggling line of Guineamen and their escorting frigate sailed across a world of deep blue and dazzling white. The sky was dotted with towering columns of boiling cloud that marched towards the unseen coast of tropical Africa that lay ahead, just beneath the horizon. They were matched by the columns of snowy canvas that the ships had spread to catch the wind. It was six weeks since the *Titan* had made her hasty departure from Portsmouth with her charges. That day had been grey and chill, the sun no more than a pale disc lost in veils of cloud. Now it was a globe of fire that sucked moisture from the waves till the air was thick with humidity. It was just after noon, and so high was the sun overhead that even the profusion of sail the frigate carried gave little shade to the group of men who sat in a line along the forecastle rail.

'You has to be more gentle than that, our Sam,' urged Trevan, as the Londoner's hook splashed into the water. 'The fish will be shy of such a commotion.'

'What! They'll take note of my little splash over the wake of the bleeding barky?' exclaimed Evans. 'How does that work, then?'

'The barky's motion is sort of constant, like,' explained the Cornishman. 'They'll be used to her by now. I shouldn't wonder if there weren't shoals of them, a-lurking under the hull.'

'If that's the case, the buggers don't seem partial to pork fat, at all,' said O'Malley. He examined the piece of rind he had saved from yesterday's dinner with distaste as he pushed it onto the hook, before lowering it down to join the other lines that bobbed about in the *Titan*'s gentle bow wave.

'Try to animate your hook a little, Sam,' suggested Sedgwick. 'Make them curious as to what it may be, like this.' He held his line outstretched in front of him and thrummed his fingers against the string. Sam tried to imitate his friend, but after several minutes without result, his attention began to wander.

'So is them the ships what slavers use?' said Evans. He pointed across towards the line of Guineamen that sailed along on a parallel course in their lee.

'No, no, your slave ship is a much sleeker and handier craft. He has to get up all them little creeks and rivers, and the like,' said Trevan. 'They be proper fast an' all, to hurry their cargo across to the Americas before they should perish.'

'That's right,' said O'Malley. 'They don't need any escort from the likes of us. They can give fecking topsails to most privateers, and still beat them in a chase easy as kiss my hand.'

Sedgwick concentrated on his line. He let the simple task of fishing calm the unwelcome memories that his friends' talk had awoken. After a moment he became aware that it had gone quiet. When he glanced up, the others were looking at him.

'Sorry, lads, I wasn't attending,' he said. 'What was said, again?'

'Sam asked how long it took them slavers to cross to Barbados,' said O'Malley. 'I thought six weeks, but Adam was having none of it.'

'I can't really remember,' he replied. 'It was hard to judge, confined as we were. I remember having no notion that it might end at all, until it did. Perhaps it was six weeks, or maybe longer?'

'I dare say it were hard to judge, Able, lad,' said Trevan. 'For them as was below decks, like.'

'So if them ships ain't slavers, what are they bleeding here for, then?' persisted the Londoner, pointing with his fishing line towards the Guineamen once more.

'It's not just your slaves as is to be had in these waters,' said O'Malley. 'There's all manner of treasure. Gold dust, elephant's teeth, palm oil, pepper – they don't call it the Gold Coast for fecking nothing. Not that we shall be having any of that. It'll be touch and go for us, drop off the Guineamen and away to the Cape, you mark my words.'

'We may not have gold dust, but we do have a bite,' exclaimed Sedgwick, as his line began to jerk in his hand. 'Help me get it landed, it feels big.'

Evans joined the coxswain and together they hauled in the large and very lively fish. They dropped it down onto the planking, were it thumped around the deck, gasping and flopping before Trevan stunned it with a blow from a belay pin. The fishermen crowded around their catch in admiration. It was a long silver fish with yellow fins and tail, and a glow of lemon on its belly.

'It be a right handsome creature,' said Trevan. 'Looks a bit like some manner of bass.'

'It is what my people call a ladyfish,' said Sedgwick. 'They are very good eating.'

The others looked at him for a moment.

'Of course you would fecking know,' exclaimed O'Malley. 'Wasn't you a fisherman from around here once?'

'I wouldn't have come out this far, but we had ladyfish close into shore, too,' said the coxswain, his eyes watching the dying animal.

'Well that's good,' said Evans. 'I was a wondering how we might tell which of these foreign fish is sweet and which is poison. Let's catch another.' He and O'Malley returned to their lines with renewed enthusiasm. Trevan waited with his friend.

'You all right, Able?' he said. 'You seem low in your spirits.'

'It's only memories, Adam,' smiled Sedgwick. 'I find it proper strange to be catching ladyfish again.'

'Over 'ere, Able!' called Evans. 'I can see a whole load of them fish of yours, gathered around some flotsam.'

'Not just one bit of sea drift, neither,' said O'Malley. 'Fecking ocean is covered with them.'

The others joined their friends at the rail. The sea ahead of the frigate was now dotted with a line of low, dark shapes in the water. Sea birds squabbled overhead, while the flotsam itself jerked and turned in the oily water as something bit at it. The nearest piece drifted closer, surrounded by a silver halo of fish.

'Shit,' muttered Evans. 'Is that what I think it is?' The others watched in silence as the corpse of a black man bumped against the side of the ship.

CHAPTER 3 FREETOWN

Once the convoy reached Freetown, the Guineamen quickly departed, splitting up and making their way to the various trading posts of the Gold and Ivory Coasts farther to the east. This left the *Titan* as the only substantial vessel at anchor in Tagrin Bay. Clay could see his ship as it swung at anchor, with awnings spread to shelter the anchor watch on deck from the sun. The tide was full, and a swarm of dugout canoes, loaded with fishing nets, were heading past the frigate as they made for the open sea. He stood at a window that looked out onto a busy square of red earth, dominated by a single large tree in its centre, with widely spreading branches. In its shade were lines of traders with their wares spread out around them on rush mats. He could see piles of tropical fruit, baskets full of squawking chickens, heaps of tubas and plantains, all being haggled over by a colourfully dressed crowd. On the far side of the tree was the beach where Clay had arrived earlier, with the bay and his ship beyond. There was a substantial crowd of locals there too, all gathered around the waiting crew of his barge. The hands seemed to be behaving themselves as they played with the little barefoot children, or flirted in mime with their older sisters. He could rely on Sedgwick to make sure that matters did not get out of hand.

But now a second crowd had started to gather in front of him, composed of locals who had been passing to and fro, but had stopped to stare at the tall white man in his magnificent captain's uniform in the window. He began to feel self-conscious, and ducked back into the room to retake his place on his battered wooden chair. Once seated again, he looked around the room. Of all the colonial residencies he had seen, that of the Grosvenor of Sierra Leone was the most modest. It consisted of a row of wooden cabins that stretched across one side of the square. Had it not been for the sun-bleached union flag that fluttered from a pole outside, he might have entirely missed that these shacks were the seat of local government. He was in the best maintained of them, in what he had been assured was the governor's office. The floor was composed of bare planks, which had been much feasted on by the local insect population, to judge from the numerous little holes in the wood. The walls had been finished with a plaster of mud and straw and then painted over with lime wash. The windows had no glass in them, and the only furniture in the room was a roughly built desk, three chairs, and a substantial bible on a lectern by the door.

'May I assist you, captain?' asked a young, ginger-haired man in shirtsleeves who came into the room, wiping his hands on a rag.

'Yes, please, young man. I had hoped to speak with the governor? Could you let him know that Captain Alexander Clay of His Britannic Majesty's ship *Titan* is here to see him?'

'Ah, yes,' said the man, offering his hand a little shyly. 'That would be me. My name is Mr Thomas Ludlam. I am delighted to make your acquaintance, captain.'

'My dear sir!' said Clay, jumping to his feet to seize the proffered hand. 'You must think me dreadfully rude. I suppose that I was expecting someone... eh... perhaps a little more senior in years.'

'No matter, captain,' said Ludlam. 'Most visitors are surprised when they meet me. White men die so readily of fever on this coast that it is not so unusual to find a printer of three-and-twenty holding such a position. Might I get you

seen near Freetown?'

'Suspicious vessels?' repeated the young man, his eyes darted towards the large bible on its stand. 'I am not sure how I would judge that. I am only a printer, after all.'

'Very well, have *any* vessels visited Freetown recently?'

'Oh, I... I am not sure about that. We have so few ships stopping here.'

'Not sure?' said Clay. 'But if visits are rare, should they not be easy to recall? You must have a port official who keeps some manner of record? Are you trying to hold something back from me?'

'I do not wish to be unhelpful, but I would prefer not to answer your questions further, captain,' said the governor, folding his arms.

'I beg your pardon?' said Clay, 'What can you possibly mean?'

'Only what I said. I am not in a position to assist you in this matter.'

'Sir, I am a King's officer, seeking to investigate a suspicious incident at sea. If you know something about it, you must tell me. I am entitled to expect your unambiguous support!'

'I do not seek to dissemble, but you must understand the position I am in,' said Ludlam. 'If such a ship were to exist, and if it was directing itself to attacks on the slave trade, its activities might not be wholly unwelcome to the Sierra Leone colony.'

'Is that what the drowned wretches whose remains I came across out there would say?'

'Many of our residents in Freetown would think them lucky,' said the governor, pointing towards the open window. 'Unlike you and I, they have firsthand knowledge of the horrors of the middle passage, and the fate that awaits those who survive it in the Americas.'

'Governor, I understand your passion for your cause,' said Clay, leaning forward in his chair. 'But if you have knowledge of a threat to our country's commerce, it is your duty to tell me of it.'

'You must also understand, captain, that the greatest threat we face here is not from the activities of privateers, but from slavers, many of whom are British,' said Ludlam. 'They pay scant regard to the official status of this colony. Any resident that strays too far from Freetown is likely to be taken by them, or by one of the local tribes that are their creatures. If this privateer is attacking slave ships, I am not likely to be displeased with their activities.'

'I can see how this must vex you, Mr Ludlam,' said Clay. 'I myself find slavery to be abhorrent, but under the law of our country the slave trade is still legal. As a naval officer I cannot stand aside and let an enemy prey on British ships.'

'There is also God's law, sir, which is surely superior to any law of men,' said Ludlam.

'That may be so,' said Clay. 'But fortunately my orders do not require me to enforce that, too.'

'Well, sir, you must of course do your duty, as I must do mine. Sierra Leone is not a Crown colony but is run under private charter. I am not going to be able assist you any farther.'

'No, Mr Ludlam, that will not do!' exclaimed Clay. 'It is plain to me that you have some knowledge of this enemy ship. I must oblige you to pass it on to me.'

'But they are not my enemy. The foe of my foe is my ally, is it not said?'

'This is intolerable! I insist that you tell me what you know!' roared Clay. 'I shall not leave this office until I am quite satisfied you have been candid with me.' He fixed the younger man with a glare from his steel-grey eyes.

*****

There were two gun ports at the very rear of the *Titan's* wardroom, one either side of the rudder. No guns stood behind them, and even George Taylor, the ship's veteran first lieutenant, could not remember them ever having been used in battle. They were placed so close to the surface of the water that it was only on occasions like now, when the frigate was at anchor, that they could be thrown open to let in some welcome natural light and a little fresh air into the gloomy cave where the ship's commissioned officers spent much of their time. Sunlight danced off the water and sent patterns of silver spiralling across the low ceiling of the wardroom.

Taylor peered through one of the square openings and across the brown water towards the beach where the captain's barge still lay, pulled up on the sand. The crew had retreated to the shade of some palm trees that overhung the beach, and the crowd of onlookers had moved on. He looked along the straggling line of wooden shacks that lined the shore and searched for a familiar tall figure.

'I wonder what can have detained the captain for such a long period,' he mused to himself, pushing a hand through his grey hair. 'Do you think I should go back on deck?'

'Mr Preston has the anchor watch, sir,' said John Blake, his second lieutenant. 'I am sure he will send word the moment his barge pushes off from the beach.' He had spoken without looking up from the leather-bound sketch book he had propped up in front of him. Taylor got up from his chair by the open port and squeezed around the table that dominated the little wardroom to look over Blake's shoulder. On the sheet of paper a strong, angular face in profile was appearing. The artist had just started, but even from the first few lines it was already clear the face was that of Tom Macpherson, the frigate's Scottish marine commander. He

41

glanced from the portrait to the subject, sitting at the wardroom table. Blake did the same, and lay down his piece of charcoal in frustration.

'Can I trouble you to stay in the same position for above a minute, Tom?' he said. 'Please disregard George in his restless pacing around the room and continue to look only at the entrance to my cabin, as we agreed.'

Macpherson angled his head back towards one of the slated doors that lined the sides of the wardroom, and the artist returned to his picture. He rubbed in some charcoal with his finger, conjuring the marine's bristling black sideburns from out of the paper.

'Perhaps I should send another boat ashore, to see if anything is amiss?' mused Taylor to himself, as he returned to his original seat.

'Oh, no, sir! I pray do not consider such an ill judged action!' exclaimed Richard Corbett, the *Titan*'s surgeon, glaring over his little steel glasses. He was a small man in his late thirties with thin, sandy hair and pale blue eyes. 'I have already agreed with the captain that we must have minimal contact with the shore, and none at all after dark. The noxious vapours on this coast are most unwholesome. The less the crew are exposed to such miasmas the better.'

'Surely the town should be healthy enough,' protested Taylor.

'Healthy!' exclaimed the surgeon. 'Doubtless it is, if you discount the risk of Yellow Jack, Ague, Bilious Fever, Plague and all manner of Fluxes.'

'He has the truth of it, George,' said Blake, still concentrating on his work. Then he started to chant.

'Beware and take care of the Bight of Benin.
There's one comes out for forty goes in.'

'Save that the Bight of Benin is a good seven hundred miles east of us here,' grumbled the first lieutenant. 'But I daresay your advice is sound, Mr Corbett.' He returned his attention to the gun port and found the square now filled with the beaming face of a large black man with a mass of grey, bushy hair.

'Upon my soul!' exclaimed Taylor, jumping back from the opening. 'Wherever have you sprung from?'

'Good day to you, Massa,' said the man, in the distinctive drawl of the American Deep South. 'Only one way to reach you folks, and that's by boat.' He indicated the canoe he was seated in to answer Taylor's question. The middle section was loaded with a pile of tropical fruit. He selected a large one from the top and held up the glossy red and green orb for Taylor to inspect. 'Got the finest mangos in Freetown, right here. You wan'a buy?'

'I daresay the purser might, but you will have to present yourself in regular form to him at the entry port.'

'Hey, Armstrong!' called Macpherson. He reached behind him with an arm and banged on one of the cabin doors, while still holding his head motionless for Blake. 'We have a fellow colonial for you to converse with.' The *Titan*'s sailing master came out of his cabin with a yawn. He rubbed his eyes and repositioned his horsehair periwig back on his bald head before joining Taylor at the open port.

'Where you from, boy?' he asked.

'Why that's a darn' New England accent, or I ain't never heard one!' exclaimed the boat man. 'I was born in South Carolina before I ran, Massa.'

'Goodness, but you are a long way from home,' marvelled Armstrong. 'What's your name?'

'Now that depends. I started with a slave name of Clinton, but I changed it to Nash, after the preacher who helped me to escape. I mainly go by that, these days.'

'So how did you come to be all the way over here, Nash?' asked Taylor.

'Just after I ran, the goddamn rebellion started,' said the former slave. 'I fought for King George an' all, but then the darn Yankees gone and won. Government had promised to look after us, so they went and settled all us loyal Negros on some Crown land up in a place called Nova Scotia. My, oh my, but them winters was cold! Well, that was no good for a South Carolina boy like me. Soon as I heard tell of this place, I was first in line to be resettled.'

'Sounds a little like my story,' said Armstrong. 'Near broke my father's heart to leave our farm in Albany County along with the other Loyalists and move away up north. Do you prosper over here now?'

Nash shrugged. 'Be good if more ships put into Freetown for us to trade with, Massa,' he admitted. 'We only had you and that other one this last month or more.' Armstrong exchanged glances with Taylor as the germ of an idea came to him.

'Nash, I am going to have a word with Mr Faulkner, our purser,' he said. 'I will see if he might not buy all these fruit of yours, you having been such a good servant of the King. In return, might you find your way to help me? As a fellow Loyalist?'

'That I will,' said the former slave, his eyes alight with greed. 'What is it that you need, Massa?'

*****

When Clay clambered up from his barge and in through the entry port, his face was even redder than could be accounted for by his wearing a uniform coat of heavy broadcloth in the tropics. He gave a perfunctory salute to the assembled line of white-gloved ship's boys and boatswain's mates as they squealed on their pipes, and strode across to where his first lieutenant stood to greet him.

'Can you believe it?' he raved. 'I have just passed over two hours with that damned man, but the sanctimonious, snotty-nosed printer refused to tell me anything.'

'Printer, sir?' queried Taylor.

'Mr High and Mighty Thomas Ludlam, the governor of this God forsaken place. Apparently he is a printer by his calling.'

'Ah, I see, sir. And I collect he refused to cooperate with you?'

'He was perfectly civil, at first,' said Clay. 'He made it clear as to how those bodies came to be in the water. He said that they would have been dumped by a slave ship who sought to avoid capture. He as good as confirmed that there is an enemy ship operating on this coast, right now. But once he got wind that I might want to deal with such a menace, he was tighter than a clam. All he would give me was some rot about their attacks on our slave ships being beneficial. Doesn't he damn well realise we are at war?'

'Then I may have some glad tidings for you, sir,' replied Taylor. 'I believe we have discovered the intelligence you seek. There is indeed a French privateer in these waters, named the *Passe Partout*. She is an ex-slaver, fitted out with a dozen cannon and a substantial crew. She was in Freetown not four days ago, flying American colours, although there is barely a man aboard who is not French. Once she had watered and taken on some supplies, with this Ludlam's permission, she left. Our source tells us she headed eastwards down the coast.'

'Mr Taylor!' exclaimed Clay. 'You have me quite taken aback. How in the name of creation did you learn all of this? Have you gone against Mr Corbett's instructions and been ashore?'

'All our intelligence gathering was performed from the comfort of the wardroom, sir,' said Taylor. 'It was chiefly Mr

Armstrong's doing, but it is a long story. Perhaps I can give you the particulars below, where your servant can relieve you of your coat before you expire? We might then plan how we will track down this privateer over a glass of fresh mango juice.'

*****

A week had passed, and the *Titan* still searched for the illusive French privateer. She sailed over a sea that changed from azure to the most brilliant of sky blues as it washed towards the white sand that lined the shore. Beyond the beach was Africa, massive and green. The coastline that slid past their port side seemed empty of human life. Only the occasional remains of long abandoned villages hinted at the thriving population that had lived here once. Beyond the last abandoned hut, thick, tangled forest sprung up. Dark and mysterious, it stretched endlessly away into the interior.

'We have another of those river estuaries coming up on the larboard bow, sir,' reported Midshipman Butler. The teenager was a little out of breath, and sweat coursed down his face. He had run the length of the ship from his position on the forecastle. Lieutenant Preston looked on him with a kindly eye. Eighteen months ago that would have been me, he thought, having to run about in this heat. Now I am a lieutenant, able to stand where I choose, in the shade of the mizzen sails.

'Thank you, Mr Butler,' he replied. 'Would you care to take the launch in to reconnoitre the river? You may find the air a little cooler close to the sea.' The teenager brightened at the prospect.

'Why yes, sir, I should like that above all things. A most agreeable diversion. I shall go and fetch my spy glass and dirk.'

The *Titan*'s launch was the second biggest of her four

boats. With a small mast stepped, and mainsail and jib drawing well, she quickly left the ship's side and headed across the rolling sea towards the land. Butler settled into the stern sheets and let his hand trail in the water. It was delightful to feel the coolness that rushed between his fingers and soaked upwards into his sleeve. He was sat next to Sedgwick, who had the helm, while the rest of the crew handled the sheets and sails. How wonderful to be away from the frigate, he thought. Aboard the *Titan* I am the most junior of officers, while out here I am as good as a captain. Cool sea water splashed up from the waves as the boat skimmed on her way, and a fresh wind flowed across them. Butler looked over his shoulder at the stately frigate as she sailed along under easy sail spread on her soaring masts. Then he returned his attention to the land that was now rapidly approaching.

'Ah, now this is the life,' he sighed, to no one in particular. The crew of the launch smiled at his high spirits. The one exception was Sedgwick, who leant forward in the boat with a frown of disapproval.

'Where are your eyes, Rodgers?' he demanded. 'Ain't you seen that boat up ahead?'

'Sorry, Cox,' replied the sailor at the jib sheet. 'Boat ahoy, Mr Butler. Fine on the bow. She looks to be some manner of dugout.'

'Signs of life at long last!' exclaimed the midshipman. 'I had begun to wonder if anyone lived here at all.'

'There was no end of folk here once, all along the coast, sir,' said Sedgwick. 'Mind, that were afore all them slavers came. Them as is left have shifted far inland.'

'I dare say they have,' said Butler. He loosened his dirk in its scabbard. 'See if you can take these two we have found unawares. It is possible they may know something.'

'Aye aye, sir,' said Sedgwick. He ran the launch down

towards the dugout. There were two figures in the crudely carved canoe. One was a powerfully built man in his prime and the second was a much younger boy. Both were naked apart from cloth kilts tied around their waists. They were so intent on pulling in their fishing net that they missed the approach of the sailors completely. It was only when Sedgwick brought the boat smartly up into the wind beside them with a volley of flapping canvas that they looked around in wide-eyed surprise. The young man let out a cry, dropped the net and grabbed for his paddle.

'Clap onto the canoe there,' ordered Butler. Several arms reached across and pulled the two boats together.

'It's all right, lads,' said one of the crew, seeing the two men's terror. 'We ain't no slavers.' He smiled widely to reassure them, an effect largely spoiled by the many sinister gaps amongst his teeth.

'Might you be able to converse with them, Sedgwick?' asked Butler. 'Reassure them, and see what they know. You did proceed from these parts originally, did you not?'

'That were ten year ago now, sir, but I can try.' He started to talk, the words returning to him haltingly at first. Both men grinned with relief and spoke rapidly in return. 'They ain't from the same tribe as me, but their lingo be close enough, sir. I have told them that we aren't slavers, and that we shall let them go with their catch as long as they answer our questions truthful like.'

'Very good,' said Butler. 'Ask them if they have any knowledge of the *Passe Partout*?' Sedgwick spoke again. He turned to point over his shoulder towards the distant frigate. Both men followed his arm, and then spoke excitedly. The younger one pointed towards the beach emphatically with his paddle.

'I said as how we was searching for a ship, like the *Titan* but smaller, that may have passed this way, sir. They both say they saw one here yesterday, but they ran away from it because they thought it were a slaver. They beached their canoe and fled inland and only returned to collect it again this morning.'

'Yesterday, eh? That's capital!' exclaimed the midshipman. 'We are getting close at last.' Sedgwick then spoke some more with the men. To Butler he seemed more animated, as he pointed to himself and then to the coast ahead. In response the older man shook his head and said a few words back, his tone sad.

'What did you ask them?' said Butler.

'Just for some more details of the area, sir,' said the coxswain. 'I learnt nothing of note.'

'Very well then, let the canoe go there, men,' ordered the teenager. 'We must go and explore this next creek.'

As the launch entered the river estuary the world began to close in around them. The fresh wind of the open ocean was cut off, and the temperature and humidity soared. Now the air was tainted with an earthier smell of decay from the line of dense forest that seemed to push in on them from either side. The blue rolling sea had turned to flat brown water and the sound of waves faded behind them to be replaced by the cries of strange birds and the constant drone of insects. As the estuary narrowed, long shiny mud banks rose from beneath the surface on either side, their tops dotted with pieces of drift wood left high and dry.

'It seems plain to me that there can be no ship-rigged privateer here,' said Butler. He ran a finger around his collar, trying to cool himself. 'God, it's damn hot.'

'We should press on a little farther inland, sir,' said Sedgwick. 'The channel is deep enough for a ship for some distance yet, and there's this proper long bend in the river ahead what you can't see around from here.' Butler looked at him in surprise.

'How the deuce do you knows that?' he asked. 'Did the fisherman tell you?'

'I need no advice from them, sir,' said the coxswain. 'I grew up on the banks of this river and fished it with my uncle. We are very close to where I came from.'

Butler swatted at a biting insect and then sat back in the stern sheets, fanning himself with his hat. The boat sailed on up the brown river, and the banks came still closer, before opening up to one side as the flow swept around a broad bend. Sedgwick sat forward with one hand on the tiller and scanned the nearest side. The midshipman followed his gaze to a big area of much lighter undergrowth and no large trees that stretched along the river bank. The shore seemed lower there. Sedgwick looked at it for a moment, then leant back in the boat.

'Is that clearing where your village once was?' asked the midshipman.

'Yes, sir,' said Sedgwick. 'But no one lives there now. Soon it will be forest again.'

Butler looked a little longer at where the coxswain's home had been, and then turned his attention to the opposite bank of the river. His eyes wandered over the forest, but his mind was still thinking about the man sitting next to him. He chanced to look at a line of particularly tall trees that grew right down on the river bank. Most were straight, but some were angled over. The water flow must have undercut their roots, he thought, although a long bank of mud obscured his view of their bases. His eye drifted over one fallen giant that rested against its neighbour at much the same angle as the forestay of a ship was to the foremast. He had started to glance away when something flashed in the sun. That's odd, he thought, shading his eyes. Whatever it was had been too bright to be the light reflecting off the water. He reached for his spy glass and focused on the shore. After a moment he pushed himself upright and looked away. He closed the telescope with a snap and sat in the boat, looking straight forward.

'Put her on the other tack,' he ordered. Sedgwick glanced around in surprise and noticed the fixed look in the teenager's face.

'Hands to the sheets, there,' he called. 'Ready to go about!' The launch spun around and headed towards the sea once more.

'Is everything all right, sir?' asked the coxswain.

'Men, keep your eyes in the boat,' Butler said, then he muttered out the side of his mouth. 'Direct your gaze over my right shoulder, where those tall trees are. What can you see?'

The coxswain looked at the patch of jungle where Butler had indicated. He scanned the forest, his eyes moving backwards and forwards, without success. And then he saw a shape emerge from out of the background of lush green.

'It's a bloody ship!' he gasped. 'With loads of creepers and branches tied aloft in the rigging. The hull must be tucked behind that big mud bank.'

'Nice and calm does it, Sedgwick,' urged the youngster. 'Let us return to the *Titan*, but keep it nice and calm.'

Chapter 4 Passe Partout

The first mate of the *Passe Partout* was a bear of a man. He had shoulder-length black hair and a pockmarked face dominated by a bristling moustache. He stood towards the stern of the privateer and peered up into masses of greenery over his head.

'Have they gone, mon capitaine?' he asked. The man he addressed had climbed part way up the mizzen shrouds and was only visible as a pair of polished Hessian boots that protruded from the abundant foliage draped over the ship's rigging. He heard his captain close his telescope, and a moment later he jumped back down onto the deck amid a small shower of leaves.

'Yes, they have gone for now, Bruno,' said Captain Andre D'Arbigny, as he brushed pieces of creeper from off his plum-coloured coat. 'But the question is why.'

'Capitaine?' queried the mate.

'Did they go because they saw nothing to interest them, or do they hurry back to their frigate with news of us?'

'They did not come across to this side of the river,' said Bruno. 'Surely if they were suspicious they would have come to our side of the mud bank, mon capitaine? I took the cutter out into the river this morning to check our cover. I swear that a hawk would have missed the ship.'

'Even so, there is something that troubles me,' said D'Arbigny. 'It all felt very strange. I do not like the way that they suddenly turned their boat around. Having come so far, why did they not search past the bend in the river? They took a glance at the abandoned village and off they went again. And I do not trust the look of the officer who sat in the stern sheets. One moment he was searching everywhere, and then he sat staring only ahead. No, I do not like it at all.'

D'Arbigny set off to pace along the deck of his ship, his hands clasped behind his back and his polished boots making a slight squeak on the planking as he went. The sloop was too small to have a quarterdeck or forecastle, which meant he could stride all the way along her uninterrupted length. He paused for a moment at the first of her little six-pounder guns and frowned. The tiny cannon balls they fired were fine to intimidate other slave ships, he mused, but would bounce of the thick sides of the heavy frigate he had seen from the masthead. He had counted her many gun ports, each one sure to conceal a huge eighteen-pounder. He could picture the hurricane of shot they would fire and how it might smash his little ship to splinters. No, it would be suicide to enter a fight with the likes of her.

An awning had been suspended from the rigging, and under its shade the anchor watch sat at their ease. Several of the men were grouped around an upturned tub where a lively game of cards was in progress, while others sat around and talked quietly. He watched them out of the corner of his eye as he strode past. Here too, all was not as he would have liked. On the surface, they were a fearsome looking crew. Most were old Africa hands; former slavers from the Vendee and Brittany, well used to intimidating large bodies of men, and capable of considerable violence. But it was one thing to dominate a group of unarmed and bewildered slaves in shackles. How well would they fight against trained sailors and marines, armed with cutlasses and muskets as they poured over the ship's sides? They might resist for a while, but once things turned nasty, he doubted if one man in three would die for him. So, I cannot win with my cannon, nor with the crew either, he muttered to himself as he reached the bow of his little ship.

'Masthead!' he bellowed, up into the masses of greenery. The roar of his voice briefly silenced the sounds of the forest. 'What do you see of that ship's boat?'

'She is out at sea now, mon capitaine,' came the reply. 'The English are just about to reach their frigate.'

'Watch them carefully. Let me know what they do next.'

'Oui, mon capitaine!' came the reply.

Captain D'Arbigny leant on the bow rail and stared over the side into the oily brown water of the river. A piece of wood drifted towards him, bumped off the steeply raked hull of his ship, and carried on towards the sea, turning with the stream as it went. Now that was something he did have in his favour, he decided, as he admired the sharp lines of the sloop. No one could touch his *Passe Partout* for speed. If ever he could once put some blue water between himself and the English ship, he would be free. He leant over the rail and patted the oak side with affection, as if he wanted to calm a nervous thoroughbred.

'We have crossed the ocean together many times, old girl,' he said out loud.

'Capitaine?' queried Bruno, who had followed him up the deck.

'I was just remembering all the voyages I and the *Passe* have made,' he said. 'Back in the year ninety we set a new record from this coast to Martinique, you know. But now the market for my slaves has vanished. The Roast Beefs captured our sugar islands and the Negros are in revolt in Saint Dominique.'

'So now we make it our business to prey on their slavers,' said Bruno. 'Your idea was brilliant! The only thing swift enough to catch a slave ship is another slave ship, and the

three marines and two sailors, one of whom was trying to row. In the stern sheets there was a little more room, but Sedgwick was still squeezed in next to Lieutenant Taylor, with Lieutenant Macpherson on one side and the gangly Midshipman Butler on the other. He tried to ignore the hilt of Taylor's sword as it dug into his thigh and concentrated instead on navigating the boat. In his head he kept a running count of the oar strokes, using this to help him feel his way into the night.

They were deep into the estuary now, and with the last of the sea breeze cut off it was almost as hot as it had been during the day. The reek of decaying plant matter seemed to flow out of the black trees that hedged them in. The air all around throbbed with the drone of an infinite numbers of insects, while larger creatures stirred in the dark. From the forest off to one side the distant roar of a big cat set off howls of derision from a troop of monkeys, while on the other side something very big shifted amongst the trees. There was a sudden swirl in the water just beside the boat, accompanied by a heavy jolt against the side. A circle of ripples twinkled in the starlight.

'Was that some manner of large fish, Sedgwick?' asked Taylor as he watched the ring of disturbed water disappear behind them.

'No sir,' said the coxswain. 'A hundred and twenty. It was a crocodile. A hundred and twenty-one.'

'Truly?' said the lieutenant. 'Well I never did. Remind me to make sure of my footing when we clamber aboard the enemy.'

'Damnation,' muttered Macpherson as he slapped at his neck. 'It is not your crocodile I fear but these damned mosquitoes. The wee beasties are worse than Highland midges.'

'The mud bank that conceals the enemy is coming up on

the port side, sir,' said Sedgwick. 'Shall I let the others close up?'

'If you please,' murmured Taylor, twisting in his seat to look behind him.

'Easy oars,' ordered Sedgwick and the boat slowed to a halt. 'Bow pair keep sculling. Hold us in this here current.' Off to one side the long dome of mud glistened in the faint light. Beyond it the *Passe Partout* was invisible against the black forest.

'Are you sure there is a ship there?' said Macpherson.

'She was moored hard up against the bank, sir,' replied Butler. 'They had covered the rigging with such a profusion of foliage you could have missed her in broad daylight.'

'And she is precisely lined up behind this bank of mud here?' asked Taylor.

'That is correct sir, with her bow pointing towards the sea.' Just behind the long boat two other nucleuses of darkness appeared in the night.

'Mr Preston, Mr Blake, are you ready?' said Taylor.

'Aye aye, sir,' drifted quietly across the water, twice.

'Here is where we divide our forces,' said Taylor. 'We will carry on, round the bank upstream and attack her from astern. You will both round the bank downstream, and attack her from in front. Is that clear?' A pair of whispered acknowledgments sounded in the night. 'Then good luck, gentlemen,' and Taylor returned his attention to the boat.

'Absolute silence now, lads,' he ordered. 'Lay us up against their stern, Sedgwick.'

'Aye aye, sir. Give way all.'

The longboat gathered way and resumed her progress up stream, while the other two boats turn around and stole away into the night. After a dozen strokes Sedgwick pushed over the tiller to take them around the top of the mud bank.

'Row steady there,' growled Taylor, as he sensed the

rising excitement in the boat making their speed quicken. Sedgwick scanned the night ahead, searching for the ship. He had expected to see at least a few little splinters of light leaking out from below deck, but all was dark. He searched the sky for the distinctive silhouette of rigging against stars, but all he could see were the huge trees of the forest towering over the boat.

'Where the bloody hell is this ship?' muttered Macpherson. 'Surely we should have....'

'Easy all!' shouted Sedgwick. 'Backwater, both sides! Boat Ahoy!' From out of the darkness ahead there were more cries of warning. Water foamed silver in the night along the sides of both boats as their oarsman desperately tried to slow them down. They struck bow to bow with a crash that threw most of their occupants from their seats, and warm river water slopped freely over the gunwale of the longboat.

'In the bow there,' said Taylor. 'How bad is the damage?'

'Whole crew, get bailing,' supplemented Sedgwick. 'Use your hats, hands, anything you can find.'

'Top strake be a touch stove in, sir,' reported a voice from the bow. 'She should be all right for a bit, like.'

'Boat ahoy!' came the voice of Preston from ahead of them. 'The cutter is all right. We have shipped a deal of water, but no serious damage. It is fortunate you hailed when you did. If we had not slowed, one of us would have sunk for sure.'

'Any sign of the enemy?' asked the first lieutenant.

'None, sir. No sign of them at all.'

'But that is ridiculous!' raved Taylor. 'They cannot have slipped past us out to sea, and in any case the captain has that eventuality covered.' He rounded on his midshipman. 'Is this the correct mud bank, Mr Butler?'

'They were here, sir!' insisted the teenager. 'Of that I am certain. Sedgwick saw them too!'

'That's so, Mr Taylor, sir. They was moored here this afternoon, right enough,' said the coxswain.

'So where the bloody hell have they gone?'

'I think I may know, sir,' said Sedgwick. 'If you was to put me on shore here, I could go and see if I am right.'

*****

It was close to midnight now, and the three ship's boats were moored amongst huge tree roots that curved down like claws to plunge into the water. Out on the river the faint glimmer of starlight brushed across the top of the moving water. Close into the bank, beneath the canopy of trees, was a cave of utter black. The forest around them had fallen silent, amazed by the strange presence of the ring of marine pickets that Macpherson had thrown out to protect the boats from a surprise attack. In the centre of the circle the officers whispered to each other as they awaited Sedgwick's return.

'And that is the last we shall see of him,' muttered O'Malley, easing himself into a more comfortable position in the crowded boat. 'If he doesn't tread upon a viper, he will be dinner for a fecking lion. It's a crying shame an' all. He had the makings of a passable seaman.'

'I tell you what, I wouldn't fancy a stroll through that there forest,' said Evans. 'I can't see me bleeding hand before me nose out here. It'll be black as a Newgate coal scuttle under them trees, quite apart from being obliged to dodge all manner of savage beasts.'

'Ah, but you be forgetting he comes from around here, Big Sam,' said Trevan. 'It may be as natural for him as you setting out for a walk through Whitechapel of a night.'

'I bleeding hope not,' said the Londoner. 'I doubt the lions in these parts are half as fierce as an East End footpad.'

'What a fecking shambles,' said O'Malley. 'Do you reckon

there was ever a ship here at all?'

'Able were proper certain,' said Trevan. 'An' he be a steady one. He said it were concealed with no end of creepers and the like, but it were here, right enough.'

'Well, where has it gone to?' asked Evans. 'I mean it ain't like we're hunting for a lost shoe. A bleeding ship can't just up and vanish!'

'Hold steady there, Sam,' whispered Trevan, placing a hand across the big man's chest. 'Something be happening ashore, like.'

Deep in the forest, Private Conway spun round towards a faint sound of movement.

'Wh... wh...who g...g...oes there!' he called towards the rustling sound in the dark, his accent pure Munster. 'You halt now, or I am after firing at yous!'

'Friend, friend!' replied the rustle as it drew closer. 'Careful where you point that musket, Ryan.'

'Holy Mary, Able,' said the marine. 'I was after thinking you might be a fecking oliphant or the like.' He felt himself patted on the arm.

'I wouldn't go worrying about those,' said the coxswain. 'You can hear them coming on from miles away. No, if I were stood out here, in the dark, it is the leopards that would truly concern me.'

'Is it the leopards, you say?' queried the marine. 'Why them feckers?'

'Because they make no sound at all,' whispered Sedgwick into his ear. 'Where can I find Mr Taylor?'

'O...over yonder. B...by the boats,' stuttered Conway, peering past him into the blackness, his musket at his shoulder.

'Have you discovered the whereabouts of the enemy, Sedgwick?' asked the first lieutenant, as he stepped out of the night.

'Yes, sir,' replied the coxswain. 'They must have seen that Mr Butler and I had smoked them, then gone and shifted that there ship soon as we left. There is another inlet, a little farther up the river. It's a narrow creek really, a proper tight squeak, just big enough for them to slip into. They have towed her up into it by the stern.'

'Good work, that,' enthused Macpherson. 'Can we come at them by boat?'

'We can, sir. It's a bit snug at the mouth, but then it sort of widens later. If we go behind each other, we should be fine.'

'How the hell did you know where to seek them?' asked Blake.

'When I saw they had gone, I remembered this place. I used to fish there as a boy with my brother.'

'Come then, gentlemen, at least we have found our quarry,' said Taylor. 'We have done quite enough blundering around for one night. It is time for us to resolve matters directly. Lead us to this inlet of yours, Sedgwick.'

*****

Perhaps the sky had grown paler out on the water, or perhaps their eyes had now fully adjusted to the dark, but to the men in the boats the river seemed easier to navigate. The broad stream was now a slate of grey, in contrast to the inky black forest on either side. They moved steadily upstream, the oarsman all swinging backwards and forwards with the creaking rhythm of each stroke. They passed another, much lower mud bank the glistened a little beside them like the back of some huge slumbering creature. Then there was a stretch of farther rowing before Sedgwick turned the longboat towards the trees. The endless hedge of dark forest reared up against the backdrop of stars, and then Taylor

64

noticed a break, a deep notch visible before the forest begun again. In the middle of the gap was a nucleus of something even darker in the night.

'There is the ship,' breathed Sedgwick. 'They are bow on to us. When we get closer you will see they have a number of lamps lit on deck.'

'Easy oars,' hissed Taylor. 'Let the rest of the men catch us up.'

Two other patches of dark slid across the water towards them. They heard muffled orders and one boat drew up just behind them while the other appeared off to one side.

'Mr Preston, Mr Blake!' whispered the first lieutenant. 'Do you mark the enemy ahead, where that break is in the trees?'

'Aye aye, sir,' came the faint replies.

'The launch will attack at the starboard chains, the cutter over the bow,' he ordered. 'We will take them from the other side. Is that clear? Good, give way all.'

The boats all surged forward, gathering speed and shuffling into a tight line ahead. The bank grew closer and closer. Taylor watched the shape of the privateer as it emerged out of the gloom ahead. The masts were high above them, still festooned with branches, but with a starry sky behind the shape of yards and shrouds were plain to him now. It was their straight lines that betrayed their manmade origins. A sharp pencil stroke of gold appeared in the night where light leaked out around an ill fitting deadlight. Soon they were close enough to detect the glow of lamps in the air, and the faint shadows of those on watch as they moved about in front of the lights. An oarsman in the cutter ahead missed a stroke in his excitement, and Taylor saw the blade foam white in the darkness.

'Qui va la?' shouted a voice from ahead, sudden and loud. Moments later a musket fired, the flash brilliant after so many hours of darkness. Then a long bowsprit was above their heads and the side of the privateer appeared like a wall beside them.

'In oars!' yelled Sedgwick, just in time. Another musket banged in the night on the far side of the ship, followed by several more, and a cheer echoed loudly from close to the front of the sloop. The longboat came to a halt and Macpherson sprung up, drawing out his long claymore with a hiss of polished steel.

'On your feet, marines! Fix bayonets!' he ordered. As the men slotted their long blades home, a head appeared over the side of the ship and levelled a pistol at the Scotsman. There was a loud bang, and his hat was whisked away to splash into the water alongside.

'Corporal Edwards, you will shoot that man,' said Macpherson without looking up from the lanyard of his sword that he was securing about his wrist. A musket flashed from the centre of the longboat, and when Macpherson turned to face the ship's side the head had vanished.

'Marines will charge!' he shouted. He stepped onto the gunwale of the longboat and then scrambled up into the fore chains of the sloop, leaving the boat rocking behind him. The rest of the marines poured up after their commander and heaved themselves over the side.

'Abbot, you stay with the boat,' ordered Taylor. 'The rest of you follow me. Plenty of noise, lads. Put the fear of God into them.'

Evans was one of the first of the sailors to scramble out of the longboat. He pulled himself up until he stood on the side rail of the *Passe Partout* and balanced himself with one hand hooked into the privateer's shrouds. He looked down into the melee that swirled about his feet. The deck was packed solid with struggling marines trying to drive forward. They were thrusting out with their long bayonets, but they were

66

'What the bleeding hell is all this about?' exclaimed Evans, still half asleep, as he looked around him. 'How am I meant to clean the deck? My bit is under that there barrel.'

'I have no clue at all,' said Sedgwick beside him. O'Malley began to whistle tunelessly, while Trevan thrust his hands deep into his pockets and stared out to sea.

'Deck there! Boat ahoy!' cried the lookout at the masthead. 'Boat approaching on the larboard beam!'

'Boat?' muttered Evans. 'But we are miles from land. What's one of them doing right out here?' The confused sailors rushed to look over the rail. Beneath them was an old mizzen top sail moored alongside the frigate. It was suspended between four floating spars and buoyed up by empty barrels to form a sort of swimming pool. Farther out they could see the ship's launch approaching. Its crew were naked from the waist upwards and wearing exotic headdresses of some kind. In the stern sat a large figure with a trident in one hand. As the boat neared them he stood up, and the men could see that he, too, was naked above the kilt of tassels that encircled his waist. His ample torso was thickly painted in all the colours of the rainbow. Around his neck was a necklace of various seashells, while the part of his face visible above his large beard of unpicked rope hemp was completely blue.

'Ahoy, yonder ship from a distant land!' yelled the figure in the distinct bass of Hutchinson, the grizzled boatswain of the *Titan*. 'Who dares to enter the realm of Mighty Neptune?'

'The officers and crew of the *Titan* crave your permission to do so, Your Majesty,' replied Clay from the quarterdeck.

'You I shall permit to enter, gracious Pipe, for I know you to be a friend of my people,' offered Neptune, 'but as for your crew I must examine them first to see if they are meat for the honour. I shall come aboard to inspect them presently.'

A few moments later the launch was alongside, and the

King of the Ocean appeared at the entry port, followed by the boat crew. He adjusted his crown, hitched up his skirt of plaited rope ends, and strode through the crowd of grinning seaman with his followers in his wake. When he was settled on the throne he looked over the assembled crew, banged his trident on the dais to gain attention and sniffed at the air.

'Tell me, do I smell the reek of griffins?' he bellowed.

'Here be two, your Majesty,' called Trevan, and Evans and Sedgwick found their arms pinioned by the veteran seamen all around them.

'Hoy, what's going on?' exclaimed the Londoner. 'An' what's a bleeding griffin?'

'A griffin is them as haven't crossed the line at all,' laughed O'Malley, as he helped to push the struggling seamen forward.

'Constables, bring them before me!' ordered Neptune, as the sailors were dragged remorselessly across the deck.

'Adam, I have got something precious in my left pocket,' yelled the coxswain. 'A little bag!'

'Easy there, lads,' said Trevan. He came around in front of the helpless man and pulled a leather pouch from out of his jacket and held it in front of his face.

'Didn't have you marked for a smoker, Able, but your backy be safe with me,' said the Cornishman. 'Can't speak for the rest of you, mind. Take him away, lads!'

'On your knees, hideous creatures,' ordered Neptune, and the two men found their legs swept from under them. 'Better. Now let us see if a gentle wash from my hand maidens may improve matters.' Both men found themselves being drenched with fire hoses to a point just short of drowning. Once it had been done, the King of the Ocean sniffed the air once more.

'No, it won't answer. I can still smell their slime. Anoint them with precious fragrances, frankincense, myrrh and such like.' The men were smeared all over with a combination of the rancid pork slush normally kept for the lubrication of the ship's rigging blocks, and wood ash from the galley.

'Better,' smiled Neptune as he regarded the two filthy sailors. 'Place them delicately in my bath tub, and bring me some more griffins.' The friends found themselves borne aloft by willing hands and dumped over the side for the long plunge down into the waiting sail.

It transpired that at least a third of the crew had never crossed the equator before, and as a result it took most of the morning to process the considerable number of griffins aboard. Once the decks had been swabbed clean and the various items of paraphernalia dismantled, it was early afternoon before the *Titan* was able to resume her way southward. Clay declared the afternoon as make and mend, so that those who had been victims could be excused from duty to clean themselves, and the rigging was soon all aflutter with freshly washed and drying clothes. By evening Evans and Sedgwick had got the last trace of pork fat from out of their hair, and were back in clean and dry clothes once more. They took their places at the mess table for their evening meal in the middle of a lower deck alive with noisy laughter after the events of the day.

'There you go, me hearties!' said O'Malley, slapping both men on the back as they sat down either side of him. 'Clean at last, which is more than can be said for the boatswain.'

'How come?' asked Sedgwick. 'He was the one ordering how all that filth was to be spread about, rather than copping it his self.' The Irishman looked conspiratorial.

'Turns out that he asked Britton to see if it could get some paint from Lieutenant Blake, as he does them pictures of his with,' he explained. 'Which was fine till Hutchinson comes to try and fecking shift it. Seems as it don't wash away in water, no matter how you scrub. Only grog will answer, so he's been and used all of his ration, as well as that of his boatswain's mates, trying to get it off, and it still ain't all gone now!'

'Serves the bleeder right,' laughed Evans. 'He was proper enjoying being that Neptune. He gave Able and me a right seeing to.'

'Still, you're griffins no more!' said O'Malley. 'Next time you find yourself crossing the fecking line, it'll be you as will be after doing the ducking.'

'Here you go, Able,' said Trevan. 'I nearly forgot your pouch.' He pulled out the small bag of leather and hefted it in his hand as he passed it across. 'What manner of backy be that? It don't feel right at all.'

'Besides, I thought as how you gave your ration to me?' queried O'Malley. The coxswain untied the drawstring to show his friends the contents. Inside was a fistful of reddish-brown soil.

'Dirt?' asked Evans. 'What you doing with that?'

'I took some in the forest that night, when I went off to find the French ship,' said Sedgwick. 'May be it were just being near to my village. Daft, really, but I wanted a little part of home, not that any remains.' He held the soil up to his nose for a moment. 'It still smells as I remember from all them years back, but I suppose that will pass with time.' The others looked at their friend quietly for a while.

'You ain't daft, mate,' said Evans. 'Now daft would be if I was to carry around a lump of Seven Dials mud on me, 'cause let me tell you, that would still bleeding stink for years.'

'There's a fair few of the Irish lads as carry a sprig of heather from the old country, you know,' said O'Malley. 'Fecking lucky that Adam took your bag, mind. Would have been no more than silt, the amount of ducking you had to endure.'

'Anyways, I reckon as you had it proper easy,' offered

Trevan from the far side of the table.

'How do you figure that, Adam?' said Evans. 'We was halfway to being bleeding well drowned!'

'I first crossed the line on a whaler,' he explained. 'We had just caught a Right Whale, so there was no end of disgusting guts and entrails for Neptune to make sport with. And I was the lone griffin on board.'

'Shall we stow that yarn till after we scoffed?' suggested Evans. 'I've only just got past the reek of that bleeding slush. Besides, it be New Years Eve an' all. Are we going to have a bit of a carouse later, then?'

'Aye, that sounds grand,' said O'Malley. 'I've not played my fiddle these past few weeks. And we should be after celebrating our fecking prize! That French ship will fetch a pretty penny. She will be snapped up for a slaver for sure.'

'A slaver?' queried the coxswain. 'How'd you figure that, then?'

'Ah... well... it's not certain like, but it is sort of what she be built for,' explained the Irishman. 'Chances are some Bristol merchant or Yank will put her back into service.'

'Damnation!' protested Sedgwick, tossing down his spoon. 'So taking that bloody privateer will just give the trade another ship?'

'Oh come now, Able, don't look so low,' urged Evans. 'We've had a right lark with all that Neptune stuff, we got plum duff for dinner and then a song and a hornpipe.... What's up with Adam?' The others turned to look at their friend. He was sitting slumped over his food. His forehead was beaded with sweat.

'Are you all right there?' asked Sedgwick, looking at his friend's full plate. 'You upset about the slaver, too, or don't you fancy your meat?'

'I don't feel right at all,' replied the Cornishman. 'I seem to have come over all odd like, just while we been sat here yarning. It's happened right sudden.'

'You do look fecking queer,' said O'Malley. 'Why, you're sweating like a virgin in a brothel.'

'Am I?' muttered Trevan. 'That's odd, is that. I was just wondering if some bugger had put a new wind sail in place. It feels proper cold down here all of a sudden like.' His friends all exchanged glances.

'Adam, it's bleeding roasting,' said the Londoner.

'I think I might be after having a puke,' he gasped.

'Easy there,' said Sedgwick, helping his friend to his feet. 'Let's get up to the lee rail for that, and then we had best find the sawbones. You don't look right at all.'

*****

'Surely not more mango for pudding, Britton?' protested Blake, as the steaming plate was placed in front of him.

'Frittered in beef dripping on this occasion, sir, with a little treacle to give them unction,' explained the steward. All around the wardroom table officers prodded at the charred brown pieces.

'It is not that some fruit in our diet is unwelcome,' continued the lieutenant. 'But have we not had mango twice a day this last week?'

'We have, sir,' said Britton. 'And like to continue to for a while yet. I suggest you take it up with Mr Faulkner here. Weren't me as bought three hundredweight of the buggers.'

'In fairness my hand was dealt for me,' said the purser as he toyed with his own food. 'Mr Armstrong had rather committed me to the transaction.'

'No matter, Charles,' said Taylor from the head of the table. 'When the first few guineas of prize money rattle into our purses from the sale of the *Passe Partout*, we shall all forget how the intelligence was obtained. A glass of wine with you, sir?'

'The cost of that victory may be higher than the ship having to consume an excess of fruit,' said Macpherson. He pointed across the table at the surgeon's empty chair. 'How many cases of this malady does Mr Corbett battle with?'

'Eighteen so far, all from the party that attacked the privateer,' said the first lieutenant. 'He will join us presently with a more current picture, but it would seem Mr Blake's Bight of Benin has bitten us most savagely.' Silence descended around the table, with those who had stayed onboard avoiding the eyes of those who had been on the boats that night. Macpherson was feeling uncomfortably hot, and wondered if this might be the start of a fever. Then he glanced down at his scarlet coat sleeve and reminded himself that he was dressed predominantly in wool, was in the tropics, and had just eaten a large meal washed down with heavy red wine. He pushed his untouched mango away and turned towards Taylor.

'How soon before we reach the more temperate Cape Town and the rest of the squadron?' he asked.

'A month at least, perhaps longer, for we have several thousand miles to go yet,' replied the first lieutenant. 'Mr Armstrong will have taken our exact latitude at noon, so I will be in a position to give you a more precise answer when he comes off watch. But while Cape Town will be fresher than the tropics, I make no doubt, it will not be temperate. February is the height of their summer.'

'Of course it is,' muttered the marine, loosening his neck cloth a little. 'Still, it will be good to be reunited with the other ships. The society of some of the other officers will be welcome.'

'I am not sure you will be over pleased with Sir George Montague, Tom,' said Blake. 'He has a reputation as something of a pedant, I understand. But I am not acquainted with the other gentlemen. Do you know any of them, George?'

'Not at all, I am afraid,' said Taylor. 'Mr Macpherson and Mr Preston are best acquainted with the commanders of the *Rush* and the *Echo*. Did you not all serve together in the Caribbean?'

'Aye, that is right,' said Macpherson. 'As did Mr Faulkner. We served with Lieutenant Sutton, as he was then, aboard the *Rush*. I found him to be of a very cheerful disposition, open and quite lacking in conceit. He was a pleasure to serve with, and he is, of course, very close friends with the captain. I never served with Mr Windham, however. Charles, you are perhaps the one who knows him best?' The purser tweaked the lace cuff of his shirt where it showed beneath the sleeve of his coat and cleared his throat.

'Perhaps I do, but it is not an acquaintance I look back on with any fondness,' he replied. 'His people have known mine for several generations, and I knew him as a boy. He was once amiable enough in his way, but then he changed into a rather uncivil cove. He became possessed by some very strange notions from which he refuses to be shaken.'

'Whatever can you mean, Charles?' said Taylor.

'His uncle, Captain Follett, was knocked overboard during a single ship action between the *Agrius*, which was Follett's ship, and a French frigate back in ninety-six,' explained Faulkner. 'A tragedy, I make no doubt, but Windham has got it into his mind that Captain Sutton was in some way responsible. He even thinks that our captain may have been involved – they were all lieutenants on the ship at the time. It is a notion he clings to like a limpet to its rock.'

'How does he mean, responsible?' queried Blake. 'Does he mean through neglect?'

'I believe he suspects there to have been foul play,' said the purser. 'I only report Captain Windham's views. Perhaps

Mr Preston can help us. He was aboard the *Agrius* that day.'

'That is correct,' said Preston. 'I was but a youngster then, a midshipman. I remember that the battle was going very ill for us under the direction of Captain Follett. In part it was because Mr Windham, who had command of the guns, was making a sad mess of his duty. It was only after the captain fell and Mr Clay took command that matters were set right. Perhaps the root of the difficulty is that Mr Windham resents the manner in which he and his uncle's failings were so publicly exposed?'

'This is all a very ill omen for our forthcoming operations together, I must say,' snorted Macpherson. 'So the commander of the *Echo* thinks the commander of the *Rush* killed his uncle with the connivance of the captain of the *Titan*? I fear that our squadron shall be no Band of Brothers, gentlemen. A knot of adders would seem closer to the mark!'

At that moment the door of the wardroom opened and in walked the surgeon. His frame was even more stooped than normal, and the pale eyes that looked out from behind the small discs of his glasses were rimmed in red. The front of his linen shirt was stained with smears of dark brown.

'Ah, there you are, Mr Corbett,' said Taylor. 'Goodness, man, you seem quite spent! Come, seat yourself. You have missed dinner, I fear, but would you care for some mango fritters?'

'I thank you, but no,' he replied. 'But if you would oblige me with a little wine, that would be most welcome.'

'Ahoy there, Britton! A glass of bishop here!' Corbett drank deeply, and then sat back in his chair with a shake of his head.

'Matters go ill with your patients, I collect Doctor?' asked Faulkner.

'They do indeed, Charles,' he replied, peering across the wardroom table. 'I warned the captain of the perils of exposing the crew to night airs. You cannot say that I did not. The party that attacked the *Passe Partout* spent much too long amid the miasmas of that putrid coast, and the result is plain to see.'

'But the damned French moved their ship to a fresh location,' said Macpherson. 'That is why the enterprise was so protracted. The captain can hardly be blamed for that.'

'I am sure no one is blaming the captain, Tom,' said Taylor, holding up a hand. He turned back to the surgeon. 'So, how many cases do we now have?'

'Still just the eighteen at present, thank the Lord, sir,' he replied, laying a hand on the wooden top of the table. 'Mr Butler, five marines and twelve seamen. I have established a separate fever ward at the bow end of the lower deck that is screened off from the rest of the men. There were no fresh cases again this morning, so I live in hope that the rest of the party will have escaped the contagion.'

'And what do you hold to be the nature of the disease?'

'Oh, that is plain enough,' replied Corbett. 'The languid circulation of the vital fluids, combined with intense fever, convulsions, ejection of vomit and the patient's sallow complexion all points towards the Yellow Jack.'

'Yellow Jack!' exclaimed Blake. 'I have heard of the devastation that can cause in the Caribbean. God have mercy on them.'

'Let us hope that He does,' said Corbett. 'In the meantime I will continue to take an ounce of blood a day from my patients, and give them Peruvian bark whenever I feel they may be able to keep it down long enough. That, together with a few drops of laudanum, may prove efficacious.'

'What prospect can you hold out for their eventual recovery?' said Macpherson.

'From Yellow Jack?' exclaimed the surgeon. 'Surely you jest, my dear sir! Three of them are already producing vomit corrupted with blood, which is a certain indication that death is near. If one from ten is still alive this time next week I shall be very much surprised.'

*****

Adam Trevan was burning hot. Sweat trickled down his face, dripping from the point of his chin and soaking his shirt as he laboured away with a long heavy oar in his hands. The sun was pitiless as it beat down on his head. He could sense that he was close to the limit of his endurance. His whole body ached and his arms shook uncontrollably. Cramp knotted painfully in his abdomen, and he knew he would be sick again soon. He leant over the side of the boat and puked up. The ball of vomit bust into a cloud of fragments as it hit the water. A number of long silver fish with yellow fins left the half eaten corpse of a black man that drifted close by to come and investigate. The body rolled in the water, and turned a portion of half-eaten face towards him. There was just enough flesh left on the skull for him to recognise that it had once been his friend Sedgwick.

'Able?' he mumbled. 'How did you come to be in the sea?'

'Never you mind about him,' snapped O'Malley. 'He should never have painted the boatswain blue, at all. Just you put your fecking back into your rowing.' The Irishman glared down at him from where he stood in the stern of the whale boat, with a steering oar tucked under one arm.

'Come on, my lover,' urged a low, female voice from behind him. 'Back to work now.' He turned to find himself looking into the sea-green eyes of his wife Molly. Her mass of red hair streamed in the wind, much to the delight of his long dead son who sat laughing beside her on the bench.

'Pull three!' yelled O'Malley, and the whale boat started to move again. Trevan did his best to row, but he felt so tired.

His whole body protested at the effort it was being called on to produce. He looked at his trembling arms as they strained on the oar, and he noticed for the first time how thin and wasted they looked. His skin had lost its usual deep tan and had an unpleasant yellow look to it.

'I can't be doing this for much longer, Sean,' murmured the Cornishman. But the helmsman was staring at something ahead. He raised one hand from the steering oar to shade his eyes. From behind his back Trevan heard a hollow roar of air and felt a warm mist drifted across the boat.

'There she fecking blows!' bellowed O'Malley. 'Pull all! Evans, get the harpoon!'

'Evans?' muttered Trevan. 'You be here, too?' He turned on the bench again, and now saw that the huge figure of the Londoner stood beyond his wife in the bow. He had one foot resting on the gunwale and he held the long shaft of a harpoon aloft in his fist. Sunlight glittered on the sharp edge of the blade. Just ahead of him was an island of dark grey skin. Then Evans hurled the harpoon, and it thumped into the whale with a spurt of crimson. The creature rolled forward and a pair of huge flukes lifted high above them before they sliced down into the boiling water and disappeared beneath the surface.

'Watch that fecking line!' yelled O'Malley. Trevan glanced down and saw there was a wooden tub at his feet. The rope coiled around the interior was streaking out as the whale dived, the line smoking and hot.

'Wet the line,' he mumbled to himself. 'That be what I needs to do. I remember it now.' He picked up a little bucket of water and tried to pour it onto the hot rope, but the smoke grew worse. It made his eyes smart and caught at the back of his throat. As he went to retch, a loop of line caught around his foot and in an instant he was plucked off the bench and sent clattering down the boat. Objects and people cannoned off him as he was dragged to the bow, and in a flash he was over the side. He had a brief glimpse of Evans' face above him, and then green water closed over his head.

Down, down he went, pulled ever deeper by the rope. Below him he could see the sperm whale as it swum powerfully downwards. Lodged in its vast back was the harpoon, with a ribbon of blood streaming out behind it. Its tail swung up and down, each thrust sending a rush of water past him. Above him the surface of the sea was a distant ceiling. Diagonal streaks of sunlight turned in the water. High above his head he could just see the little hull of the whale boat, with the wavering line still running from it, and then it disappeared from view. Now the water was getting dark and cold. The whale had vanished into the gloom beneath him. But after so much burning fever, he found that the cold was pleasant. It washed away the sweat from his face, and soothed his aching body. He was very tired, so he closed his eyes to sleep.

Someone had grabbed hold of his pigtail and was shaking his head by it. He opened his eyes to find Molly with the blond plait in her hand. Her pale face was angry and her long copper hair coiled about it like weeds as she shook her head from side to side. Bubbles erupted from her mouth as she yelled at him. Silver flashed in her hand, and she thumped him in the chest with something hard. He glanced down to see that it was the ash hilt of his open clasp knife. She pushed the handle into his hand, and closed his fist around it with her own. Wearily he bent forward in the water and sawed at the whale line knotted around his foot. It parted at last, and he felt his downwards rush ease to a stop. He dropped the knife and it spiralled away from him, turning and flashing as it fell towards the blackness underneath him. He hung in the cool gloom for a while, unsure what to do next. Then he felt a hand in his, tugging him upwards. Molly swam above him, pulling him towards the light. Her skirts ballooned around her in the water like the bell of a jellyfish.

*****

Captain Alexander Clay stood in front of the portrait of his wife that hung on the cabin bulkhead and adjusted the folds of his neck cloth. The garment was proving difficult to settle down behind the still unfamiliar Nile medal around his neck. As he pulled at the thick China silk, his eyes looked at the dark-haired Lydia, who smiled back at him from out of the picture. It was an extraordinary likeness that Lieutenant Blake had achieved. The physical form was undoubtedly that of his wife, but he had also captured her spirit. There was the merest ghost of a smile pulling at the corners of her mouth, and a sparkle in her eyes. Together they hinted at the underlying sense of fun that he knew lurked just below the unruffled surface of the grand lady. His eyes strayed towards the front of the blue satin dress in the picture. All being well, you will have long since had to abandon that garment, he told himself with a smile. If he had been alone in the cabin he would have talked out loud to her painted face. He had been embarrassed to do so at first, when the picture had been given to him by his wardroom two years ago. He would only speak to her in a whisper when he was certain he was alone. He had found the benefit immediate. It was soothing on long voyages, helping to ease some of the ache at being apart. He gave the neck cloth a final tug, and drew himself as upright as the low headroom would allow. I am a captain and master of my own ship, he reminded himself. I can do what I dammed well please. He opened his mouth say something to Lydia. At that moment his servant came back into the cabin, and the words somehow turned into a cough.

'Will it be your new sword as you'll be wearing, sir?' asked

Yates. The teenager held the magnificent black and gold weapon that the King had given him in his hands.

'If you please, Sam,' he replied, holding up his arms to allow the boy to buckle it around his waist. He glanced down at the glittering hilt. From amongst all the seed pearl that encrusted the pommel, the head of a lion snarled back at him. Then there was a knock at the cabin door. 'Come in!' called Clay.

'Good evening, sir,' said his first lieutenant, as he came into the cabin. He too was in full dress, with his own silver Nile medal hung around his neck.

'Good evening to you, Mr Taylor. Have all the preparations been made?' asked the captain.

'They have, sir. The ship is as still as I can make her, and the black ensign flies at the masthead.' Through the open door came the sound of a boatswain's call. 'That will be Mr Harrison, summoning the people.'

'And Mr Corbett is as certain as he can be that tonight's ceremony will be an end to matters?' asked Clay. 'Nothing brings a crew low like the melancholy drip of frequent burials. I want a single event at which we bid farewell to our shipmates, and then we sail on.'

'I understand, sir, and the doctor is certain.'

'Very well,' said Clay. He took his best hat and his service book from Yates. 'Let us get the wretched matter done with.'

He strode out of the cabin, acknowledged the salute of the marine sentry who stood outside, and walked onto the main deck. The ship rocked in the gentle amber light of evening. Overhead the pale blue sky was dotted by clumps of cloud turned pink in the light of the setting sun. To one side of the deck the crew were drawn up in the blocks and lines of their various divisions. All were dressed in their best shore-going clothes. Dotted amongst them were his officers, and when he looked behind him he could see the frigate's contingent of marines drawn up behind the quarterdeck rail. He returned his attention to the deck in front of him. Stretched out on the planking was a long line of mess table tops. On each one lay a hammock, stitched shut to form a cocoon around the body that it held. The job had been done thoroughly. From the bulge at each person's feet Clay could guess at the round shot placed there to pull them down into the depths beyond the reach of sharks. The stitching finished in the traditional way, over the corpse's face with the last one driven through the nose as a final test that the victim was indeed dead.

He counted the mess tables to check they were all there, then caught the boatswain's eye.

'Off hats!' roared Harrison, removing his own polished leather one with the royal arms painted on the front. Clay found himself drawn to search his grey hairline for any remaining paint.

'Carry on, Mr Harrison,' he ordered.

'Aye aye, sir,' growled the boatswain. He summoned over a party of eight sailors to lift the first table up onto their shoulders. Clay opened his service book at the place where a slip of paper marked the text, although he knew the simple words by heart now.

'One moment, please,' ordered Clay, stopping the men in their tracks with the first mess table still on their shoulders. He had just caught sight of movement at the fore ladder way. Two emaciated figures were climbing up the steps, each helped by one of the surgeon's assistants. Corbett came last of all and guided the survivors to the chairs that he had placed for them in the shade under the forecastle. Midshipman Butler and Adam Trevan took their seats, and the funeral for the others recommenced.

CHAPTER 6 THE CAPE

Two weeks later, the *Titan* dropped anchor in the open waters of Table Bay, alongside the other three ships of the squadron. Close to where they had moored were the ditches and stone walls of the Dutch fort that lay at the northern edge of Cape Town. From beneath the ramparts stretched the wharfs and whitewashed houses of the little town in a curve along the shore. Farther back from the sea, the roofs of larger buildings and church spires stood proud of the surrounding roofs. Behind the town could be seen steep slopes, chequered with green fields and vineyards. They stretched up towards the base of Table Mountain, with its flat summit, that reared above the bay like the fortress of a giant.

The first twenty-four hours after the frigate arrived were packed with activity. The *Titan* needed to be resupplied, and a full report on her adventures on the Gold coast made to Commodore Sir George Montague. The French prisoners from the *Passe Partoute* were handed over to the soldiers of the garrison, while the privateer herself went to the port admiral to be condemned as a prize. Clay found himself torn between the needs of replenishing his ship and time spent with Sir George and the other captains. The commodore was keen to draw up plans to tackle the French menace in the Indian Ocean. It was not until three days after they had arrived, that he was able to entertain his officers, together with his best friend John Sutton of the *Rush*. At long last he was able to sit at the head of this cabin table, the surface loaded with all the fresh produce the Cape had to offer and the sides lined with his expectant guests.

'I trust you will find the wine tolerable, gentlemen,' said Clay, holding up his glass to the light. 'It is of local production. Constantia, the Dutch name it. Apparently it is like to a port wine, and has been grown here since the Dutch first came.'

'It is very agreeable, sir,' said Faulkner, who had already tried his. 'I must get Britton to replenish the wardroom's pantry with a dozen cases or so. I had expected to find Hollander gin here, but not a wine as pleasing as this.' There was a rumble of agreement from around the table, and a general movement as officers half turned in their seats to have their glasses refilled.

'Let us hope the meal is a match for the wine,' said Clay. 'As you can see, Harte has procured a haunch of antelope from a butcher who insists that it is as fine as any venison, and a tolerably good selection of local vegetables. But even if he has been deceived with mule, it will make a more pleasant remove than our usual salt beef.'

'Or mango,' said Macpherson, to general laughter.

'Mango?' queried Sutton.

'Mr Armstrong here agreed to purchase a prodigious quantity of the fruit in return for intelligence of the *Passe Partoute*, sir,' explained Preston. 'In consequence we have dined on little else since we left Freetown.'

'It is a very fine anti-scorbutic, gentlemen,' said Corbett, peering around the table. 'As Doctor Lind of Haslar has long established, the consumption of fruit is an essential component of a mariner's diet. I now have little fear that scurvy will break out in the wardroom.'

'Do you remember Admiral Keppel?' asked Sutton, turning towards Clay. 'He came aboard the old *Marlborough* to dine with the captain when we were midshipmen.'

'Small, sour-faced cove who was said to never smile?'

'The very same,' said his friend. 'Apparently he suffered very badly from the scurvy when he was a youngster. He accompanied Anson on his circumnavigation of the globe, and when the disease broke out he shed every tooth in his head. That was what prompted his resolution to never smile thereafter.'

'It must have been hard to preserve such a melancholy aspect,' said Macpherson. 'Were the survivors of that voyage not all made fabulously wealthy on account of that prize they took? The Spanish treasure ship.'

'If he was pleased, Old Keppel concealed it well,' said Sutton. 'I remember him barely saying a word.'

'How did he contrive to eat?' mused Preston. 'Without the benefit of any teeth to aid him.'

'He may well have had a false set made from elm,' offered Armstrong. 'They say that George Washington has wooden ones, having lost all of his teeth to an over fondness for molasses.'

'The latest sets can be quite effective, I understand,' said Corbett. 'The wood is set with actual teeth recovered from cadavers.' Conversation around the table faltered to a stop as the officers considered this with looks of distaste.

'I live in hope that all those here present are blessed with at least some teeth,' said the captain briskly. 'Else this antelope may prove beyond us. Would you care to carve, Mr Corbett? I always find that surgeons do the most creditable job when it comes to slicing flesh of all kinds.'

While the piece of antelope was carved, polite conversation started again around the table once more. The officers of the *Titan* were an amiable group of young men, and the prospect of fresh food melded with the excellence of the wine to make for a jolly party. During a break in the flow of conversation, Blake pointed towards the stern windows of the ship. Through the glass was the squadron's other frigate, moored behind the *Titan*. A number of sailors could be seen at work on hoists mounted over the frigate's side, toiling away under the hot midday sun.

'Can the *Black Prince* really be painting her hull again?' he remarked. 'They do seem to spend a prodigious amount of time on embellishing their ship.'

'According to the sailing master, Sir George Montague has his own private supply of paint,' said Armstrong. 'It is a formulation of his own devising, and he has it applied to the ship whenever they have the leisure to do so.'

'Perhaps Mr Harrison should petition for some of his blue paint for out next line crossing,' said Macpherson, to chuckles from his fellow *Titan*s.

'I am surprised they don't founder under the weight of all those extra layers,' said Taylor. 'You have been aboard her, sir. Is the *Black Prince* a particularly smart ship?'

'Absolutely spotless,' confirmed the captain. 'The Royal Yacht could hardly be trimmer. Pipe clayed hand ropes, Turks heads on every available stanchion, and the brass could serve as a mirror to shave by.'

'But does it answer to make a ship truly effective?' asked Sutton. 'The *Rush* may be a little shabby by comparison, but I doubt if the *Prince* could match my people in gun drill. I never saw them fire their guns once the whole way here, bar the odd salute.'

'I would not want to be thought to criticise another captain's methods before they are proven in battle,' said Clay. 'And of course a certain thoroughness in the regulation of a ship is desirable; but to my mind I am with you, John. How much sail drill and gun practice the people have had is what chiefly counts when the enemy is in sight.'

'I invited Sir George to dine with me when we were at Gibraltar, and he was most put out with the condition of the

Rush,' said Sutton, accepting another large plate of roast antelope. 'He was tut-tutting over the brass here, wiping a finger across a cannon there. I tell you, it was as if a maiden aunt had come to call. The man is quite obsessed.'

'It is strange how some captains can take matters to such extremes,' said Armstrong. 'Did you ever hear tell of Captain Robert Willoughby? I served with him at the start of the war, on the North American station.'

'The name is passing familiar,' said Preston. 'Was he not rather hot in matters of religion?'

'The very same,' said the master. 'The hands named him Puritan Bob, on account of the fervour of his religious beliefs. He always shipped with a fire and brimstone parson in tow, and he made the crew attend Divine service every morning without fail, even the Jews and Papists. Then one day he resolved to bring about his people's morale improvement by preventing them from playing games of hazard.'

'How did he do that?' asked Faulkner.

'During service one morning he ordered the Lobsters to search the ship from stem to stern for every pack of cards and all dice onboard, and had the lot tossed over the side.'

'And did that answer to stop the hands from gambling?' asked Macpherson.

'It seemed to, at first,' said Armstrong. 'But then these curious circles began to appear in the tops of the mess tables, marked into the wood with the point of a knife. They always took the same form, an outer ring about the size of a hand, with an inner circle perhaps the size of a crown piece. Well, Puritan Bob had a notion they must be some manner of pagan symbol, so he had his parson redouble the fervour of his preaching. But despite that, the number of circles continued to grow.'

'Good heavens, so what did they prove to be?' asked Preston.

'It would seem that you can no more keep a seaman from gaming than you can from drink,' explained Armstrong. 'When the men were tapping the weevils out from their ship's biscuit, they would place the liveliest to one side. After the meal, the tables were cleared, and then each man would lay a wager down. At a given moment the weevils were dropped into the small circle. First man's worm to touch the rim of the outer circle took the purse.'

'An excellent tale, Mr Armstrong,' laughed Clay from the head of the table. 'What a shame we have fresh bread for once. A weevil race over the cheese might have been diverting. More antelope, gentlemen? Perhaps while Harte is serving you I might share what Captain Sutton and I have learnt from our various consultations with Sir George, apart from his advice on how to whiten deck planking, that is.' The officers all quietened down to listen.

'The situation is that the French have three of their larger frigates at large in the Indian Ocean. They have established themselves at St Paul on their island of Reunion, or Bourbon as it was before the revolution. It is an excellent roadstead, well provisioned and with good port facilities. From that base they have been fanning out to attack our East India trade, which they have been able to do this past six months with little annoyance from us.'

'Are we to root them out from their nest at St Paul, then?' asked Macpherson, sitting forward at the prospect of action.

'I think not, Tom,' said Clay. 'It is protected by fortifications and has a considerable garrison. Without a regular army we can attempt little against it. Sir George plans to defeat the enemy at sea. Destroy their frigates and they will be able to do little further to harm our trade.'

'Does he have a project in mind to achieve that?' asked Taylor.

'The next convoy of Indiaman is due to touch at the Cape

any day now,' explained the captain. 'In the first instance the squadron will convoy them across towards Bombay. He is hopeful that the French will attack them.'

'And what if they decline to make such an attack, sir?' asked Armstrong.

'The convoy is a substantial one,' explained Clay. 'Sir George is quite confident that it will suffice to draw the enemy to us. But should they not prove inclined to make such a bold move, we will split up, as they do, and hunt them down. The *Black Prince* shall take one part of the ocean, we on the *Titan* another, and so forth.'

'And the *Rush* will operate with the *Echo*,' added Sutton. 'Two sloops together should be a match for a single French frigate, if they are well handled.'

'You are senior to Captain Windham of the *Echo*, I collect, sir?' asked Macpherson. 'So will you be in command when you two split away?'

'I suppose that I shall be, yes.'

'Your first time in charge of a squadron!' announced Macpherson, rather grandly. 'Gentlemen, I give you a toast. To our honoured guest, and his first tentative step towards being named as Admiral of the Fleet, Sutton!' The toast was drunk with enthusiasm by the company. The captain's friend was well liked on board, and Preston, Macpherson and Faulkner had all served with him. Sutton bowed with mock gravity on all sides as the officers banged the table.

It was some time later that the party began to break up. First Corbett rose to his feet, profuse in his apologies, but he had an appointment ashore with an apothecary who could renew his depleted stores of drugs. Then Taylor remembered he had promised to inspect the fore main yard with the boatswain. With the first lieutenant's departure, the other more junior officers were quick to made their excuses and leave, which left Sutton and his friend at the head of the table with the last of the Constantia.

'What is your true opinion of Dismal George's plan of campaign, Alex?' he asked.

'That it is most unlikely to succeed,' replied Clay. 'I have said as much to Montague, not that he takes very kindly to suggestions from his juniors.'

'What is it in his project that you particularly object to?'

'Take his initial notion, that we should all accompany these Indiamen to Bombay in the hope that the French will attack them. That will never answer. The enemy will not attempt such a thing.'

'Why not?' asked Sutton.

'Because the convoy will now be much too well protected!' exclaimed his host. 'Four warships for an escort? The French will run a mile. They are here to menace and annoy our trade. If we are all in one place, they will simply proceed to another. No, if you truly wish to tempt them to make an attack, have one escorting ship, or at best two.'

'So if you think that his plan is so ill judged, what would you do, Alex? If you were in command?'

'I would send to Bombay for a regiment or two of John Company Sepoys,' he replied. 'It is the East India Company that has most to gain by the elimination of this French menace. Then I would descend upon this St Paul, as Tom Macpherson suggested, and destroy the place before the French have any notion that there is a British squadron in these waters at all. Surprise in a campaign is more than half the battle. Deny the enemy their base to repair and resupply their ships and the French will be obliged to return home. But no, we shall instead let them mark us as we escort this damned convoy, and thus announce to them our exact numbers.'

Clay sloshed more wine into the two glasses and stared out of the window across at the *Black Prince*. The men had moved farther along the hull. The fresh paint behind them was hard to distinguish from the old. Then he sighed aloud, and smiled at his friend.

'You would have thought by now that I might have become reconciled to the frustrations of junior rank, wouldn't you, John?' He raised his glass towards the portrait of his wife. 'Lydia generally keeps my feet on the ground at home. Perhaps you might serve in that office afloat?'

'I will if I can, brother,' said Sutton. 'But I shall have my own problems. As your officers were so gleeful to point out, when the sloops leave the convoy I shall be in command of Mr Windham. I cannot help but dwell on how much he will resent my direction.'

'Oh, he will hate it,' confirmed Clay. 'But does that not add some savour for you, eh?'

'He still believes that I killed his uncle. I can see the hatred in his eyes.'

'That is because you did, John,' said Clay, leaning forward, his face serious. His friend looked around him.

'Not so loud, Alex,' he hissed. 'Ships have ears, as well you know.'

'As you wish, brother. But make sure that you watch him closely. I do not trust our friend Windham. If he is able to serve you an ill turn I am sure he will not hesitate to do so.'

The two captains were quiet for a moment. Sutton thought back to that insane moment on board the *Agrius* three years earlier, when Captain Follett had been knocked overboard by the fall of the mizzen mast. He had rushed to the ship's side, exultant that all his friend's problems might be solved by this stoke of good fortune. Then there was the crash of disappointment when he looked down and saw that the captain had somehow managed to grab on to a single strand of rope. He had stood there, alone for a moment in a whirl of smoke and confusion, his hand resting on the hilt of the razor-sharp sword by his side. The straining rope had creaked beside him, stretched taut against the last fragment of splintered rail. It had been the work of a moment to turn what he had actually found into what he had hoped to see. Sometimes he still saw Follett's face in his dreams. It fell away from him, as slow as a feather, with an expression that moved from hope, to surprise, then rage and finally terror in the instant before the jade-green water closed over him.

'Sorry, Alex,' he said as he returned to the warm cabin with a shiver. 'I was not attending. What was it you just said?'

'I was looking at my wife's portrait, and wondering how she fares at home,' said Clay.

'Of course, poor Lydia,' he exclaimed. 'When is the child due?'

'She will be rather more than half way through her confinement, now,' said the expectant father. 'She will be stuck inside, in the middle of winter, and unable to venture out as she so loves to do, poor thing. God, but I wish I had some intelligence of how she fares. It is truly agony to be so many miles away at this time.'

'Perhaps this convoy of Indiaman will bring letters for the squadron,' said Sutton.

'If they do it will hardly answer,' said Clay. 'They can only have left a few weeks after we did. I can well remember how she was quite radiant then. It is how she is now that I wish to know.'

'I fear any letters from home will not tell you that, but they may serve me better,' said his friend, half to himself. Clay looked at him for a moment, then cleared his throat.

'Might I touch on a subject of some delicacy?' he said.

'Of course. We have never had secrets, you and I.'

'Have we not, John?' replied Clay. 'You kept Captain Follett's fate from me for many months. Remember that it

96

was Windham who first opened my eyes to what happened, but let us not return to that disagreeable topic. What I wanted to ask you is if the correspondence that you expect will be from my sister?'

'I do hope to hear from Miss Clay, yes,' he confirmed. 'As you know I was unable to fulfill a commitment I had made to visit her, thanks to the speed of our departure. I wrote to her, of course, and I am anxious to see her reply.'

'I see,' said his friend. 'Might I know the nature of the approach you made to her, before we left?'

'That would seem to be very intrusive, brother,' said Sutton. 'I must say that I am not generally inclined to discuss correspondence of a personal character in such a way. But as you are a close friend, perhaps I can put your mind at rest. What is it that you fear was said?'

'It is not necessarily that I suspect there to be something I should fear, but she is my sister, and since my father is long dead I feel it my duty to be mindful of her well being.'

'Her well being?' queried Sutton. A frown formed on his brow. 'Surely you can trust me to have the same regard for Miss Clay's happiness as you?'

'Perhaps I could, if I knew what it was you had communicated to her. I ask for no particulars, just the general nature.'

'I am not sure I am comfortable with your tone,' said his friend, putting down his glass. 'I do not recall such niceties being required when I was bringing secret love notes back to you from Lydia! This is me you speak to, Alex, your oldest friend.'

'Of course you are,' said Clay. 'But that is still not a satisfactory reply. As the senior member of my family it is I that am responsible for my sister's protection. So I ask you again, have you made any formal advances to her?'

'That is none of your damned business!' exclaimed

Sutton, standing up. 'If she has not seen fit to tell you of our relationship, I do not see how it can be demanded of me. Asking me to break a confidence is a damned impertinence.' Clay stood up too, his face flushed.

'The only possible conclusion I can draw from your extraordinary behaviour is that you have something to hide,' he said. 'Has a formal understanding been reached between Betsey and yourself, yes or no?' In response his friend turned and yelled towards the cabin door.

'Pass the word for my barge, there!'

'Kindly do not presume to issue orders on my damned ship!' roared Clay.

'Oh, I see how things stand! So now you are going to deploy your superior rank, are you, *sir*? That is a low way to treat a friend who has done so much for you. I shall put your extraordinary behaviour down to an excess of Constantia, for it is plain to me that the wine is in and the wits are out. Good day to you!' He stormed out, knocking past a chair, and the cabin door crashed closed behind him.

Clay spun around in frustration, and caught the eyes of his wife staring down on him from out of her portrait.

'What would you have me say?' he demanded. 'Oh, I know I handled it very ill, but I will not have it!' He looked around to check that he was quite alone, and dropped his voice to a murmur. 'How can I let darling Betsey marry a man I know to have committed murder, even if he is my closest friend?'

*****

Across an ocean of cobalt blue came the double line of ships, their sails white against the empty dome of sky. One line consisted of four widely spaced East Indiamen. They were big, bulky ships with their double rows of gun ports picked out in white stripes like men-of-war. On closer inspection the naval aspect of the ships vanished. On their quarterdecks could be seen groups of civilian passengers taking the air, the men in coats of green, brown or pale blue, while beneath an awning sat a number of ladies, their dresses extended in coloured fans around them. A few miles to windward was the squadron. These were lower, sleeker ships, in a tight line. At each ship's masthead was stationed a pair of lookouts to scour the empty sea. They scanned the distant horizon for the first glimpse of the enemy, expecting them to appear at any moment to snap up one or more of the rich merchantmen. But none had materialised so far. Day followed day as they headed northeast towards India.

'Is them bleeding Frogs going to show sometime, or are we to sail on and on till Doomsday?' demanded Evans, leaning on his mop while Trevan sloshed clear sea water over the planking. Although he was recovering quickly, pouring water was the only activity his friends would allow him to do in his weakened state.

'Pipe don't reckon as how we will see them at all,' said O'Malley, as he scrubbed. 'On account of Dismal George having made such a sad cock of things. The Frogs shan't go putting their precious frigates at hazard by milling with this fecking great armada.'

'I don't see why these here East Indiamen need us in the first place,' exclaimed the Londoner. 'I mean, look at them! More bleeding gun ports than the *Sovereign of the Seas*.'

'You doesn't want to go and be fooled by the look of them, Sam,' said Trevan, leaning on the rail. 'They may choose to look all warlike, but that be so much gammon. Cargo and grand folk is what they chiefly carry. Half them ports will have no gun behind them, and the rest will be little six pounders. They ain't got the crew to man more than that, for one thing. Too many stewards and not enough gunners, that be the John Company way. No, they may look fierce enough to scare away a pirate, but that'll not answer with the Frogs.'

'Who shan't be fetching up any time soon, as long as we are here,' added O'Malley. 'Leastways not according to our Pipe.'

'I can never get me neck around how you know all this stuff,' complained Evans. 'I mean, how do you bleeding know what Pipe thinks of Dismal's plan?'

'Sam, lad, you may dress like a fecking sailor, but you're still after being a city boy at heart,' said the Irishman, with the air of a sage. He tapped the handle of his mop on the Londoner's chest to emphasise his point. 'For as long as Grunters shall want seaman to serve them at table, there can be no secrets on a ship.'

'Meaning how he shares a pinch of backy with Harte of an evening hard by the galley,' added Trevan. 'And the two of them gossip like a brace of Penzance fish wives.'

'What did he have to say about all that shouting between Pipe and his mate back in Cape Town?' asked Evans. 'I heard it were a proper set to, with Pretty Boy storming off with a face like a bishop during lent. He even left his hat behind.' O'Malley looked around them before he answered, and then beckoned his two friends close.

'Harte happened to be polishing the silver in the coach when all this to-do was happening,' he said. 'He heard our Pipe layin' into Pretty Boy on account of his being a bit too fecking sweet on his sister, if you follows me drift.' The gossip tapped the side of his nose.

'What, has he and she been dancing the old featherbed jig, like?' said Evans, with a leer.

'Got to be something of the sort, for him to carry on so,' said O'Malley. 'He would hardly have ranted like that over a kiss and a cuddle now, would he? Why else would he be so vexed with his best mate?'

'Deck there! Sail ho!' roared the lookout. 'Sail fine on the larboard bow.' The sailors all exchanged glances.

'Frogs?' queried Evans.

'Maybe Dismal ain't such a fecking dunce after all,' said O'Malley.

'Deck there!' persisted the lookout. 'I can see two of them now. Indiamen from the look of their topgallants.'

'Ah, so not Frogs, then,' said Evans, slapping his mop back down on the planking and resuming his cleaning.

With the convoy and the two newcomers on converging courses, they drew steadily closer. The sailors moved to scrub the forecastle planking by the port side carronade with particular thoroughness, as it was the portion of deck with the best view of the approaching ships. First, tiny white squares appeared. Then more and more sail became visible, until the ships themselves could be seen. As the range shrank, more detail became apparent. Now they could detect tears and shot holes in the canvas, then powder stains and damage to their sides, and rigging that showed signs of having been spliced.

'Them ships look to have been in a right mill,' said Evans. The other two sailors grunted in agreement.

'There may be no Frogs here now,' said O'Malley. 'But those devils must be fecking close.'

CHAPTER 7 MADAGASCAR

Commodore Sir George Montague straightened the inkstand on his desk with care, while he waited for the captains of his squadron to settle. His steward had arranged chairs for them in a semicircle across the floor of the *Black Prince*'s great cabin, and was now serving drinks. One of the seats was already occupied by a stranger in the naval-style uniform of the East India Company. He was a small, neatly dressed man, with fair hair and very full ginger sideburns.

'Gentlemen, we at last have some intelligence of the enemy,' he announced, when all his guests were attentive. 'May I present Captain Franklin of the *Chester Castle*. He is the senior East India Company officer aboard the two vessels we have just encountered.' Captain Franklin rose from his chair and shook each of the three officers by the hand.

'Delighted, I am sure,' he said in a strong northern accent, as the commodore introduced his subordinates to him.

'Might I prevail on you to share the particulars of your unfortunate encounter with the enemy once more, Captain Franklin?' said Montague.

'Certainly, Sir George,' he replied, turning towards the others. 'We were six weeks out from the Coromandel Coast, bound for home, when we sighted a warship yesterday morning, shortly after dawn. With all the attacks that have been made of late on company ships, we were aware of the risk of such an encounter, which was why I was sailing in company with the *Madras*. The warship proved to be an enemy vessel, and she came on very boldly to close with us.'

'Can you say what manner of ship it was that attacked you?' asked Clay.

'I can furnish you with her exact particulars, sir. She was the *Prudence*, a thirty-six gun French national frigate. Once in range, she stood off us and fired broadside after broadside into our rigging, I presume because she did not want to damage our hulls excessively.'

'Undoubtedly,' said the commodore, looking at his steward with a frown. 'A coaster if you please, Thomas. Before Captain Sutton's glass marks that table. Pray continue, sir.'

'We returned as brisk a fire as we were able, but matters were looking very ill for us. We may have been two against one, but our people are not man-of-war's men. But then we enjoyed a stroke of good fortune. The *Madras* discharged a particularly well directed broadside, which brought down the *Prudence*'s foremast so that she stopped dead in the water, and in all of the confusion we were able to make good our escape.'

'That was pluckily done,' said Windham. 'Do you know what became of the enemy?'

'We were some distance away before she was able to cut herself free of the wreckage. The last we saw of her she was back underway, making off towards the north.'

'Was she returning to Reunion for a refit?' asked Clay.

'I think not,' replied Franklin. 'At least not directly. From the course they were on when I last saw them I would judge that they were making for the Madagascar coast, which was near at hand. I imagine they were in need of shelter to effect some repairs before returning across open water to their base.'

'Thank you, Captain Franklin,' said Montague. 'Do you have any observations, gentlemen?'

'This crippled frigate would seem to be a heaven sent opportunity to eliminate at least one of our three opponents, Sir George,' said Clay. 'She cannot have gone far, and even if she has contrived to rig some manner of jury mast, she will be slower than normal until she can have it replaced properly. I would be happy to go and hunt her down, with every prospect of success, if she is where Captain Franklin suspects.'

'I don't think that sending the *Titan* after the *Prudence* is a sound idea at all, Sir George,' said Windham. 'I know how Captain Clay thirsts for glory, but — '

'I do no such thing,' protested Clay, but Montague held up his hand.

'Please, Captain Clay, let him finish,' he said.

'This *Prudence* is the lesser of our three adversaries,' continued Windham. 'We have yet to locate the two superior forty-gun frigates. For all we know they may be closing with us now. Surely that is the danger that the larger *Titan* and *Black Prince* are needed to counter? I would recommend that you send Captain Sutton and me after this ship with our sloops. We should be able to defeat a damaged frigate between us.'

'Captain Sutton, you have been very quiet,' said Montague. 'What is your view of this opportunity?'

'I am obliged to agree whole heartedly with Captain Windham, Sir George,' said Sutton, avoiding his friend's eye. 'He speaks a deal of sense in this matter.'

'I see,' said the commodore, glancing between the two officers. 'I must say it is very refreshing to find you two gentlemen in agreement for once. I am not sure what has occasioned the change but let us take it as a good omen. In that case I shall go ahead and send the *Rush* and *Echo* to deal with the *Prudence*. I will naturally remain with the convoy to see it on its way to Bombay.'

'And what role do you see for the *Titan*, Sir George?' asked Clay.

'Perhaps you would afford your protection to Captain Franklin here?' said Montague. 'See that his ship and the *Madras* are brought safely through to Cape Town without any further onslaught from the enemy. Would that be acceptable?'

'I would not want to be thought of as thirsting excessively for glory by my fellow captains,' said Clay. 'Perhaps my acceptance of such a lesser role with good grace will help to refute such accusations.'

'Perhaps,' muttered Windham in a whisper that only Sutton heard.

'Excellent,' said Montague. 'That is resolved then. Let us all drink to the health of our two gallant young sloop commanders and wish them every success in battle.'

Glasses were raised around the cabin, and good wishes exchanged. Montague looked over at his captains and wondered at the strange change in the mood amongst his command. Now it is Clay and Sutton that are barely conversing, he sighed to himself, while I cannot remember when I last saw young Windham so happy. How very odd.

*****

It was early afternoon the following day and John Sutton was sat at his tiny desk, trying to work. The fierce sun had been beating down on the low deck above his head for hours now, and had raised the temperature in the little cabin to an alarming extent. All five of the window lights that ran across the back of the space had been open for most of the day, but in spite of this his linen shirt still stuck to his torso, and his dark hair was plastered down across his forehead. With a sigh he picked up the purser's indent he was meant to be studying and tried to give it his full attention. A few moments later he felt his concentration slide away from the page of numbers and towards the open windows once more. Beyond them he could see deep blue water, the sparkle of sunlight, and almost filling his vision the bow of the *Echo* as she followed along close behind the *Rush*.

It was a pleasing picture. He could admire the contrast between the black of the hull and the startling white of the bow wave that foamed up where sea and ship met. When he raised his gaze a little, he could see the elegant curved line of the head rails that framed the sloop's figurehead. The carving was of a slim woman in a flowing blue robe with both hands cupped around her open mouth. Now he could study it properly, he realised the shipyard's carver had not got the arms quite right. Instead of calling she had the look of someone who was trying to cover her mouth.

'The Puking Wench, we calls her, sir,' said Chambers, his steward, in his gravely Deptford voice. He had just come into the cabin from the quarter galley and had noticed where his captain's attention was fixed. Sutton looked again at the figurehead, saw instantly what the sailor meant, and choked back a laugh. As if to destroy the image completely, a pair of pale buttocks now appeared between the head rails next to the figurehead as one of the crew of the *Echo* took his place on the seat of ease.

'Deck there!' came the lookout's hail through the open skylight above his head. 'Ship ho! A point to larboard.' Sutton closed the account book with relief and sat drumming his fingers on the cover. If Chambers had not been present he would have leapt up and paced the deck, but under his eye he did his best to maintain the nonchalant dignity of a commanding officer. Fortunately he did not have long to hold the pretense. A few moments later there was an enthusiastic knock at the cabin door.

'Come in,' he called, once he had picked up his pen and

flipped open the book once more. A gangly teenage midshipman with a mop of sandy hair above his hazel eyes burst through the door.

'Mr Appleby's compliments, and there is a ship in sight around the next headland, sir,' he announced.

'Thank you, Mr Croft,' said Sutton, with exaggerated calm. 'Please tell him that I will be up directly.' He waited at his desk for a little longer, counted to fifty, and then rose to pull on his coat. At the moment when he had one arm in and the other out a further hail came from above.

'Deck there! She's a warship for certain, sir! Them spars is altogether too heavy for any merchantman!' He left the cabin, shrugging on the coat as he came, and ran up the ladder way onto the quarterdeck. The little space was crowded with a handful of officers, all with their telescopes trained towards the sighting. The two sloops were sliding along a barren coastline of yellowy brown rock covered in scrubby grey-green bushes. Beyond the bow, the land rose up to a line of rocky cliffs that jutted out into the ocean to form a headland. Standing proud above the top of this promontory was the main and mizzen topgallant masts of a large ship, seen side on. Where the foremast should be, nothing was visible.

'Now, Mr Appleby, what have you found?' said Sutton. He came over to stand between his portly sailing master and the much slimmer figure of Lieutenant Wise. In response the officer of the watch pointed towards the masts.

'Either those be the masts of the largest bomb ketch as ever set sail, sir,' he replied in his broad West Country accent, 'or that be a frigate as has lost its foremast. You will not find any other vessel on the seven seas with such a peculiar rig.'

'Let us hope it is the latter,' said his captain. 'What does the coastline do beyond that cape?'

'According to the chart it tapers back into an inlet about half the size of Plymouth sound, sir,' replied Appleby. 'When we round yonder headland, we should have that *Prudence* tucked up like a trout against a river bank.'

'Let us hope so,' said his captain. He looked towards the rocky shore as it slid past. Opposite him the dead skeleton of a tree stood proud against the skyline. Several large, dark birds were perched in the branches like vultures, eying the ships as they sailed by.

'They are some manner of fish eagle, sir,' said the lieutenant. 'With a glass one can see the prodigious size of their talons and the absence of feathers on their lower legs.'

'You are quite the natural philosopher, are you not, Mr Wise?'

'I would not go so far, sir, but I have always had a fondness for the study of birds,' he replied. 'These are quite unique to my experience. They may even be nondescript.'

'When the French are beat, I shall let you go ashore and shoot one, so that you can present a paper on it to the Royal Society,' said Sutton. 'Wise's Fish Eagle, it will sound rather fine, will it not?'

'As we are speaking of birds, perhaps we should not be so swift to count our chickens, sir,' said Appleby, slapping a large, fat hand down on the wooden quarterdeck rail. 'We wouldn't want to go a jinxing matters by talk of victory too early, now.' Sutton saw out of the corner of his eye a number of pigtailed heads bob in agreement as various members of the afterguard reached for the rail too. He resumed his inspection of the coast.

'Tell me, Mr Appleby,' he said after a while. 'I had always imagined Madagascar might be rather lusher. More like to the islands of the Indies. Are we not almost in the tropics? This place is barely above a desert.'

'The island is green enough, for the most part, sir. It is

only this southern end and the east side that is barren.'

'I see,' said Sutton. 'And is there anything significant set down on the chart I need to worry about in this bay of yours?'

'There are no hazards marked, although as there is but a single sounding for the whole inlet, I would not rely on that. These waters are visited by plenty of Arab slavers, but Royal Navy ships have not come here since the time of the pirates. I took the liberty of ordering a leadsman into the bow to take soundings as we approach the bay.'

'A good precaution,' agreed Sutton. 'Kindly reduce sail and set him to work. Take us around the end of that headland and let us see what we have caught in this bay of yours.'

The two sloops worked their way steadily forwards, the *Rush* still leading and the *Echo* following in her wake. With metronomic precision the man stood in the fore chains whirled the heavy lead weight around in a wide circle and then hurled it forwards. He let the sequence of leather and cloth markers run through his hand and called off the depth as the ship passed over the weight and the line went vertical.

'By the mark fifteen!' he called, as he hauled the dripping line in for the next cast.

'Plenty of water here,' commented Sutton, watching the angle of the bay start to open.

'By the deep twelve!' yelled the leadsman. The *Rush* stood on farther and Sutton looked towards the far side of the bay through his telescope. He could see a little collection of huts by the shore. Two thin native boats had been dragged up the beach, and a baggy fishing net hung drying on poles. Villagers were watching the new arrivals with interest, pointing towards them, while small children ran and splashed in the shallows.

'And a half ten!' bellowed the man in the fore chains. The

ship moved onwards, revealing more and more of the inlet. Then they cleared the end of the headland and suddenly the French frigate was in sight.

She was moored close to the shore, under the shelter of the cliffs. The water was calm there, and her long, black hull with its broad white stripe lay deep on its broken reflection. A big main and mizzen mast soared upwards, but where her foremast should be was an ugly stump that protruded six feet above the forecastle, the top jagged. Lashed against it was a thinner spar that was in the process of being rigged. All along her side the gun ports were open, and her big eighteen-pounder cannon were run out. A tricolour stirred limply from her mizzen halliard in the little sea breeze that had penetrated the bay. Sutton focused on the anchor cable that dipped into the water just in front of her. Running from it he could see a second cable that stretched along the ship's side and disappeared in through a gun port towards the rear.

'She has a spring cable mounted,' reported Wise. 'See, she's taking a turn on it now.' As Sutton watched, the second cable grew stiff and the hull creaked around to keep the frigate's guns facing towards the two new arrivals.

'She seems to be prepared for us,' he grunted, still looking the Frenchman over.

'By the deep nine!' yelled the leadsman, by way of reply.

'At least there do seem to be plenty of water, sir', said Appleby. 'I believe I can see them Frogs starting to rig boarding netting now. They have no intention of letting us surprise them.'

'Heave to, if you please Mr Appleby, and then signal to the *Echo* for her captain to come across. Mr Wise, when he is aboard, bring him down to my cabin, and let us make plans for our victory.' Sutton headed down the companion ladder, his face impassive as he tried not to smile at the shock his second gratuitous mention of winning had caused the more senior mariners within hearing.

Fifteen minutes later the three men were gathered around Sutton's little cabin table. Now that they were in the confined waters of the bay, the temperature was even hotter. Wise drew out a huge, bright blue handkerchief and mopped at his thin face. By contrast the captain of the *Echo* seemed to be unaffected by the heat. He leant forward over the chart, his eyes darting about him and his fingers drumming on the table top.

'Will this be the first time that you have commanded a ship in action, Captain Windham?' Sutton asked.

'Yes sir,' replied Windham. 'But it shall not be the first time I have been in a battle, as you will recall. That was the occasion on which my uncle was killed.'

'Of course,' said Sutton. 'So what do we make of our situation? My initial thought before we arrived was that we would cut the *Prudence* out after dark. But now I see her disposition, I am less certain.'

'I would urge us not to attempt that, sir,' said Lieutenant Wise. 'We will have no element of surprise, and tonight is a full moon. She would see our boats coming as clear as day. Taking a merchantman is one thing, but fighting our way onto the deck of a man-of-war against a crew of trained men is quite another.'

'Do you have any suggestions to proffer, Captain Windham?'

'You are the senior officer, sir,' he replied. 'I am sure that any scheme you suggest will be satisfactory.'

'Very well,' said Sutton. 'The *Echo* is equipped like the *Rush* with carronades, I collect?'

'Yes sir, we have twelve-pounders,' replied Windham. 'She carries nine per side.'

'And the *Rush* has eight. I find them to be excellent quick firing weapons, but with a worryingly short range. We will need to get in very close before they will answer against the *Prudence*.'

'That should not present too many issues against a ship that is at anchor with cliffs behind her,' offered Windham. 'She cannot stand off and use the superior range of her cannon.'

'True, but she will give us a few lusty blows as we approach,' said Sutton. 'The key to our victory will be to make certain that she cannot defeat us separately. We should both approach her at the same time, but from two different directions. That way her captain will only be able to point those big guns of hers at one of us.'

'What if the *Echo* was to wait here, while we headed towards that village we saw?' suggested Wise. 'Then we could close from that side, and the *Echo* from this. When the *Prudence* turns her broadside towards one of us, she will also be turning her stern or bow towards the other.'

'And then that ship will have the opportunity to rake her,' said Sutton. 'Even a sloop, if well positioned so as to fire down her whole length, should be able to bring matters swiftly to a resolution.'

'Meantime, what will become of the second sloop?' asked Windham. 'The one which the *Prudence* has chosen to concentrate her fire upon?'

'She will be in for a hard pounding, I make no doubt,' conceded Sutton. 'Which is why it is essential that both sloops move into their respective positions as quickly as possible.'

'I understand sir,' said the captain of the *Echo*. 'You can rely on me.'

*****

The twin roar of drums echoed across the waters of the bay as the two Royal Navy sloops prepared for action. In both ships their captains' possessions were swept down into the hold, and the bulkheads that made up their suites of cabins were knocked flat by the carpenters to leave the whole gun deck as a continuous space. Men rushed to their places around the carronades, stripping themselves to the waist and rolling their neck cloths into bandanas to protect their ears. Sand was scattered on the planking to improve the gun crew's grip, and the ships' boys were sent rushing down to the magazines to bring up fresh powder charges. Over the men's heads the sail was reduced to fighting trim with a single topsail on each mast, while in the tops marine sharpshooters settled into position, ready to pick off anyone on the *Prudence*'s deck.

After the bellow of orders and the rush of feet had subsided, the drums fell silent. The quarterdeck of the *Rush* was now very crowded. Clusters of sailors were grouped around the little swivel guns that were mounted on posts along the rail, with more marines filling the gaps between them. The wheel had an extra quartermaster in case of injury, and the afterguard were grouped by the mizzen mast, ready to trim the sails. Lieutenant Wise picked his way over to Sutton and touched his hand to his hat.

'Ship is cleared for action sir,' he said. 'The *Echo* has just signalled that she too is ready.'

'Very well, Mr Wise,' said Sutton. 'Put her on the other tack and take us across towards that village over there. The leadsman can resume his work.'

While the *Echo* waited by the headland, the *Rush* sailed across towards the centre of the bay. The blue water parted before her and ran away in long lines like folds in silk towards the shore on both sides. Sutton watched the French frigate with care. So far, apart from rigging her boarding nets and turning on her spring, she had showed little sign of responding to their arrival. All work had stopped on her jury rigged foremast, however, and she squatted low in the water, huge and dangerous, like a crouching beast.

'Mr Appleby,' he said. 'Can you take a bearing on the *Echo,* if you please. I want us to approach the enemy at ninety degrees to their line of attack.'

'Aye aye, sir,' said the master. He pulled his sextant from its place near the wheel, turned it on its side and sighted along it. The ship sailed on, and as it did he inched the arm along the scale, following the changing angle. Everyone on the quarterdeck seemed to be watching him in silence.

'By the mark seven!' called the leadsman. Appleby turned his sextant round to check the reading, then resumed his work.

'By the deep six!' came from the forecastle. The master checked the instrument again, and turned towards Sutton.

'Just passing ninety degrees now, sir,' he said. He walked over to the wheel and retuned his sextant to its place.

'Wheel hard over!' ordered the captain. 'Hands to the braces! Steer directly for the enemy, quartermaster.'

'Aye aye, sir. Steer for the enemy it is.'

'And a half seven!' added the leadsman.

'Mr Croft,' said Sutton. 'Kindly signal the *Echo.* Engage the enemy.'

'Aye aye, sir.' A seaman attached the toggles of each flag to the halliard as Croft read out the numbers, and then he hauled the message aloft. When it reached the mizzen peak, he broke the flags out with a snap of his wrist.

'*Echo* acknowledges, sir,' reported the midshipman.

'Thank you, Mr Croft,' said Sutton, staring across the bay towards the French ship.

The enemy frigate now lay at the point of a right angle. Coming down one side of the triangle towards her, parallel to the cliffs of the headland, was the *Echo.* Approaching along the side which stuck out into the centre of the bay was the

Rush. The French ship could turn herself around her anchor cable by hauling in, or letting out, her spring, but she could only face her main battery towards one of the two ships at a time.

'That has given them a poser, sir,' said Lieutenant Wise with satisfaction. 'Which way do you imagine they will turn?'

'Towards the foe that approaches the swiftest, I should think,' said his captain. 'But as to which vessel that is, I cannot say.'

As if to answer the question the profile of the frigate began to change. The two remaining masts grew farther apart and the hull seemed to stretch even longer across the water as she twisted around, foot by foot, till every one of her long line of guns pointed towards them.

'It would seem to be us then, gentlemen,' said Sutton, his throat dry. The comment was heard across the quarterdeck in the sudden quiet. A flash burst out of the frigate's side and a ball of dirty white smoke rose into the air. A scatter of sea birds flew up from the face of the cliffs behind the frigate. Moments later a chain of splashes rose up off the smooth water of the bay as the ranging shot skipped over the surface. The loud thud of the cannon arrived a little later.

'Two cables short sir,' reported Appleby, and the sloop continued on.

Sutton took the few minutes before *Rush* would be in range to look around him. He first checked over his ship. In the bow his boatswain stood with his party of forecastle men. These were all prime seaman, capable of the feats of gymnastics that would be required to repair cut up rigging high in the masts. Next he looked down into the well of his ship, at the gun crews that stood in patient groups around their weapons as they waited for battle to start. He was pleased to detect a general air of confidence about them. There were smiles and fist bumps in evidence, together with the nervous tapping of equipment on the deck. Last he looked around the bay. The beach in front of the village was crowded with people. Goodness, the whole population must be there, he thought. And why not? It was not every day that the navies of Europe did battle, a few miles from their front doors. Lastly he looked back at the enemy, just in time for her to vanish behind a wall of fire and smoke.

The first broadside was widely spread. A scatter of splashes tore up the water on either side. A single hole appeared in the foretopsail, and there was a solid thump from near the bow.

'Even our scantlings should be able to keep a spent ball out at this range,' muttered Wise. Sutton pulled out his pocket watch and flipped it open. It had no second hand, but he would be able to estimate how quickly the enemy reloaded by the movement of the minute hand. The second broadside arrived a little over a minute later. One ball streaked past his head with a sound like tearing cloth. Several cut ropes hung down like jungle creepers, and some of the forecastle men where climbing up to splice them.

'They make reasonable practice for Frenchmen,' he commented to his lieutenant. 'Although note how they fire all their guns together, Mr Wise. Their captain does not trust his men to serve their pieces independently.'

When the enemy next fired they had covered perhaps a third of the distance between them, and the bombardment was starting to tell. More holes appeared in the sails, and all of the boatswain's men seemed to be aloft as they struggled to make good their repairs. Sutton heard a double crash from the bow, and shortly afterwards two seaman appeared from under the forecastle carrying a wounded comrade towards the fore hatchway. He watched his men, noting some of the looks of unease that were starting to appear amongst them.

'This is always vexing for the men, is it not, sir?' said

Wise, echoing his thoughts. 'It is never congenial to be fired upon without the possibility of reply. They will be happier when we are alongside.'

Now they were much closer. The French ship seemed to fill the whole of Sutton's vision. The hull was wrapped in a bank of smoke, and the side of her hull bristled with cannon. Then she vanished in orange flame and shot tore into the little sloop. Splinters flew up from the front of the ship. There was a whirl of movement next to him as two marines fell to the deck, while from above came a cascade of falling blocks and cut rope.

'Steady lads,' he called, more to himself than to those around him. He glanced across the narrowing gap to the frigate's side. 'One more of those and we shall be able to say our piece. Stand by your guns there!' The smoke began to thin and Sutton realised they were so close that he could now hear French orders being shouted. There was a rumble as the cannon were run up on the enemy ship, and a row of thick black muzzles appeared all along her side.

'For what we are about to receive...' intoned Appleby, and the side of the French ship vanished in fire once more.

'Helm up, quartermaster!' yelled Sutton, ignoring the crash of shot striking home all around him. 'Lay me alongside.'

'Aye aye, sir,' replied the man at the wheel. Sutton strode forward to the quarterdeck rail and looked down on deck once more. One carronade had been dismounted, but the armourer was supervising a party of men as they tried to heave it back onto its slide. There were a few bodies lying on the deck and some of the crews were a little thinner than before, but they all looked up expectantly at him.

'Standby, starboard guns!' he yelled. 'Fire as you bear and pay those Frogs back with interest, lads!' They all cheered at that. The sloop continued to turn and the side of the French frigate appeared out of the smoke beside them. All along the line of carronades the gun captains shouted a warning to their crews and jerked on their weapon's lanyards. With a colossal roar the guns of the *Rush* spoke at last.

Now Sutton's consciousness narrowed to the single world of the two ships. Clouds of smoke billowed all around them, blotting out the sky overhead. The thin gap between the two hulls was a corridor of fire, with tongues of flame darting backwards and forwards. Above the deep roar of the guns came the lighter bang of muskets as the marines fired at any shadow they could see in the fog. Down on the main deck the light carronades barked out, pumping ball after ball into the enemy, while in reply came the slow but steady French broadsides, each one a tempest of shot that slammed into the *Rush*. The bulwark near him disappeared in a cloud of splinters and a seaman fell back, clutching at a wound that had opened in his chest. Red blood spread like an ink spot over his shirt as his comrades carried him below. A gust of wind rolled the smoke apart for a moment, and he saw the splintered holes that had been torn all along the sides of his ship. The sloop's rigging hung down in festoons and the main mast now had a jagged wound near the base. Sutton had just started to wonder how it was still standing when he saw the foremast start to topple forward. Slowly at first, but then with gathering speed it crashed over the bowsprit, sending debris pelting down over the front of the ship.

Death was all around him. Musket fire pattered on the planking from soldiers in the French ship's rigging. First the quartermaster was struck down, then Appleby, and finally Wise. Piles of dead lay along the centre line of the main deck, and still the fighting went on.

'Keep at it, lads!' shouted their captain. 'The *Echo* will be giving them hell. Raking the bastards again and again.'

'The *Echo*, sir?' replied Midshipman Croft from beside

him on the quarterdeck. 'But she has hauled her wind.'

'What?' exclaimed Sutton. 'What did you say, boy!' He rushed along the gangway of the sloop, vaulting over dead and dying seamen as he went, in his haste to get to the bow. Once there, he clambered over the ruins of the foremast till he reached the rail. A gust of wind parted the smoke a little to reveal Windham's ship, stationary with her foretopsail backed. The sloop was firing, but she was so far away that her shot fell some distance short of the enemy's stern. From behind him the cries of the wounded were briefly masked by a huge juddering crash as the mainmast came down to join the foremast over the side, and still the remorseless French fire thundered on. As if she had now seen enough, the *Echo* turned gradually around and headed back out to sea.

CHAPTER 8 REUNION

In the stern cabin of the *Black Prince*, Commodore Sir George Montague was becoming increasingly frustrated with his visitor.

'But I simply do not understand!' he said, banging his hand down on the top of his desk. 'What on earth has become of the *Rush*?'

'I regret that she is no more, Sir George,' replied Windham. 'When I returned to the scene of battle on the following day the *Prudence* had departed. The *Rush* had been beached close to the village and set fire to. There was little left beyond a few charred frames and her keel. I imagine she will have surrendered, but was too badly damaged to be of any use to the French.'

'There we have it, again!' exclaimed the commodore. 'You *imagine* that she had surrendered? Does that mean that you were not present the previous day to witness her actual defeat? I fail to comprehend how it was that you came to abandon her in such a fashion?'

'I did not abandon her, and I resent you saying that I did, Sir George!' exclaimed the commander of the *Echo*.

'You can be as indignant as you like, Nicholas, but in the absence of a proper explanation of your conduct, I shall be forced to draw my own conclusions.' said Montague.

'As I have tried to explain, Sir George, when I left the battle she was already a dismasted wreck. I withdrew so as to ensure that at least one of your sloops survived the debacle, and as a result I did not witness her final hours.'

'Very noble of you, I am sure,' snorted the commodore. 'And yet your casualties seem to have been very light, in a battle that saw a fellow ship destroyed. How is that possible?'

'It was all that fool Sutton's fault,' said Windham. 'We agreed that we would stand off from the *Prudence* and cripple her from a distance, before we moved in to finish her off. The French chose to concentrate their fire on the *Rush*, hence the difference in our casualties. Then the next thing I knew, Sutton had closed with them and was fighting yardarm to yardarm. A sixteen-gun sloop against a thirty-six gun frigate, I ask you? There could only have been one victor.'

'I am well aware of the unequal odds, Nicholas,' replied Montague, his voice icy. 'That is why I dispatched not one but two sloops of war. What I fail to understand is why you did not consider going to Captain Sutton's assistance?'

'I did try, of course, Sir George. If you care to see my gunner's indent, you will see that we expended a considerable quantity of powder and shot. But regrettably the wind was unfavourable for us to close with the enemy. By the time we were near enough, the *Rush* was barely still fighting. I am quite certain that Captain Sutton will have perished in the battle. At that point I took the difficult decision that any continuation of the action would merely serve to endanger my ship, too.'

'And so you fled,' said Montague.

'I did no such thing!' protested Windham. 'I stood clear of the battle to avoid being brought to action by the *Prudence*.'

'Which has now disappeared, presumably back to Reunion to be repaired. So I am left the weaker by one sloop, yet still have three French frigates to defeat. In fact, until the *Titan* returns from Cape Town, I only have your ship and mine.' Montague stood up from his desk with a gesture of despair. 'I must say you have made a sad cock of things, Nicholas. Do you know that I specifically petitioned the

Admiralty to have you assigned to my command, out of respect for your uncle? This is a fine coin in which you choose to repay me.'

'It wasn't my fault,' muttered Windham.

'Wasn't your fault! What kind of explanation is that? You left a brother officer to his fate! How do you imagine your fellow officers will regard these events, once the particulars are generally known? At best you will be thought of as incompetent, at worst as a coward and a poltroon! I might almost think that you were trying to gain some sort of revenge... oh my God!' Montague spun round in horror and stared at his visitor.

'What?' said Windham, his face colouring.

'Enough of this dissembling, I want you to speak plain. Did you act as you did because of that damned nonsense of yours about Percy Follett?'

'Of course not,' said the captain of the *Echo*. He cleared his throat as Montague continued to glare at him. 'No, that played no part in matters at all.'

'What have you done, Nicholas? Tell me the truth now? Did you hold back deliberately from coming to assist the *Rush*?'

'No, no, it all transpired as I laid it out,' said Windham. 'It was that hothead Sutton's fault.'

'Nicholas, I don't know what you have done, but unless you are absolutely candid with me, I shall not be able to help you.'

'The *Rush* is no more. Captain Sutton is no more. There was nothing I could have done,' Windham folded his arms and sat back in his chair. Montague tried to hold the young man's gaze but it slipped away from him whenever their eyes met. You are lying, boy, he thought to himself. I think I know what truly happened off the coast of Madagascar. Then he struck his head with the flat of his hand as another thought came to him. What if this should all come out, he asked himself. It was on my recommendation that Windham was promoted. My preferment that got him his command. What will the Admiralty say of a man who showed such poor judgment? The captain of the *Black Prince* turned away in frustration.

'Oh, just let me think, Nicholas!' he exclaimed, as if Windham had been speaking, and he began to pace up and down the deck in front of the cabin windows.

'I need to win a victory,' he muttered to himself. 'If I can fulfill my orders, fewer questions will be asked. Report failure, and those bloody nib scratchers will want to know why. But I can achieve little until the *Titan* should return. Now young Clay, he has a decent reputation as a fighting captain. If only I had sent him to bring back the *Prudence* instead of those two puppies.' He paused to glare at the surviving puppy, who was now examining the backs of his nails as if nothing had happened. With a growl of frustration he resumed his pacing.

'Very well, so we wait for the *Titan*,' continued Montague, still to himself. 'Then perhaps we can seek the enemy closer to their refuge. Maybe catch one of their frigates at sea and level the odds again.' He strode on, backwards and forwards, his head down and one hand twisting in the other. After a while he stopped in mid-stride and stared at the window next to him.

'What is it, Sir George?' asked Windham. 'Have you had an insight?'

'Only to replace my damned steward,' said the commodore. He pulled a silk handkerchief from his coat pocket and buffed at the glass. 'Bloody smudges everywhere.' Then he turned back towards his visitor, with his handkerchief poised as a fresh thought came to him.

'Nicholas, have you given any consideration as to how you

will face Captain Clay?' he asked.

'How do you mean, Sir George?' asked Windham. Montague's eyes rose towards the sky.

'Do you not think he may require an explanation as to how it was that his closest friend was abandoned to his fate by you?' he said. 'You will certainly need to furnish him with a better one that I have just heard.' Windham stared back at him, his eyes dark and unreadable.

'Well, as for that, I shall tell him that his friend died bravely in battle, just like my Uncle Percy did.'

*****

On the island of Reunion, Commander John Sutton stood on a terrace that looked out over the harbour of St Paul. A frown played across his face as he wondered what he disliked so much about the place. The location of the port was spectacular, on a promontory of flat land cut off from the rest of the island by huge, forest-covered hills that loomed above the little town and its hinterland of fields and groves. The buildings were nice enough, with their thatched roofs and colourful shutters framing the windows. Many had climbing plants sprawling up their walls, ablaze with tropical flowers in crimson, yellow or bright orange. Most of the houses were whitewashed, but there were others dotted amongst them that were painted blue, or ochre or gentle pink. Clustered amongst the buildings were trees, many bearing fruit of various kinds. The weather was warm and sunny, with a pleasant sea breeze to check the heat from becoming too fierce. And on three sides of him was the ocean, vast and blue, as it stretched away to the far horizon.

No, it was the other little details that annoyed him. Where the sea met the palm-fringed shore, the sand of the beach should have been white, but instead it was a dirty volcanic grey. It was much the same colour as the blocks of stone used to build the numerous gun batteries that protected the harbour. All were squat, ugly, functional buildings that jarred with the softer lines of the town's houses. Then there were the vessels in the harbour. Not the little fishing boats with their brown sails and pale blue hulls, or the two massive French frigates that swung at anchor. They were attractive enough, but behind them were two battered East Indiamen, symbols of his country's inability to protect its commerce, and worse still there was the *Prudence*. Her hull lay hauled down on its side against a slipway. He could hear the echo of distant hammering from where he stood, as the dockyard workers smoothed away all the damage he had inflicted on her. Soon she would be good as new, as if his beloved *Rush* had never fought her. But most of all what depressed him was the large tricolour flag that floated above his head, reminding him that he was no longer the captain of a ship, but just a simple prisoner of war.

He turned away from the view in response to a muted cough, and saw a curious figure waiting for him. The man was dressed in a shabby version of a footman's uniform that stretched no farther down than his knees. Below the torn bottoms of his britches, his legs and feet were quite bare, while on his head a dirty white wig framed his black face.

'Monsieur le Commandant will see you now,' said the servant, with a bow. 'Please to follow?'

'Of course,' he replied. He turned his back on the view and followed the footman. They left the brightly lit terrace, and plunged into the cool dark of the residency. The high-ceilinged corridor beyond had walls lined with portraits of bewigged figures and ornate chests in tropical wood. Sutton was led past doors that opened on both sides into various rooms. The footman stopped at one that was closed and knocked firmly.

'Entree,' came a deep voice from inside, and the footman swung it open for him. Inside was a large office with windows down one side. The shutters were partly closed, leaving slats of brilliant light through which Sutton could just see the lush greens and flashes of colour of a tropical garden. In the room were two other men. Seated behind the desk was a large bull of a man in a pale blue coat and snuff-coloured waistcoat. He turned his heavy, jowly face towards the door and regarded the visitor with dark eyes. The other was Enseigne de Vaisseau Chavency, the handsome young lieutenant from the *Prudence* who had looked after him since his capture.

'Ah, Commander Sutton,' he said, as he rose to his feet and favoured the Englishman with a flashing smile from his very white teeth. 'May I present Monsieur François Morliere, Commandant of St Paul. You and your men will be under his protection now.'

'You mean that he is to be my next jailer?' said Sutton.

'If you make war upon France, you must accept the risk that you may be captured, monsieur,' said the lieutenant.'

'You may call me a jailer if you wish to,' growled Morliere. 'I had in mind a more liberal regime for you and your men, but if you would prefer a dungeon, that too can be arranged.'

'Your pardon, sir,' said Sutton. 'I am a little low in spirits at present.'

'Every fighting man must face defeat at sometime,' said Chavency. 'You have no need to be ashamed of your conduct. You and your men fought bravely, that is what is important.'

'May I ask what provision has been made for my people?' asked the prisoner. 'I am particularly concerned about the wounded.'

'We are not savages, monsieur,' said Morliere. 'They have all been taken to the hospital where they will receive treatment for their wounds.'

'Thank you, sir,' said Sutton. 'And what of those who survived unharmed?'

'We are fortunate in being on an inaccessible part of an island many miles from land,' said the commandant. 'Escape is quite impossible, which allows me to grant you some liberty. The surviving seaman will be housed in an old warehouse near the docks.'

'A warehouse?' queried Sutton. 'Is that suitable?'

'It is clean and dry, and has been used by the sailors from the East Indiamen we captured without complaint,' said Morliere. 'I imagine it is better accommodation than they are used to aboard your ship. I will permit you to visit them once each day. As for the officers, it is only you and Monsieur Croft who survived unharmed. I will provide you with a small house near to here, together with your steward to attend to your needs.'

'Thank you for your kindness, sir.' The commandant's dark eyes narrowed as he regarded Sutton.

'You should know that I can also be much less kind, monsieur,' he said. 'While you are here, so long as you behave, I will grant you a degree of freedom. But let me be quite clear; if I find you have abused my trust, I will have you and your men locked up in a less pleasant location.'

*****

The weather side of the *Titan*'s quarterdeck was over sixty feet long, yet it seemed close and cramped to Clay as he tried to work off the boiling frustration within him. Like a caged animal he tramped up and down, up and down, his eyes passing over the life of the ship about him, registering little. He reached the limit of the deck and swung round to retrace his steps once more, his head bowed in thought.

Something was wrong. He had felt it the moment he had

stepped into the great cabin of the *Black Prince* earlier. Sir George Montague had been as polite as ever. He had peppered Clay with inconsequential questions. Had his trip back from the Cape passed without incident? Was the *Titan* in tolerable shape? All the time he had fussed even more than usual over the positioning of the items on his desk.

'Why is the *Rush* not with the squadron, Sir George?' Clay had eventually asked. 'I particularly wished to speak with Captain Sutton.'

'Ah, yes,' the commodore had said, tearing his attention away from his ink stand. 'I am afraid I have some bad news with regard to that. There has been a battle, and matters have ended badly for your friend.'

Clay reached the quarterdeck rail of the *Titan*, and turned back towards the stern. Behind the frigate sailed the *Echo*, keeping station, a cable length back. How was it possible, Clay asked himself, for a brave fighting officer like John Sutton to fail in battle, and yet the incompetent Windham to somehow come through the same action? The first was the veteran of a dozen fights, the other had barely fought one, and had hardly distinguished himself then. He scanned the rigging of the little sloop behind his ship, searching for clues. Those spars have been barely touched, he told himself, and yet in the same fight the *Rush* was lost? No, this whole story stank to high heaven. Something was wrong, he felt it in his bones, and he had seen in Montague's eyes that he knew it too. Thoughts of the battle brought back thoughts of his friend again. He felt his eyes begin to water as he turned about once more.

Could it be it that John was truly dead? His dear friend, with whom he had shared so many adventures? This was the man who had spoken to Lydia on his behalf when he was unable to do so. It was John who had been first to cradle his head on the quarterdeck of the *Rush* when he was struck down by a Spanish musket ball. John Sutton, who was so full of life and fun, dead? No, it couldn't be true. He swerved around the last ring bolt on the quarterdeck and headed aft once more.

Why had he parted on such bad terms with his friend? Clay's hands writhed briefly in the air in frustration, before he clasped them back behind his back. Well, the past is the past, he decided. Little can be done to remedy that matter now. But I need to find the truth. I owe John that. He slowed as he approached the rail at the stern of the frigate and paused to lean on it, his breath coming in gasps. Looking back at him from the little sloop was its strangely carved figurehead. Above the cupped hands, two painted eyes stared back at him. What did you see, *Echo*, Clay asked the carved nymph, on that fateful day? What truly happened off the coast of Madagascar?

*****

For the next few weeks, life on Reunion settled into a regular pattern for Sutton. The little, single storey house provided to the officers was furnished simply, and was clean and dry. It stood in a secluded spot on the edge of town at the top of a small rise that overlooked the beach and the coral reef beyond. A little farther along the coast was the last of the big stone coastal batteries that protected St Paul from attack by sea.

His day would begin shortly before dawn, when the sound of bird song from the trees in the house's garden woke him. He would get up, wash and shave with the help of Chapman, his steward from the *Rush*, get dressed and then leave the house. A narrow, sandy track ran past the side of the garden and down to the beach. Once by the sea he would walk while the sun was still lost in the east, behind the forest-covered mountains that formed the back wall of his prison.

It was important to walk this early on the curious dark sand. When the sun fell directly on it, it would heat rapidly until it was uncomfortable even for a man wearing leather-soled shoes. Every morning his route was the same. He reached the beach and then turned right, away from town, and walked in front of the solid wall of the coastal battery. He would glance up at the big guns that projected out above his head from between the stone embrasures, then return to his thoughts, with both hands clasped behind his back.

On one side of him was the sea. He could see the waves of the ocean as they broke far out on the edge of the reef, while the shallows closer to him were littered with pieces of driftwood. On the other side of him were lush fields and groves of fruit trees that rolled away from the edge of the beach. A mile or so along the sand was the point where the mountains met the sea amongst spectacular cliffs. Squeezed between the two was a coast road that ran in the narrow gap, but the sentries who guarded it always turned him back at this point.

As he walked, his mind was occupied with playing over and over the visions that haunted his sleep. Every night he tossed and turned through the long tropical darkness. First there were images of Betsey Clay, her long fair hair, her cool grey eyes, her neat white teeth when she laughed. Even now he could see the flash of her smile as he had last seen it beneath the shade of the apple trees back at Rosehill cottage. He now knew with certainty that he loved her, but he had no confirmation that she loved him. He had written to her before the *Rush* left Portsmouth, but that was a poor substitute for what he had wanted to do. If only he had been able to meet her and declare himself properly. In his mind he would imagine how that scene would have gone. Her eyes growing wide with pleasure as he told her, her rush into his arms, the feel of her slim body as he held her close. Then her face angled back, her eyes closing and those rose-coloured lips parting beneath the pressure of his kiss.

But then he would curse himself as a fool. What true evidence did he have that she loved him at all? His hands coiled around each other. Oh God, she must, he thought. Yet his ship had outrun any possible reply from her, leaving him in an agony of doubt. And even if she did love him, how impossibly far away was she now? There were all those thousands of long miles between her and where he stood, on a beach in the middle of this distant ocean. Then there was the ridiculous attitude of her brother that had made him quarrel with Clay for the first time in their friendship. Worst of all was the reality that he was imprisoned on this island, and could be for long years ahead. And how had he come to be here? The hands behind his back clenched into fists as scarlet rage flooded his mind.

Windham. How could he have been so stupid? How could he have let that man trick him so easily into making his fateful attack on the *Prudence*, while he had stood back from the fight? And what of all the poor souls that had died to give him his petty revenge? Like Lieutenant Wise, shot through the chest by a musket ball. He could still hear the thwack as the bullet struck, spinning him around like a doll and sending him crashing first against his captain before sliding down to the deck. He had dropped down beside him and held up his head as he spluttered and coughed. He had witnessed the terror in his eyes as his lungs filled and he drowned in his own blood.

As he returned along the beach he looked with hunger at a pair of little fishing boats pulled up on the sand, but they were much too small to cross an ocean. If he could only escape for this place, he knew what he would do. He would hunt Windham down without mercy.

Later, he would return to the little house, calmer for now, but with nothing forgotten. By then Chapman would have laid the little table on the veranda for breakfast, and Midshipman Croft would be waiting for him, up and dressed. Then the dreary pleasantries of their domestic life would descend on him. And how was the beach today, sir? What was the state of the tide? A little more of the soft tack if you please, Chapman. It seems to have turned out fine again, Mr Croft. The two officers were slipping into the behaviour of an elderly couple whose many years together had driven out any spark of originality in their conversation.

After breakfast came his daily walk into St Paul, to visit the remaining wounded in the hospital. Then he would check on those of his crew who were well, as they lounged about in their abandoned warehouse. Occasionally the officers of the garrison, or from one of the frigates, would take pity on him and invite him to dinner. Afterwards he would return to the little house with its lengthening shadows and the prospect of another hot, dark night tossing and turning with thoughts of desire and revenge clashing in his mind.

And then one morning, everything changed.

*****

'Oh, sir!' cried Chapman, dropping his basket of washing in surprise as he came out of the house. Clothes of all colours tumbled out onto the floor of the veranda. 'You gave me a proper turn! I was just going to get these here togs hung on the line afore breakfast. Ain't you going for your constitutional this morning?'

'No, not today,' said Sutton. He stood looking out to sea and shading his eyes beneath one hand. 'Tell me, Chapman, do we have a spy glass?'

'We do, sir,' said the steward, as he gathered up the wet

garments. 'It be only a small one, mind. Mr Croft chanced to have it in his pocket when we was taken. I am surprised them Frogs left him with it. It was the Devil's own job to get 'em to let me keep my clasp knife.'

'Have you seen something of interest, sir?' asked the midshipman as he stepped out onto veranda too, tucking in his shirt tails as he came.

'I believe I have. Mr Croft, could you oblige me with your glass?' The youngster disappeared into the house again, and returned with the little tube.

'It is rather indifferent, I am afraid, sir,' he said, offering it to his captain, but Sutton shook his head.

'You have the younger eyes. Direct your gaze at the horizon, two points to larboard of that palm tree, and tell me what you can see.'

'Top gallants of a ship I would say, sir,' the midshipman said. 'With a second one on its beam.'

'And all three of the French frigates are back in harbour, I collect?' asked Sutton.

'That's right, sir. The *Rhone* arrived back yesterday.'

'I can think of no reason why any Indiamen who valued their freedom would come within sight of here,' said the captain. 'Which means that it may very well be the squadron.'

Once Chapman's washing billowed on the line, he brought out their breakfast on a tray. The two men ate their meal fitfully, with frequent breaks for one or other to look back out to sea. The tiny white squares that had first lifted above the horizon were growing, stretching into pillars of white as more and more of the ships' sails became visible. From the coastal battery down by the beach came the echo of a drum and the sharp bark of orders as the guns were manned. By the end of the meal there could be no doubt.

'It's the squadron for certain, sir,' said Croft. 'I can see the

Echo now, off to windward of the other two, and I would recognise the *Titan*'s topsails anywhere.' Sutton said nothing, but he stared hungrily at the approaching ships.

'Do you think they mean to attack the port, sir?' continued the midshipman.

'I doubt it, Mr Croft, unless they have brought considerable reinforcements,' said his captain. 'The French fortifications are much too strong to attempt a seaborne attack. I imagine they mean to blockade the port. It may answer for a while, but when victuals run low on board, they will be required to return to Cape Town, and out the enemy shall come again.'

'Is that all they will do, sir?' said the teenager. 'I did wonder if their arrival might lead to our being rescued.'

'Do you very much want to escape?' asked Sutton.

'At first I had assumed that we would be exchanged before too long, what with there being so many more French sailors who are prisoners of our nation than the other way around,' explained Croft. 'But then I realised that they must all be back in Europe, and then I got to thinking how long such an exchange might take to arrange.' Sutton looked at the young man thoughtfully.

'So if the opportunity presented itself, you would favour our flight?' he asked.

'Oh yes, sir,' enthused the youngster. 'I thought at first that we might steal a fishing boat, but those in the harbour are too well guarded, and the little ones on the beach look altogether too small for an ocean voyage.'

'Too true, but perhaps we may yet contrive to escape, Mr Croft,' said his captain. 'I generally find that with new circumstances comes opportunity, for those who are open to it.' He twisted in his chair to call over his shoulder. 'Chapman! Our hats and coats, if you please. We shall be going into town.'

As the two officers approached the heart of the little port, they noticed a change in the atmosphere. St Paul was generally a relaxed place, but today they could feel the tension in the air. Instead of the usual groups of black labourers heading out to the fields, the streets seemed strangely empty. They turned around a corner to find a drummer boy in a dark blue uniform covered in red braid advancing towards them down the centre of the road. He was marching in time to the steady tattoo he beat on his instrument, and troops were emerging from some of the houses, buttoning up their uniforms as they came. At the square at the end of the street was a party of gunners, drawn up in a small column. Their sergeant barked an order and they swung away, down towards the sea. The two men exchanged glances, and then followed the soldiers.

When they reached the end of the street they found themselves looking out over the harbour. They could see that all the ocean-facing gun batteries were being manned. Some officers were grouped around the substantial figure of the commandant, who stood close to the harbour wall. He was studying the approaching ships through a large telescope that rested on the patient shoulder of a black servant. The quayside around them milled with people, black and white, civilians and military, all of whom were chattering about the ships that had appeared that morning. Sutton picked a figure out from the throng and waved his hat at him.

'Monsieur Chavency!' he called. The young lieutenant looked around, flashed a smile in his direction, and pushed his way through the crowd.

'Captain, and Monsieur Croft,' he said. 'Have you come to join in the fun? Your compatriots have appeared, how do you say it, in the hoofing of St Paul?'

'The offing we would have it,' corrected Sutton. 'Do you think they mean to attack?'

'All the world knows that the English are quite mad, but St Paul has over a hundred guns to protect her. Unless your friends have brought other ships that we cannot see, there is little such a small force could hope to achieve.'

'So you think they look to blockade you?' asked Croft.

'Doubtless that is what they will try, my friends,' smiled the young man.

'How do the repairs to your ship go?' asked Sutton He looked towards the *Prudence* and felt a pang of jealousy. 'I she is afloat once more, with a new foremast in place.'

'She is quite restored,' said the Frenchman proudly. 'In fact, I am on my way to rejoin her. We have now only her yards to set up, and some provisions to take onboard, and she will be ready to go to sea. I fear that I shall not have the pleasure of you gentlemen's company for some months.'

'Really!' exclaimed Sutton. 'You mean to sail out and fight the squadron?'

'Of course not! We French are so much more subtle than you English. The *Prudence* will slip by your cruisers very easily,' he boasted. 'We go at midnight tomorrow, when the tide is high and the moon has set.'

'But I do not understand, monsieur. Even in the dark, how will you manage to evade ships that wait just off the harbour entrance?'

Chavency tapped his nose and chuckled. 'Because we know these waters, mes amis. And your friends know them not at all. At high water there is a beautiful passage through the coral reef. In fact, it comes out just in front of your house. If you cannot sleep tomorrow night, be sure to wave to me as I depart, eh?' He laughed at his own wit, pushing at Sutton's arm, and the two British officers smiled with him.

Farther down the quayside there was a commotion amongst the crowd. It parted in a wave to make room for a man on a horse as he pushed his way forwards. He trotted smartly up to the three naval officers and pulled his mount to a halt. Sutton noticed that, unlike the blue-clad gunners he had seen earlier, this man wore a military uniform of dark green, with yellow piping and flashes.

'Non!' he called down to them, wagging a gloved finger. 'It is forbidden! By order of Monsieur le Commandant.'

'What is forbidden, Jean-Pierre?' asked Chavency.

'These men cannot be here,' replied the horseman. 'Not while the enemy are just off the port. Monsieur Morliere has ordered it.'

'But what about my men?' protested Sutton. 'I have not visited them yet.' The hand waved again, with increased agitation.

'No more visits!' he said. 'Your men are now under armed guard. I must insist that you return to your house, and that you stay there until you are permitted to return.'

'Very well, monsieur, I will of course comply with the commandant's wishes. Goodbye, lieutenant. Forgive me if I do not wish you a prosperous voyage.' He shook Chavency's hand, and the two men left the port and retraced their way back towards the little house by the sea.

*****

When they returned, the three British ships were plain to see. They beat up and down outside the entrance of the port like sentries, sailing just out of range of the coastal guns. The *Black Prince* was in the middle of the line. She was the biggest of the ships, the paintwork of her hull noticeably cleaner than the other two. Farther away was the *Echo*, like a much smaller version of the two frigates. Sutton stared at her for a long while through Croft's telescope, trying to recognise Windham from among the tiny figures on her quarterdeck. Closest of all was the *Titan*. She was very slightly smaller than the *Black Prince*, but she was being sailed the best of the three. She turned crisply at the end of her run, her sails sheeted home with a minimum of fuss, and now she was sailing back along the edge of the reef, comfortably out of range of the coastal batteries. In the little disc of magnification she grew and grew, filling the space. Now she was almost level with them, and Sutton could see individual figures on board her. Sunlight flashed from the gold epaulet on the tall figure by the wheel, and Sutton felt a surge of longing for his friend. Then the frigate turned around once more and sailed away from him. He gently compressed the telescope and placed it on the table, his eyes vacant.

'Are you quite well, sir?' asked Croft. Sutton dropped down into one of the chairs on the veranda and folded his arms.

'I am fine,' he said. 'But I do find our position to be vexing. Here we are, with vital intelligence of the enemy. We know when the *Prudence* will leave port, and even the route she will take. Over there is Captain Clay, in plain sight from where we sit. I just wish there was some manner in which we might communicate with the squadron.'

'It is very annoying, sir, said the midshipman. 'But it can't be helped. Still, if they should attempt anything, we shall have a fine view of it from up here.' Sutton glanced towards the younger man and then stopped, transfixed by what he saw. Beyond the end of the veranda was Chapman's washing, like a line of bunting, as it billowed and flapped in the keen sea breeze. He felt a rush of excitement as an idea began to form in his mind. After a pause he became aware that his companion was looking at him curiously. He cleared his throat.

'Your pardon, Mr Croft, but I have been seized by a notion,' he said. 'Tell me, how long were you signal midshipman on the *Rush*?'

'Over two years, sir. Ever since Mr Preston and I transferred from the old *Agrius* back in Barbados.'

'And how much of the code book do you retain? In your head.'

'As you know, there is no end of words and phrases in the book, each with its own numbered code, sir. I don't know them all by any means, but I daresay I could recall the common ones easy enough, with a little thought.'

'And if I collect, you have ten different types of flag on board, one for each digit?'

'That's right, plus a few extra to qualify a signal, sir. For instance, if you wished to order the *Titan* to close with the enemy, I would first put up the *Titan*'s number followed by the flag for one over the flag for six. Sixteen being the code for *engage the enemy more closely*.' Sutton nodded, and then indicated the line of washing.

'With a deal of cutting and stitching, could we make some sets of flags with the material we have? They would not need to be full size, just big enough to be seen by the *Titan*.' Croft got up and walked along the washing line, letting the clothes pass through his outstretched hand.

'Mostly blue and white, sir,' he announced. 'That will do for many of the flags, and I have a red cover on my bed we could use, but we shall need some yellow cloth. The flags for three, five and nine all have yellow in them.'

'Chapman!' bellowed Sutton.

'Sir?' said the steward as he emerged from the house, wiping his hands on a cloth.

'Did I hear that you were once taken as a cutpurse?'

'Aye, I been arrested a brace of times, like,' he admitted. 'But them traps could never prove naught, sir.'

'Which I suppose argues for you having some talent in that regard,' said his captain.

'If it's all the same with you, I would sooner not answer

that, sir,' he replied, his face a mask.

'No matter. I want you to go down into the town, and without being observed, steal some yellow garments that have been put out to dry. You might also bring back another washing line too. Enough to make a signal halliard for that palm tree over there, when long spliced together with our own line.'

CHAPTER 9 WASHING

Sunday afternoon on the *Titan* was generally devoted to make and mend, whether the frigate was far out to sea or, as was the case today, a French naval base with three powerful warships was two miles off the starboard beam. The entire wardroom had been invited to dine with their captain, apart from Lieutenant Preston, who was officer of the watch. From the volume of the officers' laughter drifting up through the open skylight in the middle of the quarterdeck, it was proving to be a successful meal. A minimum crew had been allocated to sail the ship, which meant that the rest of the hands could do as they pleased for the afternoon.

Most had congregated in the warm sunshine of the forecastle. They had washed their clothes, and as a result the rigging of the foremast was alive with garments of every shade and hue, all flapping together in the breeze. Then they had washed their hair, a considerable process for sailors who had only ever lightly trimmed their locks since the day they became man-of-war's men. Some of the more veteran mariners sat on the forecastle rail with clouds of grey hair blowing all about them as it dried. Sean O'Malley's curly black hair only reached down to his shoulder blades, and was already dry as he sat with an air of Louis XIV behind Adam Trevan. In his hands he was braiding the Cornishman's blond locks back into a thick pigtail for the week ahead.

'A deal of fecking grey in here now, Adam,' he said, as he secured the end with a length of blue ribbon.

'Aye, but only since that blasted fever, like,' moaned

Trevan. 'It was yellow as corn afore that.'

'As was your bleeding face, mate,' said Evans, while Sedgwick plaited his hair. 'Looks better now, mind,' he added. The others all looked at the Cornishman. In truth his face was still much too thin and gaunt, but the yellow hue had indeed gone, to be replaced with his more familiar mahogany tan.

'Hoy, Able,' called one of the group of hands who were fishing off the larboard cathead. 'We got one here as looks like a fat herring. Be he any good to eat?' The sailor held up a blue and silver fish for inspection that gasped and twisted in his hands.

'Can't say, Roger,' replied Sedgwick. 'He looks wholesome enough, but the fish hereabouts are all different to them as I knew off the Gold Coast.'

'I heard how some of them are fecking deadly,' added O'Malley, with a leer. 'Venomous, so they are. Full of all manner of noisome bile and the like. Drop you down dead before your second mouthful.'

'Poisonous, eh?' said the sailor to his fellow fishermen. 'We best play on the safe side, lads. I'll flog this one to the gunroom.'

'You've sailed in this here sea before, ain't you, Adam?' asked Evans. 'Did you not try the fish?' The Cornishman had now swapped places with O'Malley, and he was combing the Irishman's hair for lice.

'That be right, Sam, I was in these waters afore the war, like,' he said. 'But it were bigger fish as we was hunting. If you goes a bit farther south of here it be proper good for whaling. Plenty of big sperm whales to go after. We spent the best part of two year on my last voyage, much of it hereabouts.'

'Two fecking years!' exclaimed O'Malley. 'What was you doing for vittles, if you wasn't catching any fish?'

'Your whaler don't carry a big crew, no more than thirty men at most,' explained Trevan. 'Each hand gets a part of the cargo, bit like how we does prize money, so you don't want the profits to get shared too thin. Then you starts from home with no cargo, so plenty of room for provisions. As you scoff a keg of salt pork, a barrel of whale oil replaces it. And there be plenty of food, if you knows where to seek for it.'

'Like what?' asked Evans. Matters of food were always of importance to the huge Londoner.

'No end of whale meat, of course, although that don't have a good savour to it,' Trevan replied. 'But away south there are islands that only whalers ever visit, with creatures that ain't never seen no folk before. Plenty of seals, and birds as can't fly and the like, what will just stand and look, mild as kittens, as you slaughter their kin. Some of them are fair eating, an' all.' He finished off O'Malley's pigtail and slapped him on the shoulder.

'Right fecking cold though, I shouldn't wonder,' said O'Malley as he placed his back against the belfry so as to enjoy the sun and closed his eyes.

'Aye, it is,' said Trevan quietly. 'But I would sooner have a mountain of ice than some tropical ague again.' The others were quiet for a moment. Then Evans looked at Sedgwick and frowned.

'You got fleas in your small clothes there, Able?' he asked. 'You're jumping about like the bleeding deck's on fire.'

'There's something flashing this way from onshore,' said the coxswain. 'It keeps getting in my eyes.'

'Probably some dirty great Frog, sharpening up his sabre in case we try to land,' murmured O'Malley, as he drifted towards sleep. 'It will pass soon enough.' But Sedgwick rose to his feet and stared towards the land.

'If it were just a chance something catching the light, wouldn't it have stopped as the ship sailed on?' he asked, shading his eyes. 'See! There it goes again, from the little house on that there hill.' Trevan stood up to look too.

'You might be right there, Able,' he said. 'You reckon someone be trying to get our attention?'

'Bah!' scoffed O'Malley. 'It'll be some fecking kid, bored of an afternoon. Thought he would try and dazzle us with a scrap of tin.'

'Maybe it is, but I reckon I'm still going to report it,' said the coxswain.

*****

'Where away did this flash come from, Sedgwick?' said Lieutenant Preston, as he opened his telescope and pointed it towards the shore.

'From the white house there, with the palm tree next to it, sir,' he said, pointing towards the beach.

'The one behind the battery?' inquired the officer. 'It will doubtless prove to be the garrison at weapon's drill.' He focused on the house. As the image sharpened he saw a figure that held a small square of silver in his hands. The man tilted it in the sun, and as the angle changed the square turned into a blinding flash of light that shot towards him.

'God bless my soul!' exclaimed Preston, pulling the telescope from his eye and blinking. 'There is a man over there with what looks to be a mirror in his hands.' He looked again with his other eye. 'Well, I never did.'

'What have you seen, sir?' asked the coxswain.

'He has abandoned his looking glass and is pointing towards a most curious collection of washing hung from a tree beside him,' said the lieutenant. 'That is strange. Why, they could almost be some of our flags. Mr Russell, see what you make of this.'

'Aye aye sir,' said the midshipman, as he took the

144

telescope from him. After a glance he scoffed. 'The Frogs are making game of us, sir. With a very indifferent set of our signal flags.'

'Look again please, Mr Russell,' said Preston. 'Does the signal mean anything?' The midshipman looked again, his lips working as he ran down the flags. His mouth remained open as he reached the end.

'That's our number, sir!' he exclaimed.

'I fancied it was,' said Preston. 'What is the rest of the signal?'

'The other number was that of the poor *Rush*, sir. How the devil did the Frogs get hold of our codes?'

'So the signal reads *Rush* to *Titan*, does it?'

'Yes sir, but—'

'But nothing, Mr Russell,' said the lieutenant. 'Kindly send an acknowledgement. Sedgwick, run down and get the captain, if you please. Give him my compliments and tell him it is urgent.'

Preston continued to watch the tree. The moment the acknowledgement broke out at the *Titan*'s peak, the line of flags was hauled down.

'What is it, Mr Preston?' said Clay when he came up on deck, his face still flushed from his meal. Lieutenant Taylor and Jacob Armstrong followed in his wake.

'We are being signalled to from the shore, sir, using our own codes,' said the officer of the watch. 'So far they have signalled to us with the *Rush*'s number.' Clay stopped in his tracks, the colour draining from his face.

'Where away?' he asked, taking the telescope from the lieutenant.

'From the little white house above and behind the battery, sir. That one, by the tree.'

'New signal being hoisted, sir!' said Russell. 'Numeral, one. Enemy ship. Weighing anchor.'

'Acknowledge, please,' said the captain as he scanned the shore. 'I can see some figures in the shade, but little more than that. Here comes the next part of the message.'

'Numeral... Eight... Bells... First watch,' read the midshipman. 'That is midnight tonight, sir.'

'This must be some manner of trick, sir,' said Taylor, from the rail beside him.

'If so, it is a curiously elaborate ruse,' said Clay. He was still looking through his telescope. 'There seems to be three men, two busy arranging their flags afresh, and one with a glass looking this way.'

'Who can it be?' asked the first lieutenant. 'Is it possible one of the *Rush*'s officers survived?'

'Perhaps,' said Clay quietly, hardly daring to hope. 'There must be at least one there who knows his signal book by heart.'

'I have the complete signal now, sir,' said the midshipman as he came over with his slate. '*Rush* to *Titan*. One enemy ship, weighing anchor at eight bells in the first watch. Sailing by passage bearing north through reef.'

'Passage bearing north?' queried Taylor. 'But that would be between us and them. Is there such a passage?'

'None marked on the chart, sir,' said the ship's master.

'Aloft with you, Mr Armstrong,' said Clay. 'Take our best glass. If a channel exists, it should be visible from the main royal yard.'

'Aye aye, sir,' said the American.

'Mr Russell, signal the commodore, if you please. Captain of *Titan* wishes to come on board.'

'Aye aye, sir,' replied the midshipman.

'Shall I pass the word for your barge, sir?' asked Preston.

'If you please,' said Clay.

'*Black Prince* to *Titan*,' reported the signal midshipman. 'Come aboard when convenient.'

'Acknowledge, if you please, Mr Russell, and then make a signal back to the shore. *Titan* to *Rush*, is Captain Sutton present?'

*****

'And you received no further reply then, captain?' asked Montague, regarding his subordinate over the top of his desk.

'No, Sir George,' said Clay. 'A large patrol of French soldiers appeared on the beach at that moment, and whoever was signalling wisely decided to take down the flags. I put the ship on the other tack, so as not to draw any more attention to that portion of the shoreline, but we kept a good lookout on the tree. No further signals have been sent.'

'That is vexing,' said the commodore. 'What would you have done, if you had been able to establish who had signalled you?'

'Once I ascertained who was present, my next action would have been to pose a question to which only they would have known the answer, Sir George. I might have asked Mr Sutton for his father's name, for example.'

'Quite so,' said Montague. 'For without such reassurance, how are we to know if this message is genuine? It is quite possible that it could all be a trap of some kind. The French may have captured the signal book of the *Rush* and be seeking to make game of us.'

'That is possible, sir, but if so I struggle to see to what end. The passage through the reef undoubtedly exists, and my ship's master has now plotted it with some accuracy. It is difficult to see what the enemy stands to gain by gifting us such a valuable piece of information.' Montague sat back in his chair and stroked his neatly shaped sideburns as he thought about that.

'Might it be possible that they have revealed this passage to put us off our guard?' he said. 'Perhaps they seek to conceal a greater lie within a small truth. They want us to concentrate our forces against this passage tonight, while they shall try to escape in a quite different direction?'

'Perhaps, but such a ruse is easy to counter,' said Clay. 'If the information conveyed to me is accurate, it is only one enemy that will try and break out down the passage. So we need only deploy the *Titan* to oppose such a move. If I can catch one of their frigates in this narrow passage, with reefs all about them, I will be able to make them most uncomfortable. You and the *Echo* can cover the main exit to the harbour, and we can signal to each other if it is indeed some manner of trap. Then one force can come and assist the other. At no stage will we be particularly far apart.'

'That might answer,' said the commodore. 'How do you plan to frustrate the French?'

'I will head away from the coast at sunset, shaping to join the rest of the squadron. As soon as it is dark I will return and anchor at the end of the reef, with my guns pointing down the line of the passage, ready to rake any ship that comes through it. There will be no moon tonight, and it looks like it may rain. If the ship is silent, with no sail set or light showing, I doubt if the enemy will detect us. But we shall mark them, as they move through the water towards us.'

'What of the shore battery that covers that section of the coast? Will they not present a hazard?'

'Firing at extreme range against muzzle flashes in the dark, Sir George?' queried Clay. 'Let them do their worst. They are as like to strike their own frigate as us.' The commodore thought about all this for a moment and then came to a decision.

'Very well, let us make it so,' he replied. 'My *Black Prince* and the *Echo* will watch the normal passage out from St Paul.

If you should get into difficulty, show two Bengal lights from your foreyard, and I shall do the same if the enemy concentrates against me. Is that a satisfactory plan?'

'I believe it will answer very well, Sir George,' said the captain of the *Titan*.

'Good, that is settled. Can I move on to another matter I wish to discuss with you?'

'By all means, Sir George,' said Clay. 'What is it that you wanted to say?'

'Now that the possibility has emerged that your friend John Sutton may be behind these signals and is therefore perhaps alive, are you considering some manner of rescue?'

'The thought had naturally occurred to me, Sir George. The French battery precludes any attempt at a landing during daylight hours, but something could be tried at night.'

'I thought that might be the case,' said Montague. 'It is a course of action that I must forbid in the strongest terms.

'What!' exclaimed Clay, jumping to his feet. 'But he is my oldest and dearest friend! Should the opportunity arise to restore a brother officer to his liberty, of course I shall take it!'

'Calm yourself, I pray you,' said the commodore, holding up a hand. 'Please resume your place, captain, and give me a full hearing.' Clay continued to glare at the commodore, but he sat back down again. When he was seated Montague resumed.

'I do understand the sensitivities here, and that he is your friend, but I must ask you to place to one side such considerations. Permit me to explain my motives, which are quite honourable, I assure you. I speak now as commander of this squadron with only the good of my country at heart.'

'Go on, Sir George,' said Clay.

'I make no doubt that you would seek to lead such a rescue attempt?'

'Given the strength of my interest in its success, I probably would, sir,' conceded Clay.

'Which, given that you would be landing on a well protected and hostile shore, shall place you at considerable risk. I have already lost Captain Sutton. For the good of the mission entrusted to us by the Admiralty, I cannot lose you too. It would leave the squadron bereft of leadership.'

'If I were to succeed, I could restore Captain Sutton to you, Sir George.'

'True, but if you were to fail, I would be left with only the commander of the *Echo*. To be frank, it is not a prospect I relish. I regret to say Mr Windham has shown himself to be wanting as a commander, over this affair of the *Rush*.'

'I understood him to have been your prodigy, Sir George?' Clay looked across the desk with an unblinking stare.

'I would not put it so firmly,' said the commodore. 'I asked for him as a favour to a long dead but dear friend. Regrettably, precious little of the uncle seems to have rubbed off on the nephew.'

'Do I take it that you do not find his explanation of his actions when the *Rush* was lost wholly plausible?' asked Clay.

'Frankly no, which is the second reason why I must forbid your rescue attempt. Mr Sutton, if he is alive, is likely to bring a quite different version of the loss of his ship back with him. I cannot afford to have such ill feeling and dissension among my command at this critical time.'

'Sir George, I must protest,' said Clay. 'You speak of duty and honour, yet you propose to abandon a brother officer, because he is likely to speak ill of Captain Windham? So be it, I say! Because I hold that Mr Windham has a great deal to explain. If he has acted dishonourably, as I feel certain he has, and abandoned one of our ships to its fate, he deserves whatever censure is his due. Why do you seek to protect him?'

'Understand that my injunction against attempting a rescue is not a permanent one,' said Montague, leaning forward to urge his case. 'Captain Sutton, or whoever is signalling; for mark this, we still have no certain intelligence that it is he; whoever our mystery ally is, they are perfectly safe where they are. In fact this person is proving to be a most valuable spy. He will be returned to us in time, doubtless through a prisoner exchange. Come now, captain, let us not fall out over this. I give you my word that once we have gained an upper hand over the French, I shall make enquiries as to whether Captain Sutton lives, and how we may best exchange him. Once he is released, then we will hear his version of events, but it shall not happen tonight. We have quite enough upon our plates as it is. Agreed?'

'If that is an order, Sir George,' said Clay, after a pause.

'Good man! Now, come closer. I have an idea for what the squadron should do tonight, once you have captured your prize. Allow me to share it with you.'

*****

The sun was setting off the port bow of the *Titan* as she stood out to sea. It had rained for much of the afternoon, but the towering thunderheads had drifted away to the north. Now there was a scatter of clumpy cloud across the sky, all lit in pink from below as the sun sank amid a bed of crimson. Lower and lower it slipped, till only a slither of gold hung above the horizon. The frigate dropped into the trough between two waves, and when she rose back up again the sun had vanished and night rushed towards them from all sides. She carried on, displaying no light to the outside world, conscious of the many eyes that might still be probing the dark from the shore as they looked for her. An hour after sunset, the frigate hauled her wind, turned about, and headed back towards the shore. As she drew closer, she gradually reduced sail, minimizing the faint silhouette that might be visible against the black water.

Clay looked at the island, a dark brooding presence before him. St Paul stood out as a glow of yellow off to one side. The lights of the port thinned to single points scattered along the shore that marked where individual dwellings lay. He looked at the few clustered near to the spot he thought the signal had came from and wondered if his friend were there, on a dark veranda, looking out to sea with a lamp-lit room at his back.

'Shall I clear the ship for action, sir?' asked the shape of his first lieutenant by his side.

'If you please, Mr Taylor,' he replied. 'Pass the word, rather than using any drums. And make sure the battle lanterns are shuttered until the action begins.'

'Aye aye, sir.' Clay guessed that Taylor would have touched his hat in the dark, so he did the same, even though both gestures were invisible. Then he turned to the bulky shape of the sailing master who was stood by the wheel, giving gentle instructions to the helmsman.

'How are you managing to navigate in this dark, Mr Armstrong?' he asked.

'Tolerably well, I thank you, sir,' replied the American. 'I took a bearing on the end of the reef while it was still day, and St Paul can be readily marked. I am quite confident I will be able to navigate us into position.'

Clay looked around him in the warm tropical night. Dark, but not completely so, he thought, as his eyes continued to adjust. Through the gaps in the clouds above his head a few stars had appeared, tiny points of silver against the velvet of the sky. Where the bow of the frigate split the sea there was a tumble of phosphorescence that faded into lines of light along the ship's side. In the faint glow of orange lamplight on the main deck below him, the shadows of the gun crews grew and shrank as they moved to their places. And ahead of him were the lights of the shore, twinkling off the surface of the sea, and growing all the time. Clay let his mind wonder as he struggled to come to a decision. He paced along a portion of deck that was free from the mass of gun crews and marines that crowded the quarterdeck. Then he paused at the rail and looked towards the shore once more.

'Damn the man, ordering me not to rescue John!' he muttered. 'What gentleman uses rank to force another to abandon his friends?' Then he paused, as a though came to him. 'Ordering *me* to not to rescue John,' he repeated. 'It was *my* presence that he forbade, was it not?' He pushed himself away from the rail and turned towards the figures grouped by the wheel. 'Mr Taylor, Mr Macpherson and Mr Preston, I would obliged if you would join me at the back of the quarterdeck,' he said. 'You come too, Sedgwick.'

He walked to the stern rail, where they would not be overheard and waited until the shadowy figures stood around him. 'Now, Mr Taylor, we shall be in position at the end of the channel through the reef a good hour or more before the enemy frigate will arrive. While you are anchoring the ship and getting a spring deployed, I intend for Mr Preston to go ashore, if he is willing.'

'Ashore, sir!' exclaimed the first lieutenant. 'With what object?'

'It was you that first saw that signal, Mr Preston. Do you believe you could find the house again?' asked the captain.

'Aye, I daresay I could,' confirmed Preston. 'What am I to do?'

'Find those that signalled, and bring them off,' said Clay. 'I will not order you to do it, for it may be hazardous, and I cannot go myself. But it is just possible that Captain Sutton may be there.'

'I will go with all my heart, sir, and bring him back,' said the lieutenant.

'But what of the French frigate, sir?' asked Taylor.

'It is a bare mile to the beach, so Mr Preston will be back in good time for the action. Now Sedgwick, I intend him to take the barge. See the crew are armed and ready to go as soon as the ship drops anchor.'

'Aye aye, sir,' said the coxswain. 'I reckon as it would be best to get that there boat in the water now, sir, and tow it behind us. That way there will be a deal less noise for the Frogs to hear.'

'Good idea, make it so,' said his captain. 'Mr Macpherson, for your part I need you to select a small number of your best marines. Mr Preston can only take a handful in the barge.' The Scotsman's broad smile glinted in the night.

'I know precisely the men to take. Every one of them a former poacher, well used to moving with stealth at night.'

'Sir, I must protest,' said Taylor. 'What if the enemy should come down the channel early? Surely there will be time for this sort of escapade once the battle is over?'

'Time, yes,' said Clay. 'But opportunity, decidedly not. Once we discharge our first broadside, this beach will be alive with more French soldiers than you can wag a stick towards. I am sorry, George, but I am quite resolved on this course of action.' He patted the older man on the arm. 'All will go fine, you shall see. Now, let us make our preparations. The shore is fast approaching.'

*****

'Sails all in, Mr Taylor,' reported the sailing master, a shape silhouetted against the few lights that showed ashore.

'Thank you, Mr Armstrong,' he replied. He then turned

154

towards the starboard gangway and said in a quiet voice, 'Pass the word to drop anchor.' The order was repeated from man to man away into the night towards the forecastle. A few moments later came a loud splash, followed by a return hiss of whispers up the ship.

'Mr Hutchinson says as how the anchor is holding, sir,' said the final voice. 'And that he be fixing the spring on now.'

'Anchor is holding, sir,' he repeated to the tall figure next to him.

'Thank you, Mr Taylor,' said Clay, and he turned towards Preston. He felt for and gripped the lieutenant's hand. 'Off with you now, and see you make it touch and go. If there is no sign of them at the house, come back directly in good time for the fight.'

'Aye aye, sir,' said the lieutenant. 'I shall not let you down.'

Preston went to the main deck, past the curious glances and knuckled salutes of the gun crews, and out through the entry port. He dropped down into the stern sheets of the barge and paused as he realised an extra figure was seated there.

'Tom?' he said. 'Is that you?'

'Aye, it is,' replied the marine. 'I thought I might come along to stretch my legs. Captain Sutton is my friend too, and besides, these men I have chosen for you are not wholly to be trusted. They would steal the pearls from St Peter's gate if they thought he wasn't attending.'

'Oh, very well,' Preston said. He found it was comforting to have the solid presence of the Scot in the party, with his long claymore and his outward calm. 'Give way, Sedgwick.'

'Aye aye, sir,' said the coxswain. 'Shove off in the bow there! Pull starboard side! All together, handsomely now.' The boat turned away from the looming presence of the frigate and was soon alone in the night. Preston looked at the crew of the barge, but could make out little more than eyes.

'What is wrong with the barge crew, Sedgwick?' he asked.

'I had them blacken their faces and arms with soot from the galley, sir,' explained the coxswain. 'Well, all except Abdul and me, of course. I saw Mr Macpherson's men was doing it, and thought we should do likewise. What with muffled oars, we should be nigh on impossible to spot.'

Preston sat back and reflected how lucky the ship was to have such an able and intelligent man. After a few more strokes he felt Sedgwick point ahead of them.

'I mark that dark block there as the Frog battery, sir, meaning the place we saw the signal from would be about there. Ain't no light as I can see, mind.' Preston leant across to follow the line of his arm.

'That's the spot, right enough,' he mused. 'But as you say, no light is showing.'

'Oh, speaking of lights, do be careful of the shuttered lantern down by your feet,' said Macpherson. 'I brought it just in case.' Preston felt around with his hand till he came across the warm metal cylinder.

'I have it, Tom' he said.

They were close to the beach now, gliding along, each dip of the oars leaving a splash of light briefly in the water. From ahead they could hear the gentle crash and hiss of waves as they folded onto sand.

'Easy there,' hissed Sedgwick. 'Hold her fast.' The rowers stopped together, cradling their oar handles against their chests, the blades flat on the water.

'What have you seen?' whispered Macpherson from Preston's other side.

'Frog patrol,' murmured the coxswain. Preston looked down the beach and saw an orange light that appeared to be dancing through the air. As it approached, other sounds drifted towards them, the crunch of boots on sand, the gentle chatter of the men. In the disc of illuminated sand they could see the gaitered legs of the soldiers. They grew nearer, till they were barely thirty yards from where the boat rested on the water. Preston held his breath as one of the men seemed to pause and look their way, but evidently he could not see the motionless boat as it waited on the dark sea. He turned to rejoin the others, and the disc of light moved away.

'Carry on, Sedgwick,' he ordered, after a few minutes.

'Give way all,' said the coxswain, and the boat surged forward once more till it slid to a halt in the shallows.

Macpherson jumped out, summoning his men to join him. He sent a picket in each direction along the beach to warn of any approach. When they were in place, the other three men vanished into the dark ahead to scout the way to the house where the signal had originated. While they waited for them to report back, Sedgwick had his crew turn the barge around. He ordered half the oars kept manned, ready for an instant departure.

'What do you suppose they shall find?' asked Macpherson as the two officers waited in the dark, the shuttered lantern at their feet.

'I imagine the French will have confined the crew somewhere in St Paul, along with the wounded. Doubtless the *Rush*'s surgeon, if he survived, will have stayed with them, so I am supposing this house to be the abode of the commissioned officers. I only saw three figures signalling, but which of the officers they were I cannot say. Mr Sutton may not even be amongst—' He broke off as the marine held up his hand in warning.

'Who goes there?' he growled. One hand strayed to the hilt of his sword.

'*Titan*,' came the reply, and a dark shape appeared from out of the gloom.

'What have you found, Baker?' asked Macpherson.

'The house is there, right enough, but it looks proper deserted, sir,' replied the marine. 'Door's been left open, one of the windows is smashed, an' the furniture cast about. Ain't no Frogs there, leastways not now.'

'That does not sound encouraging, but we have come this far,' said Preston. 'Lead us to the place, Baker.'

'Aye aye, sir. Follow me, then.'

Macpherson picked up the lamp, and they disappeared together towards the dark of the land. Preston stumbled along in the wake of the others. They came to a sandy path that wound up a shallow slope away from the beach. Leaves brushed past them as they went. After a hundred yards Baker stopped, his body tense, and gently whistled like a bird. Two answering calls came out of the darkness and he waved the officers forward.

'House is off to the right, by that big tree, sir,' he said. 'Watch out for the table by the door, it's been turned over.'

The officers approached the shadowy building beneath the tree. It was visible as no more than a block of grey in the gloom. Preston heard Macpherson stumble on something and breathe a curse. Then a line of amber appeared in the night as the Scotsman inched the shutter on the lantern open and held it towards the house. Square windows, black as pitch, stared back at them from the whitewashed walls. There was a step up to a wooden veranda, and an open door behind. The marine officer slid out his sword, the edge a line of reflected gold from the lamp, and advanced towards the door. Preston drew out his own blade and followed. They skirted around the overturned table on the veranda, then the two went inside.

Once they were in the house, Macpherson opened the lantern a little more. There were only a few pieces of furniture, but what was there had been thoroughly searched. A chair lay on its side, with clothes strewn across it. A fan of papers lay in another corner with boot marks on them. Beside that were shards of broken crockery, while a thin ribbon of breeze flowed in through the hole in a broken window.

'Look at this, Edward,' said Macpherson. 'We have certainly come to the right house.' With the tip of his sword he hooked up a length of rope from the floor. At regular intervals along it was a line of crude looking flags.

'Indeed we have,' agreed Preston. He held up the remains of a yellow dress and pushed his hand through one of the large square panels cut out of the skirt.

Macpherson had moved over to look at an abandoned sea chest. The top had been flung open and its contents pulled out. Linen, a leather shaving roll, opened and then discarded on the floor, and what was obviously a Royal Navy coat. Gilt buttons glinted on the dark cloth, every one bearing the Admiralty's fouled anchor. He pulled closed the lid and held the lamp so that the light shone on the polished wood. Preston came over to his side and Macpherson pointed with the tip of his claymore. Cut into the surface and then blacked with ink was a name: J R P Sutton.

Chapter 10 Flame and Smoke

Eight hours before Preston and Macpherson discovered the sea chest of their friend, Captain Hector Sybord of the Garrison Artillery stood on the parapet of his battery and looked out to sea. He liked this particular spot on the ramparts. It was at one end of the battery, close to where a palm tree grew. The trunk was just beyond the end of the stone wall, and it bent upwards in a graceful arc over his head. The thick mass of feathery leaves at its crown shaded him from the fierce noonday sun. He knew that he should have ordered some of the men to chop it down long ago. In theory it could provide cover for an attacker, but on the other hand his battery had never been attacked, and it would be a shame to lose its shade. He decided that the palm tree would survive another day, and turned to the ample figure of Sergeant DuPont who stood beside him. Both men had been watching the steady approach of the *Titan* as she sailed along the coast just out of long cannon shot.

'Are they in range yet?' asked Captain Sybord. It was the third time he had posed the question, as if he were a child reluctant to accept that a journey was not about to end. The grey-haired sergeant shook his head once more.

'If you wish, I can try a ranging shot, mon capitaine, but they are certainly at least a hundred yards too far away,' he said. The captain stared at him in silence, a frown of disapproval on his face. After a moment Sergeant DuPont realised his error.

'Sorry, sir,' he apologised. 'I of course meant to say they

are eighty meters out of range.'

'Better,' said Sybord. 'Paris is very strict about the use of Royalist measurements, DuPont. How can we expect the men to use the new ones if we do not?'

'And yet our guns are still twenty-four-pounders, sir,' said the sergeant, indicating the line of huge cannon. 'I wonder what that would be in kilograms?'

The captain looked down at his eight guns with pride. Each was loaded and run up ready to fire. They had been trained around as far as the embrasures would allow, and the wedge-shaped quoins had been removed so that the barrels poked up at maximum elevation. Every gun captain had his linstock alight and their lines of smoke rose into the hot, humid air. He turned his head a little farther around to confirm that the collection of bare-footed slaves in their ragged trousers were squatting in the shade, ready to bring up fresh charges and balls for the guns. All was well, he concluded, except that they still did not have a target to fire at.

He returned his attention to the British frigate and sighed. She drifted along under easy sail, flaunting her country's naval ensign just outside the reach of his guns. He had to admit she was a beautiful sight, her black and yellow hull contrasting with the pale blue water all about her. She was almost side on to him now, a long sleek hull topped with towering masts. As he looked, he noticed some movement on her quarterdeck. He pulled out his telescope and focused on the ship. There were several officers, one taller than the others, all with telescopes of their own focused towards the shore. At first he felt a flutter or excitement, thinking that they were looking at his battery. Perhaps they will close in to bombard me from the sea, he thought, but then he decided that it was something else that had caught their attention. A single fag soared up to the top of the mizzen mast and broke out in the breeze, and then came down again.

'Curious,' said Sybord. He chewed at the lower fridge of his moustache as he continued to watch. After a pause, the same flag rose back up and down the mast once more. 'What do you suppose that the ship is doing, sergeant? Did you see the flag just then? They might almost be trying to signal to someone.'

'It is a mystery why the navy do half of the things they do, sir,' replied DuPont, with a shrug. 'Doubtless he is in contact with the other ships.' Sybord turned his attention to the second, more distant British frigate, positioned opposite the harbour mouth.

'No, I do not think so,' he said. 'That other one flies no signals, and besides, they would have to show their flag on the far side of their ship if they wanted it to be seen from over there,' he said. He returned his attention to the group of officers on the quarterdeck. 'It is almost as if they want to attract someone's attention on shore. Who on earth would they be communicating with? See, now they have hoisted a lot of flags at once.'

'Perhaps it has something to do with the prisoners,' suggested the sergeant. Sybord lowered his telescope.

'Prisoners? What prisoners?' he asked. His deputy pointed over his shoulder with a jerk of his thumb towards the low hill behind him.

'There are some English naval officers living in the Venner's old place. Up on top of the hill, by the lane. One of them walks past here each morning at dawn and heads along the beach.' Sybord swung his telescope in the direction that his sergeant had pointed and the little white house swam into view. He re-focused, and the crisp image of a gangly young man with sandy hair appeared. He stood looking out to sea through a small telescope, his mouth working as if he was speaking to someone else. The artillery captain panned around a little farther and saw two older men. They were busy un-pegging squares of coloured cloth from a length of rope that hung down from the tree beside them.

'Merde!' he roared. 'Aux armes! Call out the guard! The enemy is amongst us!'

*****

'It's a very long signal, sir,' said Midshipman Croft as he peered out to sea. '*Titan* to *Rush*. Then the interrogative flag, so what follows will be a question.'

'Sir,' said Chapman as he looked up from the signal line. 'Can you hear something? Like a deal of shouting, maybe?' Sutton stopped un-pegging the flags and put his head on one side. Over the sound of the surf and the rush of the sea breeze through the palm trees, he heard faint but raised voices.

'It starts with "is",' continued the teenager, still focused on the frigate. 'I can't recall what the next flag group is without a signal book, but after that they are spelling out something.'

'It does sound a little like shouting,' said the captain to his steward. 'Is it coming from the beach?'

'S...U...T...T...O...I think it's your name, sir,' said the midshipman, the telescope still glued to his eye. The roar of a drum echoed through the trees from down by the shore.

'Shit!' said Chapman. 'I reckon we've been rumbled, sir.'

'Pull these rags down and hide them in the house,' ordered Sutton. 'Quickly, man!' The sailor rushed off with the bundle of flags in his arms. He leaped onto the veranda and through the door, knocking the table over in his haste.

'Mr Croft! Direct your gaze towards the shore battery. Tell me what you can see.' The teenager swung his telescope towards the beach.

'Oh, sir!' he exclaimed. 'There's an officer with a big

moustache leading some soldiers this way. He appears to be rather angry.'

'Chapman!' roared Sutton towards the house. 'Come now! We must depart, unless you wish to be hanged for a spy.'

The three men dashed around to the back of the building and cut across to the track. They were out of sight from the beach, on the down slope of the little hill, but the noise of the approaching soldiers was growing louder all the time.

'Follow me,' ordered Sutton, and they set off at a run down the lane with little more than the clothes on their backs. The only exception was Croft, who still carried the telescope. The sandy track merged into one of beaten red earth, with small, well tended fields on either side. Ahead of them the way skirted around a grove of tall, lush banana plants. Sutton led the way into the plantation, crashing through the thick rubbery leaves, and in an instant they were out of sight. From behind them came the sound of shouted orders and smashing as their little house was ransacked.

'Come on,' said their captain, pushing his way between the trees. 'Let us try and place some distance between us and any pursuit.' The big leaves clung to their clothes as they forced their way forwards, but they also sprung back behind when they passed, concealing them from prying eyes. After a few hundred yards the grove of trees came to an end. Beyond was another red earth track. It ran across their direction of travel with a ditch of gurgling, dirty water alongside it. Sutton peered out through the last of the banana plants, checked both ways, and then waved his companions on. They jumped across the ditch and dashed over the road and back into cover. This time they had plunged into a field of dense rows of lofty sugarcane that trembled in the wind. The stalks rose high above their heads, and their motion concealed, at least partially, the signs of their passage.

'Why do you suppose that there are so few people about,

sir?' asked Croft as they made their way forward. 'Normally these fields are thick with farm labourers.'

'Because it is Sunday today,' replied his captain. 'A day of rest, even for slaves, it would seem.'

'That's a bleeding stroke of luck, sir,' said Chapman, wiping his forehead on his shirt sleeve. 'Otherwise I reckon we'd have been collared pretty sharp. Do you suppose we've outpaced them flat-footed gunners?'

'For now, perhaps,' said Sutton. 'But they will soon raise the alarm. We had best keep moving, before they can arrange a proper pursuit.'

At first all went well for the fugitives. They worked their way deeper and deeper inland, always trying to stay in cover, and giving a wide berth to the occasional plantation building they saw amid the dense fields of sugarcane. At one stage the crops proved too thick for them to go cross-country and they were forced to risk a stage along a sheltered track. Their luck held for perhaps a half mile, before the sound of approaching hooves trotting briskly forced them to dive back into cover. The noise of the horse was soon joined by the jingling of a harness, and the fugitives cowered down, sure that a cavalry patrol was on their trail. Sutton peered out from between the fronds, to see a pony trap rattling by with a family out in their Sunday finest.

'Probably on their way back from church, sir,' said Croft, as Sutton brushed himself down.

'Doubtless,' said his captain, puffing out his cheeks with relief. 'Still, it was a timely warning for us against using the roads. Let us return to the fields.'

A little later they found that they had walked too close to a dwelling and were being plagued by a farm dog. Despite their best efforts to either befriend him or drive him away, the animal followed them across several fields, barking all the time. They had just concluded that they would have to lure him close enough to kill him, and had armed themselves with heavy branches for the purpose, when the first dart of lightning shot across the sky. The rumble of thunder that followed made the dog slink off with a howl. They watched it race away under a sky of boiling cloud, and large, heavy drops began to patter all around them.

At first the rain was welcome, as it washed through their hair and cooled their sweating faces. But then the sky became increasingly dark. The thunder grew in volume and the shower of rain swelled into a considerable downpour, soaking them to the skin. The ground began to soften underfoot, slowing their progress.

'Damn!' cursed Croft. 'I left my pea jacket back at the house when we left in such haste.'

'With respect, sir, at least you had a coat to leave,' said Chapman. 'Mine had a bleeding great hole cut in the back for one of them flags.'

'This rain is not wholly unwelcome, however,' said Sutton. 'That dog we encountered put me in mind of hounds. The French may well have some, for tracking run slaves. By rights this rain should wash away much of our trail.'

They pressed on into the deluge, but it was hard going. Their rain-sodden garments clung to their bodies, chaffing and annoying them with every step. The wind got up and drove sheets of water into their faces, blinding them as they walked. Sutton pointed a little way ahead, to where there was a small wooden lean-to. It was thatched with dried banana leaves and stood next to a field of sugarcane.

'Shall we try our luck there?' he suggested, and then, 'Have a care, Chapman. There are leeches all over that bush beside you.'

'Bleeding hell,' cried the sailor, jumping clear of the long grey tubes as they reached out towards his body heat. 'I am fine with indoors, sir. So long as it ain't alive with more of them buggers.'

A short dash through the tropical downpour and they clattered through the doorway and into the little hut. Some rusting tools rested against one wall. For now at least, the floor of beaten earth was dry.

'Do you suppose that our signal will have worked, sir?' asked the midshipman, a little while later, when they were sitting in a row with their backs to the wall of the shelter, staring out through the curtain of water that poured off the roof.

'I sincerely hope so, Mr Croft,' said Sutton. 'Else all our efforts will have been in vain, and we could have been resting in the convenience of our house.'

'Aye, be good to watch this storm through a layer of glass, sir,' added Chapman, scratching patterns in the dirt floor with his clasp knife.

'Quite so,' said the captain. 'My only concern is if Captain Clay should suspect a trap. He may think we were the French, making use of a captured signal book. I had intended to transmit something to reassure him. His birthday, for example, or his sister's name, but we were detected too soon.'

'So what do we do next, now that we have been rumbled, sir?'

'Let us stay here for the moment, while the rain lasts,' said Sutton. 'To answer your question with regard to the long term, we need to get off the island. The commandant will be very unforgiving to those who have been in communication with the enemy, no matter how crude the means employed. But till we have a plan to achieve that, we may as well stay dry. I will keep watch for the enemy, while you two get some rest.'

The companions settled down on the hard floor. Croft felt the first rumblings of hunger in his stomach, and his wet clothes were chill against his skin, but he was tired from all their running and he eventually slipped off to sleep. It seemed that he had hardly shut his eyes before he was being shaken awake. He opened them to find it had stopped raining, and the light outside had softened with the approach of evening. Sutton's face was close to his, a finger held up to his lips, while behind him Chapman peered through a gap between the slats.

'We need to go, Mr Croft,' he whispered. 'A patrol is coming in our direction.' The three men slipped away from the hut and vanished once more into the cover of the tall green stems of sugarcane.

*****

By nightfall, the fugitives had reached the very edge of the cultivated area of land around St Paul. Beyond the hill they were on was a ravine with a gushing stream flowing through it, and then the steeply forested mountains of the interior. They seemed to have shaken off any pursuit for now, and on the far side of the hill was another small shelter, similar to that they had used earlier. Tired and hungry, they settled down inside and quickly fell asleep.

Later that night, Sutton was awake in an instant, wondering what had woken him so abruptly. It was quite dark in the little shack, and the packed earth under him was hard as iron. From the ache the ground had left in his limbs, he could tell that he had been asleep for several hours. He could also tell, as he pushed himself into a sitting position, that both his companions were tense and awake too.

'What was that sound?' he whispered. 'Another of those damned patrols?'

'I don't think so, sir,' said Croft. They all stopped to listen. The night was full of the noises of the tropics. Insects hummed, frogs croaked and nameless creatures rustled through the undergrowth, but there seemed to be no human sound. And then they heard it again. The low rumble of distant gunfire.

'That's a bunch of cannons firing, or I ain't never heard them before, sir,' said Chapman from his other side.

'Do you still have your spy glass?' asked Sutton. He felt cool metal press against his arm as the midshipman held it towards him in the dark. 'My thanks, Mr Croft.' He grasped the telescope, rose to his feet and went outside. The other two men followed him through the low entrance. Above their heads the clouds had been tattered by the night breeze, and patches of starlight shone through. Behind them loomed the interior mountains, dark and impenetrable. Off to one side they could see the lights of St Paul. At their feet was a rolling landscape of black fields, punctuated by clusters of light from the plantations and farms dotted here and there. It stretched down to the shoreline, beyond which was an endless, vast ocean of dark water, brushed by starlight, and stretching away to the far horizon. Then he saw a line of orange tongues flash out, sending light washing across the sea. And in that flash, before the boom of the guns could reach him, he saw the battle that was raged in the night.

Two frigates formed a shape like a T, perhaps a mile off shore. One seemed to be at anchor, to judge from the lack of sail it carried. It was bow-on to the land and was firing rapid broadside after broadside at the second ship. That frigate was under modest sail, and seemed to be picking its way towards the first ship. A pair of orange tongues showed where it returned a little fire from twin guns mounted in its bow. As it was heading directly towards the first ship, the cannon along its sides had no target to aim at. There was a third source of light and flame. One of the shore batteries was firing too.

'Captain Clay did trust our signal, sir!' exclaimed Croft.

'That must be the *Titan* at anchor, and the *Prudence* coming down the channel towards her. How marvellous! See how she pounds away.'

'Aye, that Frog ship is proper screwed,' said Chapman with satisfaction. 'Beggin' your pardon for my language, sir.'

'Granted,' said Sutton. 'I believe you may have the truth of it. If that channel is too narrow to turn in, the *Prudence* can only sail on and try and lay herself alongside the *Titan*. She will take a fearful pounding all the way in, much as our poor *Rush* did.' He focused his telescope on the scene below them. The surface of the water had become obscured with gun smoke, which drifted in clouds towards the shore. The positions of the ships were still obvious to see, their tall masts soaring above the fog. There was another flash of light as the *Titan* fired again, and he saw that the *Prudence's* foretopgallant mast hung down in a mass of severed rigging, but still she came on.

'Will you look at all that flame and smoke, sir,' said Chapman. 'It's like Vauxhall Pleasure Gardens on November the bleeding fifth.'

'It's a grand sight, sir,' agreed Croft. 'The old *Rush* is being revenged at last. God, I wish I was there.' Sutton said nothing, but he wished that he were there too, beside his friend, in the midst of the fight. Then he looked up from the telescope, deep in thought. All that flame and smoke, Chapman had said. He turned the words over in his mind, aware that an idea was forming. Flame and smoke, the first could guide them in the dark, the second would conceal them from hostile eyes. He tried to think back to his walks along that beach of black sand, just after dawn. At the time his mind had been cluttered with tortured thoughts of Betsey Clay and revenge against Windham, making him take little note of his surroundings. Then his head started to clear. He could remember something at his feet, something very important. Something he had seen, but not really noted at the time.

'Fishing boats,' he muttered.

'Beg pardon, sir?' said Chapman, looking around.

'Fishing boats,' he repeated, more strongly. 'There are two little ones, pulled up on the sand, this side of the battery. I have passed them most mornings.'

'I know the ones, sir,' said Croft. 'Didn't you say they were too small for the ocean?'

'I did,' confirmed Sutton. 'But we need not cross an ocean to reach the *Titan*. A mile and a half of paddling will answer well enough.'

'Go back down back to the beach, sir?' queried Chapman, sucking in his cheeks. 'Won't it be alive with Frogs?'

'It may well be, but every man jack of them will be looking at your Vauxhall Gardens display. With all that gun smoke, I doubt they will mark three men in a little boat.'

'Well, I did say I wanted to be out there, sir,' said the midshipman.

'And soon you shall be, Mr Croft,' said Sutton. 'Let us head down the path over there. It seems to tend towards the beach.'

*****

Sutton's flame and smoke were growing all the time as the three men hurried towards the sea. They tried their best to move quickly, but they had been running and hiding for much of the day, and none of them had eaten since breakfast. The patchwork of fields seemed like a labyrinth in the dark, with just the distant flicker of light and the thunder of the guns to guide them forward. After an hour, they struggled up to the top of a low rise, close to the shore with tall walls of sugar cane boxing them in. The sound of the gunfire was very loud, the concussion splashing across the underside of the low clouds, and they could see the battle laid out before them. The two frigates were locked together now, side by side, with both their full broadsides hammering away at each other. A glow of light swept across the sea as the guns fired, making the shape of the palm trees that fringed the shore stand out like dark phantoms for an instant. The blast of the cannon was so loud now that they could all feel it, deep in the chest, as well as a sound heard by the ear.

'That *Titan*'s got her beat all ways up,' said Chapman. 'I never saw cannon plied so brisk.' Sutton looked at the volcano of fire that lit up the sea. The sailor was right; one of the ships was being overwhelmed by the other. The fight could not last much longer. He estimated how far they still had to go. Perhaps another half mile?

'Come on, lads, we need to make haste,' he said. 'Who still has the wind to run?' He forced his tired limbs into a shambling trot, and, followed by the others, he disappeared down the track towards the beach. The groves of trees on either side towered up above them once more, like the black walls of a canyon.

Now they moved more slowly, creeping forward in short dashes between the dark shadows cast by trees. Exhaustion and fear combined to slow their progress as they neared the sea. They could still hear gunfire ahead, but the tone and volume had changed.

'I believe it is just the shore battery firing now, sir,' said Croft, as they crouched down behind a palm close to the beach. 'The *Prudence* must have struck her colours.'

'No end of gun smoke in the air, mind, sir,' added Chapman. He turned his face to the gentle breeze and sniffed. 'That or we be right close to the Gates of Hell. I would recognise that brimstone smell anywhere.' Sutton was silent as he concentrated on the way ahead. The big guns of the battery boomed out again, sending a flash of orange light into the night. In the moment before dark returned, he saw the curve of the upturned boats, close to a pair of palm trees a little farther along the shore.

'Follow me,' he whispered. The three men ran forwards with their bodies crouched over till they reached the boats. They dropped down into the sand beside the hulls.

'Not sure as this one will answer, sir,' muttered the voice of Chapman from the other side of the two hulls. 'Feels to be a might snug for three, like.'

'Help me with this other one, Mr Croft,' said Sutton, and the two men rolled it over on the sand. It was a long, shallow craft, made from overlapping planks. From memory he remembered that the hull was painted a faded blue. Both men groped around the interior, their hands busy in the dark.

'Hull is sound enough, sir,' whispered the midshipman. 'I have found a bailer stowed under this seat, but no oars.'

'I have a paddle here,' said the captain. 'But it does feel rather small. Chapman, has your boat got any oars?' There was a pause while the sailor scrabbled underneath his boat.

'Sorry, sir,' he replied. 'The owner must have taken them away.'

'Sir!' hissed Croft. 'I can see another patrol!' He pointed down the beach towards the battery, where an orange light was bobbing towards them. The guns boomed out again, silhouetting the little group of black figures. Each one had a musket over his shoulder. Their long shadows raced across the sand, then vanished into the night. The three men looked around, desperate for somewhere to hide on the flat sand.

'Under the boats!' ordered Sutton. 'Now!' Chapman heaved up one side of the smaller boat, and slid from view like an eel under a rock. The other two twisted their boat over them and lay together, tight as spoons. The night was already warm and balmy and it became even closer for the two men under the hull. The air grew stale, with an added note of tarred wood and fish, caught long ago. The guns from the shore battery boomed out once more, the shock wave reverberating on the hull as if it were the skin of a drum. Then they heard voices, quiet at first against the background hiss of the sea, but growing louder all the time. They seemed to stop near to the boats, and what sounded like an order was given. Now a set of footsteps crunched in the sand close to where they lay. A pause and then the thump of a musket butt as it struck the wood of the hull, the sound shocking as it boomed around inside the boat.

'Non, rien ici,' said a bored voice, loud and close, and the footsteps withdrew. Sutton felt his racing heart bang in his ears. He waited for the feeling to pass, and for the voices to fade. When they had, he inched up the side of the boat to create a little gap. The night air smelt pure and clean by comparison, and he sucked it in hungrily. Then he looked for the patrol's orange lamp, still dancing along the shore, but now far down the beach.

'All clear,' he said, and he held up the side of the boat to allow Croft to emerge, coughing and spluttering. The two men heaved their boat over once more, then went around it to release the steward.

'Christ, but it were close under there,' gasped Chapman, as they lifted the hull off him. 'Proper ripe, like a Billingsgate slop bucket.'

'Come on,' urged Sutton. 'Let us be away before the next patrol should arrive.' Chapman took the bow, the two officers each took a side of the stern, and between them they managed to carry the boat, stumbling, down to the shallows.

'No tiller at all,' said Sutton, feeling around the flat stern. 'That paddle must have served as one. Well, we have no oars, so we shall have to make shift with what we have. Chapman, you go into the bow to act as lookout. Kindly go in the middle, Mr Croft, and I shall paddle in the stern like a Mohawk. When I can pull no more, we can change about.'

They pushed the boat deeper into the water, coral scraping against the hull, and then it floated free. They all scrambled aboard and took their places in the little craft. The waves that lapped past them were small, and Sutton found he was able to paddle the heavy boat slowly forwards, each dip of the blade accompanied by a swirl of phosphorescence in the black water. The two frigates had long since stopped firing, giving him little mark to steer towards. Just then a line of orange flames shot out from the battery, followed by the tearing shriek as the shot flew over their heads. They all ducked down instinctively, and when Sutton looked up it was dark once more.

'Keep a good watch in the bow there, Chapman,' he called. 'Use the light of the next salvo to see by.'

'Aye aye, sir,' came the reply, and the boat paddled on into the night.

'Do you mark the *Titan*?' asked the captain, after a while.

'I ain't sure as I do, sir,' the sailor replied. 'I thought I saw the loom of a ship, half a point more to starboard, but there is that much smoke about.'

'Half a point you say,' said Sutton and he turned the boat a little farther out towards the open sea.

'We are making decent progress, sir,' said Croft as the battery fired again. 'Those guns look to be a good two cables away now.'

'I would like to say it is all my hard work with a very indifferent paddle, but I think much of the credit must go to this off-shore breeze propelling us along,' replied the captain.

'I reckon there's a couple of knots of current an' all, sir,' added Chapman, sniffing the air. 'Tide will have turned. Might I try with the spy glass, Mr Croft? Help me see this barky we needs to find, like.' The midshipman passed it forward and Chapman studied the dark night with care. The boat carried on out to sea.

'That shore battery has stopped firing, sir,' said Croft, a few minutes later.

'So it has,' replied Sutton. 'Will you take over with the paddle please, Mr Croft? I am quite spent.' The men changed places and the boat's progress resumed. Sutton massaged his tired arms and looked back towards the island. The smoke was clearing now, and he could see the occasional light from the shore as it twinkled and danced off the water, giving them at least some mark to steer by in the dark. Chapman was right about the tide, Sutton thought to himself. The glow of St Paul was much more distant than his efforts with their feeble paddle could have achieved. They must be several miles out now. In the bow Chapman muttered a curse under his breath, and turned around in the boat.

'Any sign of those ships?' asked his captain.

'Not ships, sir, but I can see some bleeding breakers ahoy!' he cried. 'We must be at the edge of the reef. Pull hard, Mr Croft!'

The sound of waves crashing against the hard coral shelf was loud in the night. Now that his attention was called to the sound, Sutton realised he must have been hearing the roar for some time, but a combination of fatigue and the lulling tropical night had meant that he had missed the significance of the growing noise. Now they could all see the thick line of silver in the darkness, lying like a wall across the ocean. Sutton stood up in the boat to gauge the state of the surf as it broke ahead of them.

'The waves seem lower ahead than to either side,' he said, pointing. 'Up your helm a touch, Mr Croft, and then paddle like fury. You and I too, Chapman. Let's get as much weigh on the boat as we can, and keep her straight!' Croft redoubled his effort, and both of the other men leant out of the boat to paddle with their hands. The surf grew closer as the tide sucked them towards it, the noise becoming louder all the time. It filled the night with spray and sound. Dark hills reared up to either side of the little boat, flecked with foam, and the bow lifted sluggishly to a wave.

'Keep paddling,' yelled Sutton, as the hull scrapped to a halt on the coral and water flooded in over the bow. The next moment a wave lifted them, the boat heaved up and corkscrewed, first one way and then the other, almost pitching them out. And then, suddenly, they were through. Croft managed a few more strokes and then collapsed over the handle of his paddle.

'Chapman, take over with the oar,' said Sutton. 'Get us clear of this coral. I will see about bailing us dry.'

Now that they were beyond the edge of the reef, the nature of the sea was transformed. They were in open water, and long waves swooped out of the night, to first lift them up and then let them sink down again. Water sloshed freely around the interior, making the little boat heavy and inert, but gradually Sutton with the bailer and Croft with his hands managed to get most of it out. Chapman lay down the paddle and got to his feet, carefully balancing against the roll of the boat. He swept the night with the telescope, turning in the boat as he did so.

'Any sign of the *Titan*?' asked Sutton.

'Can't say as there is anything certain, sir,' replied the lookout. 'There could be something in the night away over yonder, another few miles out to sea.' Sutton considered the situation. None of them had eaten for almost twenty hours now. His limbs trembled with fatigue as he sat in the boat, and he felt weary to his bones. They were all almost spent from a day of running and hiding, even before they had reached the boats. It was only the adrenaline rush of their escape that had kept them going through all the hours of paddling, and now that had drained away. In the dark he could tell that his two companions were in a similar, exhausted state.

'Two miles or twenty miles, it's too far for us this night,' he decided. 'Let's settle down and get some sleep. I am sure all we need is a little honest daylight to be found by our friends in the morning.'

'Aye, aye, sir,' said the sailor. He lay the paddle down on the floor of the boat with a clatter. 'Should we set watches?'

'Not tonight, Chapman,' said Sutton. 'Poor Mr Croft seems to be asleep on his bench already. Let us take our places in the bottom of the boat, and trust to Old Father Neptune to look after us.'

Sutton helped the youngster down onto the floor of the boat, and they squeezed in either side of him. The wood was damp, but they were past caring, and exhaustion did the rest. Even the alarming way that the boat rode the big ocean rollers, with the bow pointing to the sky as they climbed a wave, before tipping down the back of it, did little to disturb their sleep. The closeness of the squeeze at least meant that their shared body warmth compensated for the remaining trickle of water that flowed over the bottom of the boat. Croft fell asleep in an instant and Chapman and Sutton were not long to follow.

It was some time after dawn when the men awoke. The sun had risen a few hours ago, but it was only when it cleared the gunwale to shine down onto Sutton's face that he opened his eyes. The first thing he saw was Chapman's gaping mouth as he snored contentedly on his captain's chest. He shook the others awake and pulled himself upright. He had to steady himself on their shoulders, for the boat still rushed up and down with each roller that swept under them. He pointed the little telescope outwards and followed the blue horizon with care. Reunion was still in sight, but only just. The island was a small green hump on the far horizon with towering white clouds above it. It took Sutton no more than a moment to realise that it was now impossibly distant for their little boat with its single paddle, even if wind and the current were not still pulling them ever farther out to sea. He swept around in a circle again as he checked the lonely ocean once more.

'Any sign of the squadron, sir?' asked Croft.

'I am afraid not,' said Sutton quietly. He closed the telescope and sat back down again on the bench. Chapman licked at his lips.

'Has anyone got something to drink?'

CHAPTER 11 LOST

'Come in,' said Sir George Montague, in response to the knock on the door. He looked up from the slim leather volume in his hand and peered over his reading glasses at the midshipman who came through into the poorly lit cabin.

'Mr Pella's respects sir, and we have just heard from the *Titan*,' he said. 'They have secured their prize and are proceeding out to sea as ordered.'

'Have they, by Jove?' said the commodore. 'That is excellent news.' The words were right for the occasion, but there was something missing in the tone. Montague looked out of the stern windows into the black night beyond, but he could see nothing save the orange glow from the cabin's single lamp, multiplied in all the individual panes of glass. 'Is there any sign of the other enemy frigates putting out of St Paul?' he asked.

'No, sir, all quiet as quiet. It was just the one ship that came out,' said the midshipman, his voice growing in enthusiasm. 'They say it was the one that did for the *Rush*. She fell right into Captain Clay's trap. It was the first action I have seen, sir, and I never imagined such noise and fury! Why, the cannon fire lit up half the night! And the good old *Titan* gave the Frogs what for in very short order. That will learn them.'

'Hmmm,' said the commodore. He looked at the young man's glowing face. 'A night action can be mighty prodigious. This is all highly satisfactory, of course.' He continued to stare at the midshipman for a while, drumming his fingers on the back cover of his book. Then he came to a decision. He marked his page with a slip of paper and put the book down on the table beside him. Then he removed his glasses and put them into the inner pocket of his coat. Finally he addressed the teenager. 'Kindly send an acknowledgment to the *Titan*, together with my congratulations, and tell them that the rest of the squadron shall follow them out to sea directly. In the meantime, send a night signal to the *Echo*. Commodore to Echo, captain to repair on board, if you please.'

'Aye aye, sir.' The midshipman saluted and left the room. Montague let his eyes drift around his cabin, as if inspiration might be found amongst its many dark shadows and black corners.

'What the bloody hell do I do now?' he asked the dimly lit space. After a while he got up and began to pace up and down, groping for inspiration, but nothing came. From outside his cabin he heard the shrill sound of boatswain's pipes and the stamp of marines saluting. A little while later his guest was shown in.

'Brandy, Nicholas?' he asked, not looking around from the decanter. 'I know that I bloody well need one.'

'Yes, please, Sir George,' replied Windham. 'Are we toasting the *Titan*'s success?'

'That would be a right and proper thing to do, would it not?' said the commodore, still busy with the drinks. 'From a strategic point of view Captain Clay has undoubtedly made up for the unfortunate loss of the *Rush*. But I am surprised that you should want to drink to his triumph, given its possible implications.'

'Please be cautious in what you say, Sir George,' said Windham, his eyes darting around the cabin.

'Calm yourself. I have dispensed with my steward tonight,' said his host, as he came over with the glasses. 'Rest assured that we are quite alone and can speak openly with one another. Do please be seated.' Montague sat down behind his desk and contemplated his guest for a moment. 'Before we begin, may I proffer a word of advice?'

'By all means, Sir George.'

'When arriving onboard ship at four bells in the mid watch, it is normal to come by the larboard side with none of the usual naval ceremony. Your decision to insist on the boatswains calls, the marines' salute and side boys, although it is undoubtedly your right, will have roused the whole ship's company, including the watch asleep below decks.'

'Sorry, Sir George,' said Windham. 'I have been rather fatigued of late. Perhaps I was not thinking straight.'

His host slammed down his drink on his desk in anger. 'And ain't that the whole bloody problem, Nicholas?' he demanded. 'You have not been thinking straight this whole commission. I have absolutely no idea how I shall extract you from this hole that you have made for yourself.'

'What has brought this on, Sir George?'

'Do you truly not comprehend the danger you are now in?' said the commodore, raising his eyes to the ceiling. 'As a result of the *Titan*'s little victory tonight?'

'Surely it is good for us, Sir George,' he replied. 'It is as you said. It will serve to redress the balance back in our favour. Perhaps it will mean that we can now lay to one side the loss of the *Rush*.'

'Lay to one side!' Montague was incredulous. 'Good God, man, do you truly see nothing to alarm you? Have you given no consideration to the signals that Clay received from the shore? The fact that they have now proved to be wholly accurate, for example, rather than some low French trick, as I had hoped?'

'Yessss,' said Windham, his face still blank. 'And what are the implications of that?'

'Think, Nicholas, for once try to think,' urged the commodore. 'If the signals were accurate, they can only have come from officers of the *Rush*. Who else would be at liberty to send such a message? Which means that there must be survivors of your ridiculous battle, yes? And they are at large on Reunion, right now. Like Lieutenant Wise or Mr Appleby? Even Captain Sutton, perhaps? In any event, they will be gentlemen and fellow officers, not just sailors whose views might be discounted. Credible witnesses, Nicholas, to what truly happened when you and the *Rush* fought the *Prudence*?'

Windham's face went pale at the thought.

'But...but...they are still prisoners of the French,' he stuttered.

'For now they are, but we have just captured one of their frigates!' exclaimed the commodore. 'Full of officers and men who are now our prisoners, whom we can exchange for the return of our own. The French might send out a launch under a flag of truce tomorrow to arrange the parole, and the survivors of the *Rush* could be back with us within days. Will they all agree with your version of events, or will they come back demanding justice from the man who betrayed them?'

Windham buried his head in his hands but said nothing. After a pause the commodore carried on.

'Can I take it from your evident distress that I should expect them to denounce you? Oh great God, man, what have you done?'

'I thought I would—'

'No Nicholas,' interrupted Montague. 'Thinking is precisely what you have not been about. What do you suppose happens when the navy loses a ship, eh? Do you think that the Admiralty will say, "Tis no grave matter, we have another"? If Captain Sutton has survived, and his first action on his return is not to call you out and put a bullet between your eyes, he will face a court martial for the loss of the *Rush*. What do you imagine his defense will be? And even if he is indeed dead, there will still be a Board of Enquiry into the loss of his ship.'

'Oh God,' wailed Windham. 'What have I done?'

'A dreadful, dreadful act,' said the commodore. 'Not only have you destroyed a fine ship, but what of all those who were killed or injured, to no good purpose? I can see no influence of mine that will suffice to save you. You have blood on your hands, Nicholas.' Windham gulped at his brandy and then coughed and spluttered.

'When will matters come to a head, Sir George?' he asked, when the choking fit had passed.

'Perhaps not immediately, to be sure. I have now ordered the squadron out to sea. I want us to be patrolling over the horizon by tomorrow; in the hope that we may lure the French into coming out seeking revenge, so there will be no prospect of a rapid exchange of prisoners.'

The commander of the *Echo* raised his head, a little hope in his eyes. 'And we still do not know that this mystery signaller is Sutton,' he said. 'It might be one who was not privy to the intended plan of attack.'

'So you admit there was an arrangement that you disregarded?' said Montague.

'Yes, there was,' said Windham. 'But it was only Sutton, his lieutenant and I that were present when it was agreed. This man who signalled might be another officer altogether. If he is junior, say a midshipman, confused doubtless by the battle, who can truly say what he saw? It would still be my word against his.'

'Perhaps, but what of all the other crew who were on board the *Rush*, or on the *Echo* for that matter? What will they say when questioned?' said the commodore. Windham was dismissive.

'What of them, Sir George? Their view of the action was through a deal of smoke and confusion. Their account will never stand against that of a gentleman. No, so long as Sutton is dead, all shall be well, and Uncle Percy can rest easy in his grave at long last.'

*****

The boat rose up and down, up and down, in an endless rhythm as each wave swept past them. And with each motion they were nudged a little farther out to sea. The mound of Reunion faded to a tiny speck of distant grey before it vanished altogether. Now the horizon was a pure, uninterrupted line of deep blue sea below an empty sky. Above them the sun beat down, heavy and hot. It drew the moisture from the three men as they tried to shelter from it at one end of the tiny hull.

Chapman had fashioned a scrap of shade for them. He had lashed the paddle upright to the seat in the stern with their belts, and they had all donated their jackets to supply the cloth for the canopy. He had showed surprising skill in its construction, with little more than his clasp knife to help him. He had opened the seams on the garments, parting their linings from the broadcloth, and lain the pieces out into a rough tent shape. Then he had joined the various panels by first marrying the buttons on one jacket with the holes on another, and then using splinters of wood cut from the hull to pin the remaining cloth together. The final touch had been to prise nails loose from the thwarts of the boat to catch and hold the bell of material into place against the side of the boat. The sun's rays still shone through the cover in places, and with three of them huddled underneath it was hot and stuffy, but it was better than lying out in the full heat of the sun.

Sutton awoke from his fitful doze in the shade to find that Croft was watching him. The teenagers face was badly sun burnt, raw and pink in places, flaking skin in others. He tried to smile reassuringly at him, but stopped when he felt his dry lips crack with the effort.

'Time?' he asked, his tongue swollen and clumsy in his mouth.

'After...noon...sir,' answered Croft. He squinted towards the sun with an outstretched arm, then indicated how far it was above the horizon.

'Forget...sir,' replied Sutton, wagging a finger at the boy. As he did so he noticed the back of his hand was red and burnt, and he pushed it into the shade. 'You...sleep?'

'Little...then...pain,' muttered the midshipman. He pointed towards his belly. Sutton nodded. He too had been tormented by stomach cramps earlier that day. He looked across at Chapman, and saw that the sailor was awake too. 'You?' he asked, pointing towards his belly.

'Bad,' whispered the seaman, barely able to speak. He pulled himself out of the shelter. 'Going...die...sir.' Sutton was unsure if Chapman had meant it as a question or a statement. He chose a question and shook his head.

'No,' he said. Then with a further effort, 'Rescue...soon.' He pulled himself slowly up and clung onto Croft's shoulder while he settled his balance. What is wrong with me, he pondered, feeling much less stable than the motion of the boat might account for. He pulled out the telescope and searched the empty horizon. Then he sat down again.

'Rescue?' muttered Chapman. Sutton shook his head.

'Soon,' he croaked again.

'Soon,' whispered Chapman, disbelief evident in his face. 'Or...die.' A strange animal sound came from farther down the boat. Sutton turned and saw that Croft's shoulders were heaving. His face was torn in pain, and a low moan came from his mouth as he tearlessly wept.

'Not...die,' he wheezed, his voice barely audible. 'Not...fair!'

'No!' croaked Sutton, putting an arm around the teenager and pulling him close. He glared at Chapman 'Not...here. Rescue!' His eyes met with those of the seaman, who stared back at him. 'Not...die!' he repeated.

'Fff...k...ing...miracle,' muttered Chapman, rolling back under the shelter.

*****

'What would you gentlemen care to drink?' asked Montague, as the three captains sat in the pleasant early morning sunshine that streamed through the stern windows of the *Black Prince*. 'I can supply coffee, tea or small beer. Captain Clay?'

'A coffee would be most welcome, Sir George,' said the captain of the *Titan* as he held his cup towards the steward. He deliberately tried not to look at his fellow guest, hoping to control the flush of anger he had felt when he had first seen him come into the cabin.

'I will have the beer, if you please,' said Windham. The commodore shot him a glance from beneath his brows. Windham looked as if he had not slept at all for the last few days. His eyes were sunken and dark, and his speech had a slur to it already. He drank thirstily at the beer, without waiting for his host to be served.

'Just coffee for me too, please Thomas,' said Montague, laying emphasis on the word coffee. 'I trust that you gentlemen are fond of smoked fish? The hands caught some manner of local breed a few days ago, and Thomas has had it smoked for us. He used a keg borrowed from the cooper, and some smoldering fragments of oak supplied by the carpenter.

It may not be your regular Scot's kipper, by I live in hope it may be palatable. If, however, your preference is the Devil you know, then that dish there contains fried salt pork and eggs. Do please let us break our fast.'

'I will gladly make a trial of your fish, Sir George,' said Clay.

'Nothing wrong with an honest portion of bacon and eggs, I find,' said Windham, helping himself from the dish. He clattered the cover back untidily, and silence descended over the commodore's breakfast table once more.

'And how does your prize fare?' asked Montague, hoping to get some sort of conversation flowing on professional matters. He reached forward to straighten the lid of the dish as Clay replied.

'We completed the essential repairs to her yesterday evening, and sent her off to the Cape under the command of Lieutenant Preston,' he replied. 'She is a very sound frigate, a little knocked about by the rough fashion in which we fought her, but nothing that a naval dockyard will not be able to put right. I am certain the Admiralty will buy her into the service, and a fine addition she will make.'

'Splendid,' enthused the commodore. 'And the *Titan* was but lightly damaged, I collect?'

'Six dead and ten wounded, Sir George,' said Clay. 'Once I have my prize crew back, I will be in almost as good a shape as before the action.'

'What a lowly butcher's bill,' said Windham, through a mouthful of breakfast. 'The Frogs must have fought very indifferently.' Clay lay down his knife and fork and looked at him for the first time.

'And what do you mean by that remark?' he demanded. Montague lay a cautionary hand on his sleeve.

'I am sure Captain Windham meant his remark to be of a positive character,' he said. 'Naturally a triumph achieved at such a low cost is doubly welcome. But it would be instructive to understand how the feat was achieved. Perhaps you would favour me with the particulars?'

'Of course, Sir George,' said Clay. 'Captain Windham is quite wrong. The French actually fought very well, in spite of the defective position they found themselves in. Much of the credit for our victory must go to how well prepared we were for the action. The intelligence we received from the shore proved most valuable. Acting on it, we were able to deploy the *Titan* in the perfect position to ambush the *Prudence*, undetected by the enemy. The nature of the channel was such that she could only approach us bow on, without any opportunity to turn aside or retreat. The flow of the tide brought her onto our guns, and the speed and accuracy with which my men served their pieces did the rest.'

'And I am quite sure we both appreciate and value your excellent victory,' said Montague. He fixed his dark eyes on Windham. 'Don't we, Nicholas?'

'I give you joy of your victory, sir,' said the *Echo*'s captain. He drained his mug of small beer, and immediately held it out for the steward to refill. Clay turned back to his host.

'How do you propose we should defeat these last two French frigates, Sir George?' he asked.

'I had hoped that our dropping back over the horizon would prompt them to come out from St Paul,' said the commodore. 'And yesterday evening, it seemed to have worked. My lookout sighted one of their ship's topsails on the horizon, but the moment I gave chase they turned tail. The *Black Prince* is thought of as swift in the service, but could I close with them? We chased them all the way back to Reunion. And therein lies the problem, gentlemen. They seem every bit as fast as our ships, and after your capture of the *Prudence*, I suspect they shall be very reluctant to give battle. What is to stop them cutting and running whenever we hove into sight?'

'Is that such a problem, Sir George?' asked Windham. 'So long as we have them bottled up in St Paul, they can be of no threat to the John Company trade.'

'That is true,' said Montague. 'But it will take only one bad storm to push us off station, and out they will come to plunder our commerce once more.'

'And even if the weather is fine, want of supplies will drive us back to Cape Town before long,' added Clay.

'Let us keep to our plan to lure them out for now,' said Montague. 'We will maintain our station beneath the horizon. Captain Windham, you and the *Echo* will be in the centre of the line, due south of Reunion. I shall be to the east, and the *Titan* to the west. We shall be strung out like a net, ready to catch the enemy. Is that clear?'

'Perfectly, Sir George,' replied Clay.

'As you wish,' said Windham.

'Excellent,' said the commodore. 'Would anyone care for more breakfast?'

'Not for me, I thank you,' said the captain of the *Titan*. 'But there was another matter I wanted to discuss, Sir George.' He drew several sheets of paper from the inner pocket of his coat. 'I have a full list of the French complement from the *Prudence*. Their captain fell during the battle, but we took over a hundred and fifty prisoners, including two officers of lieutenant rank, and seven midshipman. We now have plenty of persons for us to exchange for the survivors of the *Rush*. I could certainly use a draft of prime seamen to make good my losses from battle and fever, and we owe it to the noble souls who gave us such excellent intelligence to see them released without delay.'

'I would urge caution, sir,' said Windham, sitting up and stifling a belch. 'Do we honestly want to strengthen the enemy by the return of so many prisoners to them at this time?'

'Now, there is a surprise for you!' exclaimed Clay. He threw down his napkin and rounded on his fellow guest. 'Captain Windham would sooner our men continue to rot in Reunion. What might your motive be behind that suggestion, eh?'

'What the bloody hell is that supposed to mean?' said Windham, rising unsteadily from the table.

'Only that I find your reluctance to have the survivors of the *Rush* released rather eloquent,' said Clay. 'What did happen when you fought the *Prudence*? Perhaps we should ask some of our new French prisoners for their account of the battle?'

'Gentlemen, can you please keep your discourse civil,' urged the commodore.

'Well, isn't that you all over,' spat Windham, leaning across the table. 'You would value the word of a bloody Frenchman above that of a fellow captain.'

'So answer the damned question!' yelled Clay, rising to his feet too. 'Why are you so reluctant for the survivors of the *Rush* to be returned to us?'

'I stated my reasons just now!' shouted Windham. 'After over a year out here I make no doubt that the French are running short of sailors. That is doubtless the real reason why you defeated the *Prudence* with such ease. I think it foolish to permit their two remaining frigates to be reinforced by returning these prisoners to them.'

'I defeated the *Prudence* because I chose to fight with her, Windham. You should try it on occasion, assuming that you have the courage for it!'

'Please, will you both moderate your tone,' begged Montague. 'Before words are said that cannot be unsaid.'

'Sir George, these are our own men we are talking about!' urged Clay. 'It may well include Captain Sutton. I hope to

God I am never made prisoner with Captain Windham to rely on for my release.'

'That is a damned insult,' shouted Windham.

'Silence, both of you!' roared Montague, thumping the table. 'May I remind you that this is my cabin, where you are both guests, not some tavern for you to brawl in! Take your places once more, gentlemen. That is a direct order!' The two officers continued to glare across the table at each other, their faces red and flushed, but they both slowly sat down again.

'That is better,' continued their host. 'Now, I am quite sure that Captain Windham meant his suggestion to delay any prisoner exchange in a constructive manner. However, not withstanding his view, there is of course no question of us leaving our men in the hands of the enemy. Captain Clay, I thank you for your list. I shall send an officer into St Paul under a flag of truce, as soon as convenient, to start to negotiate an exchange of prisoners.'

'You have my gratitude,' said Clay, not looking at Windham. 'I will leave the list with you then, Sir George. If matters are concluded here, might you pass the word for my barge? I have much still to attend to aboard the *Titan*. I thank you for an excellent breakfast.'

Once Clay had left, Windham turned on Montague.

'An exchange of prisoners, Sir George?' he whined. 'Why not simply place a noose around my neck now, and be done with?'

'Do not tempt me, Nicholas,' he snapped. 'You forget yourself! Not only am I your superior officer, I am your only friend in this dire position you now occupy. Let me remind you that both the sense of obligation I feel to your late uncle and my patience are not without limit.'

'I am sorry, Sir George,' muttered his guest. 'I meant no disrespect.'

'Better,' said his host. 'Now, were you attending to any of what was said, or were you too busy with the small beer?'

'I heard most of it, in particular the fashion in which that bastard Clay virtually accused me of being a coward.'

'Good, in which case you will also have noted that my only commitment was to promptly send a flag of truce into St Paul to commence talks. There will doubtless be plenty of delay to any negotiations, processes to be resolved, lists to be drawn up. Is a French midshipman the same as two British petty officers, and so forth. In my experience such matters can be made to take quite a time. Meanwhile, the French prisoners to be exchanged are currently on their way to the Cape, which is close to three thousand miles away. No, it is problems nearer at hand that should concern you.'

'What do you mean?' asked the captain of the *Echo*, holding out his glass to be refilled.

'No more beer for Captain Windham, thank you, Thomas,' snapped Montague. 'Please leave us, now.'

'Aye aye, sir,' said the steward. He placed down the jug of beer and left the cabin. Montague walked over to his desk, opened a draw, and returned with a large sheet of grubby paper which he held by the extreme edges. It had been folded repeatedly, and showed signs of having passed through many pairs of hands, most of them none too clean. He placed it in front of Windham.

'What do you make of this?' he said. The paper had a block of text in the centre written out in a reasonable script. All around the edge, in widening circles, were seven or eight signatures and perhaps seventy shaky crosses, each with a neat little note beside it.

'It is obviously a round robin of some description, produced in the usual cowardly manner such that none of the instigators can be identified,' said Windham. He read the mark nearest to him. '*Owen Richards, his mark.* Now, there is a coincidence for you. I have an ordinary seaman in my afterguard by that exact name.'

'Oh for God's sake, man, are you quite witless?' snapped Montague. 'What you hold is a petition from your crew! It was sent to me anonymously yesterday. You had best read the middle section.'

'*To Commodore Sir George Montague, Knight of the Most Honourable Order...*'

'You can pass over that part,' said Montague. 'Read the main message.'

'*We, the loyal hands of the* Echo,' began Windham. 'Loyal! That is rich! When they send such things behind my back?'

'Just read it, Nicholas, I beg of you.'

'*...the loyal hands of the* Echo *most respectfully petition your honour to replace our captain. For we are now much ill used by the men of the squadron, who name us shy, and cowards, and make game of us for our part in not coming to the aid of the* Rush. *This is most unjust, for we would have fought that day like True Britons had we been given our chance, but our officers did hang back most shamefully, and left the poor* Rush *to her fate.*

We humbly ask that you replace our captain with a man of spirit, so that we may show you and the squadron how we can fight for our King and our Country.'

Windham was struggling to read the paper by the end, it was trembling so much in his grasp. He looked up at the commodore and saw a face red with fury.

'When we last discussed matters, you told me that I need not worry about your men!' roared Montague. 'You said that their view was so uncertain during the battle that they would have little idea what had transpired. I believe you mentioned the quantities of smoke involved. I now find they understand all too well what went on, and are as discontent at your explanation as the rest of the squadron seems to be.'

'They are simply mutinous scum!' exclaimed Windham. 'When I get back on board, I will flog the lot of them. Let's see how bold they are when they find themselves at the grating.'

'No, no, no!' roared Montague. 'That is not how you will proceed, you fool, unless you wish to find yourself cast adrift in a small boat by your people! This has all gone beyond what can be checked by firmness. I want you to listen very clearly to me. I shall give you one, and only one, final chance to regain the trust and loyalty of your crew. Starting now! Stop hiding in a bloody bottle, and start being a damned leader, like your Uncle Percy. But understand this. I am at the very limit of my patience with you, boy. If I get one more petition, or one more hint of discontent from your crew, then I shall wash my hands of you, and that will be an end to matters.'

*****

Sutton awoke, and for a moment thought he was back on Reunion. He seemed to be listening once more to the sound of distant gunfire in the hut, high on the hillside above St. Paul. A moment later the surging motion of the boat, combined with the agony of thirst in his parched mouth, brought him back to reality. It was close and dark in their little shelter, and the three men lay packed together like stacked logs. Then he saw a flash of white light from outside, followed by the same rumble again. Not gunfire, but thunder, he told himself as he lay there. He pulled himself out into the open in a sudden panic, and kicked his companions awake, as the full implications of the noise came to him.

'Thunder!' he forced himself to croak. 'Squall!'

'Wh...at?' muttered Croft.

'Rain!' gasped his captain.

It was dark outside, with only a scatter of stars to supply any light. Waves still surged past them, rolling mounds that were dark as molten pitch in the night. But the wind felt different, cool and keen, and much fresher than it had been. Another flash of lightning seared across the sky and for a split second they could see an endless vista of black sea beneath clouds of boiling grey.

'There!' whispered Croft. He grabbed at his captain's sleeve and pointed behind them. By the time the others had turned the night had returned once more. Sutton looked around him, frantic for something to collect rain in.

'Coll...ect,' he said, trying to force his swollen tongue to work. Lightning tore above them now, the crack deafening as it boomed off the surface of the sea, and the others saw his hands clawed into the shape of a cup. Chapman scrabbled around in the bottom of the boat and brought up the bailer. It was very small. At best it might hold a couple of pints. He propped it up against the thwart and pinned it into place with his clasp knife.

'Shirts,' grunted Sutton as he feverishly stripped off his own. The others followed his lead, and then crouched down in the boat as the motion became too lively with all of them standing at once. Stripped to the waist, they waited in the dark for the rain to arrive. Another crack of lightning split the sky, close to them now, and they all saw the streaked veil of water as it swept towards them across the waves. Then it was night again.

The wind grew in intensity. It tossed their little craft about, and flapped at the linen shirts they held out. Then they could hear the rain, faint at first, but growing to a hissing roar in the darkness, just behind them. The temperature dropped again, but for a long moment of agony the squall seemed to come no nearer.

'Come... bastard!' pleaded Chapman. Sutton was desperate with thirst. He could feel his arms trembling as he held them out. Croft whimpered next to him. Then the noise of falling rain was all around them, and the first few heavy drops pattered down on their upturned faces.

Deluge. It was as if their little boat had drifted under an unseen waterfall. Rain thundered down, filling the boat ankle deep and turning the sea all about them into a yeasty foam. Sutton felt his shirt grow heavy in his arms. He squeezed the wet linen into his mouth, but the water was too brackish from all the salt in the material. He spat and gagged, then forced himself to wring out the shirt before he held it to the rain once more and squeezed it clean again. He thought he could still hear Croft whimpering beside him, then realised it was his own voice. Finally he was able to squeeze perhaps a cup of fresh water into his mouth, and he groaned with pleasure.

Hold out the shirt, wring it into the mouth, and then hold it out to the storm once more. Each wait for the material to fill was agony, but the pleasure of water running into their mouths was wonderful. Sutton drank and drank, feeling as if he had never tasted a more heavenly liquid, until he felt he was starting to drown in water. He could feel his tongue seeming to shrink in his mouth as it returned to its normal size, and at last his throat felt less raw. Then he remembered the bailer.

'Croft, Chapman!' he croaked, 'bailer!' They crouched around the little wooden container like acolytes about an idol, and squeezed their shirts into it. Sutton rinsed it thoroughly, and then they filled it to the brim. As soon as it was full, they returned to drinking the rain water, thirsty once more. The squall thundered on for a while, and then swept on across the sea. The rain grew thin before it petered out all together. The three men resorted to licking droplets from their wet skin and sucking the last water they could from their damp shirts. When they had finished, they flopped down in the boat, their stomachs distended with all the liquid they had taken on board.

'Christ, it's good to be able to speak again,' said Sutton, rubbing his throat. In truth his voice was still weak and croaky. Chapman in the bow sighed with contentment.

'I even reckon I may need the heads afore long, sir,' he said, 'an' that ain't happened for a while.' The sailor's voice was more gravely than usual. Croft went to speak, but then paused as he saw something out to sea.

'Beg pardon, sir,' he said. 'But I think I can see a light.' Sutton looked up.

'Where away?' he asked. The midshipman pointed towards the horizon, and he followed the line of his arm. A dusting of stars were visible through a break in the clouds. Stood against them was a stronger, nearer light. As the men watched it seemed to move across the backdrop of spangled night. Sutton found the telescope on the floor of the boat and pointed it towards the sighting.

'It might be a ship,' he muttered. 'Take the glass and see what you make of it.'

'Lamp at a masthead for certain, sir,' said Croft. 'She's a long way off, mind.'

'If she is still in sight come dawn, we will be able to signal to her,' said Sutton. 'See, first water and now rescue. I told you there was no need for despair. Let's us bail out our boat before it founders. I am afraid we shall need to use our hands.'

Once the boat was reasonably clear of water, the

castaways sprawled around the interior, too excited to sleep. For once they no longer felt thirsty, although hunger still gnawed at them.

'Salt pork, spluttering hot from the pan, next to some fried eggs,' announced Sutton. 'That is what I shall want when I am rescued, with hot coffee. I doubt if this ship will run to soft tack, but good biscuits with jam will serve for the present.'

'That all sounds very acceptable, sir,' said Croft.

'A simple mess of burgoo will do me, sir,' sighed Chapman. 'I have had it most mornings since I joined the navy, but right now another bowl would not be unwelcome. Mind, that does require that yonder ship ain't no Frenchie, as will clap us in irons as soon as look at us.'

'Oh, that would be too cruel,' said their captain. 'Besides, the squadron will be keeping the French blockaded in St Paul. No, nine in ten it is one of our ships.'

'A wash and clean linen,' said Croft, his voice dreamy. 'Once I have eaten my fill.'

'Been a good few weeks since I had any baccy,' added Chapman.

Sutton settled back, leaning against the side of the boat, his mind full of contented thoughts now that he had a belly that groaned with rain water. He might even find himself breakfasting aboard the *Titan* in a few hours time, his good friend Clay seated opposite him. And with survival came other delightful possibilities. He thought of Betsey Clay once more, lent over her manuscript, her coral-pink lips pursed with concentration. She was brushing the white feather of her pen against the line of her cheek as she worked. In his mind's eye she was back in the orchard at Rosehill cottage once more, in the pale green dress he remembered her wearing last time they met. It would be late spring now, warm even in the shade of the apple trees, and the grass would be studded with flowers and humming with drowsy insects.

'Can't see that ship no more, sir,' announced Chapman, hauling him back to reality. Sutton joined the sailor, staring out into the night. The storm had moved far away, but some of its lightning could still be seen as distant silver threads flickering near the horizon. Above them was a bowl of stars.

'She is probably masked by another squall,' he said. 'We will see her at first light.'

'Aye, but will she see us, sir?' queried the sailor. Sutton patted him on the arm.

'She will, when I flash the morning sun into the lookout's eyes with the lens of Mr Croft's spy glass.'

'Pray God she will still be in range!' exclaimed Croft. 'And we find some manner of rescue tomorrow.'

'Amen to that,' said Sutton. 'Come, you two had best get some sleep till then. I will keep watch, in case we get another squall.'

But the night passed quietly, with no more rain. In the stern Sutton sat, alone under the stars with his thoughts. Now that rescue seemed close, he allowed his mind to wander over images of Betsey, but he found himself turning to other, more immediate concerns. Her delicate features seemed to slide and contort in his mind into those of an altogether less agreeable countenance. The eager face of Windham, his eyes alight, as they had sat around the cabin table in the *Rush*, finalising the plan to attack the *Prudence*. Soon he would be able to confront him at last. His grip tightened on the telescope at the prospect. But then other things worried him too. He kept searching for the comforting presence of the ship, but he could no longer find the masthead light, despite the air having been swept clean by the storm.

A few hours later the first rose-blush of dawn stole into

the east. Sutton stretched and yawned in the early morning sunlight. In spite of all the rain he had drunk he was now thirsty once more. He looked at the bailer of water, licked his lips, and then ignored it. Instead he picked up the telescope and started to search the ocean all around him. As the light spread it revealed a growing circle of pearl-blue sea. There was no sign of the ship they had seen in the night.

CHAPTER 12 FOUND

'What do you mean, we ain't going to be bleeding rescued?' exclaimed Chapman.

'I am afraid not,' said Sutton.

'What has become of the ship we saw last night, sir?' asked Croft.

'It must have sailed over the horizon.'

The teenager buried his head in his hands, while Chapman kicked out at the side of the boat.

'Steady there!' said his captain. 'Don't upset the bailer. It is all the water we have.' Chapman threw himself down in the bows.

'Why did you bleeding lead us on!' he yelled. 'All that talk of what we was going to scoff for breakfast! Jesus Christ!' He turned away and glared out to sea, his arms tightly crossed. After a long silence Croft looked up.

'Why are we in this mess, sir?' he asked, his face blank with despair. 'I don't mean adrift in this boat, I mean why did the *Echo* leave us to be captured? None of this would have happened if they had played their proper part in the action.'

'I am not sure why they did that,' said Sutton. 'But I intend to find out, once we are rescued.'

'Rescued!' scoffed Chapman, spinning round, his face contorted by fury. 'There ain't going to be no bleeding rescue! We got a single cup of water, and no food. So why don't you answer the boy straight? We've followed you into this fucking mess, you owe us that at least!'

'What did you say to me?' said Sutton, staring towards the sailor. 'Keep a civil tongue in your head there! I know I have allowed you both a degree of freedom, given our predicament, but I am still your captain.'

'Beg my pardon, *sir*, for my want of respect, but we are properly screwed out here, and look sure to die, *sir*. The least we deserve is to know why?'

Sutton continued to glare at him, and then looked across at Croft.

'I am sorry, but he is right, sir,' said the midshipman. 'We all lost good shipmates in the fight with the *Prudence*. You must own there was more to that battle than a simple defeat. Just before the main mast fell, I recall how you said we should not be concerned, as the *Echo* would be busy raking the enemy. You seemed surprised when I told you that was not the case.'

'And you've been proper lively in your sleep, sir,' added Chapman. 'Doing no end of muttering to yourself, as well as all that rattling up and down the beach back in Reunion.'

Sutton looked out at the empty sea for a long moment. Every instinct of his training told him how bad for discipline this talk was, but then his commonsense reasserted itself. He wasn't the commander of a ship in anything but name anymore. His *Rush* had been reduced to ash, and what the tide had not washed away the wind would have taken. Chapman was probably right; they would die out here in this little boat. He looked back at his two companions.

'I suppose you do deserve to know the truth of it,' he conceded. 'What happened that day was that I arranged with Captain Windham for both ships to fall on the *Prudence* from separate directions, and for whatever reason he was unable to carry out his part of the enterprise.'

'Unable or unwilling, sir?' asked the midshipman. 'You were the senior officer. Surely what you term an arrangement was an order, was it not?'

'Yes, Mr Croft, it was. That is why I was so surprised when you told me that they had hauled their wind.'

'So let me get this straight, sir,' said Chapman. 'You ordered Windy to attack, and he didn't do it. That's a hanging matter, if a simple Jack was to hold back in such a fashion. What would have caused him to risk such a thing? I mean, the whole bleeding squadron knew how you and Windy weren't mates, but it must have been a proper ruckus for him to do what he done.' Sutton looked at Chapman, unsettled by the shrewdness of his questions. His two fellow castaways waited for him to answer.

'It is certainly true that Captain Windham and I were not intimate,' he said eventually. 'Our quarrel goes back some years, to a time when he and I were lieutenants together back in ninety-five, on board the *Agrius*, with you too, Mr Croft. You will recall how we fought a single ship action with that big French frigate, the *Couraguese*, and matters were not proceeding at all well. Our captain was his uncle, and when our mizzen mast came down, he was knocked into the water and drowned. I was the senior officer on the quarterdeck at the time, and Windham has always held me to be in some manner responsible for his uncle's death. But I never suspected for a moment that he would take matters so far as to seek his revenge in such a base way.'

'So in some part, you're to blame for all this, then,' said Chapman.

'Of course I am damned well not,' shouted Sutton. 'How dare you say such a thing! Hold your tongue there!'

'What a fuck up,' continued the sailor. 'No, beg your pardon, sir, but if I am to die in this bleeding boat, I wants to say my piece. You bloody officers, with all your grand notions of honour and all that bollocks! Why the hell couldn't you sort out this tiff between you? You've had nearly four bleeding years to do it, either man to man in one of them duels you *gentlemen* so love, or friendly like, over a glass of grog. It don't make no odds to the likes of me. But oh no! You have to let it fester between you both, till it spills over into the lives of the poor bastards under you. How many of our shipmates had to die because you and Windy couldn't sort out who done what in a battle on the other side of the bleeding world?'

'Now just you look here, Chapman,' said Sutton, his face resolute. 'I understand your anger, but let me be quite clear with you. Whatever the rights or wrongs of his uncle's death, I never put anyone else in danger because of it. That crime can only be placed at Captain Windham's feet. And I swear, here and now, that we shall *not* die in this boat. We will live, if only so that we are able to witness that man hang for what he did to the *Rush* and our shipmates.'

As the day wore on, the hot anger of dawn slumped back into lethargy. The delicious rain that had come the previous night became a distant memory. They tried to hoard their little wooden bailer of fresh water, but by the day's end it had almost gone. Under the remorseless sun their thirst returned, accompanied by fresh torments. Their gnawing hunger was giving them the periodic agony of stomach cramps. Even though their shelter offered them some protection it was only partial, and they were all becoming badly burnt. Croft in particular had skin that had peeled away in sheets from his raw neck and arms. To add to their woes, exposure to salt water was now creating sores on their skin that wept and bled. After yet another day huddled in the stifling heat of their shelter, the sun at last dipped towards the western horizon. As it lost its fierce heat, the three men emerged like nocturnal beasts to enjoy the cool of the evening.

'One sip each,' announced Sutton, his voice a croak once

more. He passed the almost empty bailer to Croft, who drank and then passed it to Chapman. He took his portion, passed it back to Sutton, and returned to a fragment of wire that he had been working on.

'What are you about, Chapman?' asked Croft, after a while.

'Fish hook, sir,' he replied. 'I found a bit of wire in the collar of the captain's coat.' He carried on working with his knife, using the gunwale as a bench. The others watched as, beneath his skillful fingers, the tiny piece of metal slowly changed. After a while he laid aside his knife and held the hook up for inspection. He had doubled one end over to make a barb, while the other end of the curve of wire ended with a tiny loop.

'If we ain't about to be rescued, we may as well try for some vittles, sir,' he announced. 'I've made a bit of line to go with it. It's a bare fathom long, but it may serve. I don't know about you, but I could eat a bleeding whale.' He held up a thin coil of thin rope.

'Where did you find the hemp?' asked the midshipman.

'I unpicked that little bit of a painter as was attached to the bow. It weren't long enough to serve no purpose.'

'That's very good,' said Sutton. 'What will you use for bait?

'A scrap of your gold lace, sir. Mackerel and the like back home will take anything as glistens, so maybe there be similar fish hereabouts.'

The prospect of food stimulated the three men into action. Sutton tore some more braid off one of the panels of the coat that made up part of their shelter. Croft secured one end of the line to the boat's bow post, while Chapman attached the hook. They dropped it over the side, and the little strip of gold flashed for a moment in the evening sun as it sank. All three men sat back, their eyes glued on the line, willing it to jerk into life. The sun sank below the horizon in a blaze of fire and darkness crept across the heavens. Nothing was drawn to their hook.

*****

'Come in!' called Alexander Clay in response to the knock at his cabin door. The marine sentry held it open for Midshipman Russell to enter.

'Letter from the commodore, sir,' he announced. 'It's just been delivered by the *Black Prince*'s launch.'

'A letter?' queried Clay, looking up from his desk. 'Do you not mean a dispatch?'

'No, sir,' said the teenager. 'Least ways it isn't sealed up in a package like orders normally are.' He held out the single folded sheet of paper. His captain lay down his pen and stretched forward to take the note from the young officer.

'And this arrived in an open boat?' he asked. 'Is the flagship in sight?'

'Not from the deck, sir. Midshipman Kemp who delivered it said they left at two bells in the forenoon watch.'

'Goodness, that was a fair trip for them to have made,' exclaimed Clay. 'Kindly see that Mr Kemp and his crew receive some refreshment to sustain them on their long return journey, if you please, Mr Russell.'

'Aye, aye, sir,' said the midshipman, before smartly turning away to leave the cabin.

'Now then,' said Clay to himself. 'What news warrants such a communication, I wonder?' He broke the seal and unfolded the note from Montague.

My dear Captain Clay,

Thank you for the list of officers and crews taken from the French National Ship Prudence *that you were kind enough to furnish me when I last had the pleasure of your company. I have now had occasion to send an officer under a flag of truce to enquire about the possibility of an exchange of prisoners. He has been received by a Monsieur Morliere, Commandant of St Paul, who has supplied my representative with the particulars of the officers and crew of His Majesty's late vessel* Rush, *who survived and are in his custody. I have studied the list, and it is with sincere regret that I must inform you that the name of Captain Sutton does not feature. From this absence, I fear we must conclude that a fine officer, and dear friend, fell defending his ship. I am sensible as to the distress and deep sorrow you must feel at this time.*

I shall write to Monsieur Morliere in a private capacity to see if he is in possession of the details surrounding your friend's sad demise, and you naturally have my sincere condolences.

I have the honour to be your obliged friend,

George Montague

The letter fluttered down from Clay's grasp, and his vision blurred as hot tears began to flow.

'No!' he exclaimed. 'How can this be? Preston and Macpherson both saw his sea chest in that damned house! John, dead? It isn't possible!' He stumbled up from behind the desk, his chair falling to the deck behind him, and began to pace feverishly up and down the cabin.

Had his dear, courageous friend really died bravely at his post, sword in hand, as his ship was overwhelmed? That would certainly be in keeping, he told himself, his pace faltering. But then where did his sea chest fit in? Surely it must mean something? He resumed his pacing, dashing away his tears as he tried to work at the problem. What had the officers truly seen, that night in the pool of light from Macpherson's lamp? It was certainly Sutton's chest, both men had recognized it, but what did that really prove? Had they interpreted what they had seen as what they had wanted to see? Proof that Sutton had survived, rather than just a box, looted by some Frenchman from the wreck of the poor *Rush*? But then how had it come to be in the house that the signal had been sent from? It all made no sense.

'There must be some mistake,' he muttered through his pain. He return to his desk, pulled his chair upright again, sat down and wiped his eyes dry with a handkerchief. Then he picked up Montague's letter once more, hoping against hope that he might have misread it. But the words were still the same. Think, Alex, think. If the sea chest means he survived the fight, why is he not on the list?

He returned to Montague's note, and two words seemed to grow from the page, *"who survived"*. Preston and Macpherson had said the house they entered had been ransacked. They had spoken of overturned furniture, possessions strewn around and a broken window. In his mind's eye he saw his friend being hauled from the house by rough hands, the line of homemade signal flags brandished under his nose, and the fury of the French soldiers that had caught him red-handed. They would show little mercy to a spy, caught in time of war in such a way.

He sat with his head bowed over the note as he thought again of his friend, so full of fun, now gone forever. Had his life really ended in such a way, perhaps blindfolded, against a wall, waiting for a volley of bullets? A few tears splashed down onto the paper, causing individual letters to wave and distort. Clay wiped his eyes again, blew his nose loudly and then paused. A fresh image came to him. It was that of

Nicholas Windham, somewhere over the horizon, receiving the same news and exulting in it. His hands began to tremble with rage and he screwed the note from Montague into a tight ball, his knuckles white with the effort.

'I will avenge you, brother,' he pledged through teeth clenched with anger. 'If it is my final act on this earth.'

*****

Sutton opened his eyes the next day, and wondered what was different. It was morning, and shafts of sunlight penetrated the various gaps and holes in the shelter to dot the three recumbent bodies with points and lines of silver. He could still hear the sea, but it was only faint. The sound of the waves was masked by a much more persistent noise. A shrill wall of sound seemed to come from all around him, a shrieking in the air that went on and on without end. Hunger and thirst had dulled his mind, which was why it took him so long, blinking in the gloom beneath the tent of coats, to realise the main thing that had changed. For the first time in days, the boat was no longer moving.

He pulled himself out from under the cover, making his two companions groan and shift as he squeezed past them. Outside he looked up in amazement at a sky alive with movement. His first impression was that it was snowing, but then he realised that the air was full of life. There were thousands upon thousands of black and white sea birds. They swirled in the space over his head and filled his world with tumult. All were busy as they streamed in various directions, and every one of them was calling raucously to his neighbours. The boat lay on its side in shallow water, the bow caught in the sand of a gently sloping beach. Already the roof of the shelter was spattered with excrement, and more lay all around him. He leant over the gunwale and roughly shook the others awake, and then staggered inland to explore.

At the top of the beach the sand gave way to a flat expanse of scrubby grass and little thorn bushes, dotted with patches of bare white rock. From where he stood Sutton could see the whole island. It was roughly circular, perhaps four hundred yards across, with white sand that tapered down into shallow, electric blue water all around the fringe. The interior of the island was a flat bowl of rock and desiccated vegetation. It was covered with thousands of nesting sea birds. Almost all of them seemed to be the same black and white terns that filled the sky, coming and going in an endless cloud of noise. The nearest few nests were at his feet. Their inhabitants looked up at him with unblinking dark eyes set either side of long, dagger-shaped beaks.

'What...?' croaked Croft, as he and Chapman staggered up the slope to join their captain.

'Gulls,' Sutton answered. 'Catch...eat?'

'No!' whispered Chapman, his eyes alight with greed. 'Eggs!'

Desperate with hunger, the three men began to feast like animals. They advanced on all fours into the bird colony, beating off the enraged terns and gorging on the raw eggs. At first they just crammed everything into their mouths: shell, egg, the developing chick within, driven only by the urgent desire to end the pain that gnawed in their bellies. Soon their faces were smeared and filthy with a mess of shell, raw egg and blood. Then Croft yelled out to them, his waving arms sending hundreds of terns up into the sky. The others came over to see what he had found. Before him was a shallow pool of collected rain water. The liquid was full of dissolved excrement, the water acid to the taste, but to the desperate castaways it was just palatable. They sucked their fill, till all that was left was a foul-smelling sludge. Satisfied at last, they picked a path through the bird nests back the way they had come.

When they returned to the beach, they pulled their abandoned boat a little higher up the sand, so that it was clear of the tide line. Then the three men flopped down with their backs against the shady side of the hull. They each had a distended belly from all their gorging and the strong taste of bird excrement in their mouths. All of them were breathing heavily, and Sutton felt sweat start to bead on his forehead. After a few minutes Croft let out a low groan, and rose to his feet. He tottered down the sand towards the water's edge, splashed a few steps into the shallows and was violently sick. A geyser of vomit poured from him as he emptied his stomach into the warm sea.

'Oh...God,' moaned Sutton. He pulled himself upright and his stomach churned alarmingly. He too came staggering down the beach, but Chapman was faster. Soon all three of them were retching and heaving in the shallows. Excited little fish swarmed around their ankles and feasted on the splattering torrent.

'Why...eat...filth?' groaned the teenager, still doubled over.

'Dying...hunger,' muttered Chapman. He waged a finger in the air. 'No more...eggs.'

'Yes,' agreed Sutton, leading the way back up the beach. 'Cook gull...fire?'

'Not now,' whispered Croft, clutching his stomach as he flopped back down in the shade.

'No...later,' gasped his captain. He pointed around them. 'But stay. Food...ship, perhaps.'

'Shellfish,' added Chapman, with a vague wave towards the shallows. He pulled out his clasp knife and made a prising motion. The others nodded at this.

'W...water?' asked the midshipman. 'Not ...puddle, again.'

'Rain,' said Sutton, retching a little. 'Clean...puddle...out. Then storm.' He mimicked rain falling, and scooping up water to drink. The others watched his cupped hands with desperation, as if they really did contained water.

'Now,' croaked Chapman nudging the others and pointing. Away to the east they could see clouds on the horizon, a hedge of tall thunderheads that stalked along in the keen breeze.

'Yes,' said Sutton, pulling himself to his feet. He reached into the boat and untied the paddle. Without its support the tent of cloth fragments collapsed. Then he pantomimed digging with it. 'Come,' he ordered, and led the way into the bird colony once more.

The sailors spent most of the morning at work on a large depression. The accumulation of guano was deep, and had baked onto the rock in places. Sutton and Croft dug at the filth with their bare hands, while Chapman scooped it up with the paddle and flung it away. They were very weak from lack of food, and the effort of the work turned their limbs to lead. The sun beat down on them from above, while the acid stench of rotting bird faeces made them choke and retch. After a few hours of toil Croft was completely spent, and the others could barely stand, but at least they had one reasonably clear basin in which to gather rainwater. As they made their way back towards the shelter of the boat they scanned the sky for any promising rain clouds.

'Where...gone?' croaked Chapman, searching the endless horizon with a hand shading his eyes. The others followed his example, but the clouds they had seen in the early morning had vanished.

'Tonight,' said Sutton, patting the sailor on the arm. Chapman rolled his eyes at this, then staggered onward towards the boat. Sutton followed with Croft trailing behind, leaning for support on the paddle. After a few steps, the youngster was forced to stop and catch his breath. Heat was rising up from the rock of the atoll, bending and twisting the air into a shimmering haze. Around his feet nesting terns squawked and pecked at him. He mopped at his brow with the sleeve of his shirt, and as his head turned he caught sight of something. He shaded his eyes and looked out to sea.

'Sir!' he croaked. Sutton turned wearily around.

'What?'

'Sails!'

Sutton staggered and reeled back towards him. A wave of alarmed birds took to the air as he came. 'Glass!' he gasped in a broken voice, over his shoulder towards Chapman. The midshipman held a trembling arm up and pointed towards the south.

'Sails,' he repeated. Chapman came lurching over, raising another cloud of terns, and handed across the little telescope. Sutton pulled it open and focussed on the spot.

At first he could see nothing but blurred sea and sky as his hands trembled uncontrollably. He let his breathing return to normal and clamped his arms against his side. The sea became a solid bar of deep blue in the bottom of the round field of vision, the sky pale in contrast, and then he saw them. Three tiny little squares on the horizon, in a row. They were undoubtedly the topgallants of a ship, but they were beam on to him, which meant that she was sailing past, rather than towards them.

'Ship,' he croaked, his face in despair. 'Sailing away.'

'Damn...eyes!' wheezed Chapman. 'How...mark...us?'

'Wave?' suggested Croft.

'No,' said Sutton. He looked around him as he searched for a solution. By his feet a tern looked up at him from the centre of her scrubby little nest.

'Fire!' he said. 'Nests! Now!'

Frantically the castaways pulled nests together in a heap.

Eggs tumbled out to smash on the rock, while birds flew at the sailors, clawing and pecking at them. Then, while the others gathered more nests, Sutton crouched over the pile, holding the telescope towards the sun, and tried to focus the beam onto the dry vegetation. But his arms had grown so weak that the point of light danced and wavered, while he croaked with frustration. Chapman came over and grabbed the telescope from the other side, and between them they forced the little spot of dazzling white to settle on one part of the mass. Nothing happened at first. Then a piece of grass began to char and curl, sending a tiny thread of grey coiling up into the air.

*****

'There she blows!' yelled several of the *Titan*'s hands, unable to restrain themselves. Every one had been pressed from whalers, and the sight of the huge, shiny grey backs as they broke the surface in a welter of white was too much for them. The sperm whales had appeared in a line, a matter of yards from the frigate's bow, close to where many of the off-duty sailors were taking their ease on the forecastle. Water shot up in tall geysers and a mist of warm breath drifted over the ship. Then there was a series of loud gasps as the whales of the pod sucked in air and dived down out of sight once more.

'There goes a hundred guineas of best grade lamp oil,' said Trevan. The other sailors gazed at the whales for a moment, before they returned to their various activities.

'How did you hunt such enormous beasts, Adam?' asked Sedgwick.

'From a boat no bigger than our red cutter, if you will credit it,' said the Cornishman. 'First you has to get your ship close to them, and then you launch your whale boats. You has to judge where they will blow next, and wait for them to rise. When they does, you claps yourself on to one with a harpoon and a deal of line. Then they drags you about for a while, or they dive down proper deep, but in time they has to come up for air, see, so you sticks them again each time they do, till they can't take no more. When their chimney catches fire, you know they be finished.'

'I don't follow, Adam,' said Sedgwick. 'What chimney?'

'Oh, that be whaler talk,' explained Trevan. 'A deal of gore comes out of the blowhole, like. It turns the sea all pink and frothy. It ain't easy work, mind, for they can get right lively before the end. I've had a good few boats turned to matchwood under me by one of them buggers.'

'Fecking hell,' said O'Malley. 'Who'd be after being a whaler?'

'That be just the start, Sean. Once you gone and killed him, you still have to cut him up and cook the oil out of him.' The others all thought about this for a moment, with looks of distaste. After a while Evans returned to what they had been discussing before the sperm whales had surfaced.

'So how long we going to spend, driftin' around these here waters?' he asked.

'It's Dismal George's idea,' said Sedgwick, with a shrug. 'I suppose us being out here serves to keep the Frogs in port, but they turn tail and scarper as soon as they clap eyes on us. Cats and mice ain't in it.'

'Seems clear to me them Frogs ain't got the pluck for no fight,' said the Londoner.

'Can you blame them? said Trevan, 'After what we done to that there *Prudence*?'

'Talking about them as has no pluck, you boys hear about the crew of the *Echo*?' said O'Malley. 'Word is they are fit to rise any day now.'

'Why would they do that?' asked Sedgwick.

'From what I heard they are fecking pissed at everyone naming them shy,' said the Irishman, in a conspiratorial tone. 'Windy's barge crew were all given white feathers by the lads on the *Prince*.'

'That's fair enough, Sean,' said Evans. 'You can't come back from a scrap where one ship got stuffed and the other barely scratched. What're folk meant to think?'

'But the lads on the *Echo* all say as how it was Windy what hung back, and they want him gone,' said O'Malley. 'They sent one of them round robins to Dismal. They ain't angry enough to roll cannon balls at night yet, but it's only a matter of time.' The others sat back and digested this for a bit. After a while Trevan spoke up.

'Well, that all seems proper ill,' he said. 'Frogs as won't fight on one side, captains too shy of battle on t'other. Even Pipe's been proper low since news came that Pretty Boy had perished.'

'It could be fecking worse, lads,' said O'Malley, pointing at the blue sea that ran away in every direction. 'Weather's proper grand, nice bit of prize money due us, back to Cape Town for a run ashore once the vittles gets low. I tell yous, it beats the Channel Fleet and polishing our arses outside of Brest in all weather.'

'Deck ho!' yelled the lookout. The men all glanced up, some shifting across the deck to get an uninterrupted view of the man who stood high above their heads. Having hailed, he seemed confused as to what to say next.

'What can you see?' prompted the voice of Armstrong from the quarterdeck. 'Make your report in proper form now, Hobbs.'

'Sorry, sir,' replied the lookout. 'Only I ain't entirely sure. Looks like it might be a trail of smoke, right on the starboard beam.'

'No ship? Or land?' queried the American.

'Not as I can see, sir, just that there line of brown smoke.'

*****

'Smoke, Mr Russell?' queried Clay, looking up from his desk. 'But surely there is no land hereabout. Are you quite certain?'

'Yes, sir,' replied the midshipman. 'Mr Butler has been aloft, and he can see it too.'

'How peculiar,' said his captain. 'I suppose it might be a ship that has taken fire. Alter course towards the source, if you please, and tell Mr Armstrong that I will be up presently.'

Clay sat at his desk and stared out of the stern window at the endless vista of blue ocean and wondered what this strange sighting might portend. In truth, it had come as a welcome distraction. In front of him was a blank sheet of paper, which was to be the latest addition to the letter/journal that he kept daily at sea, for his wife. He sent each installment as a bundle of pages whenever he was able. He thought about the last thick package well on its way to the Cape now, onboard the captured *Prudence,* and he cursed out loud.

'Oh damn and blast it,' he exclaimed, towards the portrait of his wife, as he thought about all the ridiculously hopeful things that the letter contained. 'It's all the fault of that damned chest!' He remembered how he had eagerly scribbled away in his spidery hand on the triumphant morning after the defeat of the French frigate. On the strength of that one sighting of John's possessions, he had created a whole world of hope. He had told Lydia that his friend had survived the battle, was alive and well, and though a prisoner of the French, he would soon be paroled. Beneath his feet he felt the angle of the deck change as the frigate swept around to head towards the mysterious fire.

'Poor Betsey,' he muttered. 'If she truly loves John, as he seems to love her, she will had taken such hope from that. But now I must bring her world crashing down, again. What a bloody fool I have been! Still, the letter cannot now be recalled. All I can do is correct it as swiftly as I am able.' He looked back towards his wife's picture. The blue eyes seemed to bore into him from out of the painted canvas, the look of accusation unmistakable.

'Yes, my dear, I know,' he said. 'I have made a sad hash of things, have I not? I have lurched from despair to hope, and back to despair, and have now dragged my poor sister along the same path.'

With a sigh he began to write, stutteringly at first, but gradually with more fluency, setting down what he thought to be the facts. When the task was done at last, he looked back at the picture. Lydia continued to stare down at him, but perhaps her eyes were a little more kindly now. Clay glanced back at his letter, and as he did so, he noticed the date. He found it hard to keep track of the seasons here in the tropics, but back home spring would be fast moving into summer now. He thought of life at Rosehill Cottage; the grounds would be at their best, thick with colour. He imagined his mother, in a cavernous straw hat, supervising the gardener in his work. At the end of the lawn, through the old brick arch that led to the orchard, his sister and wife would be busy at their writing, unaware of the dreadful news that was crossing the ocean towards them. Then he looked at the date once more and frowned with concentration as he calculated to himself.

'Oh, Lydia!' he gasped, returning to the painting. 'The child! It will arrive any day now.' Images flooded his mind of all the dangers she would be facing back in England. He had lost John, surely he could not loose Lydia too? He thought of the many women he had heard of who had died bringing new life into the world. He got up from his chair and began to pace the deck, an anxious father-to-be, as if Lydia were giving birth in his sleeping cabin beyond the bulkhead rather than in a different hemisphere altogether. So real was the illusion that he jumped when there was another knock at the door.

'Come in,' he called. The distinctly un-midwifely form of Midshipman Russell marched into the cabin.

'Mr Armstrong's respects, and he believes the smoke may be coming from some manner of little islet, sir. Masthead reports a great mass of what look to be birds.' Clay pushed aside thoughts of his wife and hurried to pull on his coat.

'First smoke and now birds? Very well, tell Mr Armstrong that I truly am coming this time, Mr Russell.'

On deck, the cloud of terns was visible as a coiling swirl of white specks, while behind them was a thin feather of brown. The bow of the *Titan* pointed directly towards it, and with a keen wind on her quarter the gap was closing quickly. Clay went across to join the sailing master by the rail.

'You suspect there may be an atoll of some description ahead, I collect, Mr Armstrong,' he said.

'I do, sir,' replied the American. 'It is the only possible explanation for all those birds. Clearly something has vexed them, to have taken flight in such numbers. I assume that will be the fire.'

'And nothing is marked on the chart?' he asked.

'No, sir, but that is not unusual. These waters are dotted with little unmarked islands. Most ships are obliged to keep to the main shipping routes in consequence. You would not wish to discover one at night, under full sail.'

'No, I should think not,' said the captain.

'Deck there!' bellowed the lookout. 'Land ho! Land on the bow!' Armstrong turned to his captain and raised his hat in mock salute. His periwig lifted from his bald pate at the same time.

'Congratulations, Mr Armstrong. Kindly have this atoll of yours noted on the chart. You may name it Armstrong Island, if you wish.'

'Thank you, sir,' beamed the American. 'I believe that I shall.'

The sighting of land sent a buzz of anticipation through the crew. Taylor and Macpherson hurried up from the wardroom, where they had been playing backgammon together, to find out what was afoot. On the forecastle, all discussion about the mutinous crew of the *Echo* had stopped, and they were clustered along the rail or had climbed part-way into the fore shrouds in the hope of seeing more.

'Mr Russell, take a glass aloft and tell me what you can see,' ordered Clay. The midshipman rushed to the main shrouds and thundered up them at the speed of a moderate sized ape. When he reached the main royal yard he hooked one arm around the thin upper mast and focused the telescope with the other.

'I think I can see the island now, sir,' said Armstrong from beside him. 'See, a low area of surf and pale blue water dead ahead.'

'Yes, I have it now,' said Clay. He looked up towards the midshipman. 'Mr Russell, can you see what has caused all this smoke?'

'I cannot make out much, in truth, sir,' he replied. 'I thought I could see a small blaze, but all these damned birds are in the way.'

'Can you see anyone who may have set the fire?'

'Maybe a figure? No, he is obscured again, sir. Ah, there he is! No, two of them! One is waving a shirt on a stick of some sort.'

'Castaways!' exclaimed Taylor. 'I wonder how they come

to be so far out at sea, sir.'

'We are several hundred miles from land, and even farther from where our shipping might be found, sir,' said the master. 'There are Arab slavers who ply these waters. Perhaps that is who they are.'

'We shall soon find out, Mr Armstrong,' said Clay. 'Kindly summon the launch crew, and pass the word for the surgeon. Tell Mr Corbett to expect some patients to attend to.'

'Three, sir!' yelled Russell from the masthead. 'I can see three of them. One is collapsed at the other two's feet.'

'Mr Corbett!' called Clay down to the surgeon, as he appeared on the main deck. 'You had best accompany the launch crew, and take some water with you.'

Closer and closer the *Titan* came, shouldering her way through the long rollers. The island grew from a little swirl of white in the vastness of the ocean to a stretch of scrubby vegetation with patches of bare rock. It seemed to be surrounded with coral reefs and warm lagoons. Much of the vegetation was now charred and some of it still smouldered close to the feet of the men. Their fire was almost out now, and the birds were beginning to alight again amidst the ruins of their breeding colony. The ship was close enough for everyone to be able to see the little figures, even without telescopes. The two men had now stopped their waving and were helping their colleague towards the beach nearest to the approaching frigate.

'That doesn't look like Arab dress those men are wearing,' remarked Armstrong. 'I could swear that the one on the right is in britches.'

Up at the masthead Midshipman Russell had the best view of all. He focused his telescope on the castaways. There was something familiar in the way one of them moved and stood. The man's face turned towards him and he gasped. Behind the hollow eyes, thick stubble of beard and smears of filth was a face he knew.

'Captain, sir!' he bellowed. 'I think one of the castaways may be from the *Rush*!'

*****

Later that day, when he came off watch, Jacob Armstrong made his way down to the wardroom of the *Titan* and disappeared into his little cabin. He hung his coat up on the hook behind the door, loosened his neck cloth, and unbuttoned the front of his waistcoat with a sigh of relief. Once he was in his shirtsleeves, he sat down at his tiny desk and went over the observations he had made earlier. After a few moments of patient work, he lay them aside with a grunt of satisfaction and pulled the chart towards him. Then he transferred his conclusion onto the middle of a blank area of ocean as a tiny pencil cross. He checked his calculation once more, and when he was certain that all was as it should be, he cut a new nib for his pen, dipped it into the ink well and made the mark permanent. He added the name *Armstrong Island* in tiny little letters next to it, with a smile of pleasure. Then he paused, his blotter hovering in his hand, and thought about the three men that had been saved earlier. He rapped his fingers on the side of the desk as he pondered what to do. A few moments later he leant forward once more, put a neat line through the word *Armstrong* and replaced it with *Hope*.

Chapter 13 Return

'All three of them have slept for over a day and a night in a most satisfactory fashion, sir,' announced Richard Corbett, as he polished his little steel-framed spectacles on a corner of his waistcoat. 'They have taken on board prodigious quantities of fluid, and are even starting to void some urine as their functions recommence. But even so, they are still very weak. I am most concerned for Mr Croft, who was quite spent when he came on board yesterday morning. If we had not picked him up when we did, I doubt if he could have survived a further day of such deprivation.'

'Do you hold that they shall make a full recovery, doctor?' asked Clay.

'Yes, sir,' replied the surgeon, reaching forwards to touch the top of his captain's walnut desk. 'With a deal of water to revitalise them, they are already much improved, but it will be some time before they can take on sufficient nourishment. These cases of enforced fasting cannot be rushed. Portable soup and a little sweetened burgoo, together with watered wine, is all that I will permit them to have today.'

'Do they have any other injuries, apart from thirst and hunger?'

'Only those you would expect from a lengthy time in a small boat, sir. The sun has quite scorched their skin in places, especially Mr Croft. Then they all have some unpleasant sores and a degree of wastage of the tissues. I have greased and dressed their various wounds. What they chiefly need is rest, and in time, adequate sustenance.'

'I understand,' said Clay. 'Yesterday they were in a truly shocking state. Even my particular friend, Captain Sutton, barely seemed to recognise me.'

'He will know you today, sir,' replied the surgeon. 'In fact he was asking for you when he awoke, just before I came up from his cabin.' Clay rose from behind his desk and started to pull on his coat.

'Then I must go to him,' he said. 'At once!'

'I had planned to administer some further drops of laudanum, but I could delay his dose for a little while, sir,' said Corbett, getting up as well. 'But I can only sanction a brief visit, and that only after I have first examined him. He is still in need of much rest.'

Sutton had been installed in the spare cabin off the wardroom. It was a dim little space, with a single horn lantern that swung from a hook in the beam above his head. He had been washed and shaved, but this only served to emphasize how gaunt his face looked. He was sitting up in his cot when the surgeon entered, and drinking from a marine's water canteen that hung from the bulkhead beside the bed.

'My apologies, Mr Corbett,' he said. 'I know you urged me not to take excessive fluid, but I do not seem to be able to stop. It is so wonderful to be able to drink water! I made a promise, when we were adrift, that if I survived, I would never allow myself to be thirsty again.'

'I am sure it will do you little harm, sir, but please be moderate, I pray,' the doctor said. He felt for his patient's pulse with one hand, while he pulled out his pocket watch with the other. 'Still a little elevated, I find,' he muttered to himself. He slid his hand onto Sutton's forehead. 'Do you feel able to accommodate a visit from the captain?'

'I would want that above all things,' exclaimed Sutton, pulling himself upright in bed.

'Control yourself, please. You must not become over-excited.' He turned towards the open cabin door. 'No more than ten minutes then, sir.' He made his way out, and the tall figure of Clay stooped in through the low door, seeming to fill the whole of the tiny space.

'Good heavens, I had forgotten how cramped a lieutenant's cabin is,' he exclaimed. 'Did we truly pass all those years in a dark cave as tiny as this?'

'Alex!' said his friend, holding out his arms. 'Oh my, but it is good to see your face! There were times when I thought that I might never look upon you again.'

'And for my part, I thought you dead, brother,' said Clay into Sutton's shoulder, his eyes welling up as he held his friend close, partly through sheer joy and partly because of the painful feel of his friend's ribs under his nightshirt. 'I experienced the greatest astonishment when Mr Russell said he recognised you from the masthead.' After a while he let him go and sat down in the chair next to the cot. 'My, but it is good to see you again!'

'What have you there, Alex?' asked Sutton, indicating the pile of slim leather volumes Clay held on his lap.

'I thought that while you are confined down here, you might like something to read. These are my sister's first two novels. I make no doubt that you will have read them already, but they may prove more diverting than looking at the underside of the main deck.'

'They will be most welcome, once I can persuade your surgeon not to render me insensible with milk of the poppy every five minutes.'

'So, Lazarus, while you are still lucid, tell me how it was that you came to be on that godforsaken little rock, instead of cold in your grave as I supposed?' asked Clay.

While his friend listened to his tale, Sutton talked and talked. He started with the battle with the *Prudence*, and how Windham had betrayed him.

'So you had ordered him to closely engage the enemy?' said Clay, his face white with rage. 'I knew that damned bastard was lying! You know that in his version of events your plan was to stand off and cripple the Frenchman from range. He shall pay for his deceit in full measure, I swear it.'

Sutton went on to touch on the misery he had felt as he surrendered the splintered remains of his precious *Rush* to the enemy. He spoke of the piles of dead and wounded men that had littered the deck, and how the ship itself had been sinking beneath his feet. Then had come the final ordeal, after the French had dragged the hull of the sloop up onto the beach: watching from the quarterdeck of the departing *Prudence* as flames consumed the *Rush*. Clay patted his arm in sympathy.

'She was a fine little ship,' he said. 'My first command, too. Remember how she was when we first went aboard her, back in Bridgetown? Her hull was so foul with weed she could barely muster five knots!'

Sutton moved on to his time as a captive on Reunion. The weeks of boredom, his daily walk along the shore mulling over his various problems, and then the day the squadron arrived. He explained how the signal was sent, with flags made from clothes. Then how they had been spotted and forced to flee, chased through the groves and cane fields by patrols of soldiers.

'We came and looked for you that night, you know,' said Clay. 'Edward Preston and Tom Macpherson landed with some of his marines, before we fought the *Prudence*. They saw your sea chest in that little house, which gave us all such hope that you had survived the battle. But then, when the list of prisoners came through from the Commandant of St Paul's, your name was absent, so we feared the worst.'

'Oh Alex,' said his friend. 'That is the sort of low trick I would expect of Morliere. He knew perfectly well that we had escaped, but must have been so vexed that we had done so that he took a little petty revenge on my friends.'

'Well, he certainly succeeded on that score,' said Clay. 'By the way, that jaunt ashore had best be strictly between us. Montague gave me an order not to attempt your rescue, which I chose to interpret as directed to me personally, rather than my people. I should prefer it if he did not discover I went against his expressed wishes.'

'Did he, now?' said Sutton. 'I wonder why he issued such an order?'

'He said it was because he could not afford to have me captured, too,' said Clay. 'It is an explanation that I do not find wholly convincing. To my mind he is altogether too close to that creature Windham, although I sense his patience is running thin with regard to his protege. Now, tell me how it was that you travelled from a shack on Reunion to a rock in the middle of the Indian Ocean?'

The rest of the story came rapidly. Sutton delivered the bare facts with little emotion, anxious not to dwell on the horror of his experience. He could trust his friend to read between the lines of the simple story, to fill in the fear and despair that Sutton would have felt when he found himself adrift, far out at sea, with no food or water. Clay in turn gave what answers he could to fill the gaps in his friend's comprehension, explaining why the *Titan* had vanished far out to sea on that the first night, and how they had seen the thread of smoke on the horizon, all those days later.

'Goodness, what a saga,' said Clay, running a hand through his hair. 'It is a miracle that you survived for so long in such a tiny little boat. You must have had many empty hours to reflect on matters.'

'Do you mean about what I will do with our friend Windham?' said Sutton.

'I can imagine that must have engaged you for much of the time. What course have you resolved on?'

'My first thought had been to call him out the moment I saw the blackguard, and shoot him like the dog that he is.'

'An understandable desire,' said Clay. 'But I note you say *had*. Have you now changed your mind?'

'I have, Alex, and it was Chapman, of all people, my steward, who made me think differently. In such an extreme position as we were in, convinced that we were soon to perish, there is a frankness of discourse that cuts across the normal constraints of position and rank. During one such debate, he said that he held me in part responsible for this whole sorry mess, and in truth he is right.'

'Because you killed Windham's uncle,' whispered Clay. 'Surely you did not share that with him?'

'No, of course not,' said Sutton. 'But he is a shrewd man. I am sure he suspects that something more substantial lies behind the bare facts that I gave him. No, his principal accusation was that I did not seek to resolve matters privately with Windham, and it was this want of action that let matters fester to a point when others became dragged in. He sees the principal victims in this matter to be his shipmates on the *Rush*.'

'There is a deal of wisdom in what he says, John,' said Clay. 'And I think you are right not to consider a duel with Windham, for it would provide you with scant justice. You well know the intolerance that the Admiralty has for such affairs of honour. If you should kill him, you will be dismissed the service and your career will be over. If he should kill you, which is frankly the more probable outcome in your current state, where will the justice you seek be for all those shipmates?'

'So what should I do, then?' asked the patient. 'I m put my orders to Windham in writing, and the only person present when I gave them to him was poor Mr Wise, my lieutenant, who perished onboard the *Rush*.'

'Go before Sir George and demand justice,' urged Clay. 'Any investigation will reveal the truth of what happened. Not only is there your testimony and that of Mr Croft, but you can ask that the French officers we captured on the *Prudence* be interviewed, too. I also understand that the crew of the *Echo* are very discontent. Sailors will tolerate much in a captain, but they have nothing but contempt for one who shirks a fight. Doubtless many of them will be happy to denounce him.'

'But will Sir George really act?' asked Sutton. 'It was he who petitioned the Admiralty to give Windham the *Echo*. If he now censures him, it will be an admission that he made a mistake. Their Lordships take a very dim of view of those that show such poor judgment.'

'That is so, but what choice does he have?' said Clay. 'He cannot make the loss of the *Rush* vanish. The best course for him to follow now is to put matters right and admit that he may have misjudged his protege's abilities. If he can defeat the French, he will hope that a successful campaign will cause their Lordships to overlook any earlier errors. I have spoken with the commodore. He may be close to Windham, and he is something of a peacock, I grant you, but he is no fool.'

'What of Windham's friends and family? Surely a court martial of a man with his connections is most unlikely to

'

case,' said Clay. 'The evidence is too
what Windham did will so disgust
considers the matter that no possible
im.' There was a knock on the cabin
surgeon came from the other side.
on, sir, but I must insist on Mr Sutton

being allowed to rest now,' he said.

'A minute more, Mr Corbett, I pray,' said Clay. 'I have but one more matter I need to discuss.'

'Hmm!' snorted the surgeon, but he went away again. Clay turned back to his friend.

'Before I leave you, there is something you must let me say, or rather unsay. It has been playing on my mind for weeks now. Can you forgive me for the intemperate way I addressed you when we were back in Cape Town? My demand that you reveal the nature of your relationship with my sister was ill-mannered and impertinent on my part. Let me withdraw any objection that I may have implied towards your continued acquaintance with her. If you are lucky enough to win her heart, no one will be more pleased than I.'

'Except perhaps me?' suggested Sutton, with a smile.

*****

On the lower deck of the *Titan*, her crew were agog to learn what the implications of the rescue of the three castaways might be. When the larboard watch came pouring down from on deck, most of them gathered around one of the mess tables, where Sedgwick sat with his friends.

'So what's afoot then, Able?' asked Davis, a slight, grey-haired seaman and one of the veteran members of the crew. He jerked a thumb towards the stern of the ship, where it was known the three new arrivals had been housed.

'Aye, how are them poor bleeders doing?' said Josh Black, the huge captain of the foretop. As a petty officer he should have been above such gossip, but he was just as inquisitive as the others.

'Pipe's mate Pretty Boy seems the best of the three,' explained Sedgwick to the crowd of his fellow sailors. 'He's stowed in that spare cabin in the wardroom. Chapman is right enough, out cold on that draught they gave him and snoring like a prize bull. The lad is still poorly, mind, but the sawbones reckons he'll pull through in time.'

'Any word of how they came to be cast adrift?' asked Davis.

'Pipe has spent a good while with Pretty Boy this morning, and Tom Britton chanced to be tidying out Lieutenant Blake's cabin next door, so heard most of what was said.'

'Funny how old Tom can still fold a shirt with his lughole pressed against the bleeding bulkhead,' said Evans. 'What was he able to hear, then?' A chuckle of anticipation ran around the deck. Those at the back craned forward, eager not to be left out.

'He was saying as how Windy dropped him right in the shit when they fought that Frog ship, plain as plain,' continued the coxswain. A growl of anger met this news.

'It never did feel right, the way that *Echo* came back with barely a scratch on her, the buggers,' offered Black, to general approval. 'What else did they speak off?'

'There was plenty of talk of how it was he came to escape,' resumed the coxswain. 'How they was stuck in that boat, without a drop to drink and all. Some stuff about Pipe's sister, who his mate is sweet upon it seems, and then a load of talk on what they would do to Windy when they get to him.'

'I reckon how Old Windy is proper done for,' said Evans with satisfaction. 'Plucked, stuffed, with an onion up his arse.'

'You be right there, our Sam,' said Trevan. 'Blimey! What I wouldn't give to see that bastard's face when him finds out that Pretty Boy be alive! Mind, it be a miracle that he is. Not killed when the old *Rush* was taken, and then enduring all them days adrift. How they managed, I don't rightly know.

You saw the boat, didn't you, Saul?' This to a fellow Cornishman who stood behind him.

'Aye, that I did,' Saul confirmed. 'I was in the launch crew. I tell you, it were no longer than our jollyboat, but only half the beam, if you'll credit it. No mast nor sails, not even a rudder. All they had was one poxy little paddle, on my mother's grave. How those poor buggers managed be beyond me. An' they didn't have no vitals to sustain them, neither. Just sea air and notions of revenge.'

'Can't wait to be back with the rest of the fecking squadron,' added O'Malley, a glint in his eye as he looked around the group. 'Can you sense what I can, in the air, like, lads?'

'What you on about, O'Malley?' said the petty officer. 'What bloody smell?'

'There be stormy weather and squalls ahead, Mr Black,' replied the Irishman. 'You mark my words.'

'What you reckon will become of Windy, then, Sean?' asked Sedgwick. 'Once we get back, like?'

'It's in them Articles of War, what Pipe reads out every week on the Sabbath,' said O'Malley. 'Plain as you like, it is. *He who holds back from a fight through cowardice, shall suffer death.* No ifs or buts, and none of that bollocks about *or lesser punishment* neither. Just fecking death.'

'That's right!' said someone. 'He should be strung up!' added another voice.

'Even with him being a Grunter, like?' queried a voice from the back.

'Didn't they shoot that admiral back in the day for being shy?' said the Irishman. 'What was the fecker called? Bang or Bong?'

'Aye, Jack Byng,' said Davis. 'That were a few year ago now, mind.'

'That don't signify, any,' said Evans. 'Shy is still shy. They would string us up soon enough, so why not that bleeder Windham, eh? Like I said, he's proper done for.'

*****

The stern cabin of the *Echo* may have been the most lavish accommodation aboard, but it was still a small, cramped space. The headroom was a bare five-foot-ten, which meant even a moderately tall man had to duck between the beams as he moved about. He would also have to avoid shouldering the hot oil lamp that swung close to the skylight. With a desk, table, chairs and a twelve-pounder carronade on each side, it seemed crowded, even with only two men sitting there.

The first was an elegantly dressed young lieutenant, with pale curly hair, hazel eyes and a receding chin. He sat and looked at his captain, who was slumped at the desk, a half empty spirit bottle at his elbow and a brimming glass before him.

'Are you sure you won't try some of this Hollander gin?' slurred Windham, his hair flopped across his forehead and his bloodshot eyes deep set. 'It is rather acceptable. Made in a Cape Town still, by one of your proper Dutchmen. None of your London gut-rot, don't you know?'

'No thank you, sir,' replied the *Echo*'s lieutenant.

'Oh, come now,' urged his captain, looking around for a second glass.

'Really, sir, I would rather not. I am due to be on watch within the hour, as I said earlier.'

'Suit yourself, Mr Noble,' he said. He drained his glass and sloshed some more gin in to it. Then he paused for a moment, and pointed a swaying glass towards his subordinate. 'That is very *noble* of you! Eh! What?'

'Very droll, sir,' replied the lieutenant, his face blank.

'Could we please discuss the crew now?'

'Those base villains again? Do we have to?'

'They are becoming increasingly troublesome,' said Noble. 'Most of the petty officers have reported some incident of curt and uncivil behaviour, now. They know, sir.'

'What is it that they know, Mr Noble?' said Windham, his tone dangerous.

'They talk about the fight with the *Prudence*,' whispered the lieutenant. 'How they were not allowed to come to their fellow sailors' help.'

'Ha!' snorted the captain. 'You really must not encourage them. The mutinous dogs seem to have ideas far above their station. They should be thanking me for saving their miserable skins, after the late Captain Sutton made such a sad hash of things. Be firm with them, Noble, and it shall pass.'

'I am not sure that it will, sir. The boatswain came to see me earlier. He has received a further delegation from the crew. They want to know why Sir George has not responded to their petition.'

'Why has he not responded?' spluttered Windham. 'He is a commodore and a knight of the realm! Who the hell do they think they are? Have they quite lost their damned senses? When did it become their place to issue demands to a King's officer? I have a good mind to call out the marines.'

'That might not answer, sir,' said Noble. 'Many of the Lobsters are sympathetic to the men. Some even signed that round robin. Lieutenant Barker says that he is sure that some of them may not be relied on.' His captain stared at him for a long moment, swaying in his chair, his eyes slipping in and out of focus.

'So Lieutenant Barker can't control his bloody men?' said Sutton. 'For God's sake, Noble, what are you saying? Can I not even trust my officers?'

'Of course you can, sir. I can assure you that they are all behind you.'

'Even that old Tarpaulin of a sailing master? That sod is forever presuming to query my seamanship.' Windham glared across the desk, but his lieutenant was unable to hold his gaze.

'I am sure Mr Fawcett only has the ship's best interest in mind, sir.'

'The *ship's* best interests!' yelled Windham. 'And when did those separate from *my* best interests, eh? For God's sake, Noble, why must you come and whine to me about all this? Just go away and deal with it! You're the bloody lieutenant. Do as you see fit and leave me alone!'

When the young officer had gone, Windham took another pull at the gin, staring into the distance. 'I never wanted to be in the bloody navy, you know,' he announced, as if Noble were still opposite him. 'It was all that bitch of a mother's fault.' He put on a lady's voice. '*Oh, but Uncle Percy's son has died. Very tragic, I am sure, but he has such influence in the service, and no one else to prefer now. It is your chance, Nicholas.*' He paused to take a pull from his glass. 'My bloody chance,' he muttered. 'A God sent opportunity, she said. And now look at things. Uncle Percy killed in his own ship, by the hand of that bastard Sutton, God rot his soul. And when I try to put things right, what happens? Everyone starts to turn on me. Even Montague.' He felt tears start to course down his cheeks, but he dashed them away. Then he returned to the comfort of the bottle.

It was quiet in the cabin. The thick glass of the window lights deadened the sound of the ship's wake. With the wind behind, there was very little creaking to be heard from the frames. He put his head on one side and listened. Behind his door he could hear the marine sentry as he shuffled from foot to foot. I wonder how reliable he is, thought Windham to himself. Will he turn back the tide of angry crewmen, if matters get out of hand? From beneath his feet came the low sound of his officers as they talked in the wardroom. He got down on all fours and pressed an ear to the planking, but the murmur of their voices was pitched just out of the range of comprehension, as those of plotters would be, he decided. From the quarterdeck above his head came the tramp of the officer of the watch, walking backwards and forwards like a prison guard. He stared around him at the oak walls. They seemed to be drawing ever more tightly about him, like the sides of a coffin. He drank thirstily from his glass of gin as he tried to wash away the feeling of impending doom.

'Sail ho!' came a distant shout.

'Where away?' yelled the voice of Noble, much closer.

'Larboard quarter, and coming up fast, sir. Looks like the old *Titan* to me.' Windham looked up towards the cabin's skylight. He knew he should go up on deck, but his legs felt weak and unreliable. He felt so much safer in his cabin, away from the hostile gaze of his crew. The *Titan* had disappeared several days ago, pursuing one of the French frigates, and now she had returned. Windham emptied his glass and reached for the bottle of gin. Just as he started to pour, a thunder of knocking at the door made him spill some over the desk.

'Eh ...come in,' he called, mopping at the drink with his handkerchief.

'Mr Noble's compliments, sir, and he believes the *Titan* is in sight, off the larboard quarter,' said the midshipman.

'And where is the commodore?' asked Windham.

'In view, two miles off the starboard bow, sir,' said the teenager, his eyes transfixed by the sopping handkerchief as his captain made several ineffectual attempts to return it to his coat pocket. Windham glared back at him.

'Did you just wrinkle your nose, boy?' he demanded.

'N...no, sir, not at all, sir.' The youngster looked terrified.

'Don't give me the lie, in my own damned cabin,' roared Windham. 'You just pulled a face!'

'I d...d...did not intend to, sir,' stuttered the midshipman, his face becoming pale.

'How dare you disapprove of the actions of your superiors!' yelled the captain. 'My compliments to Mr Noble, and tell him that when you come off duty you are to report to the boatswain to be given a dozen strokes of his cane. Is that clear?'

'Aye, aye, sir.'

Once he was alone again, Windham drank more of the gin.

'So the bloody *Titan* is back again, like some bird of ill omen,' he said out loud. 'It is always that bastard Clay, reading damned signals, capturing blasted prisoners to exchange.' Then he began to chuckle to himself. Still, I wiped you in the eye, Clay, when I had your friend killed, he thought. No possible exchange there. From over his head he heard a dash of footsteps, and a voice calling.

'*Titan* signalling, sir,' called a voice with a Scottish accent. There was a long pause and then a further knock at the door.

'Come in,' growled Windham. The same midshipman came and stood at attention, his face fixed and immobile.

'Mr Noble's compliments and the *Titan* is signalling to the commodore, sir,' he said. 'Have on board three crew from the *Rush*.'

'What did you just say?' said the captain, his voice low with menace.

'T...T...itan has three survivors from the *Rush* on board, sir.'

'That is not possible,' said Windham firmly. 'The crew of the *Rush* are all imprisoned on Reunion. Are you seeking to make game of me? If you are, you will wish you had never been born. I can see that the boatswain's cane will be working hard tonight. Who took the signal?'

'M...midshipman Galbraith, sir,' replied the teenager.

'Well you can tell Mr Galbraith to check the signal again, unless he wants to spend the rest of the commission at the masthead,' yelled Windham. 'Now get out!'

What nonsense was this, he said to himself, but the words sounded false even in his own mind. He started to brood once more, asking himself the same question that he had done late into the night for weeks now. Who could have survived the destruction of the *Rush*? He had searched the list that Montague had shared with him, but there were no significant names who could denounce him. The most senior officers were the surgeon and purser, both of whom would have been below deck treating the wounded during the battle. There had been a very junior midshipman; some sailors, of course; a few petty and warrant officers; and one master's mate. No, he would be fine, he told himself. But in his bones he felt something was wrong. Who were these survivors that bastard Clay had somehow found? Other images seemed to dance before his eyes. What if it was the solid, reliable Appleby, the sailing master, who was somehow alive? Or worse still Lieutenant Wise, who had been there in the cabin when the plan of attack was agreed? He started, as if he had heard a noise in the silent cabin, and half turned in his chair to glare towards the darkest corner. There it was again, the slight trace of a whisper, drifting through the air. Sutton, it seemed to hiss. What if Sutton has survived?

*****

The *Titan* was over the horizon now, bearing down on the other two ships of the squadron. Her pyramids of sail caught the keen trade wind in curves of white that drove her through the blue waters of the ocean. The *Echo* and the *Black Prince* came up into the wind with topsails backed to await her approach.

'The commodore is signalling again, sir,' reported Lieutenant Taylor. From over by the flag locker Midshipman Russell scratched on his slate, noting down the groups of numbers as they were read to him by his seaman assistant. After a while he came over to where Clay stood with Taylor, together with the thin figure of Sutton, who looked lost in one of his friend's spare coats.

'Signal from the *Black Prince*, sir,' he said. 'Commodore to *Titan*. Who from *Rush* is on board?' Clay turned towards the former captain of the sloop.

'Are you ready to release a fox into the hen coop, John?' he asked. 'We will be passing the *Echo* quite close on this tack. She will be able to read any signal.'

'How do you suppose Windham will react?' asked Sutton.

'Not unlike Macbeth at the feast, I shouldn't wonder,' said Clay. 'It is not every day that a ghost returns from beyond the grave to denounce you.' His friend laughed at this.

'I am to be cast as the avenging spirit, am I? Well, let the haunting commence, then.'

'Mr Russell, kindly send this signal,' ordered Clay. '*Titan* to commodore. Have on board Sutton, commander; Croft, midshipman; and one seaman. You will need to spell the names, I fear.'

'Aye aye, sir,' replied the midshipman, still busy with his chalk on the slate.

It took two hoists for the entire signal to be transmitted. While the lines of flags were hauled aloft, Clay looked towards the other two ships and wondered what the reaction would be to the news. He noticed for the first time that the forecastle of the *Titan* was thronged with crew, with more joining them from below all the time.

'Mr Taylor!' barked Clay. 'Is this a King's ship or a Spanish Bumboat? Why, there must be every idler onboard up on the forecastle.'

'The men have taken a keen interest in Captain Sutton's return, sir,' replied the first lieutenant. 'I should imagine they do not want to miss anything.'

'I don't care if they wish to witness the second coming of Christ, I will not have the ship disgraced in this way! Look at them, gaping like village idiots that have just seen their first stagecoach! Kindly have them cleared away below, if you please. If they have no duties to attend to, I shall find them all employment cleaning the heads.'

'Commodore signalling again, sir,' announced the signal midshipman. 'Report on board with Captain Sutton.'

'Acknowledge, if you please, Mr Russell,' said Clay. 'And have my barge crew summoned.'

The *Titan* stood on, the gap to the other two ships shrinking all the time. As she neared the little sloop, Clay thought he heard something, drifting across the sea.

'What on earth is that noise?' he asked.

'It is cheering I think, sir,' replied Russell. 'It seems to be coming from the *Echo*.'

They were very close now, about to pass behind the ship. There could be no mistaking the sound, as it rolled across the narrow stretch of water. He could see individual crewman who had climbed part way up the shrouds and waved their hats towards them. Others were gathered along the sides, arms aloft as they yelled. All seemed to be straining to get a glimpse of Sutton. Then they were level with her stern. Clay could see the sloop's name picked out in gilded letters across her counter. For a brief moment he thought he saw a pale face looking back at him from one of the window lights, but then it vanished.

'Sir, may I come in?' asked Lieutenant Noble. He had the door ajar and was peering around it.

'What the hell is it now?' demanded Windham, his voice angry. The gin bottle was almost empty, and the air in the cabin was fogged with alcohol fumes.

'Only Mr Galbraith reported there was no answer when he knocked earlier, sir,' said the lieutenant. 'He wondered if you were quite well.'

'You can tell that little Scottish shit I don't care for his damned signals,' said Windham. 'Damn and blast his eyes!' Noble came into the cabin and stood over the slumped figure of his captain.

'You must see this signal, sir,' he said. 'May I take a seat?' There was no response from Windham, and after a pause Noble sat down anyway. 'The *Titan* has signalled that they have Captain Sutton and Midshipman Croft onboard, sir.'

'Sutton!' yelled Windham. 'I don't believe it! He is dead! I saw the list of survivors and he wasn't on it!'

'The signal is quite certain, sir,' continued the lieutenant. 'The names had to be spelt out, letter by letter. There can be no mistake.' Windham looked straight into his lieutenant's eyes, his vision clear for a moment, and then his shoulders slumped.

'I just don't believe it,' he muttered.

'Now come on, sir,' said Noble briskly. 'The *Titan* is almost up with the squadron and is closing with the *Black Prince*. If there is truly some confusion, I am sure it will be resolved shortly. The commodore has ordered her captain and Mr Sutton on board to report. She will pass astern of us at any moment.' Windham's bloodshot eyes began to fill with tears.

'All I ever wanted was justice, for my uncle,' he spluttered. 'Was that too much to seek?' Noble looked away as his captain's shoulders worked with grief and he sobbed over his empty glass.

'I imagine that Sir George will want to see you soon, too, sir,' he continued. 'I will get your steward to make some coffee, and a bite to eat. Lay out some new clothes for you to wear, sir. You need to be ready for when he signals.' His captain made no response, and after a moment Noble stood up and left the little cabin.

For a long while Windham continued to sit at his desk. Then he looked up as a new sound echoed through the ship. It was the sound of the crew cheering. At first it confused him, and then the implications of it hit him.

'The damned bastards,' he muttered. 'How can they cheer him, and yet loathe me?' The level of light dropped in the cabin as a dark shape appeared astern of the sloop, looming over the little ship. He lurched up from the desk and staggered towards the stern windows. The *Titan* slid past, a seemingly endless hull of yellow and black. He peered up at the quarterdeck and saw the tall Clay, looking back at him. Stood next to him, also in a captain's coat, was the unmistakable shape of John Sutton.

He ducked back from the glass and stood, swaying uncertainly as he wondered what to do. The warmth of the gin leaked away, leaving behind only cold despair. This was it, the end of the road, he thought. Sutton will denounce me to Sir George. At that moment his steward came through the door with a steaming pot of coffee on a tray.

'Get out,' ordered Windham, his voice almost calm, with hardly a trace of the black feeling inside him. The cabin door clicked shut again, and he was alone once more. He sat back down at the desk, sure of what he would do. He pushed the empty glass and bottle aside with a sweep of his arm and both smashed on the deck, sending shards of glass far across the planking. He drew a sheet of paper towards him, dipped his pen into the ink well and scratched off a brief note. He folded it closed, rose to melt some wax on the cabin's oil lamp, and sealed it shut. When the wax was hard he turned it over, wrote *Commodore Sir George Montague, His Majesty's Ship* Black Prince, on the front, and propped it up against the ink stand. Then he reached for the bottom drawer of his desk and pulled out a large, polished mahogany box. It required both his hands to lift it to the desk top, such was its weight. He opened the lid and looked into velvet-lined interior.

The metal of the pistol felt cold against his lips. A few grains of powder dropped onto his tongue, leaving an unpleasant, gritty taste. He tried to hold the heavy gun steady, but he found his hands trembled too much. The hard barrel rattled against his teeth in an unpleasant way and seemed to fill his whole mouth. He suppressed the feeling of being choked, and felt with one finger to check that the steep angle of the pistol pointed towards the roof of his mouth. Then he closed his eyes, pulled back the lock with a smooth click and gently squeezed the trigger.

Chapter 14 Plan

A few months later, the remaining three ships of the squadron lay at anchor once more in a line beside the ramparts of the Dutch fort in Table Bay. Close at hand was the little naval dockyard, where the hull of the captured *Prudence* had been hauled out of the water to be repaired before her long trip back to Britain. It was deep winter now in the Cape, but the weather was little different from a spring day at home. The heavy rain clouds of the morning had been swept inland and were draped around the bulk of Table Mountain. Behind them, down near the coast, the sunlight sparkled off the choppy waters of the bay.

All three ships rode high in the water, with long strips of copper sheathing flashing in the sunshine amongst the little waves. After months at sea they had all consumed their many tons of food and water. The *Titan* rode highest of them all, having blazed off a portion of her powder and shot into the unfortunate *Prudence*. Yet in spite of this, there seemed to be no great urgency to resupply the squadron. No lighters, packed with hogsheads of beef and sacks of biscuit, were rowed out from the deserted dockyard. The French frigate lay on her slipway, her hull only partly repaired, with no one attending to her.

In contrast the great cabin of the *Titan* had been a hive of activity for much of the morning. Just after dawn, the planking had been scrubbed clean, the windows and the woodwork polished and the stone grey paintwork refreshed. Once the floor covering and furniture had been returned to the room, the table had been covered with a snowy damask cloth, borrowed from the steward of the *Black Prince*, and laid with a blazing array of polished silver and cut glass. In his day cabin Clay pulled on his full dress coat and settled his Nile Medal around his neck. He caught it in a button hole, so that the heavy disc would not swing around as he moved. He may not have a ribbon and glittering order like Sir George, he thought as he touched the warm metal, but he was one of only a handful of captains entitled to wear this.

All these preparations were for the benefit of just three naval officers. Two bells rang out from the belfry on the forecastle, and the sound was echoed faithfully from the other two ships. Clay hurried out of his cabin and grabbed the hat that his servant, Yates, held out to him. He then made his way across to join the throng of men grouped around the entry port. Moments later his two guests arrived, amongst a squealing of boatswain's pipes and saluting marines. He greeted them both on the sunlit main deck, and then led the way down to the freshly cleaned cabin.

'I fear that we must wait till the morning before we can be resupplied, gentlemen,' explained the trim figure of Sir George Montague as he settled himself into the chair of the principle guest. 'I have pleaded on bended knee to the superintendent, without any effect. Apparently all the dockworkers are Hollanders. Dutch Reform zealots to a man. War or no war, not one of them will stir from his home on a Sunday, save to attend divine service.'

'Fortunately the wine merchant my steward engaged with must be a papist,' said Clay. 'He was quite content to stir himself to supply a dozen bottles of his best Cape bishop. Would you care to try some, Sir George?'

'With pleasure,' said the commodore. 'Perhaps when our glasses are charged, we might drink to the health of the captain of the *Echo*.' The two frigate captains held their wine up towards the last guest, and then drained them.

'I must say, it is good to see you restored to health once more, Captain Sutton,' continued Montague. 'You start to resemble more your old self.'

'Hear him!' said Clay, drumming a hand on the tabletop in approval. 'The waif we collected from Hope Island was as skinny as the sop of a midshipman I first met in the gunroom of the old *Marlborough*, if you will credit it. That was back in the year eighty-four.'

'I confess that I have been quite gorging myself,' replied the commander of the *Echo*. 'They say that absence breeds fondness, and that is certainly true where food is concerned. I shall need to stop soon, else I will be unable to fit into any of the uniforms that have been made for me.'

'Not too soon, I trust, John,' said his friend. 'Harte has a splendid pudding for us to sample later.'

'And how do you find the *Echo*?' asked Montague. 'The people were very unsettled before the unfortunate demise of Captain Windham, and such tragedies can have a pronounced effect.'

'It has not been easy, Sir George,' said Sutton. 'Apart from Mr Croft and my steward, I have no followers with me aboard. I do not want to speak ill of my predecessor, but the men had been allowed to become rather slack. Some of their more rebellious urges had not been properly checked. But the officers are on the whole sound, and a few months of sail and gun drill has served to improve matters. They are not yet a match for the crew of my *Rush*, but they will be able to take their place in the battle line against the French with some credit, before too long.'

'Whenever that shall be,' muttered the commodore. 'The damned cowards refuse to stand and fight us. Yet now we are driven off station to resupply, you may wager your commissions that they are abroad once more and busy preying on our commerce.'

'We will be back in a month or so, to put pay to their mischief,' said Clay.

'Aye, but then they will simply fly back to hide behind their damned guns at Reunion!' exclaimed Montague. 'The whole thing is very vexing.'

'Might something not be tried against Reunion, Sir George?' asked Sutton. 'If we were to deny them the comfort of their base, they would have little alternative but to return home.' Montague toyed despondently with his food.

'But how is that to be achieved?' he asked. 'You know the defences of St Paul better than most, captain. Are they not quite formidable?'

'From the sea, certainly, but less so from the landward side,' said Sutton. 'If you had a body of troops that you might throw ashore a little farther down the coast, something might be attempted. I even know the spot to choose. I used to walk that stretch of beach most mornings.'

'But we have little more than the hundred-odd marines we carry between us,' said Montague. 'No, unless we receive some troop reinforcements from home, we shall just have to return to our station, and hope for some chance circumstance to fall in our favour.'

'On the subject of reinforcements from home, there was a very pleasing quantity of mail that awaited us in Cape Town,' said Clay. 'No less than twenty letters from my wife, if you will credit it.'

'Any news?' asked Sutton. 'Of the child, I mean?'

'Of course! Your wife was expecting when we left, I collect,' exclaimed Montague. 'Why, the blighter must have been born by now!'

'Born, and several months old, if all has proceeded satisfactorily,' said Clay. 'But her last letter still predates the event. She speaks only of being very large and rather vexed at not being able to ride of a morning.'

'Let us trust to Providence that all is indeed well, and toast the health of young Master or Miss Clay,' said the commodore. 'Come, charge your glass, Mr Sutton.'

'Did you have much correspondence, John?' asked Clay, once the toast had been drunk. He glanced significantly across the table.

'I did, thank you,' his friend replied with a grin. 'And it was all of a very satisfactory character.' Clay smiled back, and mouthed 'Good' at him, before rising from his place at the table.

'I almost forgot,' he said. 'I also received a package from my sister, containing a most intriguing item.' He picked up a thin volume bound in brown leather from his desk, and brought it over. 'What do you make of this, Sir George?'

The commodore picked up the book and flipped it open to the title page. It was dominated by an oval engraving of the head and shoulders of a solid looking man in sailor's garb.

'He looks vaguely familiar,' mused Montague. He reached into his coat, produced a pair of silver reading glasses and perched them on his nose. '*The Interesting Narrative of the Life of Ablanjaye Senghore, or Able Sedgwick, the African,*' he read, and then looked up. 'By Jove, Clay, ain't he your coxswain?'

'That's right, Sir George. It is an account of his life to date. He spent much of his leisure time on my last commission setting it down. My sister has assisted him with finding a publisher.'

'Did she now?' said Montague. 'And has it been well received?'

'According to Miss Clay, it has caused quite a sensation back home. The abolitionists have made much of it, and all want to know where the author is to be found. Reports that he is thousands of miles away and fighting the enemies of the country that once enslaved him, has merely added to his fame, apparently.'

'That all sounds well and good,' said the commodore, putting the book down. 'But I find this talk of ending the slave trade to be very ill-judged. Fact is that the country needs sugar and the navy needs rum. It won't answer for our folk to work on these plantations in the Caribbean; they all die like flies of Yellow Jack or the Ague. What these dashed abolitionists don't say is what will we do should the trade end? Without any Negros to cut the cane, where shall we be then, what?'

'When I first served on the *Rush*, Sir George, it was in the Caribbean,' said Sutton. 'Our surgeon at the time married the daughter of a plantation owner in Barbados and subsequently left the service. His father-in-law freed his slaves, and then re-employed them as labourers. He found the change worked passing well, for although he had to pay them, they were much more productive.'

'One enterprise don't prove much,' sniffed the commodore. 'I hold all this talk of freeing slaves to be very ill-judged. Besides, I have always understood slavery to be the natural state of your Negro, back in Africa. If the trade was to end tomorrow, the condition of most Africans would hardly change.'

'Perhaps you might care to borrow my copy of Sedgwick's book, Sir George,' suggested Clay. 'Then you could judge for yourself?'

'I could, but only if I thought his account to be genuine,' he said, returning the book to its owner. 'How do I know his head has not been turned with all manner of abolitionist nonsense, eh? Or that it is even a genuine account. Who ever heard of a Blackamoor who could write a book? No, he must surely have been assisted by someone.'

'It is true that he learnt his letters from another shipmate, Sir George,' explained Clay.

'There you go,' said the commodore. 'Doubtless this other man or your sister are enemies of the trade and steered this narrative appropriately. Is this other sailor still aboard?'

'No, he was killed at the Battle of the Nile, Sir George,' said Clay. 'As for the work, I need to read it myself to judge properly, but I believe it was chiefly Sedgwick's own creation. Certainly I think that he had no more than a little assistance from my sister with finding a publisher.'

'Sedgwick's creation is certainly right,' muttered the commodore.

'I can assure you that Miss Clay would not be party to any work that was untruthful, or sort to dissemble, Sir George,' said Sutton, glaring across the table. 'I happen to know that she has an unimpeachable character.' Montague stared back at him.

'Careful with your tone, Captain Sutton,' he said, his face angry. 'I can take the *Echo* away as easily as I gave her to you. But wait, it is all coming back to me. I had forgotten your distress back in Portsmouth, when you were unable to visit Miss Clay before we departed. Perhaps you are less impartial in these matters then you would have us believe?'

'I am sure that John meant no disrespect, Sir George,' said Clay, holding up a restraining hand. 'Gentlemen, it is I that am at fault. I only thought to divert by mention of this book. I imagined that you might find the notion of an author emerging from the lower deck of interest. I certainly did not intend to provoke a quarrel. Come, a glass of wine with you both, and let us not mention it further.'

The three men drained their glasses, and Sutton and Montague avoided each other's gaze by looking around the cabin. The commodore settled on the portrait of Lydia that dominated one bulkhead.

'That is a fine looking lady, Clay,' he said, pointing towards the picture with his wine glass. 'I assume that she is your wife?'

'That is Mrs Clay, yes,' he confirmed. 'And it barely does her justice. Where pictures of ladies are concerned, I find it is always best to ascertain, as you just did, the precise nature of the relationship before passing comment. I served under Lord Nelson last year, in the Mediterranean. The first time I dined on the *Vanguard* the portrait in his cabin was of Lady Nelson, which occupied much the same position as that which Mrs Clay does now. Then, in Naples the pictured vanished for a while, and for several months the bulkhead was bare. On the final occasion that I visited the cabin a fresh likeness had appeared, which was that of Lady Emma Hamilton.'

'Is that so?' chuckled Montague. 'Fine admiral though he is, I hear he is a thorough satyr where another man's wife is concerned. If your wife looks anything like that, I would keep them apart. But I must say the artist who produced that picture must be a talented cove. The blue satin of the dress looks almost real, and the features are so well produced one might almost image she were here with us now. It is quite remarkable what he has achieved with only paint and canvas.' Clay said nothing in return, and after a moment his two guests looked towards him.

'Alex, are you quite well?' asked Sutton.

'My dear sir,' said the commodore. 'You look as if you have seen a phantom!'

'Apologies, gentlemen, I am fine. It is just that all this talk of Lydia's picture has given me an idea. I think I may have found a way that we might defeat the French.'

*****

While the officers sat with their wine in the stern cabin of the ship, farther forward Sedgwick's copy of the book was being passed with reverence around the lower deck of the *Titan*. From hand to hand it went, with each recipient solemnly opening the leather cover and leafing a little way into the text, before they passed it on to their neighbour with a smile of comprehension. Not one man in ten could read the words, but all could recognise the face that stared out from the title page as that of their very own captain's coxswain. It was a proud moment for the *Titans*.

'I'll wager that fecking arse at the Elm Tree tavern back in Pompey is feeling right foolish today,' said O'Malley as he observed the book's passage across the lower deck.

'Assuming he be still alive, after Sam lumped him, like,' added Trevan.

'I barely touched the bleeder,' said Evans. 'He will still be around, his sort always are. The Devil looks after his own, don't you know?'

'I hope that he is alive,' enthused the Irishman, 'I can just picture the scene. Your landlord comes greasing over to some fancy arse in a shilling booth, who is a-reading that there book. He glances over his shoulder, like, and there will be Able givin' him the eye from out off the page. "Not the Blackamoor again!" he cries. "I cast that fecker out!" And then your learned gent will give him a full broadside. "What! The Great African scholar himself? He was here, in all his pomp? In this very tavern, and you showed him the door, you fecking rogue!" Now that would be worth seeing.'

'This here foreign name, Able,' said one of the few readers amongst the crew. 'A blank sing, a bonk sinking... any road, we meant to be a calling you that now?'

'Able Sedgwick is fine,' laughed the author. 'It was Miss Clay as wanted me to use my African name. She thought folk would not credit the tale if some bloke what sounded English wrote it.'

'Very deep, that wench,' said O'Malley. 'I would never trust a fecking word writ by an Englishman.'

'Well, I shall still be going by my regular name in the service,' concluded the coxswain.

'Pity, that,' said Evans. 'Can you imagine the bleeding lark we'd be having if Josh Black or the boatswain had to holler for him in African?' The lower deck laughed long and loud at the absurdity of the thought.

'But will you be continuing in the service, when we get home, like?' asked Trevan, when the mirth of his messmates had past. 'Won't you be giving up the sea to be one of them there philosophers?'

'I don't rightly know, Adam,' said Sedgwick. 'I never figured much beyond the setting down of my tale. It took that long to do, and then I gave it to Pipe's sister a good year back now, and sort of forgot about it. Next thing I know, that there book shows up, with it all printed like, and a letter saying how it be selling in droves, and that she has a pile of guineas waiting for me in consequence. It's all a bit sudden, in truth.'

'Fecking go, mate,' urged O'Malley. 'Why would you want to stay and be shot at, flogged or drowned, when you have all that lucre at home?'

'He's not bleeding wrong, you know, Able,' added Evans. 'You could have soft tack to scoff every day, as much grog as you liked. Bleeding hell, what about all of them fancy doxies up in London, all randy as badgers for a bit of Jack Tar. I can't see what you would be waiting for.'

'Miss Clay said she would want me to leave the ship, she wrote so, but look at me, lads. Could you honestly see me yarning with all them grand folk, with a wig and a coat of plush an' all? At best I would just be some manner of curiosity. No, I reckon I might just stay as I am.'

'That sounds right good, Able lad,' said Trevan, patting his arm. 'Barky would be a strange place without your chubby hereabouts. Their loss be our gain.' Sedgwick looked about him and registered all the nods and smiles of his fellow shipmates. He wanted to say more, about friendship, and acceptance, but that wasn't the lower deck way.

At that moment Midshipman Butler came running down the ladder and stood by the shaft of the main mast.

'Listen now, you men,' he bellowed. 'I need volunteers. Does anyone have any facility at painting? Lieutenant Blake is in need of some assistants.'

'I done the odd tavern sign, afore the war, like,' announced a voice.

'I worked in a printer's back in York, inking up the plates,' said another. 'Does that count?'

'You should try on board the *Prince*, Mr Butler,' said Evans. 'I hear them buggers do little else but paint.' The midshipman ignored the big Londoner and the laughter his comment had provoked, and selected all those with any modicum of artistic talent. They followed him across to the main ladder way.

'What be all that about?' said Trevan to the others. 'Do you reckon Dismal George wants us to tart up Old Henry?'

'The figurehead?' queried O'Malley. 'To be sure, your man loves the smell of fecking paint, but Henry looked all right last time I was on the seat of ease.'

'Well, just so long as they leave his eyes be,' added the Cornishman.

'What's that got to do with anything?' asked Evans.

'No, Adam's got a fecking point, Sam,' said O'Malley. 'We don't one some arse painting over his eyes. That would be dreadful.'

'Is this a bleeding joke?' exclaimed the Londoner. 'Are you two making game of me?'

'It be serious, Sam,' said Trevan. 'A ship has to have eyes.'

'What the bleeding hell for?' exclaimed the Londoner. O'Malley looked towards the heaven, while across the lower deck pigtailed sailors shook their heads in disbelief. Trevan took the Londoner by the arm, and spoke to him in a tone normally reserved for discourse with idiots.

'How does you reckon the barky will know where to go, if she...ain't...got...no...eyes?' he asked, pointing at his own piercing blue ones.

'Ships with eyes!' spluttered Evans. 'I've bleeding heard it all now. I tell you, if there are any sailors locked up in Bedlam, folk would pay a guinea a minute to hear this stuff. Ain't I the lucky one, getting it all for free!'

CHAPTER 15 THE TRAP

The wolves had broken free, and now had the run of the sheepfold. The remaining two French frigates had ventured out from their base on Reunion many weeks ago, when they had found that the ocean was theirs once more. They had known that this moment would come. Their stubborn opponents were sure to exhaust their supplies eventually and be forced to make the long trip back to the Cape to resupply. And they knew that those same ships would return as soon as they were able, so the frigates had made haste to gorge themselves on unprotected East Indiamen. They had worked as a pair, capturing five of the huge ships without so much as a sight of the Royal Navy.

Captain Olivier of the *Rhone* was the senior French naval officer in the whole of the Indian Ocean. He was by nature a cautious man, whose long career had only served to make him more so. An iron-haired veteran in his late fifties, he had fought the Royal Navy in three different wars now, and had found himself on the losing side in each. It had been his decision to keep his two remaining frigates together at all times, even though this halved the amount of sea they could search. The loss of the *Prudence* had served as a warning to him, and he would permit no possibility of one of his ships being surprised by the enemy on its own. He had calculated with care how long it might take the British to first reach and then return from the Cape. He had repeated the calculation just last night, in the semi-dark of his cabin. Beneath the flickering lamp, his dividers had strode stiff-legged across his chart, while Captain Olivier silently counted. First from Reunion to Cape Town, a day or two to replenish their stores, and then back to the current location of his two ships, astride the sea lane to India. He had stared at the map as he pondered the conclusion he had reached.

The following morning his cabin was a much more cheerful place. The builders of the *Rhone* had generous ideas as to the space that they should allocate to her captain, and the room ran across the whole thirty-foot width of the ship. The interior was light and airy, the bulkheads painted in a pale blue that contrasted pleasantly with the lemon-coloured upholstery of the furniture. Sunlight streamed in through the row of window lights that ran in a curve across the back of the space. All of which added to the cheerfulness of the group of officers as they ate their breakfast at the table.

'We have fish today, gentlemen,' announced Captain Olivier to the officer of the watch and the two midshipmen who had just been relieved on deck. 'Some of the Breton hands have considerable skill with a line, and sell the best of their catch to my steward.' He lifted the silver dome from the plate, and a delicious smell filled the cabin. 'Please, help yourselves.'

'Back in St Paul, while we were blockaded, they made lobster pots from bamboo, mon capitaine, and deployed them all around the reef,' said the lieutenant, transferring the largest fish to his plate. 'They supplied their catch to the wardroom and much of the garrison. I sometime wonder if they were making more from their fishing than from all our prizes.'

'Perhaps they did,' smiled Olivier. 'And they may soon have to rely on lobsters for their fishing once more. I expect our English friends to return to these waters shortly.'

'Really? So soon, mon capitaine?' queried one of the two midshipman, through a mouthful of food.

'It has been over two months that they have been away,' explained the captain. 'I have made the calculation with care. We must expect the enemy to return any day now. If they have had favourable winds, they may be close to us already.'

'That is excellent, mon capitaine,' said the lieutenant. 'Capturing these merchantmen is all very well, but it becomes tiresome after awhile. It will be good to cross swords with another warship for a change.'

'Like the *Prudence* did?' said his captain. 'Be careful what you wish for, lieutenant. Unlike you, I have fought the English, and spent long months as a prisoner in consequence. Our mission is to attack commerce, not to die, however bravely, in a fight with the Royal Navy. Let me be clear, if they should appear, it will be our duty to withdraw to St Paul once more. Steward, more coffee here.'

'But why do we not fight them?' The young man wagged his fork in frustration. 'We always live in fear of the damned Roast Beefs.'

'That is because we have a much smaller navy,' said Olivier. 'I salute your courage, but there is a difference between that and folly. Our mission is to attack our enemy where he is weak, and fly from where he is strong. In this way we shall wear him down, make him expend his ships, men and treasure. The longer we can keep him in this distant ocean the better. There is nothing that our enemy wants more than to fight us, because once we are defeated, the threat we pose will have gone. No, the very last thing we shall do is to battle with their warships.'

'Deck there,' came a cry from the masthead. It echoed down through the open skylight above their heads. All four officers looked up. 'Sail ahoy! Sail on the starboard beam.'

'Another East Indiaman?' queried the lieutenant.

'Or the arrival of the enemy, perhaps,' said his captain. 'Will you gentlemen excuse me? Please, stay seated and continue with your breakfast.' He rose from his end of the table, wiped his mouth and dropped his napkin beside his plate. Then he held his arms out behind him so his steward could pull his coat over his large frame. Once it was settled and the sleeves adjusted, he took his hat from its hook by the door and left the cabin. When he had gone, the lieutenant threw down his fork.

'Not fight the Royal Navy!' he said in exasperation. 'How are we to win a war if we do not fight!'

'I am sure Papa Olivier knows what he is doing, sir,' said one of the teenage midshipman. 'He is very experienced.'

'Papa Olivier has been beaten once too often, and now has forgotten what courage is,' said the lieutenant. 'Look what General Bonaparte has done with the Army! No one now dares to oppose him in the field. That is the sort of leader we need in the navy too, my friends.'

*****

When he reached the quarterdeck, the crowd of excited officers parted to let their captain through. He made his way over to his first lieutenant.

'What do you have for me that is more important than my breakfast, on this fine morning,' asked Olivier.

'A convoy, mon capitaine,' he reported. 'Outbound and heading for India. There are two East Indiamen together with a small warship to protect them.' The captain shot him a glance from under his bushy grey eyebrows.

'A warship, you say?'

'Yes, but only a very small one, mon capitaine. Nothing to compare with our two frigates.'

Olivier looked about him, sensing the mood of his crew. They seemed to be boiling over with anticipation. Too many easy victories these last few months, he concluded. They have lost the need for vigilance, like that young puppy of a lieutenant, and are spoiling for a fight. After a moment's reflection he decided he would see these ships for himself. Better safe than sorry, he told himself as he looked up towards the top of the *Rhone*'s enormous main mast. He was a large man with a slight paunch, and the breakfast he had just eaten sat heavy in his stomach. In his youth he would have scampered to the top of a frigate's main mast in under a minute, but today it would take him rather longer. He turned back towards his first lieutenant.

'Jean-Claude,' he said. 'I am going aloft. You may close on this enemy, but you are to stay out of range until I return. Understood?'

'Yes, mon capitaine,' said the officer, touching his hat, and the older man made his way over to the main shrouds.

'Now I have no choice,' he muttered through gritted teeth as he gripped the thick black ropes and began his ascent.

As he climbed, he concentrated on looking upwards. Lines of rigging ran away from him in all directions in curves and arcs, but he fixed his gaze only on the route that seemed to stretch endlessly ahead. As he reached the main top, he transferred his weight to the backwards-sloping futtock shrouds, his grip manic in its intensity as he felt gravity try to suck him backwards into the void behind him. He pulled himself up on to the topmast shrouds, and once more the slope was no worse than a steep ladder. Higher and higher he climbed, the wind shrill through the taut ropes, causing the tails of his coat to flap. Now his legs began to protest at the unaccustomed effort required of them, and for a moment he tasted grilled fish again in his mouth. He forced himself onwards and upwards until he arrived, with a final gasp, on the topgallant yard. He sat for a moment while he allowed his breath to return to normal, then mopped his brow with a red silk handkerchief, returned it to his pocket, and pulled out his telescope.

'Where are these ships of yours, Leclerc?' he asked, calling up to the figure perched on the royal yard above him. In response the lookout pointed towards the far horizon.

'One point ahead of the starboard beam, mon capitaine. Two big East Indiamen, fat as plovers, with just that little sloop to protect them. Magnificent, is it not?'

Olivier tried to ignore the delighted chuckling of the lookout and concentrated instead on the ships. Closest to him was the escorting sloop, which had sailed out to place herself between her charges and danger. Through his powerful telescope he examined her little yellow and black hull. The rake of her foremast seemed familiar to him.

'What do you make of the warship, Leclerc?' he asked. 'Do you recognise her?'

'Maybe, mon capitaine,' he replied, after a pause. 'Perhaps it is the one that was in the offing outside St Paul?' Olivier cast back in his mind to the ships that had appeared, the day before those prisoners escaped.

'Yes, you are right,' he announced. 'She was certainly one of the English squadron.' They had sailed closer now, and he could see that she was busy preparing for battle. As he watched, her gun ports opened along her side, transforming the line of yellow into a checkerboard, and a line of stubby little cannon were slowly hauled out. Her Royal Navy ensign fluttered in her mizzen rigging, while lines of tiny, red-coated figures made their way up into her masts. Marine sharpshooters, he concluded. Let her prepare for battle, one sloop with nine tiny guns a side, against two forty-gun frigates. If she was foolish enough to get in his way, he would crush the little ship like a walnut.

Next he looked at the pair of East Indiamen. They were sailing in a line ahead, a mile or so beyond the sloop. They were a little wider apart than a pair of warships would be, but they still kept reasonable formation. He could see few signs of preparation for battle on them. No sharpshooters in their rigging at all. Each one flew the red and white stripped flag of the East India Company. He looked over their hulls with care. In overall size they were much the same length as his frigates, but they were taller, with a double line of gun ports. He could not see that any of them had been opened yet. They would doubtless be shifting the cargo around to free up some space for at least a few of their guns to fire, he concluded.

'Very well,' he muttered to himself. 'So the sloop has returned, and is now escorting two merchantmen. Where are your big sisters, little ship?' He scanned the sea with care, looking for a slender masthead peeking just above the horizon that might indicate where the frigates lay. Nothing. He tilted his head back and called up to the lookout again.

'Leclerc! Can you see the other two English frigates? The one that defeated the *Prudence,* and that bigger one?'

'No, mon captaine,' he replied. 'There is nothing in sight. Perhaps they have gone to seek us at St Paul?'

'Perhaps they have,' said Olivier, 'Or perhaps they are just over the horizon, ready to come the moment they hear gunfire. Listen to me, Leclerc. I want you to forget any fighting that may be going on beneath your feet. You are not to take your eyes from the horizon. Is that clear? I want to know the moment that the enemy appears.'

'Yes, mon capitaine,' he replied. 'No one will surprise you, I promise.'

*****

'I do declare that the ruse may be working, sir,' shouted Midshipman Russell, from his perch on top of one of the quarterdeck carronades of the *Titan*. 'They seem to be ignoring the *Echo* and closing in on us.'

Clay was already regretting his strict orders that only Russell should be allowed to peer across at the enemy. It made sense, of course. Nothing would give the game away quicker than a line of gawking faces, but he would have dearly liked to have done some gawking himself. He strode up and down the quarterdeck in his full dress uniform, opening and closing his telescope as he marched. Sunlight penetrated down through the rigging to flash from the polished gold of his Nile Medal and the pommel of his new sword. He ran a hand over the warm metal of the lion's head. It may not be a knighthood, but for the matter in hand the King's gift, with its astonishingly sharp edge, would prove much more useful. The sound of a distant roar echoed across the sea, and he turned back towards the young officer.

'*Echo* has opened fire, sir!' announced the midshipman. 'Let fly into the bow of the first frigate, and is now hauling out of the way. Now the Frogs are returning fire with their chasers.'

'It is strange how muffled the sound is, sir, remarked Armstrong. 'Why, she can be no more than a mile off our quarter, and yet all this canvas has deflected much of the tumult.' Clay looked down the length of his ship, the deck oddly dark in the bright tropical sun. Running like a wall along both sides, a mass of timber framing had been installed, then covered in taut canvas panels. Like the back of scenery in a theatre, it was messy to look at from the deck of the ship; all wooden batons, loose canvas and a cat's cradle of lines. But he thought back to when he and Montague had been rowed around the two frigates, when the work had first been completed. It was remarkable how close they had been able to come before the illusion that the ships were not East Indiamen vanished.

'Congratulations, Mr Blake,' he said to his second lieutenant, as he had then. 'Our disguise seems to be tolerably effective. You truly are a most gifted artist.'

'Thank you, sir,' said the young man, blushing, 'but it was your idea. I just put it into practice with a deal of help from the carpenter and the sail maker. What was it that made you think of it?'

'In truth it was a remark of the commodore's,' said Clay. 'He had just seen your splendid portrait of my wife and spoke of what paint and canvas could achieve. I had been pondering how we might lure the French into making an attack upon us, so his words found their mark. But do not be so humble, Mr Blake. Your execution of the plan has been superb.'

'I was only directly responsible for the finer details myself. My team of assistants applied most of the paint.'

'Indeed,' said Clay. 'I hear that Sir George's private supply is sadly depleted, much to his annoyance. Let us hope it will all be worthwhile.'

'I trust so, sir,' said Blake. He pointed towards the panels next to them. 'I am particularly proud of the section positioned along here. It includes a *trompe-l'œille* of the steering wheel and binnacle which will be quite destroyed when the time comes for the quarterdeck carronades to open fire through it.'

'On the subject of guns, you had best take command of the main battery now,' said his captain. 'And remember, you are to fire as indifferently as drunken Spaniards, until you hear my call.' He held up the silver whistle that hung around his neck. 'When I blast on this, you may commence in earnest.'

'Aye, aye, sir,' replied the lieutenant. 'Lubberly practice it is.'

'Frogs are coming on faster now, sir,' reported Russell.

'On the same course as us, and edging steadily across. The lead one looks to be lining up with the *Prince*, the other one with us.' There was another roar of cannon fire, the sound distorted by the canvas cocoon all around them.

'There goes the *Rush* again, sir,' announced the teenager. 'Letting them have another broadside from range. She looks to be firing into their top hamper.'

'How far away are the frigates, Mr Russell?'

'Couple of cables outside of long cannon shot, I would say, sir,' he reported. 'But the range is closing. You may even be able to see the tops of their masts from the deck now, sir.'

Clay walked to the far side of the quarterdeck and looked back. Rising above the canvas screen were two sets of masts and sails. The second of them was almost level with the *Titan*. So you are to be my opponent, he thought to himself as he levelled his telescope towards her. The figure of a sailor in a red waistcoat came into focus, standing at her masthead. He was busy scanning the horizon, one hand sheltering the sun from his eyes, the other holding on to the mast beside him. As Clay watched the lookout, the man turned through a full circle, searching everywhere, except towards where the danger lay. Excellent, he thought.

'I am surprised how airless it is behind yon wall,' said Tom Macpherson as he mopped at his brow. 'I am perishing hot and I have no jacket on. You gentlemen must be fair roasting.'

'It is warm,' conceded Taylor, looking at the nearest panels. The sun was shining on the outside, making the material glow with light.

'Are your men ready, Tom?' asked Clay.

'Aye, they will come boiling up from below when the signal is given,' he replied. 'They know to wait for the peal of your whistle. Till then, no scarlet coats will be seen on deck to spoil matters.'

'I think the enemy may be about to open fire, sir,' announced Russell. 'The one that has taken station on us has run out her guns.' As if to prove his point a cannon ball shrieked over their heads, and a cut line pattered down onto the deck. A moment later the sound of the broadside boomed off the canvas wall.

'They are firing high,' commented the first lieutenant, as he watched Hutchinson on the forecastle directing some of his men to repair the small amount of damage. 'They mean to disable us.'

'All to the good then, Mr Taylor,' said Armstrong, rubbing his hands. 'They are still persuaded that we are harmless cargo ships and they do not wish to knock us about excessively.'

Clay walked to the front of the quarterdeck and looked down into the well of the ship. The space below him was crammed with men. Not only were there the gun crews grouped around their pieces, but all of Macpherson's marines in a block of red, together with the crews for the forecastle and quarterdeck carronades.

'Mr Blake,' he called.

'Sir,' replied the lieutenant. He pushed his way through the crowd and looked up towards his captain.

'You may open an indifferent fire on the French, if you please. Nothing too troubling for the enemy, I pray.'

'Aye aye, sir,' replied Blake, touching his hat. A muffled cheer started to rise from the men, quickly stifled by the petty officers.

'Silence, there!' roared Clay. 'Remember you are to play the part of frightened lascars. Only when I give the signal are you to act like *Titans* once more.'

*****

When Clay disappeared out of sight, Blake contemplated the row of eighteen-pounder cannon. They were big, heavy pieces, squat and low on their dull red carriages. Each long black barrel was worn with daily use and adorned with the names that their proud crews had given them. The one nearest to him had *Dan Mendoza* in flowing white script, painted across the breach. None had been run out yet, but each one was loaded and ready. The gun crews were stripped to the waist, with their neck cloths tied about their ears, and they crouched like sprinters around their pieces. Each gun captain held a glowing linstock in one hand, and looked towards his divisional officer, eager for the action to begin. The gun deck felt like a wound spring, ready to burst into life.

'This is not going to be easy, Mr Butler,' muttered Blake to the midshipman who stood next to him. 'For two years now we have drilled the men every day, to make them one of the briskest set of gunners in the service, and now we need them to act like lubbers.'

'Let us hope they will not forget all their training when we wish them to fire in earnest, sir,' replied his deputy.

'Precisely so,' said Blake, and then he called out, 'Larboard battery, gun four, seven and nine only! Up ports!' A grumble of disappointment swept the deck as those crews not selected stood upright again.

'Gun seven!' exclaimed O'Malley from where he stood at the rear of his piece. 'That's us, that is. Open the hatch, Sam, we're in fecking business, at last.' The big Londoner leant forward to unbolt the flap, and then pulled hard on the lanyard to swing the lid open. A square of dazzling blue sea appeared, making the gun crew squint. Framed in the hole was the second of the two French frigates. Her big solid hull filled the gun port, and her long line of guns pointed back towards them. Above the hull her huge masts seemed to tower over her, like the spires of a cathedral. Craning round a little, Evans could see the *Echo,* as she harassed her huge opponent from astern. At that moment the sloop yawed around to fire a broadside that fluttered through the French ship's rigging, sending down a shower of debris to patter into the water alongside her.

'Run out!' ordered Blake, and the men threw themselves against the rope tackles till the cannon thudded into place against the ship's side. 'Number four gun, fire!' There was a roar from forward, and the gun hurled back inboard. Its crew leapt forward as they sped to reload it.

'A hit,' yelled O'Malley, watching a burst of splinters fly up from the Frenchman's side. 'Got the fecker!'

'Too good,' pronounced Blake, from his position behind the gun that had fired. 'O'Malley, I want you to fire indifferently.'

'Beg pardon, sir,' said the Irishman, linstock poised over the touchhole. 'What manner of fire was that again?'

'It means that he wants you to miss,' translated Midshipman Butler from behind him. 'Fire across her bow, so you do not endanger the *Echo.*'

'Miss, sir? With a fecking beautiful target like that? Why in all creation would you be ordering me to miss, at all?'

'Just do it, O'Malley,' ordered the teenager. With a grumble of disappointment the gun crew levered the carriage around until the barrel of the eighteen-pounder pointed at a patch of blue water well ahead of the Frenchman.

'Easy lads,' muttered the Irishman. 'We wouldn't want to go hitting the other Frog ship, would we now?' And then he shouted. 'Stand clear!' He brought the glowing linstock down on the touch hole. There was a brief hiss, a roar, and the gun thundered back across the deck. As it came to a halt the crew sped to reload it. Evans thrust the wet sponge end of the rammer down the barrel to extinguish any sparks, while on the other side Trevan waited with the serge bag that held the next charge of powder, poised to push it into the muzzle. 'Take your time lads,' said O'Malley. 'No need to raise a sweat, like. It's fecking indifferent we're after being today.'

He peered back at the target as the third gun fired from farther along the deck. As if in response, the Frenchman disappeared behind a wall of smoke and a storm of shot howled overhead, bringing down a pattering torrent of cut rigging and blocks thudding onto the deck.

*****

'Afterguard! Have this trash taken away,' ordered Clay as he stepped over the shattered remains of a block that had fallen from high in the mizzen mast, only narrowly missing him. While the debris was removed he turned back towards the figure on the quarterdeck carronade. 'How far away is the enemy now, Mr Russell?'

'Three cables, and closing steadily, sir,' reported the midshipman. His first lieutenant looked at him with raised eyebrows, but Clay shook his head.

'Too distant, Mr Taylor,' he said. 'If we bare our teeth at this range, they will simply shear off and return to Reunion, and we shall be back where we started. Let them commit themselves more fully, so there can be no escape. Remember, I have a new born child to meet back at home, God willing.' He stooped down to touch an oak plank, before he continued. 'I would sooner not pass another six months pursuing shadows on this blasted ocean. Let us get the job done today.'

'The *Echo* is doing a passable job of wounding the enemy's rigging, Mr Taylor, sir,' added Russell.

'I doubt it is as thoroughly cut about as ours,' snorted Taylor. Clay looked up and winced. All of the sails had at least one shot hole in them now, and cut lines hung down like jungle creepers. The rigging was alive with sailors as Hutchinson struggled to keep up with the repairs. Just then another broadside from the Frenchman tore over the ship, sending down a fresh cascade from above. One cannon ball punched a hole in the canvas screen with a noise like a drum being struck. He held his breath as he willed the structure to remain upright.

'Let us hope that some French officers is not puzzling as to why no shower of splinters accompanied that hit,' said Macpherson.

'I can smell their powder smoke now, sir,' said Taylor. 'Must we wait till I can smell the garlic on their breath before we engage them properly?'

'Perhaps not that long,' smiled his captain. 'How far now, Mr Russell?'

'Cable and a half, I should say, sir,' he replied. Clay looked at the upper masts of the two frigates. He could see the topgallant masts in their entirety now, and a little of their topmasts. A big tricolour streamed in the breeze, the colours bright in the sunshine.

'Very well, Mr Taylor, you can have the carronade crews come up from below and man their pieces now. They are to do so quietly, if you please, in small groups.'

'I presume I still can't deploy my lads for a wee while?' asked Macpherson.

'Not yet, Tom,' said Clay. 'Nothing will give the game away faster than that. But the moment we run up our own ensign in place of that red and white rag, bring them up.'

*****

A hundred and sixty feet above the battle, Seaman Leclerc was finding it difficult to concentrate on the far horizon as his captain had ordered. For one thing, there was nothing out there for him to see. Try as he might, the line where deep blue ocean met a sky paled to white was smooth and uninterrupted in every direction. And there was so much to draw his attention closer at hand.

There was the little enemy sloop, for example, as she harried the two big frigates like a terrier confronted by bulls. Whenever one of the frigates made a ponderous move to turn their main batteries on her she would shy away, using her superior manoeuvrability to spin onto a different tack. But the moment the frigates returned to their pursuit of the two East Indiamen she would close in behind them, where none of their guns would bear. From his lofty position he could admire how well she was being handled, yawing first one way, then the other, and sending her little broadsides flying into their rigging. Strange that, thought Leclerc. He had always heard that the English only fired at the hull of an enemy. Kill the men and take the ship, was said to be their motto. Perhaps they hope to bring down a mast with a lucky blow.

Little by little they were making progress with doing so, thought the lookout. One shot had struck his mast a glancing blow earlier, the shock almost unseating him from his place on the royal yard. If he leant right out he could just see where the cannon ball had struck. Far below him was a white scar in the wood, like a bite from an apple. Then, moments ago, one of the thick topmast backstays had been cut by another ball, parting with a crack like a pistol shot. Now the play of the mast he sat on was noticeably more than it had been, as if a sea was running, rather than the calm conditions below him. But that shot had come from one of the merchant ships, rather than the little sloop.

He looked across at the one closest to him. The tall hull was partly obscured by a haze of gun smoke from the few cannon they had managed to get into action on the lower deck. Through a break in the smoke he saw someone moving on the deck. A seaman had made his way up a ladder and out onto the forecastle. A few moments later another figure followed him. Curious, thought the lookout to himself. He turned his attention to the quarterdeck. More sailors were coming up from below, in ones and twos. He could see the little foreshortened figures as they emerged from the hatchway below him. They seemed to be running with purpose, going this way and that. And then Leclerc started in surprise. As the man he was watching approached the ship's side, he had vanished. Where could he have gone? Leclerc watched the flow of men more intently. Another man ran across the deck to join the first, and he disappeared too. It was almost as if they had gone behind something. He puzzled over what it might be. He could see the side of the East Indiaman plainly enough, a long double row of gun ports, most of them still closed, running the length of the hull and topped by a rail. Leclerc studied the ship's side with care, and after a moment the lines of perspective seemed to move and resolve themselves into a quite different shape.

'Sacre bleu!' he exclaimed. He filled his lungs to hail the deck, but as he began to shout the *Rhone* fired yet another broadside, and his words were masked by the thunder of the guns.

Far beneath where Leclerc sat, his captain stood by the quarterdeck bulwark as the latest broadside roared out. A wall of gun smoke swept up from below him, making the two East Indiamen vanish and tainting the air with a smell of burnt sulfur. He turned from the cloud of smoke and waved his first lieutenant across from his position by the wheel.

'Tell me, Jean-Claude,' he asked, 'what size of guns did the merchant ships we have captured so far carry?' The younger man shrugged his shoulders.

'It varied from one ship to another, mon capitaine,' he

explained. 'Most had a strange mixture of pieces. Four-pounders, six-pounders, sometimes a nine-pounder. The last ship we took had three of those.'

'But nothing bigger?' queried Olivier. 'That is curious, for I do not believe any nine-pound canon ball could have made a hole like that.' He pointed with the toe of one shoe at where a large jagged gash had been torn in the ship's side. 'Six inches of best Vendee oak, and yet the enemy's shot has gone clean through it.'

'Perhaps there was a weakness in this section of timber, mon capitaine,' suggested his lieutenant. Olivier was about to reply when he was distracted by a shout from above. He looked up to where the lookout waved at him from the masthead.

'Deck there!' roared Leclerc. 'The enemy frigates! They are here!'

'Where away?' called his captain. 'What direction are they coming from?'

'No, mon Dieu, they are *here!*' yelled the lookout. 'The merchant ships...' His last words were lost in a fresh broadside from the *Echo*, as she continued to harass the *Rhone* from astern. Olivier held his hands over his head as fragments of wood and rope peppered down.

'What is he saying, Jean-Claude?' he asked.

'Something about the merchant ships,' said his deputy, turning towards them. 'But there is nothing to fear there. Look, they are surrendering to us.' The officers watched as the red and white striped flags were hauled down on both ships. A moment later naval ensigns soared upwards to replace them. At the main mast peak of the leading East Indiamen, a commodore's broad pennant then broke out, while across the narrow gap between the ships came the sound of a blast on a whistle. Captain Olivier's mouth opened wide in astonishment as all the remaining lower deck port lids on the two ships swung open, and with a faint cheer full batteries of cannon were pushed smoothly out into the warm tropical sunlight. A moment later the view was masked by a billowing wall of fire and smoke, and the *Rhone* was struck by a whirlwind of hammer blows against the side of her hull. Splinters flew across her deck and men tumbled to the planking as they were scythed down. From farther forward came the ringing sound of a direct hit on the iron muzzle of a gun. The noise echoed through the ship like the mournful toll of a bell.

CHAPTER 16 BATTLE

'This is more like it, sir!' exclaimed Tom Macpherson, buttoning up the scarlet tunic that his sergeant had handed him. He followed the lines of his sharpshooters as they made their way up into the tops, each man festooned with swinging pouches of extra cartridges. Nearer at hand, other marines crowded along the rail of the ship, bashing holes in the canvas screen with the butts of their muskets to give them a sight of the enemy. He turned in a full circle, arms outstretched, as he exulted in the roar of firing cannon and the smoke that billowed over the deck. All along the side of the frigate tongues of flame stabbed out towards the big Frenchman towering up next to them. The concussion of the guns had caused sections of the canvas screen to fall down, while what remained trembled and shook to the roar of the battle. The strip that had masked the quarterdeck from the French had been blasted into tatters by the big carronades firing through it. The Scot stooped to peered through one of the rents towards the *Rhone*. 'Hard to tell with all this smoke hereabouts, but we look to be firing a good deal faster than she is. Ah, and here comes Mr Sutton in that wee ship of his, joining in from their far side to close the jaws of the trap. Splendid! Why we have barely taken a casualty.'

As if to give the lie to his words, a number of crashes sounded from beneath them, one accompanied by the cries of wounded men.

'We caught them unawares, Tom,' said Clay, 'but they still seem game enough. Mr Taylor, kindly get the afterguard to clear all this canvas away so I can damn well see what the enemy is about.' He watched as the men set to with boarding axes, hacking at the last of Blake's masterpiece and tossing the fragments down into the sea. A last wooden upright broke with a crack, the final line was cut, and with a rush of falling screens Clay had an uninterrupted view.

The two French frigates were sailing along one behind the other on a parallel course to their British opponents, perhaps a hundred yards away. Their long hulls and huge mass of rigging filled his view. When he looked forward he could see the *Black Prince* locked in what seemed an evenly matched fight with her opponent. Neither ship's captain trusted their crew to fire independently, and instead they were trading broadsides. Each colossal roar filled the space between the hulls with a billowing mass of smoke, which slowly rolled away before being renewed by the opponent's cannon all firing as one. Clay found it hard to judge who was winning that battle. The commodore's ship had lost its mizzen topmast, but then the French ship no longer had a fore topgallant mast. On the far side of the fight he could see the masts of the *Echo*, as she closed in to attack the lead French frigate on her disengaged side. Good, he thought. Between the two of them, they should have the beating of their opponent. He could ignore that fight for now, and concentrate on his own battle.

Like the other two frigates, the *Rhone* was also firing in broadsides, walking the crew through the steps of reloading together and delivering her shot in a single blast. He watched as the row of cannon emerged through the ship's side, every one of them seeming to point at him. He could see that she had been hit hard. Already there were three barrels missing. One he could see; jammed in its gun port and pointing uselessly upwards towards the sky, but the others were as obvious as missing teeth in an otherwise perfect smile. A wall of orange light stabbed out from the side of the *Rhone*, and she disappeared behind a blanket of smoke.

A fan of splinters flashed across the deck as a cannon ball ploughed along the planking, leaving a long scar in the wood. Two of the crew men from the aft-most carronade tumbled down, one clutching an injured arm, the other with a long barb of wood in his thigh.

'Afterguard!' roared Clay. 'Take these two down to the surgeon.'

'I just needs a rag, sir,' said the sailor with the wounded arm as he struggled to his feet. 'No need to trouble Mr Corbett any.' Clay looked at the sailor. Blood flowed freely down onto the deck, and the man's tanned face was growing pale before his eyes.

'Take him below,' ordered Clay, turning away to concentrate on the battle. From behind him the man continued to protest as he was led away.

'Not the sawbones, Joe,' he pleaded. 'I can't go losing me arm!'

Spectacular as the *Rhone*'s broadsides were, Clay was content with how the battle was going. The Frenchman was firing solidly, with no mistakes, but only at the speed of her slowest gun crew. By contrast his own men had been drilled over the years to a pitch where each crew could be trusted to fire independently. Continuous gunfire ran backwards and forwards, up and down the side of the *Titan*, her guns shooting in and out of the hull below him like the stops on an organ. He could hear the crash of each ball as it struck its mark in the fog of smoke that hung around the enemy ship. A gust of wind tore a hole in the murk, and he saw sprays of splinters fly up from the Frenchman's hull. One shot produced a tall column of water, hard up against her side.

'Good shooting, that!' exclaimed Taylor from next to him. 'A hit, right between wind and water! There is nothing quite like the sea flooding in to distress a crew in battle, I find.'

Clay didn't reply. He was too busy studying the *Rhone*, trying to reach through the gun smoke, across a hundred yards of water, to feel the morale of his opponent. Like a prize fighter, he looked for the first trace of fear, deep in his enemy's eyes. That moment when the fight started to swing his way. All appeared well on board the *Rhone*, but his senses told him that his enemy was starting to wilt under the remorseless barrage. Perhaps it was a slight lengthening in the time between her broadsides that hinted at a growing reluctance on her gun deck. Or the patter of small arms fire from the marines along her sides that was not quite as intense as it had been. Another rent in the smoke gave him a glimpse of the run of the sea as it rushed along her side, and he saw that her helmsman was edging away from him.

'Bring me closer in towards her, Mr Armstrong' ordered Clay. 'Half pistol shot, if you please.'

'Aye, aye sir,' said the sailing master. 'Closer in it is.' Now the hull of the French frigate seemed to stretch even farther across the water, her battered masts towered ever higher above them as their courses converged. The impact of her next broadside seemed to slam the *Titan* back, so close were the ships, and Clay heard a fresh chorus of screams from below his feet, accompanied by calls for help to take the wounded away.

'There goes her main mast,' exclaimed Taylor. Clay looked back at the French ship. The top of the mast was swinging forwards, while the base seemed to be falling towards him, broken half way up its length. He could see the tiny figure of her lookout as he clung to a spar that had started to fall away beneath him. He had just time to recognise the terrified man as the sailor he had studied earlier in the red waistcoat, before the man vanished from sight. The whole mass of spars seemed to hesitate for a moment, but then some shrouds parted in a series of whip cracks, the released lines snaking through the air. With a rush of broken wreckage and flapping canvas the colossal mast came down, dragging in the sea alongside the *Rhone* and masking many of her guns.

'Now is our time,' said Clay, thumping the rail with his fist. 'Mr Russell, run down to Mr Blake as quick as quick. Tell him to arm his men for boarding, and load the guns with canister. He is to fire on my command, secure the cannon and then bring his men up. Mr Taylor, see that the upper deck carronades are loaded with canister too.'

'Aye aye, sir,' replied the first lieutenant.

'Back the foretopsail!' yelled Armstrong from beside the wheel. Their opponent was almost stationary in the water now, and they were in danger of overshooting her. Closer and closer the two ships came. Next to where Clay stood, the foremost of the quarterdeck carronades was being loaded with canister. The big copper cylinder needed two men to lift it up to the muzzle.

'Must be hundreds of them musket balls in that their box,' muttered one sailor to the other. 'That'll learn the bastards.' The *Titan* had stopped firing altogether now, as her crew completed the loading of the guns. From under his feet he felt the vibration of cannon being run out, and then silence. A pair of guns from close to the bow of the Frenchman banged out, but most of her crew were fighting to clear their helpless ship from the dead grip of the fallen mast. They were so close he could hear her captain as he bellowed orders through a speaking trumpet. He was a large, grey-haired man who had lost his hat at some stage of the fight. In response to his urging, his men worked away with axes and knives on the mass of wreckage draped across the frigate. It was only when the shadow of the *Titan*'s sails fell across his ship that he looked around. His eyes were drawn to the gold braid on Clay's coat and the bright medal at his throat. He raised a hand to his brow, and Clay returned the salute.

Sixty yards. The detail of their opponent was becoming clearer all the time as the last of the gun smoke cleared. Her black and white sides were heavily stained with powder burns, and punched full of holes like a colander. Her huge main topsail lay draped over her side, covering at least a third of her cannon. He could see the last of her gun crews pouring up from below, grabbing pikes and cutlasses from the racks before they came to the side to help repel boarders.

Fifty yards.

'Out quoins, larboard guns!' ordered the voice of Blake from his place beside the base of the main mast. Clay watched the line of cannon beneath him all tilt upwards as the range shrank.

'Marines will fix bayonets,' ordered Macpherson, somewhere behind him at the head of his men. He heard the rasp of steel being drawn from scabbards, followed by the double click as they were locked into place, then a clatter of something falling to the deck.

'Conway, you useless turd,' growled the voice of Corporal Edwards. 'Pick it up, then, before I'm minded to shove it up your bleeding arse.'

Forty yards, and his coxswain appeared by his side, pressing something cold and heavy into his hand.

'Fresh loaded just now, sir,' he reported. 'I have the other one here if you need it.' Clay glanced down at the pistol, checked it was uncocked, and then thrust it into his waist band.

'My thanks, Sedgwick,' he said, looking around. His barge crew were all massed at his back, armed with cutlasses and pistols, while the marines stood in a block of scarlet behind them. He looked over at Macpherson, who swept out the claymore he always carried in action and held the heavy blade up to his face in salute. Clay touched the brim of his hat to the Scot before returning his attention to the *Rhone*.

Thirty yards. Faces were clear now as they lined up opposite him, their petty officers pushing and cajoling them into position. Angry faces, and scared faces. Nervous faces, and empty faces. Old and young, moustached and baby-faced. All of them seeming to stare back at him. He could see the other captain as he yelled at his men, his drawn sword flashing as he brandished it in the sun. Now some of the soldiers mixed in with the crew were firing. Little puffs of smoke appeared as the muskets banged out. One levelled his weapon at Clay, and he forced himself to stand still. The old musket wound in his shoulder seemed to throb as he waited for the shot to come. The man's face disappeared behind a puff of dirty white cloud, and he heard the ball whistle past him. There was a cry of pain from one of the barge crew, and the sound of a body falling.

Twenty yards. A cannon onboard the Frenchmen barked out, sending a blast of canister fire towards the *Titan*. It swept away the entire crew of one of the quarterdeck carronades, tumbling them to the deck, most killed outright but one shrieking in pain. Musket balls howled off the metal of the barrel, leaving it peppered with smears of silver.

'See that gun will be fired, Mr Taylor,' ordered Clay, steeling himself not to react to the carnage. Then he strode over to bellow down to the main deck. 'Now is the time, Mr Blake!' A moment later the deafening roar of the *Titan*'s broadside boomed in the narrow space between the ships. The *Rhone* disappeared once more into a thick fog. A stunned silence followed, and then a mass of screams echoed in the smoke.

Ten yards. The side of the frigate was resolving itself in the gloom. From the ladder way came the thunder of feet as

Blake sent the gun crews running up from below. Clay looked round to see the huge figure of Evans pulling out a cutlass and dropping the sheath on the deck, and then he too was stepping forward to the ship's side and sweeping out the blue steel of the sword the King had given him.

Five yards, and there was the sound of splintering wreckage as the *Titan* forced her way through the remains of the Frenchman's fallen mast. Muskets and pistols popped away on both sides. Then four, three, two, and with a shuddering crunch the two hulls came together.

'*Titan*s away!' yelled Clay, as he pulled himself up using the mizzen shrouds. He leapt across the small gap between the ships, and with a roar the men of the frigate followed him.

*****

After the main mast fell, Captain Olivier found himself surrounded by officers, all of who needed him urgently.

'The water level has already risen over one metre in the well, mon capitaine, and I only have the starboard pump still in action,' moaned the carpenter from one side. 'I need ten more men to help plug the holes in the hull, or I cannot guarantee we will still be afloat in an hour.'

'An hour!' scoffed the boatswain, from Olivier's other side. 'We do not have ten minutes, unless I can free the ship of all this wreckage. The butt of the main mast is wedged solid, mon capitaine. I can rig up a block and tackle, but I need twenty more men to man it.'

'It is like a slaughter house down there, sir,' exclaimed the lieutenant in charge of the guns. 'Four of the larboard cannon are destroyed, and barely a gun has more than five men to serve it. I need more men to—'

'Enough, gentlemen, please,' exclaimed the captain. 'The

surgeon is dealing with almost a hundred killed and wounded. There are no more men for me to give you! Holes in the hull must wait. If we are still fighting in half an hour, I will come and plug them myself with my head, and then I shall cut free the mast with my teeth. Look over there!' He pointed at the scarred hull of the *Titan* as it closed in towards them. 'The time has long past for such matters. Forget the hull, leave the mast, abandon the cannon, and arm every sailor that can still hold a weapon. Bring all your men, gentlemen, and man the bulwarks. The enemy is upon us.'

When his officers had dispersed, Olivier rubbed at his temples. His head ached from the concussion of the guns and his body felt drained and weary. He had tried so hard to be cautious, and yet somehow the enemy had tricked him into the very battle he had wanted to avoid. He looked towards the other French frigate, hoping for some help from that quarter, but she was caught in a close embrace by the *Black Prince* on one side and the *Echo* on the other. Her foremast had gone completely, as had much of her main mast. He thrust down the feeling of rising helplessness and returned his attention to his own foe.

The British frigate that had pounded his ship remorselessly was almost silent as it slid ever closer.

'How do they manage to do that?' he asked out loud, shaking his head.

'How do they do what, mon capitaine?' said his first lieutenant, who had appeared unseen beside him. Olivier pointed with his speaking trumpet.

'How can they be so quiet? Listen to our men, or any French crew for that matter. They can never be like that in battle, making hardly a sound. It is both terrible to behold, and very cunning. It gets into the minds of our sailors, persuading them that they fight against automatons rather than men of flesh and blood like them.' He could see that they were preparing to board him now. Their red-coated soldiers had been pulled back into a solid block on the quarterdeck, the officers stood at the head of their men, and all her guns were run out to deliver one final broadside.

'They are certainly well organised, mon capitane,' said the younger man. Olivier looked at his first lieutenant and noticed how his right hand clenched and unclenched around the pommel of his sword.

'The waiting is the worse part, Jean Claude,' he said. 'Once the fighting starts the men will be brave enough. You will see.' Then he returned to his study of the enemy frigate, if only to conceal his anxious face from his nervous subordinate.

He knew exactly what was to follow, for he had been here before. In an earlier war, he had been a young lieutenant, just like Jean Claude. His hair had been long and glossy black then, and he had burned with ardour to do wonderful things for his King and country. He had summoned all his men around him, urged them to fight to the last, as he was pledged to do for his ship. But the British had approached like this, so calm, so silent. One final devastating broadside, and then they had swarmed across in the smoke, like mad barbarians pouring out of mountain fog, and every bit as savage. He looked at the surviving members of his crew, lined up along the ship's side, and sensed their fear. Battered by those remorseless cannon, fired so much faster and truer than their own, they had little left to give. He sighed to himself. During the last war he had spent two long years as a prisoner in the cold and rain of England, dreaming of his home in sun-drenched Provence. His face set in a look of determination. That would never happen again.

'Come on, my brave children!' he called as he drew out his sword. 'See how battered their ship is. We have hit them hard. They have tried to bombard us into submission, and failed. Now they shall try to board us in a last desperate ploy. Be true to your country; be true to your shipmates; follow your officers and all will be fine.' That raised a muted cheer, and the men returned to their places, fingering their weapons.

Olivier turned his attention to the British ship. They had come very close now, yet still they had not fired. He watched the tall officer with the glittering medal at his throat on the other quarterdeck. He seemed young to be a post captain. He smiled to himself. Perhaps it is you who are too old for this, mon ami, he thought. He raised a hand to the man as their eyes met, and to his surprise the gesture was returned. Now the range was very close. This broadside will be dreadful, he thought. He found he was looking almost straight into the muzzle of an enemy carronade. A seaman was staring along the huge barrel at him, his linstock poised over the touch hole with a line of smoke drifting up over his shoulder. The young captain of the ship started to step across toward the rail at the front of his quarterdeck, his mouth opening to give the order, and Olivier knew that his men would never survive what was to follow.

'Everyone down,' he yelled. 'Take cover! Now!'

*****

Gun seven roared out one final time, and dashed back inboard. Wisps of smoke coiled out from her muzzle to drift through the open port. Outside it was thick with smoke, and then grew dark as a wall of oak loomed up, blocking out the light. Her crew rushed to secure the cannon, then Evans dropped his rammer to the deck and O'Malley thrust his smoldering linstock into the water bucket with a hiss.

'Up to the gangways!' roared Lieutenant Blake. 'Take your

weapons and get moving. Look alive there!' The mass of sailors streamed towards the bottom of the ladder ways, and poured up them and out into the light.

On deck the side of the ship was packed with a mass of boarders. Many had climbed part way into the rigging; others were balanced on the rail, peering into the smoke. O'Malley shoved his way to the front, followed by the other members of the gun crew. The side of the French frigate appeared out of the gloom. She was at least a foot lower than the *Titan* now as the bigger ship continued to settle in the water. Her bulwarks were peppered with little white holes where the blizzard of canister had struck, and a curtain of rigging lines hung down, sliced through just above the deck. Those who had been too slow to heed their captain's warning lay in bleeding heaps, but many more were busy picking themselves up, amazed to still be alive. Just in front of him a soldier, barely out of his teens, stooped to pick up his battered hat, pulled it on to his head, and turned to face towards them. All those around him had been killed or wounded by the canister, leaving him alone on the blood-sodden deck. His little face looked lost in a uniform several sizes too big for him. Standing next to O'Malley at the rail stood the huge figure of Powell. He was one of the *Titan's* boatswain's mates, and was second only to Evans in size aboard the frigate. His battered face was a thing of nightmares, with a long red cutlass scar running across one eye. Powell pointed at the youngster with his boarding axe, and then drew a finger across his throat. O'Malley watched the terror grow in the boy's eyes.

The hulls came together with a squealing crunch, and the voice of Clay sounded from the quarterdeck.

'*Titans* away,' he yelled, and the madness began. The young soldier stood with his musket braced, the tip of the bayonet towards the enemy as Powell leapt across the narrow gap like a panther. He landed in front of the boy and clattered the weapon aside with a swipe of his boarding axe before closing with the small figure. For a moment he loomed over him, his axe raised high. O'Malley could see the horror on the boy's pale face. Powell jerked forwards, downing his opponent with a stunning head butt before he pressed on to find his next victim. The Irishman felt pleased that the petty officer had not followed through on his threat to kill the boy. Perhaps a heart did beat in Powell's huge chest after all.

He followed the trail of destruction behind the boatswain's mate as he advanced along the gangway, swinging his axe from side to side and felling opponents with ease. Off to one side of him was Trevan, dancing and thrusting with his cutlass, the blade clashing against that of a fleet-footed opponent. On the other side Evans was driving back the enemy, with no one wanting to square up to the giant sailor.

'Come on, you bastards,' the Londoner roared. 'Who wants a bleeding mill?' Now there came a counterattack, a block of French sailors running into the melee from the side. O'Malley found himself crushed between an opponent and the hard body of Powell. Both men wriggled like eels to get free, but neither of them were able to raise their arms in the crush. The Irishman twisted around, won a few inches of space, and managed to rip his pistol from his waistband. He pushed it against what he judged must be his opponent, and saw fear grow in the Frenchman's eyes as the hard barrel thrust against his belly. There was a bang, a scorching pain on his thigh and a gush of smoke rushed up into his face. His opponent let out a scream and slid down onto the deck.

And then the fight was over. All around them French sailors and marines were melting away with a clatter of dropped weapons.

'Quarterdeck, lads!' O'Malley yelled, as he ran towards the stern of the *Rhone,* where the fighting was still fierce. But as they arrived their French opponents were backing away here too, laying down their weapons and holding their hands up in token of surrender. By the wheel stood a large man with grey hair in a torn and stained uniform. A ring of his enemies stood about Captain Olivier, the circle marked by the limit of the bloody sword he still held in his fist. Sweat poured from his face as he gasped for breath.

'Yield, sir, I beg you,' Clay was saying, the King's sword held in front of him, but the tip down. 'There is no dishonour in your doing so. You and your men have fought bravely, and achieved all that could be expected.' Behind their captain stood a crowd of sailors, officers and marines. Olivier looked around him in desperation and then back towards Clay.

'I have sampled enough of your nation's hospitality,' he said. 'One visit to an English prison is quite enough for a single life.' Suddenly he thrust at his rival, the speed of his sword extraordinary for such a large man. But before the blow could land, there was a loud bang, and he lurched back. His sword slid from between his fingers, and he followed it down to the deck. Blood welled up from a wound in his chest, and his eyes glazed over. Next to Clay stood the figure of Sedgwick, a leveled pistol in his hand.

EPILOGUE

A world away from the gun smoke and chaos of battle, late summer was tending towards autumn once more in the garden at Rosehill cottage. Another year's crop of red fruit hung heavy from the boughs of the moss-covered apple trees. It was a sunny morning, and the old brick wall that surrounded the orchard was warm to the touch. The same table was back in position in the spotted shade, and Betsey and Lydia sat opposite each other once more with their damask wraps about their shoulders against what little breeze there was. Breakfast had just been cleared away by the maid, and the two ladies had settled down to do a little work.

Just as a year before, Lydia struggled to concentrate on the letter she was writing. This year, however, distraction did not come from a falling autumn leaf, but from the baby that slept in her wet nurse's arms. Nurse and baby sat in a wicker chair in the shade of a separate tree, with a carpet spread at their feet, dotted with wooden toys. Lydia gazed at the tiny, white-clothed shape for a moment. A small pink fist, like the knuckle of a ham, clenched briefly in the sunlight, and for a moment she thought her son would wake. But then it was drawn back into his satin gown, and she returned her attention to her companion.

The pile of closely written manuscript pages that Betsey had been working on the previous year had been replaced now by the finished proof sheets for the novel. She was busy on them, her blue pencil poised as she corrected here and underlined there. As she worked, she held her head on one side, the tip of her tongue protruding, and a single honey-coloured curl spiralling down to brush the surface of the paper. Every so often a little smile played across her lips, smoothing away her frown of concentration. Her friend continued to watch her, and after a moment their eyes met.

'You seem to have a very cheerful disposition this morning, Miss Clay,' said Lydia. 'Can it in anyway be connected with the letter in a mysterious hand that arrived from the Cape, together with Alex's latest correspondence?' Her friend laughed out loud, her joy obvious.

'After all Alex's dark hints that John might have been captured, or even killed, it was so wonderful to hear directly from him at last,' said Betsey. 'He would seem to have had a most unpleasant experience in a small boat, but he says he is much restored. And he has been put in charge of another ship. It is very unfortunate that poor Captain Windham was killed, but I feel sure that the commodore's decision to give John the *Echo* must mean that he is not to be censured for the loss of the *Rush*. What did Alex have to say? His letter to me chiefly addressed inconsequential matters.'

'He is delighted to have his friend restored to him, naturally, and was quite certain that no blame will be attached to Captain Sutton over the loss of his ship,' confirmed Lydia. 'I understand he will need to face a court martial over the *Rush*, but Alex sees that as but a formality.'

'John is eloquent in his letter,' continued Betsey. 'His prose is quite overwhelming. He seems to have had much time to consider matters while adrift, and has become a deal more decided in his views about us.'

'Ah, now we approach closer to the truth!' said Lydia, folding her arms. 'There is to be an "us", is there? No wonder you cannot help from smiling every other moment. Has a formal declaration been made?' Her friend flushed pink.

'No proper understanding has been reached, perhaps, but

John has made his intentions very clear in his letter,' she said. 'He even states that Alex has given his blessing, which implies that it has been discussed between them.' Lydia reach across and took one of her hands.

'I am teasing you in a most cruel fashion,' she laughed. 'I am delighted for you both. If voyages in little boats prompt eligible young men to declare themselves at last, then I am all for them! Perhaps he thought he might perish? I know Alex became very decided about me after he took that wound in his poor shoulder.' The baby woke at that moment and both women looked towards Lydia's child. The wet nurse cooed gently over her charge as she unbuttoned the front of her dress and drew him close into the curve of her arm.

'I imagine the contemplation of new life may very well change Alex, too, whenever he will return to meet young Master Francis,' said Betsey. Lydia nodded, a smile playing on her face below eyes touched with sadness. She felt the ache once more in her breasts as she watched the nurse feed the baby. For the first few weeks after the birth, a cry of hunger from her child had been agony for her. It would wet her undergarments with unneeded milk. The pain was more dull now, but the sense of longing in her heart to feed her baby remained undimmed.

'I have never fully understood why it is so wrong for ladies of quality to attend to the needs of their own children,' she said.

'Why, because it would be so ruinous to your health, Lydia!' exclaimed Betsey. 'The physicians are all quite in harmony on the matter.'

'Yes, perhaps I am being foolish,' said her friend. 'I wish for things that cannot be. Most of all I wish that Alex could be home, and share some of my pleasure in our son.'

'I wonder when they will return?' asked Betsey.

'Not for months yet,' warned Lydia, her eyes pricking

with tears. 'Alex's last letter spoke of them returning to the Indian Ocean, and back into danger.'

*****

The same morning sun that warmed the garden of Rosehill Cottage shone through the stern window of the *Black Prince* as the frigate led the squadron and their prizes westwards towards Cape Town, and the onward journey home. Sir George Montague sat at his desk, staring past the line of ships that followed in his wake to the distant ocean beyond. The surface looked calm and blue, but in his mind's eye he saw what lay beneath the waves. He thought of the man he was leaving behind. Somewhere in the cold, dark depths, where no sunlight ever came, would be the corpse of Nicholas Windham. They had buried him in the traditional manner, many weeks ago. He had been stitched into a canvas hammock, with his shattered head swaddled to prevent any gore seeping through the cloth to stain the union flag that covered him. An eighteen-pounder cannon ball had been placed at his feet to speed his passage into the depths. But eventually his rapid descent, wreathed in bubbles, would have ended down there, in the cold dark. He doubted if much now remained of his closest friend's nephew, once all the nameless, blind creatures that lived in the deep ocean had finished feasting on his corpse.

'No, there is something of him left,' he corrected himself. He reached for the folded note that had been found by the slumped body aboard the *Echo*. The writing was very poor, scratched in haste through a fog of gin and despair, and the surface of the paper was dotted with little brown stains, but still the words could be made out.

By this, my final act, I bear witness that

Commander John Sutton did murder Captain Percy Follett aboard His Majesty's frigate Agrius, and furthermore I call on those who come after me to avenge my uncle's death.

N P Windham, Master and Commander

Montague looked towards the ship's wake once more, as it foamed up from beneath the counter below him in a long line across the sea. It would be the work of a moment to screw the paper into a tight ball, open one of the window lights, and drop it into the ocean to join its author. He rose from his chair, resolved to do it, but then something made him stop. He stood, midway to the window, patting the stiff paper against the open palm of his other hand. Then he seemed to come to a resolution. He returned to his desk, slipped the paper into the top drawer, and turned the key. There would be plenty of time to dispose of the note later.

THE END

NOTE FROM THE AUTHOR

Historical fiction is a blend of the truth with the made up, and *The Distant Ocean* is no exception. For readers who would like to understand where the boundary lies between the two, the *Titan,* together with all the other ships that appear in my book are fictitious, as are the characters that inhabit them. That said, I have tried my best to ensure that my descriptions of those ships and the lives of their crews are as accurate as I am able to make them. Where I have failed to achieve this any errors are my own.

Other characters that appear in *The Distant Ocean* are historic. George III did spend considerable time in Weymouth in the hope of finding a cure to his bouts of insanity. Earl Spencer was First Lord of the Admiralty in 1797, and Prime Minister William Pitt's Income Tax was introduced as a temporary wartime measure in the period following the Battle of the Nile. Over two hundred years later its repeal is still awaited.

Thomas Ludlam was the young governor of Sierra Leone as portrayed in my novel. He would have been twenty three at the time, and was a printer by trade. The colony had been created in the way I describe to provide a home in Africa for black loyalist supporters of Britain who found themselves on the losing side in the American War of Independence. Many had been previously resettled on Crown lands in Nova Scotia. The colony's foundation predated the more famous colony of Liberia by over thirty years. Francois Morliere, the governor of Reunion is also a historical figure, although Captains Sybord, Olivier and the other Frenchmen in my book are not.

The campaign I describe in the Indian Ocean is of my own invention, but is based on the historically possible. The island of Reunion was used by both French privateers and warships to attack Britain's East Indian trade during the war. Linois operated French ships from Reunion in 1803, including the *Marengo*, 74. By 1810 four large frigates were causing such destruction amongst British merchantmen that a substantial military expedition was despatched to capture the island.

Places that I mention in the book are as geographically and historically accurate as I am able to make them. The tree I describe in the square in Freetown is still there, if rather larger now. The exception to this rule is Hope Island which comes purely from my imagination, although plenty of such atolls exist in those waters, and many are havens for bird life. The animals I have included in my book are essentially accurate, as are the details of the signaling system used by the survivors of the *Rush*.

ABOUT THE AUTHOR

PHILIP K ALLAN

Philip K. Allan comes from Watford in the United Kingdom. He still lives in Hertfordshire with his wife and his two teenage daughters. He has spent most of his working life to date as a senior manager in the motor industry. It was only in the last few years that he has given that up to concentrate on his novels full time.

He has a good knowledge of the ships of the 18th century navy, having studied them as part of his history degree at London University, which awoke a lifelong passion for the period. He is a member of the Society for Nautical Research and a keen sailor. He believes the period has unrivalled potential for a writer, stretching from the age of piracy via the voyages of Cook to the battles and campaigns of Nelson.

From a creative point of view he finds it offers him a wonderful platform for his work. On the one hand there is the strange, claustrophobic wooden world of the period's ships; and on the other hand there is the boundless freedom to move those ships around the globe wherever the narrative takes them. All these possibilities are fully exploited in the Alexander Clay series of novels.

His inspiration for the series was to build on the works of novelists like C.S. Forester and in particular Patrick O'Brian. His prose is heavily influenced by O'Brian's immersive style. He, too, uses meticulously researched period language and authentic nautical detail to draw the reader into a different world. But the Alexander Clay books also bring something fresh to the genre, with a cast of fully formed lower deck characters with their own back histories and plot lines in addition to the officers. Think *Downton Abbey* on a ship, with the lower deck as the below stairs servants.

IF YOU ENJOYED THIS BOOK VISIT

PENMORE PRESS

www.penmorepress.com

All Penmore Press books are available directly through our website, amazon.com, Barnes and Noble and Nook, Sony Reader, Apple iTunes, Kobo books and via leading bookshops across the United States, Canada, the UK, Australia and Europe.

The Captain's Nephew

by

Philip K.Allan

After a century of war, revolutions, and Imperial conquests, 1790s Europe is still embroiled in a battle for control of the sea and colonies. Tall ships navigate familiar and foreign waters, and ambitious young men without rank or status seek their futures in Naval commands. First Lieutenant Alexander Clay of HMS Agrius is self-made, clever, and ready for the new age. But the old world, dominated by patronage, retains a tight hold on advancement. Though Clay has proven himself many times over, Captain Percy Follett is determined to promote his own nephew.

Before Clay finds a way to receive due credit for his exploits, he'll first need to survive them. Ill-conceived expeditions ashore, hunts for privateers in treacherous fog, and a desperate chase across the Atlantic are only some of the challenges he faces. He must endeavor to bring his ship and crew through a series of adventures stretching from the bleak coast of Flanders to the warm waters of the Caribbean. Only then might high society recognize his achievements —and allow him to ask for the hand of Lydia Browning, the woman who loves him regardless of his station.

PENMORE PRESS
www.penmorepress.com

A Sloop of War

by

Philip K.Allan

This second novel in the series of Lieutenant Alexander Clay novels takes us to the island of Barbados, where the temperature of the politics, prejudices and amorous ambitions within society are only matched by the sweltering heat of the climate. After limping into the harbor of Barbados with his crippled frigate *Agrius* and accompanied by his French prize, Clay meets with Admiral Caldwell, the Commander in Chief of the island. The admiral is impressed enough by Clay's engagement with the French man of war to give him his own command.

The *Rush* is sent first to blockade the French island of St Lucia, then to support a landing by British troops in an attempt to take the island from the French garrison. The crew and officers of the *Rush* are repeatedly threatened along the way by a singular Spanish ship, in a contest that can only end with destruction or capture. And all this time, hanging over Clay is an accusation of murder leveled against him by the nephew of his previous captain.

Philip K Allan has all the ingredients here for a gripping tale of danger, heroism, greed, and sea battles, in a story that is well researched and full of excitement from beginning to end.

PENMORE PRESS
www.penmorepress.com

On the Lee Shore

by

Philip K.Allan

Newly promoted to Post Captain, Alexander Clay returns home from the Caribbean to recover from wounds sustained at the Battle of San Felipe. However, he is soon called upon by the Admiralty to take command of the frigate HMS Titan and join the blockade of the French coast. But the HMS Titan will be no easy command with its troubled crew that had launched a successful mutiny against its previous sadistic captain. Once aboard, Clay realizes he must confront the dangers of a fractious crew, rife with corrupt officers and disgruntled mutineers, if he is to have a united force capable of navigating the treacherous reefs of Brittany's notorious lee shore and successfully combating the French determined to break out of the blockade.

PENMORE PRESS
www.penmorepress.com

A Man of No Country

by

Philip K.Allan

In 1798, the Royal British Navy withdrew from the Mediterranean to combat the threat of invasion at home. In their absence, rumors abound of a French Army gathering in the south of France under General Napoleon Bonaparte, and of a large fleet gathering to transport them. Alexander Clay and his ship, Titan, are sent to the Mediterranean to investigate. Clay verifies the troubling rumors but is unable to learn where the French fleet and the army will be heading. When Admiral Lord Nelson arrives from Britain with reinforcements, Clay and Titan join Nelson's fleet heading for Southern France. But on their arrival, they discover Bonaparte's fleet is gone, and Nelson, aware of the dangers of an ambitious and ruthless general, orders an all-out hunt for Bonaparte's armies before it is too late.

As the Titan searches for Napoleon's forces, another threat has already gained passage on the ship. After engaging and destroying a Russian Privateer, the crew capture a mysterious stranger, claiming to be an English sailor who has been serving from childhood on Barbary ships. Shortly after he joins the ship, there begins a rash of thefts followed by the murder of another sailor. With the officers baffled as to who is behind this, it falls to Able Sedgwick, the Captain's coxswain and the lower deck to solve the crimes.

PENMORE PRESS
www.penmorepress.com

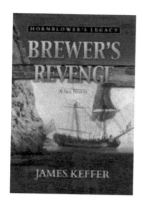

Brewer's Revenge

By

James Keffer

Admiral Horatio Hornblower has given Commander William Brewer captaincy of the captured pirate sloop *El Dorado.* Now under sail as the HMS *Revenge,* its new name suits Brewer's frame of mind perfectly. He lost many of his best men in the engagement that seized the ship, and his new orders are to hunt down the pirates who have been ravaging the trade routes of the Caribbean sea.

But Brewer will face more than one challenge before he can confront the pirate known as El Diabolito. His best friend and ship's surgeon, Dr. Spinelli, is taking dangerous solace in alcohol as he wrestles with demons of his own. The new purser, Mr. Allen, may need a lesson in honest accounting. Worst of all, Hornblower has requested that Brewer take on a young ne'er-do-well, Noah Simmons, to remove him from a recent scandal at home. At twenty-three, Simmons is old to be a junior midshipman, and as a wealthy man's son he is unaccustomed to working, taking orders, or suffering privations.

William Brewer will need to muster all his resources to ready his crew for their confrontation with the Caribbean's most notorious pirate. In the process, he'll discover the true price of command.

PENMORE PRESS
www.penmorepress.com

MIDSHIPMAN GRAHAM AND THE
BATTLE OF
ABUKIR

BY

JAMES BOSCHERT

It is midsummer of 1799 and the British Navy in the Mediterranean Theater of operations. Napoleon has brought the best soldiers and scientists from France to claim Egypt and replace the Turkish empire with one of his own making, but the debacle at Acre has caused the brilliant general to retreat to Cairo.

Commodore Sir Sidney Smith and the Turkish army land at the strategically critical fortress of Abukir, on the northern coast of Egypt. Here Smith plans to further the reversal of Napoleon's fortunes. Unfortunately, the Turks badly underestimate the speed, strength, and resolve of the French Army, and the ensuing battle becomes one of the worst defeats in Arab history.

Young Midshipman Duncan Graham is anxious to get ahead in the British Navy, but has many hurdles to overcome. Without any familial privileges to smooth his way, he can only advance through merit. The fires of war prove his mettle, but during an expedition to obtain desperately needed fresh water – and an illegal duel – a French patrol drives off the boats, and Graham is left stranded on shore. It now becomes a question of evasion and survival with the help of a British spy. Graham has to become very adaptable in order to avoid detection by the French police, and he must help the spy facilitate a daring escape by sea in order to get back to the British squadron.

"Midshipman Graham and The Battle of Abukir is both a rousing Napoleonic naval yarn and a convincing coming of age story. The battle scenes are riveting and powerful, the exotic Egyptian locales colorfully rendered." – John Danielski, author of *Capital's Punishment*

PENMORE PRESS
www.penmorepress.com

Penmore Press

Challenging, Intriguing, Adventurous, Historical and Imaginative

www.penmorepress.com

Lightning Source UK Ltd.
Milton Keynes UK
UKHW040635270119
336297UK00001B/80/P